"WE GOT A TANK!"

It wasn't a tank, because tanks don't move across the lunar surface on four stumpy legs; but apart from that, the description fit the bill perfectly. The intruder seemed to be about twenty feet long and heavy-bodied. Its whole exterior was covered with a seamless layer of flexible metal whose color quivered between violet and cobalt blue.

There were two arms beneath the dome that might be a helmet. The arms were longer than the legs, and in the hands was a backwards crossbow that the creature raised to its shoulder. . . .

"Gatewood, get the hell out!" Yesilkov shouted. "Move! Move! Move!"

TARGET

JANET MORRIS
and DAVID DRAKE

ACE BOOKS, NEW YORK

This book is an Ace original edition, and
has never been previously published.

TARGET

An Ace Book / published by arrangement with
the authors

PRINTING HISTORY
Ace edition / July 1989

ISBN: 0-441-79955-8

Ace Books are published by
The Berkley Publishing Group,
200 Madison Avenue, New York, New York 10016.
The name "ACE" and the "A" logo
are trademarks belonging to Charter Communications, Inc.

PRINTED IN THE UNITED STATES OF AMERICA

10 9 8 7 6 5 4 3 2 1

BOOK ONE

COWBOYS AND ALIENS

Chapter 1

HARD LANDING

Everybody left alive on the *KirStar*'s bridge was already scream-ing when the Rillian torpedo hit her just aft of the command module. Afterward, in his escape capsule, Channon kept replay-ing the *KirStar*'s flight-deck transcript, trying to sort things out.

It wasn't easy, sorting things out. The first missile had caught the crew entirely by surprise as *KirStar* came out of the Rift into clock-normal spacetime. Half of the *KirStar*'s passenger deck and all of her cargo bay had vaporized when the bonded-potential torpedo hit. Corkscrews of flaming hull and nonnative molecules had torn through her bulkheads, igniting everything flammable in their path, including oxygen.

The flames had been walls of green, blue and white-hot death as the Rillian cluster-weapons, tailored for airbreathers by a race who were not, sped throughout the *KirStar* in a deadly chain reaction. The Rillian explosive pulled matter apart and used the gluons between as fuses to ignite the energy potentials available from seven additional dimensions, once the skin of "normal" spacetime had been pierced. The result, on the unarmed Unity Vessel *KirStar*, was catastrophic and nearly total destruction.

But the worst was yet to come. If and when Channon got home, or got a message home, the news that the Rillians had attacked an unarmed peacekeeper would send shock waves through the Unity, which might shake the alliance apart and begin an all-out war with an enemy whose firepower was inar-guably superior.

Rillian explosives were tearing Channon's universe apart—literally. That was what *KirStar*'s mission had been about. Those aboard had all been volunteers. But none of the Kiri Unity's volunteers had expected an unprovoked attack, with no warning, on a Unity vessel broadcasting diplomatic call-signs on all in-

3

terstellar hailing frequencies. *KirStar* couldn't fight back; worse, she was hit so hard and so fast that she hadn't gotten out even an alarm before her systems went down.

Channon stabbed with his little finger at the toggle that would return the recording to the top of the sequence. He'd seen it fourteen times, but he needed to understand what had happened, to cycle the shock, the loss, the grief that made him shiver in his capsule. And he had nothing better to do. He needed to keep his mind off the anomalous readings his instrumentation kept offering, and the weird topology his viewscreens were showing him.

Even replaying the debacle was better than wondering where he was. Or how he'd gotten wherever this was. Or what he was going to do about it. The explosives that the Rillians were using got their power by punching holes in spacetime. Channon's capsule had been caught up in a blast it barely survived, and shoved—or sucked—or propelled by the advance wave of the blast . . . somewhere.

Somewhere unfamiliar. His onboard astrogator hadn't been able to match the starfields outside with any loaded topo maps. Band-hopping and frequency scanning weren't turning up so much as a familiar beacon. Channon knew he was somewhere far, far away from the Rift and the Rillion menace and the Kiri Unity's stubborn attempts to fight firepower with the power of reason. He just wasn't ready to think about it yet.

Every civilian on *KirStar* had been dear to him, a friend of his, or an admirer. His reputation had brought the team together, a team comprising some of the Unity's finest negotiators and conflict specialists.

As for the crew, there wasn't one he hadn't made into an ally. There might be tensions among the twelve races of the Unity, but the Rillian threat had made true colleagues of them all.

The Kiri Unity, he'd said in his farewell speech, with his arm around his wife and his son beaming at his side, was reaching for its finest moment while it faced its greatest challenge—the Rillians' warmaking prowess and aggressive superiority.

There had been some murmurs at that point in his address, among the leaders and the press gathered in the Unity hall. Channon had flatly stated the problem: The Kiri Unity wasn't able to fight the Rillians on the aliens' own terms. No Unity scientist understood Rillian weaponry well enough to field an effective counterforce. Not yet.

And even if the weapons could be made, there was debate as to whether they *should* be made. Planet-killers and spacetime-rippers, field-potential beams and multi dimensional cluster bombs—these were against every treaty and protocol that made the Unity the interstellar peacekeepers they'd become.

Channon shook his head savagely, as if he could shake away the cobwebs of memory that threatened to shroud what remained of his future. He had to find a haven, the capsule only had so much life-support. He needed a Unity outpost, or a provisional colony world, or a chance-met freighter . . . or a hospitable planet, anyplace with breathable air, food he could eat, and a communications emplacement capable of punching through 11-space with the emergency communiqué he desperately needed to send.

That was why Providence had spared him, he was certain. There was no other reason for him to have survived, other than blind chance and bad luck, but to send back a message—and a warning.

If the Rillians had grown so bold as to destroy the *KirStar*, that could mean only one thing: They were massing for an all-out attack upon the civilized worlds of the Kiri Unity. The *KirStar* must have stumbled into the midst of a forming armada.

Otherwise, there'd have been no reason for total annihilation. One thing the Rillians were well aware of was the value of Unity hostages. This time, there had been no burbled demand to surrender, no boarding party, no atrocities, no interrogations. . . .

All the volunteers had been prepared for capture. Each had a suicide capsule and a memory-wipe ampule, to be utilized at personal discretion. Even his wife, Terri, one of the translators aboard, had understood the risk and undertaken it bravely.

He squeezed his eyes shut. Terri. Terri had faith that the universe would not have breathed both volitional consciousness and temporal spans into her children for no purpose. She'd always maintained that life was a gift, and the best use of it was in protecting life, facilitating life, and improving life for generations to come. Terri's six toes would stroke his legs in bed and she'd tell him it didn't matter that their son was adopted, that it was Providence's way of making sure she did her best for the whole family of conscious beings—for the Kiri Unity, and for all the young races who'd someday join the Unity.

Was Terri already dead by the time the cockpit was engulfed? Had she been aft when the first blast holed the *KirStar*? He had to know. Since he'd regained consciousness he'd been scanning the migrated data in the escape pod, trying to ascertain the truth of it.

For his peace of mind he wanted to tell himself she'd died in the first instants of attack. He didn't want to spend what was left of his span wondering if he'd deserted his wife, if she'd been one of the last to die, if she'd died in agony, whimpering his name. . . .

Channon punched savagely at the escape capsule's console, enhancing and analyzing the cockpit recorder's data one more time, one more way. The pod held all that was left of *KirStar*'s noble peace mission to the Rillian frontier—a pale and shaken diplomatic trouble-shooter named Channon, and a host of distorted, flickering images from the *KirStar*'s flight recorders.

The Rillian InterStellar Defense Armada could still be countered, Channon told himself, if he could get a warning home, tell the truth about what had happened when *KirStar* came out of the Rift.

Lights dimmed in his pod and a more immediate fear clutched him. He was draining power, running the flight recorder's data over and over. He needed to calm himself, to pay attention to what he was doing.

He couldn't risk losing power to his beacon. He couldn't risk dying out here, so that the *KirStar* was logged lost in space, the victim of an unfortunate accident. The destruction of *KirStar* could be the event that catalyzed the Unity into wakefulness, stopped the endless debates and began preparations to somehow meet this soulless enemy.

But only if he got word home. Only if he survived that long. Decided, he toggled off the data feed, diverting power to his beacon.

The things he didn't want to remember he probably wasn't seeing, even if they were displayed on his monitor. He should simply accept that his wife never made it to the capsule, and that he did. Years of training in specific emergency procedures had seen to that—plus the happenstance of being in the right place at the right time, within thirty meters of the capsule bay.

Even now when he closed his eyes he could still see the explosions, the red and yellow of flesh meeting fire, the results of shrapnelling metal on the cockpit crew. . . .

He fell asleep there, at last, his little finger still depressing the emergency beacon, hurtling through space that was as alien to his topo-matching astrogator as failure was to his shocked and grieving soul.

When Channon awoke, the beacon was dead and his consoles were alive with crash-landing indicators and warnings that the moon toward which the capsule was hurtling had insufficient atmosphere for his needs.

He followed the indicated procedure: He struggled clumsily into his atmosphere suit; he clapped himself into his auxiliary life-support harness; he braced himself for a hard landing in the pod's crash cocoon.

As he was waiting for the concussion of impact, he noticed that the beacon's contact light had changed from red to yellow: from *message sending* to *message sent.*

First Channon thought: *Fine, I can die in peace.* Then he thought: *Sent where?*

But there was no time to let go of the crash mesh, and he was too well-trained to kill himself trying. His eyes darted everywhere in the capsule's cabin, gleaning what he could from his instrumentation, wishing that he'd stayed awake.

He knew, in the back of his mind, that if the beacon had been received by a Kiri substation, ship, or planet, a Unity response would have lit a green light instead of a yellow one on his console. But he told himself that it didn't mean the worst, necessarily: The push sensor could have detected a colony-world receiver, or an automated 11-space relay somewhere within range.

Or, since the moon where he'd crash, according to his monitors, wasn't uninhabited—only sparsely so—his beacon could have been picked up by the locals, whoever they were.

The emergency system didn't know who they were, but it knew there was oxygen-breathing life beneath the surface of this moon—and on the planet beyond.

He had only instants to acquire the coordinates of the large, inhabited installation and an estimate of distance from the projected crash site.

Then the moon came up and slapped him, jarring the air from

his lungs and everything from his mind, despite the hydraulic mesh of his crash cocoon.

While his brain sloshed in its skull, unconscious, the redundant automation of the capsule spat out the now-closed cocoon, and its passenger, in one last volitional act of paternal micronics.

Then the remaining fuel of the capsule ignited in a single, clean and cold explosion that shot a geyser of lunar regolith starward, as if a fast-moving meteorite had struck the dark side of the moon.

Chapter 2

DESK JOB

Sam Yates crossed booted ankles on his littered desk and put a pained hand over his eyes before he asked the speaker grille, "Say again, Gatewood? Slow and simple-like, okay?"

Yates's long, lanky form had been tilted back in his chair before the voice-only transmission had ruined his morning. He massaged his eyeballs gently with thumb and index finger, listening to the voice-actuater clip the syllables coming from Entry Level One's Coordination office.

Gatewood's voice came up from Entry Division's parking garage; the chief ticket-taker and customs man sounded decidedly unhappy: "I say again, Commissioner, I've got a guy here with no papers and a crazy story, best I can make out from his dialect. He won't take his suit off; it's like nothin' I've ever come across. I think you should take a look at him."

"Where's Supervisor Yesilkov? Why can't she vet this guy?" Yates knew he sounded cranky. Hell, he *was* cranky. He had the whole damned Mars-mission entourage to take care of—all he needed was some crazy with no papers and a thick accent. . . . Yesilkov had gotten his old job when he got booted up two slots and over one, to Commissioner of Security for the whole UN Headquarters, Luna. Now let her do it.

"Ah, sir, Yesilkov's rotated her dark time; she's working nights."

"She must have designated somebody . . ." Yates's voice began to rise in amplitude. He sat up and forward, slapping the desk with his elbows. "Never mind, I'll talk to her. Now, what's this guy's story—and have you made sure he's not some suicide commando, toting his weight in explosives in that funny-looking suit you say he's got?"

"Ah yeah, nothing's scoping like explosives. He says he

9

crashed farside. He says he wants diplomatic immunity, at least I think that's what he means. I really think you should see this guy, Commissioner. . . .''

"You *said* that already, Gatewood. So noted, on the record. Tell you what—he fascinates you so much, you bring his butt up here personally. Pronto.'' Yates switched the toggler off.

Yates had acquired a human secretary with never-ending legs, along with his new desk job. He buzzed her: "Find Supervisor Yesilkov and inform her that her presence is required on a Yellow Emergency, my office, ASAP—Security Code Five.''

No matter who she was in bed with, the Yellow tag would shake her out. Code Five meant no questions on the horn, just get here because whatever it is, it's "eyes only.''

Feeling even crankier, Yates got up and started pacing off the wait. He was going to wear a track in his office rug before he got used to this job. You did a little something like save a couple of darker races from annihilation by a genetically tailored virus, and what did you get? A nice bonus and a rotation home to Earth? No way. You got your butt booted into an executive slot that was the next best thing to suspended animation, where you could grow ulcers and listen to the cholesterol collecting in your arteries.

The State dinners he was required to attend weren't helping his weight, either. Not to mention his temper. At least when he'd been Entry Level Supervisor for Headquarters Security Directorate, he'd managed to get out of bed with something more to look forward to than lunch, dinner, and getting back in bed again, with only a sea of paperwork in between.

He hated this Commissioner's slot. His black-tie dinner suit itched and the shirt collars irritated his neck and, if it weren't for his ex-wife, Cecile, he'd probably have found a way to get transferred groundside again.

But it must be burning Cecile something fierce that Sam Yates was so successful, in her terms, up here on the Moon. Every time he was confronted with three forks and six spoons at dinner, he thought of how much Cecile would have given to be there beside him, and it helped. A little.

Or had, until the Mars expedition turned UN Luna into an observation deck for the rich and spoiled and made Sam Yates wish he could change places with Gatewood, taking tickets and stamping passports down at Entry One.

Or with Yesilkov, who had his old job and whatever action

there was to have. . . . Yesilkov had been a patrol officer when he was Security Supervisor, and they'd kicked some high-powered arse together, in the old days.

He still couldn't figure out how, when the smoke had cleared, Yesilkov had ended up in his old office, crotchety holotank and all, chasing perps and smugglers, and he'd ended up in the squeaky-clean paperwork business, chasing data filing codes and trying to remember faces floating over badges that said "Hello, My Name Is . . ."

And how come today, the one day when he didn't have time to play twenty questions with some guy in a non-reg get-up, Yesilkov had rotated herself to dark shift?

Well, the security check for tonight's Mars Observers mixer would just have to wait. He grinned with vicious satisfaction. Maybe he'd be too busy with whatever Gatewood had in hand even to attend.

He hated A-list functions, now that he was one of the determiners of who made the A-list, even more than he'd hated them when he couldn't have gotten into one with a plasma rifle and a platoon of army regulars. And of all the A-list parties he didn't want to go to, this one took first prize. Introducing New York University's finest, Elinor ("Ella") Bradley and friends, to the rest of the lunar-based academics monitoring the Mars expedition wasn't Yates's idea of a good time. Especially not when the mixer was hosted by the U.S. mission's new Undersecretary for Science and Technology, one Taylor McLeod, as blue-blooded a spook as you'd ever want to meet, and Bradley's lover.

Bradley's other lover. Bradley's *current* lover, Yates amended, silently and savagely, because Ella Bradley was history as far as Sam Yates was concerned. And because this job was getting to him, if he was thinking of her as a "former lover" instead of somebody he'd been fucking because they'd both been available. . . .

Yesilkov was still available, when their shifts matched. This wasn't the time for the two of them to be passing like ships in the night—professionally as well as personally, he'd tell her, when she got her big Slavic butt up here so that he could chew it out.

If there was one plus about the promotions they'd both received, it was that Yesilkov was directly under his supervision these days. But it was about the only plus he could think of as, pacing back and forth before his desk, he waited for Gatewood and the Unidentified Foreign Person.

His was a big office, by UNHQ standards—a suite fourteen meters square. The private portion of it had a couch he made frequent use of, as well as a passable holotank, combank behind the compudesk, and two visitors' chairs in front of it. The Isfahan rug was a gift to his predecessor from some friendly Persian, but you couldn't take any gifts with you when you left this job. Anything more permanent than a pickle on a toothpick was logged in as UN property, yours for your tour's duration, theirs when you left.

He had a Tokarev from the early twentieth century on the wall which Yesilkov's people had given him in recognition of his "glorious and heroic service to the cause of peace and understanding."

The Soviets—Sonya Yesilkov's people. The pistol must have been Sonya's idea. She knew Sam Yates well enough to guess what would be appropriate and appreciated.

Which meant that the Soviets were damned glad that bioplague hadn't gotten loose among their nonwhite races.

So was Yates. The only thing wrong with being a hero was this job they'd given him. His hatred for it was renewed every day when he began the morning's paper-chase he'd earned with blood and sweat and not a few cutaneous layers that had happened to get in the way of the perps' plasma fire while he was saving humanity's bacon. . . .

When Gatewood finally arrived, Yates had nearly forgotten he'd sent for the Entry One officer. The morning paper avalanche had begun, spitting out of his fax slot an inexorable flow of EYES ONLY/NO DISTRIBUTION/EACH AGENCY IS RESPONSIBLE FOR THE DESTRUCTION OF THIS DOCUMENT sheets that his secretary couldn't divert or hold because she wasn't cleared for raw intelligence.

Among the message traffic and shift synopses there wasn't anything as pertinent to Yates's mood as tonight's black-tie soiree for Bradley, and again he resolved to do his best to balloon Gatewood's mysterious visitor into a reason for giving Ella's party a wide berth.

"Send him in, Sally," Yates told the grillwork hiding the speaker that connected his office to the desk out front, where his secretary demonstrated just what Mom and Apple Pie could produce in the way of cheesecake.

"Sir, Mr. Gatewood's got a—"

Yates's speaker phone overrode his secretary's transmission, one of the prerogatives of command: "Right. I forgot. Send *them* in." Had Sally's voice been shaky? Or was it just her usual breathy, tremulous affectation that he was doing his damndest to ignore? She'd come with the office, like the rug, and her daddy was a congressman back home, so you looked but made god-damned sure you didn't touch. . . .

Where the hell *is* Yesilkov? Yates thought querously, and demanded that Sally find out.

Then Gatewood ushered his charge through the door, into Yates's office, and the security commissioner forgot about everything else.

The door sighed obediently shut behind Gatewood and the guy in the weird spacesuit, who was half a head taller, easily Yates's height. Yates stepped forward, big hand outstretched to shake, thought better of it, retreated and sat on his desk, arms crossed.

Gatewood was as pale as a ghost, as pale as the space suit that the stranger was wearing. The Entry One officer's voice was too loud as he said, "Security Commissioner Yates, I'd like you to meet Chan Un. . . ." Gatewood paused and looked around at the office, as if he didn't know what to do next.

"From?" Yates prompted. He was familiar with every kind of pressure suit and flight suit and space suit that anyone was issuing these days, or had issued for the past few years, and this guy's didn't match any standard template. There was some kind of coating on the faceplate that he didn't recognize, one that looked like abalone. The suit had air tanks and hoses, but none of them looked right, either. And there was a grille and punch pad in the middle of the stranger's chest.

"From . . . ?" repeated the stranger in a metallic voice that might have been the speaker.

"Okay, let's sit down," Yates said as Gatewood looked at him with a desperate plea for understanding. Yates went behind his desk. Gatewood started to take one of the two chrome-and-leather visitors' chairs, then paused, looking back at the suited figure standing so still in the middle of Yates's office.

Then the weird stuff started: The guy reached up to finger the grille box at his chest, and Yates hoped to hell Gatewood was right about there being no explosive secreted on the alien's person.

Alien seemed like the right word: The gloved hand had six padded digits. So did the other hand, Yates noticed.

"Sir," Gatewood said, looking younger by the minute, "I don't think he understands 'sit down.' "

"Then sit down and show him, Gatewood," said Yates. His temples were beginning to pound. If this was some practical joke, or a surprise readiness exercise drummed up by McLeod, who was no friend of Yates, heads were going to roll. . . .

Gatewood sat. The guy in the suit turned his head—or his helmet—slowly in Gatewood's direction. Gatewood patted the chair beside him.

The alien still had his hand on that button and Yates had an irrepressible desire to pluck the Tokarev off the wall. He did, though if he shot it in here, he'd have more explaining to do than he liked.

"Chan Un," said Yates to the man whose finger was pressed against a stud at his chest, "please take a seat and we'll begin."

"Begin," said the grille above the button.

Yates was beginning to wish he'd shifted to dark, like Yesilkov. He used his keypad to peck out a text message for Sally: *Get Yesilkov up here NOW! And six LARGE security men, fully armed; station them outside my door. Run redundant log tape from NOW!*

Christ, what did this crazy have up his sleeve? Six-fingered gloves didn't have to mean . . .

"Sit," Yates tried again, and motioned to the empty chair.

"Sit," the man in the suit repeated, and this time stepped back clumsily until his knees bumped the chair.

Human legs bent only one way. The suited man seemed to peer down at Gatewood, who had his legs crossed, for guidance. Then he sat and crossed his left leg over his right, just like Gatewood.

Gatewood rolled his eyes at Yates and said, "Maybe Mr. Un will tell you, Commissioner, what he told me."

"You're sure it's Mr. Un, not Mr. Chan?" Yates asked when the man in the suit didn't say a word. Chinese, Japanese—the name didn't sound right for either, and the mass under that suit wasn't right for an Oriental. But then, who knew what was inside the suit?

"Chan-non," said the suit's grille.

"Mr. Chan-non, you'll have to tell me your problem." Yates leaped at the opportunity. "How can we help you?"

"Help," said the suit's grille.

Gatewood shook his head. "See, I told you the dialect's a problem. Chan Un, tell the commissioner what you told me, about your ship crashing farside, about you wanting asylum."

"Crash. As-aye-lum," said the suit, and this time the helmet nodded. "Commissioner. Help."

"If I'm going to help you, Chan-non, we've got to trust each other. Where are you from?" Yates found himself talking very slowly, distinctly, and a bit too loudly as he tried to make himself understood, as if volume would help the situation.

"Kiri. Help Kiri. Trust you; trust me," said the suit.

"Chan-non, take that damned helmet off," Yates demanded, exasperation getting the better of him. He wasn't going to fall for this joke; he wasn't that damned gullible.

"Gatewood," he warned the Entry officer, "if this is some kind of game—"

"No sir, I did some checking. I mean, I tried . . ."

"What kind of checking could you do?" Yates was watching the guy in the suit as he began giving Gatewood a well-deserved hard time.

Chan-non was playing with his chest box again. Yates played with his Tokarev as well, and Gatewood looked wide-eyed between the two, explaining what he'd done:

"I checked what he told me, at least what I think he told me. He had enough crater dust on him to plug up half the toilets on-station, so we decontaminated him. No hot stuff, but some far-side dust . . . different trace elements, too, than anything we've got from nearside sampling."

"What are you saying, that he crashed out there and we didn't log it? A ship crashed and nobody tripped to it? What about distress—?"

"Sir, we did log a concussion. At least, the Geological Survey boys did. The concussion registered nearside and was logged as 'a meteorite of exceptional velocity striking, farside.' Since nobody at the UN here reported a distress call or a lost vehicle on farside, nobody questioned the seismic data or followed up on it." Having delivered his rote speech with precise desperation, and gotten his tail out of the door therewith, Gatewood shrugged and smiled a crooked smile.

The young Entry officer had thinning blond hair that was overlong by the book. It flopped on his forehead as he realized what the man in the suit was doing, and his head snapped around to watch.

The stranger was taking off his gloves. First he fiddled with one sleeve seal, then with the other.

Yates was absolutely positive that he'd never encountered the suit's type before; he was beginning to wonder whether he'd ever encountered the materials of its construction before.

Then Yates stopped wondering about details, as the gloves came off. The skin of the stranger's hands was reddish brown, the tone of a deep and recently refreshed suntan. That alone wasn't enough to make Gatewood's eyes bug or cause the kid to jump out of his seat and back up against the door, which opened briefly to reveal the security personnel Yates had called for.

And closed, when Yates motioned Gatewood savagely away, telling the men beyond, "As you were, gentlemen. False alarm." Then: "Gatewood, sit the hell down."

The youngster did, but with a look on his face that would have been more appropriate if Yates had asked him to take a walk, na-ked, in vacuum. His eyes were fixed on the hands of the stranger—the reason Gatewood had bolted for the door in the first place.

The fingernails on the exposed hand were nearly white, and they had a multicolored sheen like mother-of-pearl. And there were six of them, just like the gloves had six digits.

Yates's stomach flipped and settled. Probably a freak, some kind of weird albino, somebody's genetically manipulated mu-tation, or the kid of an early moon worker, irradiated in the womb. Had to be, because mankind had been looking hard for other intelligent life—hell, other any-kind-of-life above lichen level, and had come up dry.

There wasn't anybody out there, the UN was sure of that.

So this guy was . . . what?

Chan-non took off his other glove, and the second hand was just like the first. You could have heard a pin drop in Yates's office. His own breathing sounded like an industrial vacuum cleaner in his ears.

So he heard Yesilkov yelling, even through the soundproof partition. Or he thought he did. He toggled his com: "Sally, Yesilkov's coming in, alone. Now."

Yesilkov was disheveled and out of uniform, and by the flush in her cheeks, ready to read him the riot act. Her mouth was open to start things up once the door was firmly shut. He locked the door with his desktop override as soon as she entered.

Then her quick mind followed her eyes around the room and she stepped smartly to one side of the door, her hand reflexively going to her hip, where—if she'd been ready for action—a weapon would have been holstered.

"Supervisor Yesilkov, your man Gatewood's brought us a present. This is Chan-non, from we don't know where, who says he crashed farside and wants our help. Chan-non, meet Super-visor Yesilkov, head of Entry Division Security."

Every time anyone spoke, Yates realized, the guy with the weird hands depressed the button on his chest. This time, he also swiveled in his chair in a way Yates wasn't quite sure a human could, and said, in lots better English: "Meet you, Yesil-kov. Channon, who crash-landed farside and wants your help, from Kiri"—the next word was totally alien—"need to know where Channon is."

Yesilkov took a deep breath, ducked her head and said, "Gatewood, get out of here. Send up all your data on this— every piece of transcript, every quantizable bit. Then wipe whatever's down at Entry One. And wipe your own memory. Until we say so, this didn't happen. Make sure anybody else who encountered Channon knows what I said. And gimme a list of parties privy. Da?"

"You bet, Supervisor. I'm on my way. If the Commissioner concurs . . . ?"

"Well, *Commissar*?" said Yesilkov snottily, arms over her breasts, the flush back in her cheeks because Gatewood was going over her head to Yates, right in front of her.

"Do as you're ordered, sonny. And don't ever even imply jumping command chain again, where I can hear you, or you'll be on latrine security for the duration."

Damned kids. Never learned not to brown-nose if somebody didn't teach 'em.

He wasn't sure Yesilkov was right, letting Gatewood go now, after what he'd seen, but she sure was right that letting him go later might be more difficult, so far as security went.

He should have thought of it himself.

Yesilkov took Gatewood's seat as soon as Yates relocked the door behind the departing Entry officer.

For a moment their eyes met. He could see that Yesilkov still wasn't ready to take at face value what she saw beside her.

She said, "Okay, Sam, what's this really about?"

He said, "Our friend Channon's language skills are getting better by the second." He pronounced it, now, as Yesilkov had— as the alien had. "I think that's a vocab box he's got there. Is that so, Channon?"

"Vocab. Language." The helmeted head nodded.

"We'd like to see your face," Yesilkov said, "if you don't mind breathing our air."

"Breathe air, yes," said Channon, his reddish, white-nailed

finger on the button at his chest. He seemed to nod but made no attempt to take off his helmet.

"If we're to assume you're our friend, not our enemy—that you're not hiding something—you should take off your helmet so that we can see your face," Yates said, tapping his temple, wondering where this sort of patience came from. If this *was* some sort of practical joke fielded out of the American mission, he was going to spend the rest of the week making Taylor McLeod's life so miserable that this little escapade would pale by comparison. . . .

The suited Channon thumped his chest with a naked red-bronze hand. "Friend. Help Kiri friend. Hiding nothing. Enemy make crash. . . ."

"Kiri?" Yesilkov wanted to know.

Yates shook his head at her. *Enemy?*

One of Channon's red fingers was on the grille box again; the other hand was going to the helmet. Yates found himself stroking the Tokarev's barrel as if it were a pet.

His gut tensed when it became clear that the helmet was going to come off after all.

The alien had to use both hands to execute the maneuver. He lifted the helmet off his head and balanced it on his knee, just like any other spacer might in similar circumstances.

Yesilkov's hand had gone to her mouth, not to stifle a scream but to cover, before the fact, any errant or inappropriate facial movement.

Now, from behind her hand, she said, "Just who are you, and where are you from? Nobody's leaving the room until we know the answer to that, and know who these enemies are that made you crash, and how come you picked us to ask for political asylum."

All the while, she was looking at the face revealed when Channon took off his helmet.

The man—Yates was almost sure it was a man, a humanoid male, a cousin by evolution out of the law of averages—looked at Yesilkov through eyes with swirling colors in them and oblong, rapidly pulsating pupils. His teeth were that luminescent mother-of-pearl like his nails, and the incisors protruded a bit, like short fangs. The nostrils, in a nose that seemed almost vestigial, flared at a thirty-degree angle from the mouth. Between the mouth and nose was a suggestion of a harelip, and whiskers that were chin-long and sparse and droopy. The hair on his head was dark, straight, and sharply cut so that it stood out from his skull like a wire brush. The skull itself was markedly platyencephalic, by human standards.

What the hell was this thing before him? Yates fought a nearly overwhelming desire to shoot Channon where he sat. The guy smelled funny, acrid and metallic and . . . objectionable to Yates's nose.

Then the red-brown alien said, "Political asylum, yes. Am political, Kiri political. Need help. Tell Kiri about enemy."

"Man, I don't like this 'enemy' part one bleedin' bit," Yesilkov said under her breath, but not so low it was lost on Yates.

"Neither do I, honey. Channon, are you getting vocab—words you can use—from us speaking them and your box picking them up?" There was a wire—at least he hoped it was a wire and not a tendril of some sort—snaking from a dark hole in what was surely Channon's ear, down past the helmet seal, into his suit. Those ears were the flattest ears that Yates had ever seen.

And then they weren't. They seemed to twitch forward as Yates spoke, as if to catch the sound.

Yates rubbed his arms, where gooseflesh had risen. The reaction made him angry. This was just the sort of problem he was here to handle, never mind if it was a *real* alien contact and not an alien as defined by the UN book—that is, anybody not of your national origin when you were on your nation's turf, or anybody not permitted for UN presence, or any other damned apocryphal definition.

With a real live alien sitting in front of him, he knew what defined the term, knew it with every fiber of his being that longed to put a slug between those oblong-pupiled eyes.

He didn't. He said, for the computer log and on the record, "Yesilkov, this here's a real live alien, and aliens are our business according to charter and mandate, job descriptions and the like. You and me'll handle this far's we can—no anthropologists or biologists or any other 'ists.' "

"Yes sir, Commissar—no diplomats, no academics, no need to disturb any University personnel . . ." Yesilkov smirked at him briefly, letting him know she knew what he *didn't* want: Bradley et al involved. And continued: "But soon enough, word will leak. Everyone'll want a piece o' this fucker, and y'know that—your people, mine, all the rest."

And Channon said, this time through his mouth, in a voice that didn't sound so metallic but was somehow harder to understand as his unaided tongue tried forming unfamiliar words: "Diplomats, me. Kiri, my people. Diplomats fucker." He pointed to himself gravely.

Yesilkov broke into explosive laughter and the alien bolted out of his chair and backed to the farther wall.

Yates, trying to control his own laughter because Yesilkov's was contagious, put the Tokarev back on its rack before he went over to convince the alien that Yesilkov was going to be all right.

"Laughter," Yates explained. "Relieves tension. Humor is . . . good, a sign of friendship."

By then, Yesilkov was sobering, palming her eyes and telling Channon she was "fine, y'know. Friends, you bet. We're the best friends you got, you lucky sod. Come over here and sit back down."

Yates helped her coax the alien back to his seat. Channon *was* big: Yates's size, with more meat on him.

But Channon wouldn't sit. He'd seen the electronics on Yates's desk and he wanted to play with them.

"Friend?" Channon, it seemed, wanted to put his helmet on the console. "Good?"

"No big deal, go ahead."

Channon put his helmet slowly and carefully on Yates's compudesk. Then the red-bronzed fingers pulled a wire with a flat end out of the helmet, held it out to Yates, and said, "Vocab, friend."

"Uh, yeah. Sure." Yates went back behind his desk and punched up a *Webster's 209th*, starting with *A*. "There you go."

Without another by-your-leave, the red fingers smoothed the flat-ended wire against the display, then stepped back and nodded. "Vocab, go ahead," he said, and motioned in a startlingly human gesture for Yates to page through the dictionary.

"Whaddya think, Yesilkov? We givin' up state secrets?"

"Only in English," she said lightly.

He showed the alien what to do and stepped back, his own body between Channon and the Tokarev on the wall.

What did he have here, a superior intellect? Yates hoped to hell not. He was already wondering if his decision to keep Channon to himself could be supported before the inevitable inquiry. Not for long, probably. But before he gave the alien up, and secrecy he couldn't get past clamped down like eternal night, he wanted to know just what kind of alien he had here, and where it was from, and whether anything like a real enemy had had a hand in its appearance here.

There was no reason to take Channon's story at face value— or to think of him as an "it." Maybe Channon was the only enemy worth worrying about. If that was the case, Yates wasn't about to trust this situation to anybody else. Where UNHQ security was concerned, he was the final on-site authority—that was what being Commissioner meant.

Where his personal security was concerned, he was the *only* authority—that was what being Sam Yates meant.

While Channon was feeding *Webster's* into his helmet, Yates caught Yesilkov's eye and pantomimed: *What do you make of this?*

And she said aloud, "Damned if I know, Commissar. But damned if I want somebody telling me I'm not cleared to find out."

"You are now," he promised, hoping against hope it was a promise he'd be able to keep. So far, nobody knew squat about Channon but the grunts at Entry One, and the security officers in his outer office with his secretary.

Even if the International Geological Survey people had flagged the jitter they logged and sent it up through channels, it still wouldn't have gotten a second glance by any overseeing authority unless someone was tracking a valuable piece of space-junk that had national importance to one of the richer powers on the Moon. And nobody was. Nobody had lost anything worth watching for, or Yates would have been notified in his morning memos.

All the technical means that the UN mission had—communications, radars, optics and signature tracking—were trained on Earth, orbital habitats like Sky Devon, and the Mars expedition at the moment. Everyone was overworked and underpaid and no one gave a tinker's damn about farside taking another crater.

Yet.

Chapter 3

ANOTHER WORLD, ANOTHER CHANCE

Stretched out on the pallet in Yates's office, waiting for sustenance to arrive, with only Yesilkov present to watch over him,
Channon lay very still, eyes closed, trying to integrate what he'd
learned.

The aliens were achingly primitive, clearly dangerous, perhaps paranoid. But they were personally brave and mutually protective in a way that touched Channon's heart.

If they had not been all of the above, they'd never have been
dug in on their poor and pockmarked moon, under hazardous
conditions, coping with all the strains of close quarters and disparate objectives on individuated minds.

These were not sensitive beings. Nor did they share thoughts,
or even goals beyond survival. Each was locked unremittingly
inside his skull, communicating only through spoken language.
Their philosophies and moralities were a dizzying complexity of
differences. Their societies had become civilized at different
times and their ethics had evolved at different rates.

All this he had learned from their *Webster's,* which the one
called Yates had so freely given. This was a good sign, a good
beginning.

Channon needed to take formal note of the positive aspects
of his first contact with the race called Humanity, for much of
what he saw here, and what he'd learned from the dictionary,
was disheartening.

Yates and Yesilkov, he could only hope, were high enough in
their society's hierarchal structure to aid him. Otherwise, he'd
never get his message through to the Kiri Unity.

Even with the help of these suspicious beings, he might not
get through. The technological level displayed in *Webster's* was
grossly insufficient to his needs. All data here was value-

determined and access was compartmentalized. He must learn if the humans holding him could and would help him ascertain whether the sort of message he must send could be sent. And if it could, whether their inherently mistrustful society would permit such a thing.

He was unsure of even that much. He could feel the emotions of these humans, sloshing against his skin like the passions of animals in a zoo. They had no control of their feelings, or at least none of their broadcast ability.

At first, this had daunted him. All their fear and suspicion and uncertainty and hostility had spoken much louder than their words. Civilized persons did not broadcast their emotions so blatantly.

Yates had wanted to kill him. Then, Yates had fought rising xenophobia and won. Channon must take this as a good sign, even though the two security officers were obsessed with their vocations.

Yesilkov, the female, was throwing increasing heat as she paced before the "couch" on which he lay. While his eyes were closed, custom dictated that she forestall further questioning—unless that questioning was to be construed as unfriendly.

He wished he had another dictionary. Each nation had its own, with only a few words cross-collateralized. And Yesilkov was of a different nationality than Yates.

So many differences amid so much sameness reminded Channon of the basic majesty of life. The Kiri Unity was not so different from the primitive United Nations of Humanity, except in sophistication and realization of goals.

Terri would have loved to see this place. Terri would have loved to meet this female, Yesilkov, and her mate, Yates, who was from a different culture. To Terri, the two would have been proof of the root sameness of life, the universe over. No matter how primitive, certain rules of conduct must apply once the climb from the mud to the stars began. . . .

But Terri was dead, exploded molecules drifting near the Rift, and Channon was lost on some blasted heath of an airless moon, at the mercy of creatures no more animate than his most far distant ancestors had been. . . .

And Channon must find some way to contact the Kiri Unity, if it was not already too late. If time was not the problem . . .

He shied away from that thought. The Rillian weapons' advance wave had spun his capsule beyond the ken of Kiri exploration. He mustn't let his mind drift beyond his objective, into negativity and hopeless speculation. Thinking beyond his situation could only make his heart sore. . . .

And Yesilkov's heart was sore enough for both of them. Every time she crossed before the couch in her repetitious circuit of the room, her heat washed over him, her distress upstepped his own. They were dangerous, these humans—to one another, and more so to him.

They'd never met anyone truly different from themselves, yet they hated the ephemeral differences they saw in one another so much, they dared not look into each other's hearts and minds.

Spoken language was their only tool of negotiation; force and violence, more Rillian than Kiri, formed the rest of their diplomatic arsenal.

They were warmakers. Even the woman in front of him, who should have been the gentler, the more patient, the born nurturer, was full of violence. She kept one eye on him, in case he should move aggressively.

He shifted on the couch and she immediately came to stand over him.

"You awake, Channon? 'Cause I gotta talk to you about this stuff you been sayin' . . . before Yates gets back, okay?"

He took his arm from over his eyes, very slowly. She wanted him to trust her more than he trusted her partner. He didn't understand why, only felt the truth of it.

Careful not to move too quickly, he sat up. His suit was hot; he was chafed and pinched inside it. But he wasn't ready to take it off, not among these strange beings.

He said, with his new command of their English: "Talk, sure." He looked up at her, stretching his lips back from his teeth the way they did to indicate cooperation. "Thirsty, okay?"

"Water's all I can give you till Yates gets back. . . ."

She got him a serving in a clear flask. He smelled the chemicals and put it by untouched, setting the flask on the table. Could he survive here? Or was that the wrong question? Shouldn't he be asking himself merely if he could survive long enough to construct or convert a transmitter?

He said, "Make questions."

"Great." Yesilkov dropped onto the couch beside him as if she'd lost control of her body. He shied from contact. She smelled of putrefying flesh and chemicals similar to those in the water.

He found his buttocks clenching tight. He was beginning to lose heart. If he should die here, he could still find his wife in the spirit pool. . . .

He closed his eyes and then opened them. He must keep his purpose in sight.

And Yesilkov, as if sent by Providence, began asking questions that focused him on the present, not on his lost beloved: "What's Kiri? Who's this enemy? How'd you happen to crash here? What can we do to help you get home? Is anybody going to come looking for you, from your own people? Or chasing you, from the enemy you—"

The thought that the Rillians would follow him here was so horrid, so unwelcome, and yet so incontrovertible, Channon spat out a stream of invective in his own language.

Then he stopped. Yesilkov was blinking uncomprehendingly, anyway. She hadn't meant to bring down an evil upon his venture; she didn't understand that one never suggested to the universe a result one wished to avoid.

Hers was a paranoid, warmaking race, he reminded himself—like the Rillians. And it was entirely possible that the Rillians were asking themselves the same questions she'd just asked him, if they had received his ship's open beacon. . . .

She was waiting for his answers, her skin folded above her eyes as if his words had aged it.

He said, taking her questions in order: "Kiri is . . . my people, eleven other peoples—Kiri Unity." He used the closest English word for the amalgam that was the Kiri Unity, but it did not convey the whole truth. "Like United Nations—much old, strong. Peacekeepers, us. Settlers." Was that the right word for negotiators? "Specialists in conflict, fixing. Spread wide, civilizing. Minds alike, souls coalesced."

"Where?" said Yesilkov. "Where's this Unity based?"

He knew that humans nodded to indicate understanding, or shook their heads to indicate incomprehension. Now he shook his head. "Nowhere in *Webster's*. Must show more dictionaries, star-kind—data."

"That data's classified to you, buddy, until we know you better," she said, broadcasting distrust and crossing her arms over her mammaries. "Next you'll be telling me we're so primitive,

so far out in the boonies, you never heard of us before and got
here by accident.''

"Good story. Fits analysis," he said, pulling back his lips to
compliment her acumen. But he wasn't sure it was truly a right
assessment: The starfields in *Webster's* were all wrong, as if the
spacetime itself were non-native to him. If so, this would answer
some of his questions. But others then followed. If not just *Where
am I?* but also *When am I?* pertained, then perhaps he never
could get a message home. It needn't be that simple, or that
complex. There were many possible reasons that nothing in the
sky or in *Webster's* looked familiar. The phenomenal universe was
made up of many dimensions. It could be that, in an 11-space
manifold, the advance wave of the Rillian explosion had thrown
him into a branch universe; or it could be merely time-slip. The
truth might be that time itself must be factored into the equation
he needed to develop to send any message home.

Yesilkov touched his arm and shook it. The contact, even
through his suit, was jarring. She was full of conflicting emotions, not the least of which was fear that he represented a scout
of an invading race.

She removed her hand and he relaxed. "Think easy about
Kiri Unity. Friends, always. Not aggressors, ever. Communal,
us. Not annex civilizations. Invite. Share. Communal."

"Communists? Oh boy, this is going to make Yates real nervous. Well, don't invite us into anything, until we ask you, okay?
Like maybe we'll ask you for higher tech, if you're so interested
in sharing. . . ." She showed her own small square teeth.

"Channon"—he pointed to himself—"send message home.
To make, need think beside good people, Yesilkov . . . ." He
searched his memory for the word: "Technologists. Can do?"

"Once we're satisfied that you're peaceful like you say, and
that we can vet the message, sure thing. They'll be crawlin' all
over you for gadget upgrade, you bet."

So he could look forward to securing aid, if not more generally, then from Yesilkov's superiors. "From you Soviet people?
Word of Yesilkov give Channon to do this?"

"My word, Comrade? For what it's worth, you got it. Nobody
turns down equipment revision," said the woman, broadcasting
slyness and a hunger he didn't understand. Then a proprietari-
ness followed. "We keep this between you, me, and Yates's log
tape till I say, okay?"

He said, "Okay." It didn't seem to mean much more than a blanket affirmation of intent. *Webster's* hadn't contained a Usage Note on "Okay," although there'd been much in other Usage Notes he'd found helpful.

Yesilkov changed tack, and he felt the tension in her as she touched him again. This time she didn't let go, but squeezed his suit sleeve as she spoke: "If Kiri Unity's the good guys, who's the enemy that's chasing you, and why?"

"Now take appendage—hand—from me." He was shaken at the primal emotion telegraphed to him by the contact. "If Rillians—enemy—were . . . is . . . *are* . . . coming here to me, what you do? Nothing here stops, protects. All you technology . . . baby young. Rillians angry, make hurt if find." He nodded to show her the truth of what he was saying. "If find, kill me. Kill worlds. Kill all difference from them. . . . But not find." He looked at her bloodless face as he spoke, but he felt the unreasoning fear his words engendered more clearly than he saw it.

Her face folded up, above the brows. Her mouth drew tight across her teeth. "I think we better wait for Yates, for the rest of this."

"Good," he nodded.

"Fine," she said, crossing all her limbs as she sat back, as far from him as she could be on the couch.

Then, after only a short silence, she began again: "You don't think these bad guys—these Rillians—are chasing you? How come?"

"Sky wrong. Time wrong. Space wrong. Un-native, us," he said truthfully. "If Channon can't find home, Rillians not find here."

"Not in your native *what*?"

"Not *in*—" He struggled with the grammar of this cumbersome language and began again: "My home not in your *Webster's*. Your home not in my . . . manifold, matrix—spacetime." He shook his head. "You have no vocab."

"Try me, buddy. Now, you ain't in your what?"

"Rillians kill Kiri ship, peacekeeper." Patiently he started again, farther back along the event chain. "I escape. They look after no survivors, suspect none. Rillian weapons . . . complex-icated. Hard to think workings of." He pointed to his temple, as he'd seen Yates do. "Channon escape . . . ship banged. Advance wave happens before kill, push Channon through—from—home spacetime. Wave come before time event: field effect. Near Rift, so everyplace near and far, same. This place, by chance, for escape. Not near Kiri Unity. Not near Rillian. Chance. Eleven-space very large. This space, time, dimension—all strange. Maybe no finding again, on purpose. Access back and fro . . . not certain.''

''You think these guys whacked you right out of your dimension?''

''Out of spacetime, do think. Or time only: big universe—all moves, do Yesilkov see? Here now, gone later. What now is here, when time displaces me much, not here later, not here former. This place no Kiri explores, ever until today.''

''Shit,'' said Yesilkov.

''Not,'' said Channon. ''Important understand, Yesilkov. Attend lecture: Rillian weapons feed much power, universe power. Know English number-crunching, Yesilkov?''

Her eyes met his and held. ''Some,'' she said.

''Rillian weapons derives—strengths power from—controlled''—he took a deep breath and closed his own eyes, sifting *Webster's* through his mind's eye for the proper terms, and continued—''A-field potential effects on eleven-space manifold.'' He nodded.

She didn't.

He tried again. ''Yesilkov familiar with friend Maxwell's equations. Take field 'A'—''

''Whoa, Channon.'' Yesilkov's palm was up, facing him, a clear warning sign that matched the distress he was receiving from her physical person. ''Don't snow me with math. Ain't my area of expertise. You got all that from *Webster's*?''

''All got *Webster's*,'' he admitted, not adding that what he'd learned was pitifully inadequate to his needs. To build a transmitter . . . perhaps it was possible. To build an escape craft . . . this he had known, since *Webster's*, was impossible.

He would die here, among these children of the apes.

All the strength that training and force of will lent suddenly went out of him and he slumped. He wanted to die now. He wanted to sleep in Terri's spirit arms. But he couldn't, not until he'd made certain that there was nothing more he could do for the Unity.

Yesilkov was an implacable interrogator. She saw him slump

and he felt her instinctive need to pounce upon displayed weakness. "How about your people sending a rescue craft? Ain't that likely? And how about your ship—you're sure there's nothin' left on farside?"

"Nothing left. Kill complete. My people, I sent warning, beacon. If they receive, all done. Channon can sleep."

"Sleep?"

"Go beyond body. Find . . . spirit home. You say, God. Heaven." He was rather proud of that correlation, though Yesilkov was looking at him blankly. "Go to afterlife. Good. But—"

"Not till we're done talkin' to you, you don't. Promise me you won't try nothin'." The distress in Yesilkov overpowered him: All her horror of death and of the consequences of his death while under her scrutiny inundated him.

"Yesilkov, do not be distress. Talk other." He changed the subject, to save them both discomfort. "Timely beacon sent would warn Kiri Unity. Escape beacon—Channon not sure who receives this. Ship says, 'Message sent.' Not where. Even received home, Unity not know how, where . . . not attempt rescue. Channon thinks . . . doubts . . . anybody find me. No Rillians, even."

"You keep trying to tell yourself and me both how you believe that. I wish you were better at convincing one of us. Let's just say maybe the Rillians could—then what?"

"None Kiri know Rillian weapons. Limits of Rillian field effects are questions. They master killers, not we."

"You're sayin' they're stronger than you?"

"Indubitably." He liked that word. He nodded to make sure she understood. Then added: "Overpoweringly. We not war make anymore."

"And they do?"

"This all they do, heart and soul."

"Terrific. So if they come lookin' for you, they're going to find us. . . ." She stood up abruptly. "You know, Channon, I don't like you half so well as I did a few minutes ago."

"Understand," he said. He could feel her sudden change of heart. But there was nothing he could do about it. To motivate these humans to help him, they must know what they could comprehend of the truth.

This time her distress gave him physical pain, as if she had a hand around his heart and was squeezing it. He knew he was feeling a translation of what she was feeling, but that didn't banish his discomfort.

He said, hoping it would give them both some relief, "Rillians not send killing ships now. Channon one diplomat. Kiri Unity many . . . targets. One target, many targets: choice simple. Rillians seek whole Unity for killing. Channon single escaping target. One negotiator. Rillians have more to do than me."

This made the creature named Yesilkov feel somewhat better, and that allowed Channon to breathe more freely. But he hadn't the strength to continue leading the conversation to the point where Yesilkov would take him to a scientist or diplomat capable of getting him the sort of help he needed.

He was exhausted—by Yesilkov, by culture shock and physical differences in his new environment, by the loss of everything he held dear: his mission, his friends, his world, his wife . . . his life.

If he could send a beacon from this benighted airless hulk, through 11-space and the Rift, to a Kiri substation or even to his homeworld, would his warning be in time?

Should he merely curl up here and let his heart stop, count on the escape pod's yellow-lit *Message sent* indicator having done its job?

He might have, if Terri's face didn't swim before him every time he closed his eyes. Or if he didn't believe, in his deepest self, that there was still something left for him to do.

These humans had not done anything to him, or to Kiri Unity, or to any other race of starfaring peoples—nothing to deserve a visit from the Rillians. More and more, the suspicion that Rillians, not Kiri, might have picked up his beacon was disturbing Channon.

Coupled with that possibility—that he had exposed a young and hapless race to Rillian scrutiny—was his concern as to where in space and time this Earth of theirs might be.

Kiri did right in the universe: nurtured life and exalted it. He couldn't sleep until he knew that if he had not helped these creatures of Humanity, then at least he had not helped destroy them, whenever and wherever they might be.

Could the Rillians come chasing him through spacetime?

Would they try?

If they did try, and succeed, what would that mean to the confrontation brewing between the Kiri and the Rillian Armada?

If the Rillians could find him, and he was temporally offset to Kiri current time, would he then have been instrumental in the Rillian discovery of a new sort of warfare—one against which contemporary Kiri Unity would have no defense whatsoever?

It occurred to him then that sleep might be the best answer: If he was not living in this spacetime, would that perhaps prevent the consequences?

If it would, he would be glad to still his beating heart.

But until he learned more it was incumbent upon him as a Kiri citizen and diplomat to continue learning. It was the Kiri way.

Chapter 4

PARTY FAVORS

Sam Yates really didn't want to thread through this overdressed crowd of UN luminaries, find Elinor Bradley and Taylor McLeod, make polite noises and then tell McLeod all about the red-skinned, six-fingered package of sleepless nights Yesilkov was holding in Yates's office.

But somebody had to be informed, somewhere up the chain of command, or Yates's fine white neck was going to stretch over this one.

Technically, Taylor McLeod was a U.S. official, while Sam Yates worked for the United Nations. But Sam was an American citizen, and he didn't have to guess how far the Secretariat would back him if the U.S. Government made his removal a condition for further payments of America's UN dues.

"Informed" didn't necessarily mean "brought into the picture." Yates was going to feel things out and see what he could see.

Yesilkov was already champing at the bit to bring in higher-ups on her side. He avoided nationalistic maneuvering. But people did it, all the time. Yates wasn't even sure it was pertinent. Even when you had the first alien ever to come visiting in all of recorded history sitting in your office offering to share technology with you, if you'd just help him build a little transmitter so he could get a message home . . . The whole thing was making Yates nervous.

He'd reviewed his office log, at Yesilkov's suggestion, of the Q & A she'd had with Channon while Yates had been getting them their dinner and changing for his. It hadn't been the sort of session you could annotate as inconsequential and file under "Miscellaneous." Although he'd done that anyhow, for security reasons.

It occurred to him that if he went up to McLeod and told the spook the truth, the whole truth and nothing but, then if Channon wasn't still there when McLeod and a Who's Who of the U.S. mission got back, Yates would be spending the rest of his foreshortened tour on the Moon in a padded room somewhere.

But Yesilkov had promised that Channon would be right there when Yates got back. Of course, neither Yesilkov nor Yates knew squat about the alien's capabilities. Or whether they should believe a single thing he said.

Yates hoped to hell that Channon wasn't some advance scout for Armageddon. What if they built this purported beacon and it turned out to be a transdimensional gate through which little green men breathing fire came pouring in wave after wave, until there was nothing left of Yates's civilization but a couple of underdone barbecued human ribs and some dirty napkins?

You could really let your imagination get away from you on this one.

He kept trying to rehearse what he was going to say to McLeod, and kept failing to get beyond a nasty exchange that had too much to do with Ella and too little to do with Channon.

That didn't mean he gave a good goddamn. It just meant he understood human nature—his own, and McLeod's. He wasn't sure whether it was good luck or bad when he ducked around a canapé-bearing Latino and stood face to face with the guest of honor.

Ella Bradley was wearing prismatic contact lenses again and, given what was sitting in his office, Yates found them more than a little disconcerting. She still had the palest skin in the room, and dark, untinted hair—and a taut fine body that he remembered with more fondness than he wished.

"Sam, I wasn't sure you'd be able to make it."

Always the diplomat. And she was going to air-kiss him on both cheeks.

Hell, why not? He held out his arms and let her come into them for one of those chaste society hugs, then couldn't resist the temptation to really close his arms around her. If nothing else, his was still the hardest body she was likely to have encountered for some time.

And he liked pushing her to the edges of her precious propriety. Her lips brushed his right ear, then his left, and she was saying, "Now Sam, let's be civil."

She arched back and he released her the way he was supposed to, suddenly wishing he was more at ease with this sort of charade, that he'd been the one to be cold, that no one was watching.

But of course everyone was. She was the guest of honor. She was the reason for the NYU banner and the ice sculptures on the buffet. He wasn't the only one who'd become a hero over the biohazard thing.

"Congratulations on your promotion," she said to him in a voice meant to carry to the closest of the black-tie onlookers.

"Likewise, I'm sure," he said clumsily and thought he shouldn't have come. But he *had* come, and if he didn't say something pertinent, she was going to float away among the rest of the gowned women. . . . "You look lovely," he offered, and it sounded so strange coming out of his mouth that her lids narrowed above the accursed contacts.

"Are you all right, Sam? You look a little haggard."

He leaned toward her. Damn the eavesdroppers and the embassy types watching from the corners of their eyes. "I need to talk to you. Privately. Or to your boyfriend, I don't care which." To make it clear it was business, not any attempt to resuscitate a dead issue, he added: "Now. Or not at all."

"Yes sir, Commissioner," she said. "Step this way." She'd always been quick, had Ella.

He wasn't expecting her to turn around and lead him straight to McLeod, who was huddling with his staff by the buffet.

Yates waited on the other side of the ice replica of some arch from Washington Square College. McLeod disengaged and came over, letting Ella guide him with a hand on his arm.

Yates really didn't know why he'd played it this way. What the hell was he going to say to this guy?

"Hello, Commissioner," McLeod greeted him smoothly. "Ella says you need a minute with both of us. Come this way."

Another conga line through the crowd brought them to a shadowed alcove. McLeod held up a hand for silence until he'd fished a wallet-sized black box out of his pocket and enabled it. He looked at the meter on it and then nodded. "Go ahead, then."

Yates just couldn't resist. "I got a six-fingered, red-skinned, white-eyed alien in my office that says he's from another dimension and wants help building a beacon to send a distress call home before the bad guys chasing him show up here and turn us all into meat pies. You're the highest ranking spook I know around here. You and the U.S.A. want a piece of this? Or should I let Yesilkov and her Russian delegation have all the fun?''

"What?" McLeod, to his credit, kept his volume low, but disbelief was acidic in his voice. "If this is some kind of tasteless joke, Yates, you're going to find yourself stamping passports in Juarez quicker than you can say chicken-fried redneck.''

Yates was already backing away, one hand up. "Just thought I'd give you the option, Ella being an ace anthropologist and you bein' . . . what you are. See ya. Gotta practice up on my Spanish.'' He jammed his hands in his pockets, where they wouldn't hurt anybody, and, shoulders hunched, headed for the far door and the safety of his office. Alien and all, it beat the hell out of this celebrity parade.

He heard Ella's footsteps: fast and determined. You don't sleep with someone and not know what their footsteps sound like, not in Yates's business.

He slowed to let her catch up, feeling only slightly mollified.

She said, "Sam, how could you?'' when she caught up with him. Then: "Stop, damn you, and talk to me.''

He stopped, right before the bandstand, where a string quartet was tuning up. No expense spared.

"Here I am, stopped. I had to tell you—or somebody. Now I've delivered the message, I can go back to doin' what I do.''

"Is there really a . . .''

"Yep.''

Her face seemed pinched and very sharp. If she smiled, it would light up from within. But she wasn't smiling. "Are you inviting me to come and meet . . . it?''

"I'm just going on the record about it. It's up to you and your friend, what you do.''

"Yesilkov's . . . involved.''

"You bet. Up to her—''

"Sam, do you *want* me to take a look?''

By now, McLeod had caught up, but was standing a discreet distance away, although not so discreet he couldn't hear what they were saying.

So Yates had to make things clear. "I—Damn, I just want to cover my butt. I'd like a couple scientific types to come talk to him, but that's up to somebody like your friend McLeod. It's what the—it's what my guest wants.''

"We'll put something together. What kind of expertise?"

"Ah, commo, I guess . . ."

Up came McLeod, leisurely as all get-out, but quickly enough to interject, "Siginters?"

"Yeah, one. That's 'signals intelligence' types to you, Ella—electrospooks." He wished he didn't get such satisfaction from making McLeod uncomfortable, but he wasn't here to make McLeod's life easier. Taylor McLeod and he wore the same size suit; that was as far as the similarities went. He didn't have to pretend he cared what men like McLeod thought. . . . The truth meant something to Yates, that was the difference between them.

"Anybody else?" McLeod wanted to know, his dark-haired head down, his well-bred features precisely neutral.

"Maybe a space scientist or an astrophysicist or somesuch—maybe not. The guest just wants to build a ham radio. He doesn't think he can get home from here no matter how hard we try to help. I think we want to keep the party real intimate. One, two others beyond yourselves—Ella's the only one of her type I'll vet for this. Send files on who else you'd like and I'll look 'em over. We'll be working all night."

"I'm not sending you any files. We'll be along. You'll have to take my people at face value."

"I'll take two beyond present company at face value. That's all the slack I gave Yesilkov. That's all I'm giving you. This is one sensitive situation. I don't want any kind of incident. And I sure as hell don't want a circus that ends up the size of this one."

Yates turned on his heel and left, figuring that as Security Commissioner, he had a right to look busy, and cranky, and distracted. That was what he was.

He didn't care if Bradley came or not. He'd let the proper authorities know what he had. If McLeod didn't come to the party, he'd work with whoever Yesilkov's people sent.

The point was to avert a problem, develop a threat analysis, slap together a readiness scenario—for something that nobody knew anything about.

Except the red-skinned, white-eyed guy in Yates's office, who was having trouble figuring out where he was and sure as hell wasn't telling Yates and Yesilkov half of what he knew.

Chapter 5

COUNTRY OF ORIGIN

Class will tell, Elinor Bradley reminded herself, trying not to let her irritation at Sam Yates's behavior show as she walked stiffly through the remains of the Mars Observers' mixer. But show it did, to those who knew her, in the rigidity of her limbs and spine, in the tilt of her sharp-featured head and the thin line of her mouth.

Ella forcibly shoved thoughts of Yates's bad behavior out of her mind. He was, after all, not the only one whose comportment had been less than perfect during that little interchange. She must rise above all that, concern herself only with how soon she might leave the festivities without giving offense to their hosts.

Since Taylor McLeod was one of those hosts, the question should have been moot. McLeod was as anxious to leave as she was; he was already dispatching functionaries to slide through the celebrants, toward the NYU and UN bigwigs, to make the appropriate excuses.

She wasn't even sure what excuses those were, yet, but she trusted her fiancé implicitly. Taylor "Ting" McLeod had asked her to marry him last year, while he was acting USIA director and she was . . . recovering from the rogue Afrikaner plot to make all of Earth white by loosing a bioengineered plague to wipe out the colored races.

The wedding was set for June, of course. In Virginia, of course. And there was nothing Sam Yates would be able to do to spoil it—nothing—not if he had six aliens in his office, all of whom wanted to enroll in NYU extension courses specializing in the anthropological considerations of interspecies cultural mixing, and offering her exclusive access and unlimited aid in what would then be a Nobel-quality paper that only she'd be qualified to write. . . .

She said farewell to the college dean and pecked his wife's

cheek. Three more murmured apologies, and she'd be at the door, where McLeod already waited.

Taylor McLeod had rotated down to Earth and then back up here to be with her when her old grant ran out and she'd been offered first the lecture tour back home, then a second stint on Luna. She hadn't readjusted to the one-sixth gravity completely, yet. She had to watch her step in high heels. . . .

McLeod's boys came and went in the passageway like warrior ants while he leaned against the door and talked first to this one, then to that. He always gave her a feeling of competence, of American right and might, and of the value of culture—especially their native one. And of intelligence, as a human attribute and as a career.

Whenever she'd needed to do the impossible, or merely the improbable or the difficult, a call to Ting's various offices had done the trick. For as long as she could remember—when she was in the field in North or South Africa, and later here on Luna—whenever she'd been in trouble, he'd been the one to call.

So it had seemed natural that some day they'd formalize the arrangement begun in the Atlas Mountains one summer when she'd been trapped on a mountain road in a broken-down Rover and his limo had happened by. Yet the closer she got to their wedding day, the closer she looked at the man she'd always assumed she'd known.

Like tonight: He'd told her three times over the last week that "Yates will pull something, find some way to interpose an ugly note at the NYU affair. I know his type. We'd best invite him, anyhow. But don't expect the invitation to forestall anything unpleasant."

Ting was always right about that sort of thing. She wished he wasn't. The only trait that kept his knack for anticipation of human behavior from becoming oppressive was his hesitancy to volunteer his opinion unless asked for it.

Still, nothing excused McLeod openly threatening the security commissioner. She couldn't let him think she approved, or would even silently endure his hostility to someone who just happened to be a former lover.

The world was full of real conflict. The UN was riddled with it, even on the Moon. There was simply no need to create more ill feeling. Taylor McLeod was a consummate politician when he wanted to be. She must make it clear to him that her concerns, her friends, her best interests, must be handled with as much delicacy as his own. Otherwise, the marriage would never work.

"Ting," she said when she reached his side, "I need to talk to you about what happened between you and Sam Yates. . . ." As she spoke, she raised her eyes to his face. When their eyes met, her words dried up in her mouth.

McLeod's gray eyes were nearly slitted. A muscle ticked in his jaw, which seemed almost blue against his paled skin. "He wasn't fabricating," McLeod said. "Let's go, Ella. The rest of the team's waiting."

McLeod took a step down the hall, realized she hadn't followed, and turned in place. When he was tense like this, his eyelids seemed to disappear altogether. "Unless you'd prefer that I get another anthropologist, of course? Tell me now, before we ram this through channels and you're seconded to me for the duration—"

"Do you think an anthropologist's an appropriate choice?" she said dumbly. Of course it was. No exobiologist was as ready as she to deal with a being who brought a set of cultural biases with him, who'd come from an alien societal matrix.

And she did want very much to see the alien, now that she was sure there was one. But she would have appreciated being asked by McLeod, not just by Yates—asked before Ting's office went into bureaucratic overdrive and she found herself attached to him like a piece of carry-on luggage.

McLeod didn't answer, just quirked his lips and held out a hand to her. She took it. He was high-powered, she'd always known that, a doer in a world of talkers. She couldn't change him. Most times she knew better than to try.

She need only determine whether her free will and his could coexist in as static a structure as a marriage. This working interval he was proposing would go a long way to answering all her remaining questions. No matter what the alien contact brought her careerwise, she still had much to gain from working directly under Taylor McLeod on something more pertinent to real life than floral arrangements and guest lists.

He had a limo out front, with dip flags on its front fenders, and a driver, as well as a security car waiting in front of it to clear traffic. She could count on her fingers and toes the number of times she'd been in private ground cars up here instead of taking slideways or tubes—and all but two of those times had been with McLeod.

Inside the six-place limo with USG plates, he toggled the speaker and told the driver beyond the glass to take them by way of the Strip and stop at a restaurant there to pick up another passenger.

Then he sat back and turned to her with a pensive look. "You're angry. I'm not sure that I blame you, but I'm not sure at whom . . ."

"You have no right to treat a friend of mine like—"

"I wasn't treating him like a friend of yours. I was treating him as what he is: an overachieving beat cop with a knack for stumbling into the middle of delicate political situations. I've got to teach Yates to heel, fast, or pull him out of play. He's not mentally equipped to deal with—"

She was not mollified, but she wouldn't rise to Yates's defense, either: "That's not the point. You're making a differentiation between people you consider assets—your friends—and people you consider inconsequential—my friends. That's not healthy for—"

"If you want to consider Sam Yates your friend, then put him on the guest list for the wedding."

That stung her. She hadn't put him on the guest list, and the invitations had already started going out. And McLeod *knew* she hadn't. The car pulled away from the curb, into traffic thickened by the UN/NYU affair's attendees, and she looked out the window blindly, biting her knuckles where McLeod couldn't see.

Why did spats like this bother her so? Why did she lose her temper at the smallest impropriety, yet routinely find herself calm in the midst of the worst sort of crises?

She had to answer that question for them both. She tried one more time. "By devaluing the need to show even simple courtesies to the people you meet through me, Taylor McLeod, you're saying that there is no 'us' that extends far enough for it to matter what you say . . . that what's in my interest isn't necessarily in yours. And I don't like that. As a matter of fact, I won't accept it."

"And you won't accept my judgment that coddling a china-shop bull like Yates isn't in your interest?"

"If it's not, then tell *me*—privately. Don't embarrass me in front of . . . people. Ever." This time, she'd stopped herself before she referred to Yates as a friend.

McLeod reached for her, slipping his hand along the button-tucked seat-back until it gently caught the nape of her neck.

The contact broke the tension between them and she slid along the seat to lay her head on his shoulder.

"I'm sorry," he said into her hair. "I'm overprotective by nature. And you're right, I shouldn't try to precipitate situations that make your judgments for you. I'm a manipulative son of a bitch and I still don't know what you see in me."

"I'm sorry too," she told his collar. "But there has to be some overriding 'us' that bridges both careers, or our jobs are going to divorce us before we've picked out furniture. And you know how much"—she grinned wickedly and craned her neck so that he could see her expression—"I'm looking forward to picking out furniture."

He made an exaggerated grimace full of pain and trepidation. "I've had my secretaries looking to see if I left any paychecks in the bottom of my desk drawers, but I'm still worried about turning you loose in a showroom. Tell you what, when we're done with Yates's alien, we'll go groundside and get it over with. Just promise me you'll buy States goods; we'll get enough Continental crap as presents."

She could feel him relax; the inconsequential banter was doing the same for her. They had a life, they were telling one another, beyond their offices and their colleagues. They weren't children, embarking upon some shotgun marriage, but willful adults, each used to having the last word. A divorce would be not only personally difficult, but proof of poor judgment. Someone they both knew had said they weren't marrying, they were merging portfolios.

Sometimes she thought that someone was right, though she'd never met anyone else even vaguely suitable in age or provenance who excited her the way McLeod did. . . . Except men like Yates, of course, who weren't vaguely suitable.

When the car stopped outside an Italian restaurant on the Strip, she noticed one of McLeod's boys outside, holding the restaurant's neon-framed door open. A man in a duster came hurrying out and approached the car, two more of Taylor's people flanking him.

One staffer opened the door, ducked his head in to say, "On schedule, sir. Quint will meet you on site," and then got out of the way.

The man in the duster slid into the facing seat, beside the bar. "Good to see you, as always, Ting. Thanks for the lift." He was heavy, jowly, red-haired and bushy-browed. Ella liked him even before he added, "And who's this?" and held out his hand to her.

"We can talk in front of Ella. Elinor Bradley, Montague Sanders. Sandy, our UN Security Commissioner, an Amcit named Yates, says he's stumbled onto an alien who's asking for diplomatic immunity."

The heavy man called Sandy had barely settled back into his seat as the limo pulled away. "For this, you get me out of the Basso Profundo? Do you know what those women in there are like?" His mobile mouth stretched into a pleasantly lecherous grin. "Sorry, Ms. Bradley, but the Moon's the Moon, and the Strip's . . ."

"The Strip. I know, Mr. Sanders. I—"

"Call me Sandy. And tell me what you're doing on the Moon."

"Sandy. I'm with the NYU contingent."

"She was," McLeod cut in. "Ella's on the team for this one. So you *can* talk about this in front of her."

"So you said, Ting. I believe you. I just don't understand what the flap is. So another alien wants political asylum. . . . I trust you to vet it and give me the downside, as well as a sense of what he knows."

"No sir, General, you don't."

"*General* Sanders? NATO Command Luna Gen—" Ella stumbled, stopped. "I thought we were bringing a scientist and a sig—signals person."

"Yes ma'am," said the general, winking one eye that sparkled with amusement. "I'm the siginter—one of the oldest of the Old Crows, which is what they call us. And let me put your mind at ease—I haven't eaten a baby all week. *Does* that ease your mind, Ms. Bradley?"

Sanders was possibly the highest-ranking American soldier on the Moon. "Oh yes, sir," she said, feeling her cheeks grow hot.

"Good," said the grizzly-haired man. "Now, Ting, what was that about I can't trust *you* to call this one?"

"Sir, this is a nonterrestrial alien, as in 'from outer space.' "

"Okay, Ting. We'll talk about it later." The Air Force officer looked from McLeod to Ella, and back to McLeod. "Privately," he added, still with a jocular edge to his tone.

"I repeat, sir: Ella's on the team. You, me, Ella, and Dick

Quint from Space Sciences. That is, besides whomever the Russians are bringing."

The car was picking up speed. In front of it, the security vehicle had begun using its flasher. In the intermittent pulses Sanders' face seemed to be hung with flaps of swinging skin.

"Maybe you'd better brief me from the top then, McLeod. I thought I heard you say nonterrestrial alien and Russians in the same breath."

"Yes, sir, from the top," said McLeod.

She hadn't seen Taylor McLeod sit so still or heard him bite his words off that way since the Afrikaner mess.

"All this is from Security Commissioner Yates, and not yet fully substantiated," McLeod began, "but here goes: Yates, and subsequently a Soviet citizen named Yesilkova, who's an Entry Supervisor, had a walk-in whose physiology supports his claim of an alien origin. This party has officially asked Yates for political asylum, claims to have crashed farside—we have seismic data to support some correlating impact at the appropriate time. The alien's offered to trade technical knowledge for help in building something that's beginning to sound like a subspace radio, if you'll pardon the lay description. So we said, 'We'll think about it,' and he—it seems to be male—is still in Yates's office, waiting for technical support if official sanction, and sanctuary, are to be forthcoming. That's it so far."

"No, that's not it," said General Sanders. "You said 'subsequently' a Soviet citizen became involved. The implication there is that initially there wasn't one. On whose authority was another nation brought into a situation like this?"

"Ah . . . on Yates's authority, sir."

"So who's the alien asking for asylum—us or them?"

Ella saw McLeod take a deep breath and his eyes begin to narrow. "Us, sir—at least we can certainly maintain that position. The first contact officer was an Amcit—Entry Level One Security Officer Gatewood—and, although Gatewood was told by Yesilkova to send all his files to Yates's office and wipe his duty log for containment, we've already acquired that data and verified it. If it's a matter of primacy, that primacy's ours."

"Where was this Yates when Yesilkova started giving orders to wipe log tapes?"

"Ah . . . in the room, sir, as far as we know. Yates and Yesilkova have worked closely together in the past. I don't think harm was meant, but I do think things could get a little murky, if the Soviets want to contest just whose little boy this alien is. . . ."

"Sam never would do anything to hurt—"

Both men turned so sharply to Ella that she stopped in mid-sentence. "The alien's the focus of this, isn't it? I'm the anthropologist on this team, and my professional opinion at this point is that we work with the Soviets, while maintaining our primacy. It was one of our people who was asked for asylum. If we give it immediately, there should be no problem with the USSR, as long as we share data with them. . . ."

"Lady, Ms. . . . Bradley, that's what worries me. This Yates, he invited the Soviets in *before* consulting you, Ting?"

"I'm afraid so, Sandy. If this is anything more than a badly timed hoax, we'll have to work with the Russian experts."

"But the defector's ours! See that they realize that," said Sanders. "Just where in outer space did you say he was from?"

"I didn't, sir. We haven't correlated that data yet."

"Well, see that I have a chance to review the whole case file—and to talk privately with this Yates."

Ella wanted to groan. A real live alien, and all this NATO general could think about was what colors were going to fly above the debriefing desk.

She sank down in her seat as McLeod continued the briefing: "The Soviet team consists of Ruskin, whose rank is approximate to yours; Silov, an astrophysicist; Minsky, my opposite number here; and we couldn't find out whose the fourth slot is, if they've filled it."

"You know, McLeod, if I thought this was your fault, I'd do my damndest to get you busted to filing Export Lists on Fourteenth Street."

"I know that, sir. But *(a)* it's not my mess, it's Yates's; and *(b)* I don't think you could do it in any case."

Ella sat up very straight. Had she misheard her fiancé? Had he said that? Would he dare?

Sanders' jowls flopped. His eyes nearly disappeared in their fatty sockets. He said, "What was that, son?"

"I'm trying to tell you that this isn't an Air Force operation, that it isn't a military coup, that it isn't simply a matter of national security. This is, unless we're being deceived, a major spike in history. I ran it up my own command tree and I got a carte blanche back. This is my baby, whatever he looks like. I want that clear to all parties.''

"Just make it clear to the Russkies. And don't think I won't check to make sure you've dotted all the *i*'s and crossed all the *t*'s on that ticket you say you've got.''

"I will. I'm sure you'll find all's in order. That's what I do, General—make sure that things like this don't cause external problems.''

"You mean there've been others—other aliens?'' the general demanded.

"No sir, that's not what I mean. There have not been any other alien contacts of which my agency is apprised. Or by any other agency we can shadow. And we're not sure we want this one to have happened, either—not officially.''

It went on and on. McLeod told the general he wanted a complete security lock-down, and the general said that was impossible, with Soviets involved. They argued until the car stopped at the squat and utilitarian Government Center entrance closest to Yates's office.

Then everyone got out before the men running to open the limo doors reached them, and Ella said softly, "I know where to go, if you don't want a parade. . . .''

"Good, let's do that.'' McLeod waved his people off. "After you, Ella. General.''

She led the way, wondering why she had ever doubted McLeod's judgment, or his intentions toward her, or his good faith.

This alien better be worth all the trouble that Taylor McLeod had gone to, all the risk he'd already taken.

When she reached Yates's outer office, she was sure that all the risk was worthwhile. Even downstaffed for dark shift, she could feel the tension in the building.

She wanted to tiptoe. By the look on the faces of Yesilkov and Yates's secretary, so did they. "Hi, Yesilkov,'' she said brightly. "Let me introduce my colleagues . . .''

"That won't be necessary. Just get this Yates out here,'' the general said as Yesilkov heaved herself up out of one of the chairs crowding the little office, to examine the newcomers' documents.

"Commissioner Yates,'' said the achingly pretty blond secretary, "has gone to the commissary. Supervisor Yesilkov must check your papers. And I've got to log you-all in and out. The commissioner left strict orders.''

"Yates left the alien alone in there?" the general thundered.

Yesilkov put her sturdy body directly in the general's path and said, hands on her gunbelted hips, "He's with Soviet experts. Hardly alone. Now, if I can see your documentation so I know who I'm talking to . . ." Yesilkov paused and, when the general just glared, said, "Bradley, I know you and your friend. You can go right in."

Ella winced but McLeod's hand in the small of her back propelled her away from the confrontation and through the door into Yates's office.

She wasn't sure what they'd done was fair. She whispered in McLeod's ear, "We ought to be ashamed of ourselves, leaving General Sanders with Yesilkov—"

Then she saw the alien, sitting on the couch with two men she didn't recognize, talking quietly.

All three looked up, suddenly silent.

Ella Bradley knew she should move out of the doorway so that the door could close. She forced her suddenly clumsy legs to obey her, her eyes fixed on the alien.

He had red-bronze skin and everything else that Yates had described. He smiled, revealing sharp teeth. Then he said, "Channon," and touched his space-suited chest.

Ella Bradley's whole world came down around her in a kaleidoscope of shattered assumptions as she said, in a voice that seemed to belong to someone else, "I'm Ella Bradley. This is Taylor McLeod. We're honored to meet you, Mr. Channon."

Channon said, "Honor mine. Friends of Yates or friends of Yesilkov?"

The alien learned fast. McLeod said, "Friends of Yates *and* of Yesilkov, Mr. Channon."

The alien nodded his head vigorously and said, "Good story."

Then, in quick succession, General Sanders, Yesilkov, Yates, and two men arguing animatedly in Russian crowded into the room, behind Bradley.

In the confusion that ensued, the alien didn't say a word, just watched everyone through his abalone and ebony eyes, his finger on the box at his chest the whole time.

Chapter 6

LEARNING CURVE

Channon said, "Where are Yates and Yesilkov?" to the woman named Bradley, for the third time in as many days.

"They're not cleared for this, Channon. I've explained this before: What you're telling us is secret."

"Yates's office. Yates and Yesilkov know Channon secret. Want Yates and Yesilkov." He crossed his arms over his chest as he'd seen Yesilkov do. "Not remove suit until they come."

The matter of his space suit had become a stumbling block in negotiations with these humans. They wanted to "test" it—they weren't lying about that. And he wanted to get out of it, wash himself, clean his elimination and cooling systems, scratch his back if he chose.

"Channon, you can't stay in that suit forever. Be reasonable."

"Am reasonable. Humans unreasonable." They seemed somewhat less so now, with only Bradley present to broadcast just one set of emotional collisions he couldn't help receiving.

When the whole team was there or, more usually, the split shifts of two from each regional faction, the noise in his head and heart was almost deafening. The emotional cross talk of this race was clearly the reason it remained deaf and dumb in those frequencies. Channon was beginning to wish he could hear only what their mouths said.

What those mouths said, however, so seldom reflected the impulses behind their speech that he despaired of ever making sufficient accommodation to secure the sort of cooperation he needed.

Sultanian, the mathematician from the Soviet group, was the only one who seemed to understand him at all. The rest were listening to their own hearts only, and projecting their fears upon Channon as if he were a blank screen or a wall for painting.

And now he was sensing something else, an additional and more serious hostility, a violence beyond what these humans could project. He *needed* Yates and Yesilkov. They were the humans concerned with security, and Channon knew beyond doubt that his security was about to be threatened.

And perhaps everyone else's security as well. But how could he tell this to the xenophobes who surrounded him? Only Yates displayed the right group of reactions. Only Yates was qualified, in their hierarchy, to deal with the sort of threat Channon sensed.

All the rest were concerned with the threats represented by one another, and the information they were gathering from him. Each was here to learn as much as possible, while keeping his fellows from learning what he'd learned.

Channon said to Bradley, the woman who was in the midst of mating with the team's designated leader: "If not Yates, then need say story to McLeod."

Bradley massaged her skull and looked at her right hand for guidance from the timekeeper there. Then she said, "You need McLeod—alone? Tell a secret?" Her voice was hopeful; her mind was tired. "Before the others get back from their meeting?"

"Now," said Channon. "Next instant."

He mustn't frighten these folk any further. "Yates and Yesilkov, with."

"Look, Channon—no Yates, no Yesilkov." Frustration radiated from Bradley's delicate person. "I can't learn anything from you if I spend all my time teaching you about bureaucratic protocols that aren't any of our concern. Why aren't McLeod and I as good as Yates and Yesilkov, when we're . . . permitted to talk to you and they're not?"

Channon tried to control his exasperation, but he slapped at his chest translator, scrolling through his dictionary files once again for something that might help. There was nothing among the words in English, Cyrillic, or any other language which gave him a clue as to how to proceed. He clicked his tongue loudly. Since she didn't know what it meant, Bradley couldn't take offense at the disparagement.

As if talking to a retarded child, he said very slowly: "Yates not McLeod. You not Yesilkov. If Yates and Yesilkov not per-

mitted Channon, Channon not permitted tell any more stories."
He sat back to see what effect his words had.

How could he tell Bradley that he'd sensed a Rillian presence?
A wisp of undeniable Rillian perception, a brush of minds. He
wasn't sure from how far, or what it meant. Truth be told, he'd
panicked.

When he'd calmed, the Rillian probe was gone. He'd gotten
his helmet then. It was beside him on Yates's couch. He could
put it on and leave, go outside—if they'd let him refresh his
atmosphere supply. He could, and would, walk out of this hab-
itation, up onto the surface, over onto the dark side, where—if
the Rillians found him—he'd be all they found.

But to do that, he needed help. Or at least an absence of
constraint. And he knew with certainty that there would be attempts to constrain him if he tried to leave without explaining.

So he must explain to someone expert in security matters,
who could judge the quality of his reasoning, and might agree.
None of these selfish creatures, seeking self-aggrandizement
through "discovering" his knowledge, would let him go easily.

Only Yates and Yesilkov were properly focused to evaluate
the threat he sensed.

"Channon, don't do this to me. Don't stonewall. And don't
threaten us. You don't understand mankind well enough to evaluate what a threat like that can mean to your own health and
welfare. Don't say 'no more' unless you mean it."

She was trying to be kind, to protect him. She was also trying
to frighten him into doing what she thought was good for him.

He said, "Get McLeod, say Channon says no more stories
until Yates and Yesilkov comes."

"Fine, I'll get Ting and we'll see." Now she was purely
angry. Her pride was outraged. She got up stiffly, went behind
Yates's desk and stabbed at the primitive communications devices there.

From what he overheard, McLeod would come.

He settled back to wait, closing his eyes.

Bradley's voice intervened: "Now don't go to sleep on me,
you red-skinned bastard. McLeod is on his way. The least you
can do is prepare me for whatever bombshell you're going to
drop."

"Bombshells of Rillian, not Kiri, manufacture. And not certain—"

"I'm sorry Channon. Metaphorical coloration of language, that's all. You made me . . . angry. Implying that I'm not qualified to hear what you've got to say or to help you. Like you angered Silov, the Soviet astrophysicist, when you couldn't find anything familiar in your star atlases, remember?"

"Channon remembers." None of the people who'd met with him had gone away happy, except for the single mathematician, who'd gone away worried. But then, all of the so-called experts had been lying to him, and to one another, holding back information. Whether that information would have helped Channon or not, it was the perception of each warrior on the interrogation teams that such revelation would weaken the faction he or she represented.

It was beginning to seem to Channon that it would be impossible to build even a beacon. He was no scientist. If the scientists and their warlords claimed ignorance of the workings of the necessary machinery, and even of the power sources known here as A-field potentials, then Channon could not provide the missing data, any more than he could have constructed a Rift-capable starship from the components of Yates's office.

Thus it was a standoff: their ignorance and paranoia against his ignorance and need.

He had acclimated himself to their water; he had found plant life he could ingest; he was teaching them whatever he could. If not for the Rillian probe he'd sensed, he would never have threatened Bradley, who was status conscious and fighting to prove herself competent to act as his interpreter, if he understood her correctly.

If not for the Rillian threat, he could have spent a life here and died on his day with no regrets, as many other missionaries before him had done.

It was not the work for which he was trained, but it was close enough. And helping humans was still helping cognizant life. Therefore it satisfied his sworn mandate—until he sensed the threat.

He did not open his eyes to Bradley. He needed to find a position from which to inform the team leader, one which would not engender terror in these humans. He needed Yates. He needed Yesilkov. He needed those who'd sworn friendship to him, not these who only wanted to learn from him what would make them more powerful among their own kind.

When McLeod came, the diplomat in Channon sensed the diplomat in the human male, and he was somewhat encouraged.

But McLeod was unhappy. These people were almost always unhappy. They had not learned that unhappiness was a poor choice for a span; that it was no better, no more noble, to be unhappy than to be happy; that life proceeded temporally to spend itself, and only pleasant or unpleasant memories remained when life was done, to be collateralized in afterlife; or even that the universe gave what was expected of it.

Like the Rillians, humans offered violence, aggression, hostility, and mistrust. If human society had been older and stronger, it might have been the perfect race to send as point negotiators to the Rillians. They proceeded from the same intuitive base. Thus they might, in a thousand of their years, have met with the Rillians and prevailed by might, if not by right of respect and reason.

But the humans were children and the Rillians were abroad in spacetime, adult in power if not in morality.

And Taylor McLeod, who coordinated the American and Soviet team holding Channon, stood over him with both hands on his hips and demanded, "Okay, Channon, what's the damned problem?"

"Rillians," Channon said truthfully, opening his eyes and patting the couch beside him as Yesilkov liked to do. "Sit comfy and talk story with Channon."

"We know about the Rillians, Channon. What's this about needing Yates and Yesilkov? Bradley says you're refusing to cooperate unless you see them. Is this true?" McLeod didn't sit, or even remove his hands from his hips. The threatening posture matched his broadcast.

Behind him, Bradley sat at Yates's desk, an odd satisfaction coming from her person.

"Yates," Channon said patiently, "Yesilkov. Security stories." He stood up also, to show he too was adamant in his concern.

McLeod took a step backward, scattering fear and then bold control around the room. "Tell me your security needs and I'll evaluate them. Then we'll see about Yates and Yesilkov. They have other duties, you know, Channon—like the rest of us. This unit doesn't exist in a vacuum."

"Vacuum, good," said Channon. "Channon go back to dark

of moon side. Fill atmosphere tanks. Okay?'' Perhaps the obvious approach would work if Yates and Yesilkov could not be provided.

"Vacuum, bad. You're not going anywhere—at least not alone. You want to see the farside crash-site? Sandy would love that. You think there's something out there that's important?''

"Important. Rillians. Go vacuum. Safe there.''

"You're safe here. What's the matter, do you feel sick? We're about ready for a complete physical, whenever you are.''

Channon had refused the idea in principle, whenever it had been broached. They couldn't help him determine what he could eat or what microorganisms of theirs might be harmful. They had sent someone to take his blood and he had refused with fervor and physical repulsion, knocking the needle from the person's hand.

They were very primitive, he must never forget that.

"No physical invasion. Channon in perfect health.'' Well, close enough, all things considered. "Go vacuum, or see Yates and Yesilkov.'' He put his fists on his own hips, matching McLeod's body language.

"Channon, give it to me straight: You've got a security problem, is that it?''

"It.''

"What kind of security problem?''

"Yates, Yes—''

"Not Yates. Not Yesilkov. Yates and Yesilkov work for me. You tell me what the problem is. I know you can if you want to.'' McLeod's eyes met his. McLeod was the most intelligent, or at least the most comprehensible of the Humans. "Come on, friend. You won't scare me. I won't desert you. I'm here to help.''

Bradley moved in her chair and vocalized something too softly or too idiomatically for Channon to understand what she'd said.

But McLeod had understood. "Okay, get 'em, Ella. But nobody else. And detente my two o'clock with the others; have my office keep them at the luncheon.''

"Yates? Yesilkov?'' Channon asked hopefully.

"On their way. Now, you were going to tell me the good story?''

"Good story, but not pleasing. Rillians touch Channon's mind. Know is here.''

"What? Shit." McLeod stepped back until his hips met Yates's desk, where he sat. "Let me make sure I've got this straight: You think the Rillians have pinpointed your location? How do you know?"

"Feel minds hunt, catch." He pointed to his temple.

"Terrific." McLeod swiveled from his hips and said to Bradley, "Ella, scramble this whole session tape. All logs. Call my office and say we're bringing Lucky over there until I can get a Space Command briefing set up. Have them send my ADC over. We're going to goose security up to—"

"Security: Yates and Yesilkov."

"You think Yates and Yesilkov can protect you, Channon?" The inflection in McLeod's voice belied the interrogatory structure of his sentence.

"Yes," said Channon. "Better than others. Channon want to go to crash—"

"Yeah, I know. You stay here with Ella while I go put some questions to the right people. Yates and Yesilkov will be along, okay?"

"Okay," said Channon.

At the door, McLeod stopped. "How time-dependent is this, Channon? You don't expect the Rillians to come out here looking for you, really, do you?"

"Expect? Never," said Channon, making a sign over his chest meant to ward off the evil of negative expectation.

At least Yates and Yesilkov would be coming to see him. He had much to tell them. If not from the Rillians, then they could provide him security against the onslaught of their own colleagues.

And Yates would understand Channon's decision to go back to the crash site, if the situation demanded, rather than involving so young and vulnerable a race in something that need not be the death of them.

Terri would be saddened if he came into her spirit arms with the sacrifice of a whole toddler race on his conscience.

If the Rillians came after him, it was possible he could distract them from the humans who barely registered on the technology scale. *If* Yates would keep his duty to his race in the forefront of his consciousness, Channon could still manage to behave in accordance with the Kiri way.

If Yates could help Channon escape from these pushers and

prodders of his physical and mental person, in a human spacecraft, he might be able to lead the Rillians away from this poor
moon and the fertile young planet it orbited.

Channon was aware that the chance was slim. But the chance
of the Rillians actually finding him had been slim. He still
couldn't fathom what the Rillian presence he'd sensed bespoke.

What he had felt was definitely a Rillian contact, but brief
and weak. If the Rillian armada were to come chasing him, even
these poor consciousnesses would know it eventually. And when
it came, it would be neither a brief contact nor a weak one.

What Channon had sensed was not anything as notable as a
major Rillian incursion.

But it had not been his imagination, either. He tried to concentrate on what such a contact might signify, but Bradley was
resuming her never-ending flow of questions, and she was even
more demanding of his attention than she'd been previously.

Finally he said, when she stopped for breath, "Bradley, want
learning? Or want famous name? Not game, this. Not contest
who learns most. This learns nothing. Need Yates, need Yesilkov—need mathematician, Soviet. Need help, Bradley. No time
for stupid questions anymore."

"Channon, you arrogant red—" Bradley seemed to bite her
own lip.

This he could not understand. Her eyes brought forth water
and she wiped it across her cheeks, which must have been
parched. "For somebody as paranoid as you are, you sure can
dish it out."

"Not dish. Not hungry. Need to make security plans. Now,
Bradley. Now."

"Right. Now." Bradley fingered the console before her and
said in an unfriendly voice, "Sally, find that cop you work for
and get him in here, or I'm going to write you up as incompe-
tent. And find Ting and tell him the alien's asking for the Soviet
mathematician, now."

She got up, came around the desk and, blinking, stared down
at him. "You know, I really wanted to like you, Channon. Truly
I did. But you're just like the rest of them."

"Not."

"Are." Her lip curled. "All your talk of Unity, and you're
not cooperating with us worth a damn. You might be fooling the
rest of them, but you're not fooling me. You're not going to give

us a damned thing. You want Yates—fine. You two deserve each other. He's sure you're bringing down the wrath of God on us, anyhow. Just mark my words: Don't go farside with Yates and Yesilkov all by your lonesome.''

He still had trouble following their most idiomatic speech. And he was, as she said, lonesome. "God not wrathful, Bradley. But Channon all alone against wrath of Rillians, here with just your kind." He shrugged, as she so often did, to indicate that he was doing his best in difficult circumstances. Then he added, for good measure, "Your civilization, God loves. Universe loves. Only humans not love. Like Rillians, not love."

"Go fuck yourself, Channon," Bradley advised.

But he couldn't do that, in his suit, even though it might have made him feel better. He could only wait for Yates and Yesilkov and hope that the liar McLeod would truly produce them.

Otherwise, he would languish in this chamber and endure whatever Providence had in store for him: Rillians, starvation, some intentioned or unintentioned evil brought down on him by his human caretakers, or merely endless questions as unenlightening as those posed by Ella Bradley.

He wasn't sure that fleeing in an expropriated and primitive spacecraft into the hinterlands between the worlds was a worse fate than being cooped up here with Bradley and her ilk.

At least, in space, nothing smelled as bad as a frightened human being.

Or an angry one. Bradley came back to stand before him once more. Her voice was tremulous and her skin was changing color, developing red spots on the cheeks and nose. He thought it must be from the ocular secretions she'd smeared over them.

"You know, Channon, no matter what you say, nobody's going to let you go farside—not with Yates, not with the Devil himself."

And as easily as he could smell human fear and sense human lies and feel human anguish, he could tell that Bradley was not lying now. This was the truth.

So he said, "Then must prepare security. Still need Yates and Yesilkov."

"Somehow," Bradley told him with a brief baring of teeth, "I knew that was what you'd say. You know, I don't need this crap. I'm getting married in a few months."

He hoped her race would have those months. He said, "Blessings, Bradley, upon your union and upon your mate, McLeod. Many offspring and the wisdom to teach them be yours."

"How'd you know Ting's my fian—?"

Channon pulled back his lips to calm her. "Your bodies talk, Bradley. Human bodies talk much, and minds are noisy also."

"Sweet Jesus, are you saying you can read minds?"

"Read? No. Listen. You too can, Bradley. Just listen. All life speaks. Must only listen without fear."

If time was short, Channon must teach these people what he could, while he could. Even Ella Bradley could learn, if she only ceased thinking about herself long enough to try.

And he must learn what he could do to help himself, and them. He would not lose hope. He would find a way to send his message home; he would find a way to protect these beings, or divert the Rillians' attention from them.

If he had to, he would still his heart. Then there would be nothing here to draw Rillians. It was a clear and cogent option, previously. Now it might be too late to do any good.

If the Rillian probe had taken a bearing from his presence, then some contact must be anticipated, prepared for, a countering measure concocted in case Rillians appeared here in force.

His race would never have chased another so far. He still held out hope that the contact had been sufficient to the Rillians' needs: Wherever he was, he was no threat to them.

But they knew where he was, or they knew he was somewhere a Rillian mind-support probe could reach. Channon felt deep regret, and something more uncharacteristic:

For the first time in his span, Channon wanted to destroy a threat, rather than defeat it by reason or guile. Was he learning from his hosts? Or merely feeling what Bradley felt, sitting across from him, glaring at him as if he were her mortal enemy?

He didn't want to hurt these people. He held out a hand to her, remorse and compassion overwhelming him. "Friends, Bradley? Not argue silliness? Be friends?"

Her face blanched, then wriggled into a great grimace.

He nearly withdrew his hand before she lunged to take it and started pumping it.

"Oh yes, Channon. Friends. We'll be great friends, and I'll take wonderful care of you. I won't let those others manipulate you, I promise."

"Not promise, Bradley, what cannot deliver," he scolded her, but she didn't seem to hear.

Chapter 7

THE RILLIAN WAY

The Rillian soldier had a name, but in Human terms it amounted to a few clicks, rather than sounds, in the 49-meter shortwave band. Not that his name mattered at the moment. He was the only one of his kind within—light years certainly—and perhaps the only one within this bubble universe.

The Rillian had a name, and a weapon, and a purpose: He was to locate the survivors of the Elevener craft his navy had attacked; and, having located the survivors, he was to destroy them utterly.

Thoroughness was the essence of the Rillian way.

The section controller had added a personal stricture to the orders he received from the ground-force commander: If possible, his troops were to bring back proof of their success. Heads would be suitable; or ears, if the Elevener species involved was among those with external ears.

Each time the Rillian transferred from one segment of the search-pattern to the next, he felt his guts shrink to a point of ice and then invert to envelope him. Familiarity with the sensation did not make it a pleasant one. Familiarity did not make the sensation even acceptable, but he had to accept it. It was part of his duties, and nothing could release a Rillian soldier from duty.

The Rillian hated the ground-force commander. He hated the naval personnel even more—for not doing their jobs properly the first time. The navy commander had been verbally fluffing his scales in triumph only moments before the distress signal from the Elevener survivors came in. . . .

Most particularly, the Rillian soldier hated the Eleveners themselves, whose survival had damned him to this hideously uncomfortable situation. He and his ground-force fellows were locked into a series of tests of an experimental technique, using the die-effects of A-field weaponry to rip paths through sponge-space. The series would end only when the ground-force commander gave up.

The Rillian knew his commander too well to expect him to give up while any of his troops retained the modest degree of sanity required of a combat soldier.

His guts settled back into their normal location—convulsing—to indicate transfer was complete. He did not know how much more of this he could take.

The soldier's suit-instruments, flickering madly during transfer, flatlined. For a moment the Rillian thought he had outlived his hardware—for however long it would take him to drown in his own wastes. And then he had full instrumentation again.

With a track, and a tracking vector. He'd found the Eleveners.

When the Elevener signal was received, the ground-force commander had committed all the troops at his disposal in over a thousand three-person search teams. The teams operated as trios of individuals, weaving and crossing so that they rotated through each of the sectors of probability assigned them in the search pattern.

If the Eleveners still had the power of movement in spacetime, they might attempt to cut back across the track of their escape. The interlacing search pattern would take care of that possibility.

He was alone. If the Rillian soldier went mad in this endless kaleidoscope of spacetime, his controller would check on his failure. When the controller himself failed—as even a controller would inevitably fail in hideous infinity—the ground-force commander would examine the circumstances.

But so long as the Rillian soldier functioned, he was alone with his duty.

No one—least of all the troops involved—doubted the ability of a single Rillian soldier to deal with the target once it was located, even if the whole Elevener vessel had managed to flee ahead of the navy's claims of destruction.

Equally, no one had thought the searchers *would* locate the target. The encounter had been very near the Rift, and the effect of the navy's massive A-field weapons would have been to send the Elevener ship—or the surviving portion of it—corkscrewing through a potentially infinite segment of spacetime.

The technicians had thought they could calculate probable

courses, so that the search patterns would have a possibility of success . . . though not, they admitted, a statistically significant possibility.

That was enough for the ground-force commander, particularly in view of the navy's failure; and enough for his troops, because they had their orders.

Rillian soldiers understood the theory of probability. Probability meant that if you destroyed one of three opponents, the other two still survived.

The answer to probability was to destroy all of your opponents.

The target vector was so unexpected that the Rillian's first thought was that his instruments had failed after all. He checked them as he hung in space, trying to ignore the fact that he felt as helpless as an infant in the jaws of its father. It was no good saying that his suit was a spacecraft itself. The suit had the properties of a spacecraft, but that did not make it one. . . .

Nor did it make a Rillian soldier into a sailor. He wanted all four feet on the ground, and he wanted something to kill with his new weapon.

He would have both very shortly. His tracking apparatus completed self-test, and the vector shifted when the Rillian twisted his body in the hard alien vacuum. Yes, he'd found the Eleveners, all right.

Instead of fleeing farther, they had made groundfall on a star system within light hours of where they punched back into normal space. Very likely their vessel was damaged; not even the navy could fail completely, with all the resources of the energy sea for their weapons to tap.

The Rillian soldier gave his suit its orders, then waited for the software to come to a decision about how to execute them. The location sensors were reporting garbage, because they had no base line in this universe from which to compute. First, the suit had to set a base line—an artificial one, but only after it had exhausted the possibility that there was a real point of reference within the present reality. That settled, the suit determined a course.

For a binary planet rotating in a common orbit around its star. The Eleveners had touched down on the lesser member of the pair, only an eighth the diameter of its fellow. Its cold core made it a satellite rather than a planet—to a technician, in an excess of precision which a Rillian soldier could neither understand nor appreciate. Effectively airless, which was more desirable than not, given the Rillian soldier's task. An atmosphere would only complicate things, not that it would keep him from—

The suit decided transfer through sponge-space was the most efficient means of crossing the remaining distance. The Rillian soldier was not expecting the total nausea again, but this time it scarcely mattered.

He was thinking about killing.

Chapter 8

MOTHER HEN

"Yes sir," Taylor McLeod was saying into the handset of his NSA-encrypted, digitized, voice-and-data only, milsat-bounced secure phone, trying to ignore the palpable lag-time between his office and the Department of State, far below in Washington. "If it's what you need, then of course you have my personal assurances that bringing the . . . respondent . . . to Earth would pose health risks not only to him but to the general population as well. For the record—"

He turned when his office door opened, covering the mouthpiece with his hand, although the unit had the ability to mute all ambients, including background conversation. "Sit down, Quint; I'll be off in a moment."

McLeod swiveled his chair one hundred eighty degrees, not to further shield his side of the conversation from Dick Quint, the space sciences expert on the U.S. alien team, but so that he could concentrate on the conversation he was having with the Undersecretary of State for Lunar and Cislunar Affairs, whom General Sanders had sicced on him.

"For the record," he resumed, "I'd like to make it more than an epidemiological caution, which we can't sustain for long—certainly not against what you're implying are Congressional calls for an appearance by the respondent before a joint session." McLeod took a deep breath, considered pausing long enough for an objection to be satellited up from Earth, then thought better of it: "We can't risk an argument with the Russians—or with anyone else—about who sees him on Earth, for how long, and in what order. He's our baby, we've got to take good care of him. I can't guarantee his cooperation, let alone his health and safety on Earth, where everyone who's anyone from science and academia, plus half the sovereign nations we're bound to by treaty considerations, will be demanding to interview him. And then there's the stickiness with the Soviets, who might, under such circumstances, contest our primacy. He's our walk-in; until we're finished with him, he doesn't leave the American lunar mission. That's my final word, as head of the alien task force and ranking officer of the lead agency undertaking this debriefing.''

Now McLeod did wait, his eyes closed, for State's response. His pulse was pounding in his ears as he listened to the whispery silence of the secure line. He really didn't need this alien in his life right now. He didn't need the enemies he was making over the Channon affair; he didn't need the notoriety. He'd codenamed the alien ''Lucky'' because it was just McLeod's luck that the friendly fugitive from Fugawi had showed up on his watch. McLeod wasn't angry any more, he didn't have time to be angry. He was scrambling just to cover all the bases. He'd long subscribed to the fatalist catechism that taught: When things can't get any more complicated, they simplify themselves by getting a whole lot worse than complicated. A complete and utter disaster is the simplest thing in the world; it's preventing one that's complex.

This pressure from Sandy's groundside friends to throw a ticker-tape parade for Lucky, all the way down E Street and around the Beltway and back into the Russell Building, wasn't anything he hadn't expected, just something he'd hoped somebody else would table on a Langley desk. Maybe they'd lost their ''Dumb Idea'' rubber stamp, down there.

The Undersecretary wasn't giving McLeod a break today, either. His satellited voice came through finally, reedy with oscillator telltales: ''And off the record?''

Anybody from McLeod's side of the tracks who still thought State had an ''off-the-record'' mode deserved to be Lucky's wet nurse. But McLeod said: ''Off the record, sir, the alien's fearful for his life as it is. The Russians want as big a piece of him as they can cut, and I refuse to be responsible for his security—or the data's—or even to sign off on any order that moves him one inch from his present location. Any further discussion by us on this is a waste of the taxpayers' time and money; put that on the record as well. I've got a debrief to run.''

He swiveled the chair again, the phone cradled between his jaw and shoulder, and waited for the inevitable threat to crawl across all those nanoseconds from Earth to his ear. In the meantime, he pawed through the papers on his desk and held out a notepad to Quint.

Dick Quint, the balding, big-eared Space Command scientist took it, read it, and frowned.

The Undersecretary's frosty, "I'll get back to you on this," when it reached McLeod's ear, was a welcome relief. He cradled the instrument without looking away from Quint.

"What do you think, Dick?"

The bird colonel pulled on his nose. "Lucky's worried that the Rillians, whatever they are, might come after him. What's new about that?"

"Wanting to go darkside? Wanting to visit the crash site? Wanting Yates and Yesilkova because he's got a 'security problem'? What do you make of it? Any bogeys out there that SpaceCom's tracking that don't look right?"

"You're not beginning to believe this crap, Ting?"

"Which crap is that? That we've got a bronze-skinned, kaleidoscope-eyed alien with six fingers and funny organs, in the Security Commissioner's office? Nah, I never believe the evidence of my five senses. It must have been something I ate."

"You know I don't mean the presence of one alien. And you know I didn't appreciate you skipping that luncheon altogether and leaving me to muddle through alone, the sole voice of reason to outshout General Sanders' overt hostility to the whole Soviet team. . . ."

"Sorry. Couldn't be helped. But look at those notes again. Lucky's saying he felt 'Rillians touch Channon's mind.' Then: 'Feel minds hunt, catch.' Next he's asking for Yates and Yesilkova to take him darkside, to the crash site. That's all new. Something's changed. . . ."

"Maybe he's bored to tears. Maybe he lost a contact lens out there and just realized." Dick Quint scowled at the notes in front of him, culled from McLeod's meeting with the alien.

"I'm moving him over here. I want you to huddle with my ADC on any special precautions you'd like. And—"

"Are you going to let him?"

"Let who what?"

"Let Lucky go darkside with Yes and Yahoo?"

"Christ, I can't even find Yates and Yesilkova. They're probably making passionate love in a suit-room. Won't answer their phones. Some Security Commissioner. But the answer's *no*, not darkside. Not unless you think it's worth the risk . . .''

"Risk?'' Quint looked up at McLeod and his expression was impersonal. "The only risk you're taking that's quantifiable is from terrestrials—Soviets, our people, the usual motley crew.''

"Okay, the answer's still *no*: no moonwalk. Let's get this Space Command briefing roughed out so that I can scrounge enough time to suck a soup canister in the shower before we're due there.''

"No problem. First, I'd like to ask for a mathematician of our own. I'm good on general stuff, but you need somebody who's up to the Russian expert, Sultanian. Second, I think if you're worried about Lucky's security, the less people who know where he is, the better.''

"I don't follow you,'' McLeod said cautiously. Quint's comment seemingly had nothing to do with the briefing. But McLeod knew Dick Quint as a dedicated professional, with ten years more experience in the trenches than he himself had. Quint could have written his own ticket in private industry, but he hadn't done that; he cared as only a military career-man could. And McLeod wasn't enough of a fool to think that gung ho meant stupid.

Quint was anything but. "*You* don't follow me?'' he said. "It was eavesdropping on your groundside call that gave me the idea, although I admit I'd been looking for a likely scenario to fly. I think if I were you, I'd introduce a sudden and all-pervasive quarantine—at the SpaceCom briefing, since the Russians are going to sit in on it. Say the alien's not feeling well and, as lead agency, your people can't risk any more contact—with anybody—until we find out what's wrong with him and see whether any of the already exposed humans catch it. That takes care of my problem with Soviet kibitzing, and yours with security: Everybody who's been with Lucky is confined to quarters, under close monitoring for, say, a week. . . .'' Quint's eyes were very bright.

"It'd make an awful flap,'' McLeod said, fighting a grin that threatened to spread over his face. "You really need to play catch-up that badly?''

"I need to bring some quantum-mechanics guy up from groundside who specializes in the theoretical. A-field potential is something we haven't done half as much with as the Russians have.''

"And they're not sharing with you?" McLeod's attempt to sound concerned sounded sarcastic instead. When Quint stiffened, he said, "Sorry, Dick. I feel like my brain needs a laxative, and everywhere I look, all I see is burgeoning complexity."

"Give me a week or two alone with Lucky, and get me an A-field specialist up here, and I'll show you some results. Otherwise, you might as well give whatever science advantage this alien offers to the Soviets, out of hand."

"That bad?"

"It's not bad; it's worse: We're outgunned by their team. Promise me you'll replace Yates with a mathematician, and I'll go into that SpaceCom meeting and scare everybody there so completely that none of them, including our beloved General Sanders, will go near that alien without a direct order from a head of State.''

"Yates? Who'll run security for the debrief?"

"Ting, with you heading this team, the only one you're fooling with this drivel about Yates being needed for security is Yates. Unless all those big healthy boys of yours are hanging around hoping to challenge the Moscow soccer team to a low-g match . . . ?''

"All right, Dick. You've got it. All of it. As soon as I find Yates and Yesilkova, that is. Sending my people to hunt them up personally ought to be enough of an excuse—out of the command chain during an emergency, that sort of thing."

"Terrific. Let's go over the rest of these points, then."

"In a sec. You know that Lucky likes Yates and Yesilkova better than all the rest of us put together?''

"No, I don't know that. I know that he thinks he's threatened, and they have the right job descriptions. Don't anthropomorphize his behavior, Ting, just because he looks a little like us—the way Ella is doing.''

"Have you a problem with Ms. Bradley's performance?"

"Not that I'll go on record with, no. But as I said, I'd like specialists—I'd really like an astrophysicist of our own in Bradley's place. Anthropology isn't exactly an action discipline.''

"Military specialists, no doubt—pet two-stars with Space Command patches on their Ph.D's. You know, I'm annoyed at Yates myself, and I admit I'm not unbiased where Ella's concerned. But replace both with military-fielded experts to make the Soviets redundant? This isn't the Cold War, Dick, at least not so far as I'm concerned.''

''Isn't it? I think it's getting colder than hell out there.'' Quint's chin jutted to the ceiling, and the airless surface beyond.

''We're supposed to be cooperating with the USSR, remember. If we bring in a mathematician to match theirs, and an astrophysicist to match theirs, and bounce Ella and the Security Commissioner for the UN, then we're saying (a) we don't trust you and (b) we don't trust the UN. We're also admitting that I'm doing more up here than playing backgammon with Minsky. Sorry, Quint, I've rethought it: All the players stay the same. You want a mathematician, bring him up; we'll smuggle him in to see Lucky. Best I can do.''

Some things never changed. McLeod was so tired he'd almost fallen for it. Well, you couldn't expect miracles. Agencies would jockey for position and the Space Command had a vested interest in anything extraterrestrial. But as long as McLeod was running this show, the only foxes in the hen house were going to be his—and the Soviets', of course.

Chapter 9

COMPANY COMING

It was a crash site, not a landing.

The Eleveners would have attempted to destroy their traces, anyway—that was basic; no Rillian soldier could imagine a race too peaceful, too passive, not to have learned that. They could not have been successful in hiding from his sensors, of course. . . .

But this was no attempt at concealment. Impact; a massive cold explosion; and the track of one survivor.

The Rillian soldier twitched his ear-points sideways, further broadening the lines of his broad, flat skull. It was his equivalent of a grin, and as he made it he checked the fit of his weapon against his shoulder. He began to follow.

Since the track and the vector were generally congruent, the Rillian soldier decided to follow the former. The planet's low gravity was no handicap; his four stumpy legs fell into the rhythm of a trot and took him skimming over the irregular surface in a series of low arcs.

He was used to operations in low gravity and in zero gravity. Used to high gravity as well, though to a Rillian, "high gravity" implied metals sagging against their own crystalline structure. His suit amplified his movements, almost turning his thoughts into motion; but even without that help, the soldier could maintain his rocking pace for days.

If the vector diverged abruptly from the track, the Rillian soldier would reconsider his course of action. He would reconsider, for instance, if the Elevener again boarded a spacecraft and left the planet.

That was a possibility, because—to the soldier's amazement—this airless ball was inhabited. There were satellites in powered stasis above the surface, shouting incessantly at pitches higher than Rillian speech but well within the range of the soldier's hearing.

His suit would block the noise if he asked it to, but the notion of deafening himself on the verge of combat gave the Rillian soldier a twinge reminiscent of sponge-space transfer. The noise was probably speech—certainly speech; the inhabitants had not gone to the effort of maintaining satellites just to shout shrill garbage at the first Rillian who arrived. His suit hardware was capable of sponge-space navigation; it could easily have translated the noise into intelligible sound, if anybody had bothered to program it to do so.

No one had, of course. He was a Rillian soldier, and the ability to communicate with lesser races was not esteemed as a virtue except at the highest levels of the Rillian polity.

And only then to the extent that communication was a matter of getting one's point across . . .

The Rillian scanned his surroundings, then raised his weapon. Its stock nestled against his shoulder. Lifting the weapon threw up automatically the targeting display as a ghost image, a holographic vacuum quivering against the empty reality. He could have let the suit aim for him, but there was no need of that; and besides, he was proud of his marksmanship.

The noise source was moving in a slow orbit. Another of its screaming ilk was just coming over the horizon, to take up its duties when the first passed on—there must be a trio to maintain unbroken communication across the planet. The Rillian soldier panned with his upper body while his left hand slid on the forestock to extend the sight picture. A flicker, a shape—

A communications satellite, festooned with solar panels, reaction motors to hold it in unstable equilibrium—and microwave dishes that shrieked down on the Rillian soldier and made his scales quiver in hideous sympathy.

He fired.

The casing of the Rillian weapon was a single integral crystal with a pair of horns flaring twenty centimeters to either side of the muzzle. The horn-tips pointed forward like those of a bull. Nothing visible happened to the weapon when the soldier triggered it; but at the point of intersection of the fields generated by the two horns, a hole opened in spacetime.

The comsat disintegrated like a spark from a star's coronal display. Fragments of crystal and metal blasted out in the fury of their own destruction, streaming trailers of glowing plasma. For as long as the Rillian soldier triggered his weapon the infinite sea of energy underlying the universe—underlying *every* universe—spewed out and devoured whatever was in its path.

In the relative silence the Rillian surveyed his surroundings again.

He was overlooking one of the planet's population centers. It was clearly an outpost of the larger planet in the binary system, the blue-white ball which had dominated the sky almost as soon as the Rillian started to follow the Elevener's track. Here, they burrowed into the planetary rock or trenched and backfilled over themselves, huddling in wretched wormholes for protection.

The soldier's scales rippled in his equivalent of a shudder. Given time, his weapon could excise the whole of this warren, despite its thick, refractory covering. Silica, alumina, titanium oxides . . .

He could burn it out the way a surgeon had removed a boil from the muscles beneath his dense neck-scales. But that had taken time. He shrugged reflexively; needles that were partly memory, partly scar tissue, answered the movement.

With the weapon the Rillian soldier carried, destroying this installation would take hours. During that time, the ravening fountains of destruction spurting from the energy sea would overload his sensors.

Assurance of destroying the installation was not at all the same thing as being sure of destroying his quarry.

If he disturbed spacetime to that degree, he would lose his vector. He might lose the Elevener's track as well, burying it in an avalanche of spacetime transients from which even the fleet's battle-management computers could extract only a spiderweb of possibility.

That was the error the navy had made. If the Rillian soldier repeated it, the ground-force commander would not have to order his execution. His section controller would flay the soldier, scale by scale, before he reported the situation.

On request, the soldier's sensors located and tracked vessels in ballistic arcs between this planet and the greater one. Occasionally a vessel would vary its course by using reaction motors.

The local inhabitants were not folk whom a Rillian soldier needed to fear. Neither were the Eleveners. So . . .

The Elevener's track led to a small surface installation, an airlock at one end of the rail-and-pylon roadway. At the other end of the roadway was the site where the local spacecraft took off and landed, a cautious distance and the wall of a meteor crater away from the population center.

The Rillian soldier started for the airlock, trying to keep from bouncing high in hormonal elation. Success. After so much discomfort, success.

And a city to gut.

Chapter 10

FIELD EFFECT

Channon had sensed the Rillian probe, then it was gone. First he'd panicked, alone with only humans in this alien dugout on an airless moon.

Subsequently he'd convinced Bradley to summon McLeod, and McLeod to summon Yates and Yesilkov, and his panic had eased. Providence would guide him; the universe was a blazing panorama of options. He would find one.

Or he would not. Still he was isolated from most humans, from scientists and technologists of the sort whose help he needed to attempt building the warning beacon. But he had regained control of his emotions, often the most difficult task among these beings who broadcast their feelings unceasingly.

Once he'd buttressed his person against the onslaught of their frightened hearts, he knew that stopping his own heart was no option he might consider.

The Rillian probe's passing had taught him that. When it was gone, he'd realized its coming had been a gift in disguise. Providence had sent him a sign. He was not alone, adrift in spacetime irremediably, or—worse—lost in time itself. If the Rillian probe could reach him, then Channon could reach the Kiri Unity.

Given time, given constancy, given strength of purpose and firm guidance levied upon the humans here, he could build the beacon which would warn the Kiri Unity of the massing Rillian threat. Using the fate of the *KirStar* as a catalyst, an object lesson, and a prod to action, Channon could still serve his purpose, even from this great distance. Civilization must meet the Rillian threat and overcome it, by moral rectitude or counterforce.

And the passing of the Rillian probe had answered a question that Channon had not dared pose. It was not already too late. He was not marooned somewhere in the future, or so far in the past by standard clock time that no warning he sent would ever reach an ear that could heed it.

Now that he'd been gifted by Providence with new hope, he realized that he missed the Rillian probe once it had gone. He was alone again, among these children of a faint and long-lost star.

So when he thought he sensed a second Rillian mind, he discounted the sensation. He was not a telepath of note, but he was a trained empath; he heard with his body's extra-low frequency receptors, as did all Kiri.

He thought he heard a Rillian, a primal killer splashing out reactions of fear, pain, destruction, triumph.

Then he did not. He heard only Bradley, who was increasingly uncomfortable because Yates and Yesilkov had not yet arrived and she could not leave.

By slitting his eyes where he lay on the couch, Channon could see Bradley slumped over Yates's desk, head in her hands, without alerting her that he was "awake."

If any of these humans had truly been "awake" by *Webster's* definition, Channon's task would be easier here. But they all slept yet, merely promises of what they someday might become.

And among them, Channon must perform a miracle. He could not stop his heart; he could not lose hope. He must create the spacetime beacon that would warn the Kiri in time.

He was so grateful to the parent universe that had spawned him, he at first thought he had conjured a second Rillian presence here—to ease his loneliness, to prove his thesis. Time was not the problem. He was not cast adrift in spacetime on some distant shore that could not be bridged through the Rift because 11-space did not contain it.

Whatever spacetime this was, it was accessible through the Rift; it was part of the 11-space matrix. He hadn't been blown so far along the temporal axis that a message from him would fall on deaf ears in a universe that had not yet spawned the twelve races of the Kiri Unity. If the Rillians could probe here after him, then he could probe Kiri spacetime from here as well.

Therefore, his original mandate was yet in effect. The beacon, once constructed, would fulfill Channon's purpose, but until then, there was no chance of doing less.

He couldn't summarily decide to terminate his span; he couldn't sleep in Terri's arms; he could do no less than complete the task he'd undertaken when *KirStar* set out for the Rillian frontier.

For this answer to his quandary, he thanked the Rillians, his self-appointed enemy. When he came face to face with a Rillian emissary, or when one of his successors, armed with the message he'd send, did so—then this true emotion of gratitude would be invaluable.

But until the day, as his people said, only right thought and right action would teach the future what to bring as its greeting gift.

Terri would be so pleased, when their spirits met again, to know he'd found a way to appreciate the Rillians. Hate was the destabilizer, the sentient being's equivalent of molecular degeneration.

Like certain atomic structures that replenished lost energy from the energy sea and remained stable thereby, the Kiri Unity's stability was assured by the replenishment of respect and good will among all races. It was one of the cornerstones of the Kiri way.

With his purpose firmly in the forefront of his mind, Channon sat up on the couch, knowing that Bradley would immediately react to this "wakefulness."

She sat up straight. She scraped her limp hair from her face. She grimaced at him. "Now don't start with the 'where's Yates, where's Yesilkov' line again. We're doing our best to find them. They can't stay incommunicado forever. Would you like some jasmine tea, or a cucumber sandwich?"

"Water with flowers, yes; thanks upon you." The drink was stimulating, heady. He must be careful not to become addicted. But his throat watered, thinking about it.

Bradley got up. Her motions were jerky. "Well, I'm going to eat something, and you'll just have to watch me kill those poor, helpless fruits and vegetables, if you won't join in." She showed him her teeth again so that he would understand that this was a pleasantry.

They'd discussed the difficulties of eating sentient plants while those plants were still full of life, but she saw no alternative: Very little that nourished humans was not either still living, or killed for the purpose of being eaten when newly dead.

It was repulsive at first, but not horrible beyond tolerance. Life transmuted to higher forms, leaving behind cellular carcasses, which in their turn were transmuted into renewed cellular life in the bodies of these human omnivores. Until humans developed the technology to produce nonsentient nutrients, they would subsist as killers of all lesser species.

Again he was struck with an instinctive desire to equate human and Rillian behavior. But to discuss it with Bradley . . .

She was talking to the desktop communicator, ordering food. "Fruit salad with cottage cheese, yogurt on the side, jasmine tea, coffee, salad no dressing—for three. And buzz Undersecretary McLeod's office for me. Tell him I've ordered him a light supper and I'm expecting him to join us as soon as he's done at SpaceCom."

As she was straightening up, a wash of stimulus seemed to erase her from Channon's perceptions. In her place he saw . . . something: a sight picture; a ball exploding.

Simultaneously, he felt a cascade of jaw-numbing emotions. First, fury came and went—so intense it made his throat close up. Then he was inundated by vertigo, a sense of gut-wrenching anguish. After that, a horripilation enveloped him from head to toe. Finally, he felt a solid reintegration of his person. But that person had four legs rather than two, and clutched a weapon like curving horns, down which its attention was directed . . .

. . . to the portal through which Channon had entered the underground city.

"Friend Bradley," Channon said. "Kill dinner, one thing; kill higher life, other thing. Bad thing. Not kill Rillian, for Channon's sake, okay?"

"Channon, if we find a Rillian and have to kill him, it won't be because of you. Don't worry." She was moving toward him, displaying what he'd come to know as a panoply of body-expressions meant to transmit total attention.

She sat on a chair she pulled before the couch. "Don't worry so, Channon. We'll protect you as best we can. And help you as much as we can. We're committed. You say you're psychic; you should know that."

"Not kill Rillian. Channon negotiator. Channon needs talk with Rillian. Very important talk."

"Yes, your government. We know. We want to talk to your government too, Channon, as soon as we get your transmitter built. But you'll have to be more helpful—"

"Not then, now. Say, friend Bradley, that Channon will talk with living Rillian—"

"Channon, what makes you think some living Rillian is going to come here? Or that if he does, we wouldn't want to talk with him as much as we want to talk with you?"

"Rillian coming here, is now. While we speak, coming. Exploding—destroying—your ball communicator not make you kill Rillian?''

''You think that when a Rillian comes here he'll destroy a comsat? Well, that'll give us some warning, anyway.'' Bradley's eyes were very shiny; her whole body telegraphed approval and the hope that he'd keep talking to her.

Channon didn't understand what it was he was failing to communicate, how he was misusing her language so badly that what she thought she understood was not what he'd said.

So he tried one more time to communicate the urgency of his message, using the present tense as forcefully as he could: ''Rillian is coming here now. Comsat is past. Promise Channon humans not shoot—''

A blare of broadcast Rillian angst, disassociation, and vertigo silenced him.

When he could see Bradley again, she was assuring him that ''It's been centuries since we shot first and asked questions later, Channon. Don't worry so. We'll help you get your message to your people, you just wait and see.''

Channon took extraordinary measures in the face of the Rillian's broadcast discomfort: He reached over beside him and took his helmet from the couch. He put it on.

Bradley was distraught. ''Channon, don't. Please, Channon, I didn't mean to upset you. Don't start this farside madness again. You're not going anywhere until Ting's satisfied that such a trip is safe for you. We value you very highly, remember. You're the first alien contact we've ever had.''

Inside his helmet, Channon could filter his naked person's reception of the extra-low frequency waves that the Rillian was broadcasting during the stress of whatever twisted him inside out.

''First, not last,'' he muttered in his own language. And then, using his suit's speaker, he said again to the human who would not understand the simplest thing he was trying to tell her: ''Yates and Yesilkov, Bradley. McLeod promised Channon Yates and Yesilkov.''

Yates and Yesilkov would understand what Channon was trying to say. He must communicate to these feral creatures how much lay at stake on their airless little moon in this backwater of spacetime. He must convince them not to kill the Rillian, until he had a chance to convince the Rillian not to kill the humans.

It was what Terri would have wanted. It was a chance beyond price, an opportunity beyond measure. If he could sit down with this Rillian and begin a dialogue, the Kiri Unity would be forever in mankind's debt.

But it had already destroyed one of their satellites. And it would destroy more before he could get to it, even with the help of Yates and Yesilkov.

This plan, Channon knew, was not without danger. But the danger approached in any case. The Rillian would surely kill him, as it had doubtless been ordered here to do, if he could not reason with it first—unless the humans killed it before it got to him.

Channon still wanted desperately to send a message of warning to the Kiri Unity. But Providence was nudging events in a different direction. Time was increasingly short—for all of them.

"Yates," he said implacably to Bradley through his helmet speaker. "Yesilkov."

And within his helmet, he arranged his features in a display of contemplative acuity: The Rillian was here; he was no longer alone. If nothing he did served to further his cause, he would be in Terri's spirit arms sooner than expected.

This did not displease him. When events conspire, intelligent beings take the message from the moment. It now seemed that his entire span had been leading him toward this confrontation with the Rillian emissary.

He was ready. It was what he was trained for; it was what *KirStar* had journeyed across the Rift for. He was no longer contemplating running away, to distract the Rillian from the primitives he hid among. If that had been appropriate, a way would have been provided.

He only regretted that lives of higher consciousness than vegetables would be spent to secure this meeting—human lives.

The crew and team aboard the *KirStar* had been composed of volunteers willing to take such risks. Looking at Bradley, he could not convince himself that she, or any of her species with the exception of Yates and Yesilkov, would volunteer to do the same.

Chapter 11

GOVERNMENT BUSINESS

If the Commissioner of Security commandeered the office of a Supervisor in Entry Division while the Commissioner's own office was being renovated, nobody was going to complain . . . except maybe the supervisor herself.

And God knew, Sam Yates had given her enough reason to complain recently.

Sonya Yesilkov sat in the jump seat folded down from the back wall, staring at Yates—glaring at him—across the desk that'd been his before it was hers; and was his again. He could be brusque and put-upon; tell Supervisor Yesilkov that they were both in this other thing, this fucking alien thing, and she could stop sulking about him transferring into her office for the duration.

He could *act* put-upon, but that'd be a lie, a denial of the real problem.

It was the sort of lie that provided a great way to sweep things under the rug: Pretend something was something else, deal with the something else, then act hurt and superior when the other party burst out in frustrated rage. He'd handled his marriage that way; and if it wasn't all his fault, then he wasn't *about* to claim he was putty for somebody like Cecile to shape any way she pleased.

He'd done what he'd done. He wasn't going to do that particular thing again if he could help it.

"Sonya," he said, realizing this was the first time they'd had alone since the mess—the mess he *hadn't* made—blew up. "I screwed up. Bad. When I rousted you on the Code Yellow."

The wall behind Yesilkov kept her from leaning over the back of her chair. She twisted sideways on the seat and stretched her arms over her head and backward. Tendons stood out on her bare forearms as they strained against her interlaced fingers.

Now that she'd been promoted, Sonya didn't wear uniforms much, any more than Yates had done when he was in the Supervisor slot. Today she was in pale green slacks and a silk pullover of the same hue but slightly greater color saturation. There was probably a bandeau beneath the blouse, but the silk rippled as if the deltoids and large, flat breasts were unconfined.

Yesilkov's eyes focused on the low, stained ceiling. Her blond hair was so short that it only fluffed a little instead of hanging down in this position. She said, "Gettin' some flak, are we, boyo? Shouldn't have let the nasty Russkies in on the deal of the century."

All that passed for humor was on the brittle surface of her voice.

"Bullshit," Sam Yates said calmly, because now that he'd started, there was nothing left but calm.

He'd never told Sonya Yesilkov that he loved her. He *didn't* love her.

But he knew he didn't want to lose whatever it was they had. Especially because he'd been jealous and acted on it, proving that he was her boss and he could move her around like a poker chip if he felt like it.

She shrugged out of her contortions and met his eyes, waiting for him to go on.

"I work for the UN," he said. "So long as I do my job right, the whole U.S. Government can collectively fuck itself for all I care."

As he spoke, Yates let anger heat and tumble the words to make them real, believable. Not that he had to pretend the anger . . .

"They could have—" Yesilkov said. Her tone and eyes sharpened. "Taylor McLeod could have your job, *and* your ass, so fast you wouldn't be able to clean out your desk. Don't give me that crap about 'I don't work—' "

"I don't work for Taylor McLeod," Yates said in a gun-barrel voice under gunsight eyes.

Yesilkov stopped speaking as abruptly as if he'd shouted her down. She'd seen Sam Yates that calm before.

"If they want the job," he said, "they can have it. If they

want the rest of me, there's enough of 'em they can have that too.''

Licking his lips—it didn't help, because his tongue and mouth were dry and he wasn't faking anything now—Yates said, ''I didn't think about it when I called you in. If I'd thought, I'd have done the same thing. Because it was the right choice. And maybe some people don't much like what I did, but''—he started to grin, his eyes focused somewhere else—''none of 'em have had the balls to say so yet to my face.''

Sonya laughed and stood up. ''Didn't they?'' she said with a kittenish lilt he remembered also. ''I had a fella wonder if there hadn't been some way I coulda took you out of play when I realized how hot this thing was.''

Yates raised an eyebrow.

''His secretary was coming by the next shuttle,'' the stocky blond continued. She shook her head sadly. ''The poor thing's entry approval got lost in the computer, so she spent twelve hours in a holding cell.''

Yates stood up cautiously. Quick movements in lunar gravity meant you bounced off the far wall or the ceiling. ''They wouldn't have to think real hard,'' he began, pressing upward against the ceiling at the spot he'd used for isometrics when this was *his* cubbyhole—''to figure out this was a bad one to play Cowboys and Indians over.'' He continued pressing upward, against the megatons of living rock, not even backfill, that covered the old section of UN Headquarters.

''The way you and McLeod are doing,'' Sonya gibed.

The comment was pointed, but there was none of the bitter control of moments before.

Besides, it was true. It had taken Sam Yates a while, but he'd finally learned not to get mad when somebody jabbed him with the truth. It was that or go into some business where the truth didn't matter; and he'd have made a lousy spook.

So he laughed now and said, ''Well, nobody ever expected *me* to have good sense. Besides—'' his voice wasn't laughing anymore, ''nobody died and appointed Taylor McLeod God. Whatever he may think.''

''Or what Ella thinks?'' Yesilkov asked softly.

Yates shook his head, not to the question but the whole subject.

He relaxed his body and looked around the tiny office. It was more crowded than he remembered it. Partly that was Yesilkov's style. There was no sacrosanct space in the uniformed patrol substations, so she'd gotten into the habit of stacking material anywhere, everywhere. If you didn't fill the space, somebody on the next shift would.

In addition to what was already there, a lot of communications and data transfer equipment arrived with Yates when he shifted his office back here. Three of the ceiling corners were filled by the heads of a hologram projector that could produce high-resolution images of twice the volume of this Entry Section office.

For now he'd cut all incomings, but if he wanted to, he could conference-call with Earth and the asteroid belts, through the quarter-meter cube of the secure phone bank which took up half the surface of the desk. And—

Yates blinked. "When'd you get that?" he asked, pointing at the holotank against the wall next to Sonya. It was a standard unit, nothing special; but it looked brand new. The balky unit he'd cursed and struggled with throughout his tour as supervisor was gone.

" 'Bout three days after I moved in," Yesilkov said through the curtain of caution that dropped over her eyes. "The guys installing it said it was a priority request from the Commissioner of Security."

"Damn," Yates said. "Damn. Yeah, I did do that. I forgot, Sonya." He closed his eyes and rubbed his forehead hard with the tips of his fingers. This fucking job was getting to him. . . .

"We been pretty busy, you'n me," Yesilkov said softly, a little closer to Yates than she'd been when he closed his eyes.

He opened them. She was reaching for his shoulder. He took her hand and held it gently as he said, "Sonya, I called you five minutes before I should've on Channon. Because I was pissed, because—"

He couldn't say, "Because I was jealous." She was *married* for chrissake! And Sam Yates wasn't exactly a celibate himself, to wonder who was dipping his wick in Sonya Yesilkov.

"Because I was jealous," Yates said, because that was the truth. Saying it didn't make him more an idiot than he was already. "I—won't do that again."

"We been pretty busy," she repeated, fingering his ribs with her free hand.

The office didn't have a solid door, just sound-absorbent strip curtains. Yesilkov glanced toward them as Yates cupped her butt with one hand, squeezing her closer, while the other hand slid beneath her blouse and bandeau, like the old friend it was.

If the Commissioner of Security didn't care, she sure as hell didn't; though with all her mess stacked double-height to make room for the extra hardware, they were going to have to lean against a wall if things progressed much farther in the direction they were headed.

Yates had never been the sort to back off when he thought he had a good idea.

"Here, let me—" Yesilkov said, reaching for the touch-sensitive fastener of her slacks.

A phone rang with a loud Priority warble.

Yates turned to the big unit on the desk. "I told my people that *nobody* was to disturb me," he said conversationally as he reached for the handset. "Whoever misunderstood is out of a—"

There was a dial tone on the handset. The emergency call sounded again.

"Sorry, Sam," Yesilkov muttered. She reached past Yates and keyed the speaker of her own phone, still connected. "Go ahead," she said as her hands rearranged her blouse.

"Sir, it's the Main Gate!" cried a voice she couldn't recognize because of its distortion. "We got something coming and you *gotta* look at it! We got a tank!"

"Calm down and give us the feed, Gatewood," said Yates. He *did* recognize the voice—and he seemed to be able to get back to business in a way Yesilkov didn't find altogether flattering. "We'll take care of it. Address the feed Alpha Romeo Alpha Mike Star, that's ARAM Star."

"Hologram, project feed," Yesilkov said.

"Hologram, project feed," Yates repeated, because the big unit had an interlock keyed to his voice, not hers. They pressed back against the walls as the projector filled the center of the office with a three-dimensional view from the holocameras mounted above the buried city to deter smuggling and terrorists.

"Jesus Christ," Yates said. The Russian woman muttered something scatological.

It wasn't a tank, because tanks don't move across the lunar surface on four stumpy legs; but apart from that, Gatewood's description fit the bill perfectly. The intruder seemed to be about twenty feet long and heavy-bodied. Its whole exterior was covered with a seamless layer of flexible metal whose color quivered between violet and cobalt blue.

There were two arms beneath the dome that might be a helmet. The arms were longer than the legs, and in the hands was a backwards crossbow that the creature raised to its shoulder—

"Gatewood, get the hell out!" Yesilkov shouted. "Move! Move! Move!"

Chapter 12

POINT OF CONTACT

The doorway was big enough to pass a Rillian soldier. That was important, because the Rillian did not want to even consider scraping and blasting his way along after he got inside.

Not that he would refuse to do whatever was necessary.

The door was a massive structure of titanium alloy, hardened against meteor impact and braced to withstand quakes without losing its seal. If the inhabitants were aware of the Rillian's approach—and by now they must have been aware—the portal would be locked and guarded by every means available.

None of that mattered in the least. The Rillian aimed his weapon at the lower left corner of the door valves, then swept across and up while squeezing the trigger.

Rock bubbled and split an instant before the airlock doors shattered like bomb casings. The heart of the thick panel was opened to more energy than was contained in the universe of which the panel was a part. The alloy's toughness contained the plasma at its core for a microsecond; then the airlock blew to fragments in a dazzling white flash.

A piece of titanium the size of a card table blew back, tumbling into the Rillian soldier's helmet. His suit's dynamic armor, powered by the same A-field source that energized his weapon, reacted.

The Rillian staggered and swore.

When his armor went live, the Rillian was invulnerable; but until it returned to stand-by, he was as blind and isolated as if he were in a sponge-space transit. For all practical purposes, he *was* in sponge-space transit: Everything within the bubble formed by his armor had dropped out of normal spacetime, untouched and untouchable.

The Rillian soldier's suit went live at a rate faster than that of light in normal spacetime, but its return to stand-by was based on a computed delay rather than observation. When the suit dropped out of the universe, so did *all* its sensing apparatus. The lag-time was insignificant, a mere eye blink, the technicians said.

The technicians had never gone utterly blind and deaf in the middle of combat, their instruments cartwheeling and their guts shrinking to a pinhead. An eye-blink is enough time to imagine plucking out a technician's claws, then his scales, then his—

The soldier's vision cleared. He felt his legs thrash onto the surface, stutter-stepping because they had lost the pace as surely as his conscious mind had done. The outer lock was clear except for quivering sparks, spacetime transients. You could not pull a handful of the universe through a hole in itself and expect it to snap back unaffected when you let it go.

The piece of self-made shrapnel had been a cheap warning. The locals might not be able to harm a Rillian soldier, but the soldier could cause himself enormous inconvenience unless he was careful.

He stepped sideways and aimed at the inner door from a safer angle than that at which he'd blasted the exterior. He fired.

Of course. This time only a few beads of blazing metal sprayed outward, onto the stabilized surface of the entrance apron. Almost all the effect had been expended toward the community's interior.

The Rillian soldier strode forward, forcing himself to ignore the twinkling transients. They could not hurt him in his suit, but—

He saw flickers of false memory: creatures with long necks and bodies massive even by Rillian standards, ratcheting their jaws backward and forward as they stared at him with dumb brown eyes.

Not here, not now, not him. Merely a harmless side effect of the weaponry.

But the soldier did not fire again as he stepped through the blazing airlock, as he might otherwise have done.

There was a body just within the airlock: four-limbed, erect when living. The nub of a door valve was ablaze with some private fury, though the Rillian had given it only a short burst with his weapon.

Balls of plasma, blue and yellow, skittered down the broad corridor beyond, guided by the dielectric patterns of buried pipes and cables. The balls burst when the spacetime bubbles containing them reverted to the local standard. Each crash of release was further muted as the internal atmosphere vented to the lunar surface.

An oxygen atmosphere. That was good. The Rillian's weapon had a lock-out to prevent it from affecting a chlorine atmosphere like that bathing the soldier himself. Inverted effects were not only possible, they were inevitable under field conditions.

The Rillian soldier dropped out of spacetime—back and out again—back, out; back, out; back—

Strobe-lit by the lag-time of the suit's protective reaction, the Rillian saw one of the locals aiming a hand-sized weapon at him and spraying a stream of darts that would have been entirely harmless to the soldier even if he stood in his bare hide to receive them. . . .

As the local stood—with neither armor nor breathing apparatus, though by now the atmospheric pressure must have been far below that necessary to sustain the creature's life. And every time one of those *ridiculous* darts struck, the Rillian suit—as mindless as the moronic technicians who had programmed it—threw itself into limbo. . . .

For about the same time-delay as it took for the next dart to strike.

The Rillian came out of subspace and stayed. He turned, squeezing the trigger of his weapon while his guts flip-flopped in momentary expectation of being flung back into sponge-space. His holographic sighting display tumbled like a kaleidoscope as the weapon's muzzle slid sideways and reality dissolved before it.

The local threw his dart gun after he emptied it. He was jumping back toward an alcove beside the airlock, but its door had slammed automatically with the lowered pressure.

The Rillian soldier squeezed his trigger and then, catching his breath, surveyed the interior of the habitat.

There was a long corridor bounded with closed doors and, in some cases, transparent walls displaying the interiors. There were banks of lights in the corridor ceiling, emitting in a range close to that of the system's sun when filtered through a thin oxygen/nitrogen atmosphere.

The local atmospheric pressure was rising. Behind the Rillian, green foam bubbled across the gap where the airlock had been, expanding and hardening. He ignored it. He could blow another opening whenever he chose.

The soldier strode forward, following the Elevener's track. Doors opened along the corridor; he fired to convince the locals to stay out of his way. Though he was careful to keep his burst short, the A-field weapon followed laws beyond those which the technicians had devised to govern it. A spear of blazing oxygen, on a reciprocal of the direction in which the weapon pointed, enveloped the Rillian soldier and forced his suit to fling him back out of current spacetime.

He returned from his protective envelope, cursing the technicians, cursing his commander—and cursing himself, for the terrible fear that swallowed him every time his armor flashed live. A line of molten rock and metal had danced across the side of the corridor he'd targeted, thickened occasionally by paired whorls as nearly symmetrical as the arms of spiral nebulae.

The soldier knew already that he could never be sure of what effect he would achieve when he triggered his weapon. Just that the effect would be sufficient.

The local with the dart gun, for instance, was now melded with the door he had been trying to enter when he became the focus of the A-field weapon. The legs were thrust back into the corridor. The Rillian soldier thought he had seen them twitch for an instant after the event.

An orange-painted vehicle on wheels spun out of a cross-corridor ahead of the Rillian. It shrank in on itself when he fired, the center of a universe expanding inward until it vanished from present spacetime.

Because the Rillian soldier was concentrating on that target, he almost missed the blue vehicle with six locals aboard when it skidded into the central corridor from the next crossing up. He fired, but a burst of those infuriating darts sleeted across his armor and knocked him out of existence.

The Rillian swung back to objective reality in a state of nausea that was half anticipation of the seesaw of darts and more darts until he managed to—

But he already had. The distant vehicle was a glittering chaos of fire and spacetime transients. He'd triggered a burst before the darts hit him, and his reflexive aim had been true.

They could not hurt a Rillian soldier, these soft, four-limbed folk who spat darts at him. But they were determined to interfere to the full extent they were capable, instead of letting him get on with his task.

He fired a long burst, steeling himself against the backblast that failed to occur—this time. A line of cold fire swept up the corridor, choosing to fling offshoots to either side at intersections, like a vine seeking sunlight. There was a great deal of noise, but nothing in the Rillian's vocal range except the hash generated when spacetime ripped and compressed.

The folk of this warren chose to resist? So be it. It would have been easier if the Rillian soldier had not been alone, but the problem of safeguarding his back was one he could deal with.

The Rillian moved on, shifting from side to side and firing into each doorway as he passed.

Chapter 13

THE WELCOMING
COMMITTEE

Gatewood had aligned the sending cameras on the intruder, not the main airlock, and the creature's weapon didn't do anything visible in the display in Yesilkov's office.

When a huge chunk of the airlock sailed through the center of the holographic display, Yates didn't have much doubt about what had happened.

The dust and gas that blasted from the ruptured airlock formed a momentary atmosphere, dazzling in the lunar sunlight. Maybe that was why the intruder's image flickered—but what the hell had happened when the piece of door hit the creature? A half ton of titanium alloy moving at that speed should've taken care of the problem, even if the six-limbed thing was armored like a battleship.

If the chunk didn't demolish the creature—and it hadn't, there was no doubt about that—they should at least have bounced apart . . . instead of the creature staggering in the visual spectrum, and the lock panel passing through the same location with no apparent contact.

Yates had more pressing concerns right now, but he'd want to run that scene again, later.

If there was a later.

"System, General Alert," Yates said. "Meteor impact, main lock breached. Out."

Nothing like the reality he watched striding out of the ho-lofield Gatewood no longer controlled, but something everybody in the headquarters complex could understand and react to in-stantly.

And as for "breached"—a second ground shock proved the inner lock door had gone the way of the outer one.

A System Alert by the Commissioner of Security gave him

priority control over every communications device in the Headquarters net. The speakers of Yesilkov's phone and holotank rapped out Yates's orders a microsecond after he gave them.

A miniature image of the creature formed in the holotank's heart. Sonya'd realized they were going to need data. She was switching her own unit to follow the intruder's ambling progress on the internal-surveillance cameras at each intersection.

"All security personnel," Yates continued, switched to a more limited distribution by his opening control code. "An armored vehicle has just crashed the main gate. Off-duty personnel, report to your stations with weapons and breathing apparatus. On-duty patrol officers, take your teams to the site *carefully*. This thing's really dangerous, and I'm not sure what we've got up here that'll stop it. Officer of the Watch, take command of operations. Passing control *now*."

While Yates watched the holotank, his hands jerked open the middle drawer of Yesilkov's desk and scrabbled within it. She leaned past him and opened the bottom drawer.

"Here," she said, slapping a needle stunner into his palm. It was her desk now, and Sonya didn't keep her hardware where Yates used to keep his.

He shouldn't take her gun. She needed—

Yesilkov's small, flat purse was sprung to her belt, the usual fashion for women in a low-gravity environment. When light caught the purse directly, the side panels looked white; but as the woman's short, capable fingers flexed it open, the purse fluoresced through the lower end of the visible spectrum—yellow and orange and sullen, sticky red.

"My treat," she said. Her hand came out of the purse with a stunner of her own. Unlike Yates, she hadn't stopped carrying a weapon regularly when she took off the uniform.

"But it ain't gonna stop *that*," she added. She nodded toward the holotank as the creature moved forward in a series of half-pirouettes. At the end of each upper-torso arc, the facade at which the thing aimed its weapon blazed or slumped or simply disappeared.

"Hologram, off," Yates muttered to the artificial intelligence controlling his room-sized display. It turned off the innocent moonscape, which Yesilkov's body blurred and shadowed.

That was possibly the most useful order he'd given thus far.

The creature had reached the first intersection but had continued its progress up Corridor E—after blasting in both directions along the cross-corridor, with a fury that extinguished the ceiling lights. From the way flames spat and guttered, the blasts had also ruptured the colony's integrity again.

Nothing that Utilities Division couldn't handle, so long as Security managed to keep the creature from repeating his performance indefinitely.

Security was Sam Yates's responsibility. He could no more carry it out with what he had to hand than he could breathe vacuum and live.

Which also looked like it might be a useful skill now.

Sonya had grabbed her phone. Yates didn't hear her address the call, and it probably wouldn't have helped him, since she was speaking in her native language. His Russian was about good enough to thank somebody at a party for the glass of vodka.

Hell. Of course.

"Data bank," he said. "U.S. mission. Sort by military ranks. Phone display."

In the holotank, a limousine that must have bulled its way through the police cordon was burning at the intersection of E and 25. The occupants, members of a Latin American delegation from the look of them, were running away in three directions.

A name-list flashed up, filling the forty-line display of Yates's phone. Normal display would throw the entire file into the center of the room—which left no space for the two people in this damned cubbyhole to *do* anything.

Curlicues of fire twisted from the vehicle in the hologram display, moving with the apparent sluggishness of icebergs calving into the North Atlantic. They closed with the running figures, ignoring all else, and began to devour them with the same coruscant display in which the vehicle itself was vanishing.

General, General . . . bird Colonel . . . Military personnel in the diplomatic missions didn't necessarily wear their uniforms, but their backgrounds were in Entry Section's files.

Bingo! *Lieutenant Colonel Rufus William Birdwell, USMC.* An attaché to the mission's Acting Officer for Southern Regional Affairs—which didn't matter a damn, certainly to Yates and very possibly to Birdwell.

"Phone," Yates said. "Birdwell, Priority One."

If you wanted people to charge a machine gun head-on, you

chose Marines. If you just wanted the machine gun silenced, there were usually better ways—and better personnel—to do it . . . but sometimes plowing straight ahead in disregard of rules and reason was the only possible answer.

Times like this. The intruder in the holotank had just turned up Avenue 20. The purple suit vanished occasionally; usually when a gout from its own weapon rippled back to engulf it. Uniformed bodies, part-bodies, and crumbled blue vehicles witnessed the vain attempts of the Security patrols to stop it.

"What the hell is this!" snarled the flat-plate image of a red-faced man with no hair at all. Birdwell's phone didn't have speaker-display capability, but its pickups transmitted the colonel's picture to the top-of-the-line unit that was one of Sam Yates's perks.

"Colonel, I'm the Commissioner of Security," Yates said, banging out his words with the flat calm of heavy machine-gun fire. "Samuel Yates. American citizen. Nicaraguan campaign ribbon, Silver Star with V, Purple Heart."

He didn't add that he'd been a staff sergeant when he slogged through the jungles, looking for the things he was supposed to kill . . . and finding them, very often finding them. The colonel wouldn't have been impressed by enlisted rank.

"What the hell?" said Birdwell, his tone different enough that the words weren't really a repetition. He'd been wearing pajamas. He tossed the top away and pulled on an undershirt as he spoke, oblivious of the fact Yates had a viewscreen, or ignoring it.

Yesilkov was shouting into her own phone; someone shouted back at her through the speaker. The noise didn't bother Sam Yates. Not when he was in this mode. The shots and screaming hadn't bothered him when he called in artillery, knowing that a fifty-meter error in his coordinates would mean the spics didn't have to finish the job.

"Colonel, we have an intruder, a kind of tank, that's shot its way through the main gate and is now proceeding up Avenue 20. My—"

"Russkie?" Birdwell barked as he closed a khaki shirt with three rows of ribbons over the left pocket and a pair of unit citations on the other side. "Is this a Russkie coup?"

There were pluses and minuses when you called in a Marine. . . .

"Negative, sir," Yates said crisply. "That's a negative. It's terrorists of some kind and the Reds are helping us try to stop it. My men"—back to where he'd been interrupted—"have only needle stunners. We need automatic rifles, we need plasma weapons. We need you and the U.S. mission."

"Commissioner, I can neither confirm or deny—" Birdwell sputtered.

"Colonel, there isn't time for bullshit!" Yates snapped. "My people are out there dying with needle guns and I'm about to join them. I—"

"Sir, I don't have the authority—"

"Have your people liaise with my XO," Yates continued as though he hadn't been interrupted. "He'll direct them. Colonel, I can't give you orders. But if you're a man and an American, I don't have to. Yates out."

Colonel Birdwell was blinking as the screen went blank.

Sonya slammed down the handset of her phone, still snarling in Russian.

"No go?" Yates asked as he slid past her toward the door.

"Bullshit," Sonya snapped as she got to her feet beside him. "We'll have plasma guns on the bastard an hour before your people get their fingers out."

"Yeah, b-but ours'll work," Yates replied with an adrenalin stutter.

As they pushed out of the office, gas grenades burst around the creature in the holotank. A pair of men in civilian clothes crouched and fired; their projectiles roiled the enveloping white clouds. The creature flickered. A spot of light bloomed, sucking both the gas and the gunmen toward it—clothing afire, faces shriveling.

"Only thing is . . ." Yates muttered. "I'm not sure that's going to be enough."

Chapter 14

CHAIN OF COMMAND

The Space Command briefing had barely started when an Easter Parade of various ADC's came scuttling down the aisles, looking for their particular masters, urgency in every line of their crouched bodies and pale faces.

General Montague Sanders waved his man over imperiously, unconcerned about his own unmannerly display: He needed to make sure the aide saw him even though he was sitting with the Soviet mathematician, Sultanian, and not with the U.S. contingent.

Since Taylor McLeod was on the podium introducing Dick Quint to the audience, McLeod's man would have to wait in the wings until his boss's speech was done, giving Sandy a head start on whatever the problem was.

Sandy smacked his lips in satisfaction. It wasn't every day you one-upped the Company crew. Then he began wondering what the problem was, as he watched his man and others scurrying through the aisles of seats.

Meanwhile, Sultanian, a Soviet Armenian built like a bull, was telling him, "Don't think I am the mistaken guy, General Sanders, my friend. You must realize that, so far, we are using scalar fields only as primitive devices to derive other fields, as in Aharonov-Bohm, and maybe a little for communications/detection systems based on A-vector potential fields having physical significance, yes? Treating scalar fields as more than mathematical tools can make the gigantic impact on national interests of our—"

"Excuse me, Dr. Sultanian," said Sandy as soon as the messenger from his office reached his aisle. "I'll be right back, and we can continue this." He clapped the Soviet on the knee; they liked physical display. "So far it's been very enlightening. Very."

About like listening to Radio Moscow. Whatever message Sandy's office had sent was bound to beat the hell out of listening to the Soviet mathematician trying to allay his fears that the Russians knew more than the U.S. did about the technology the alien brought with him.

The only thing was, there were Soviet runners here now, too, giving whatever data Sandy was about to receive to Ruskin, the florid Warsaw Pact general who was Sandy's opposite number on the Moon; and to Minsky, the fair Slav who was the KGB resident.

As a matter of fact, from the look of things, this was one time when Taylor McLeod was going to be the last to know whatever it was that, so suddenly, was obviously the only thing on the Moon worth knowing.

"What is it, son?" Sandy demanded as soon as he reached the waiting lieutenant who stood at attention, his back to the wall.

"Sir," said the youngster through blue lips as he leaned close to whisper in Sandy's ear, "we've lost our B-sat; looks like foul play. Headquarters wonders if you'll come back to the office, sir, since we think we want to raise the DefCon. We'll need you to look at the data—"

"Look at the data," Sandy snarled, just barely controlling his volume. The shock of something actually *happening* nearly made him stagger in the aisle. "Look around you, son. You see those Russkies scrambling? There's your data for you. What else? You can brief me as we go."

He took the kid by the arm and hustled him toward the doors, McLeod nearly forgotten. Playing points with McLeod was something you did in peacetime, which this suddenly wasn't. Destroyed the B-phase comsat? What were those damned Soviets thinking of?

"We've never seen anything like this, sir." The youngster's words stopped Sandy's suppositions in mid-leap and drained everything from his mind. Pleasure at acing McLeod, fury at the Soviets, shock that the interval of nerve-grinding détente which had made his life miserable was suddenly ended and that action against his boyhood enemy finally was called for—all disappeared into a chasm of thoughtless cold from the bottom of which he could hardly think at all. Was this the Big One? World War Last?

"Sir," the aide said again, actually covering his mouth with his hand as he spoke, to fend off any later attempt to reconstruct his words by having a lip-reader view the inevitable surveillance tapes of the hall. "Something's shot up Entry One as well. We think it's the same thing that took out the B-sat. It's inside now, and it's destroying everything in its path. Nothing we've got seems to be effective against this thing; we're sustaining substantial collateral damage. Security's calling for plasma weapons, but so far, nothing's stopping it. Maybe a SADEM—"

"*What's* inside?" Who the hell was authorizing Special Atomic Demolition Emergency Munitions—fusion backpack bombs—for use in the habitat?

Sandy's head spun; his fists balled. Then he realized that nobody was authorizing the use of SADEMs—yet. That was why the aide was here: to bring Sandy back so that as ranking on-site U.S. military officer in this emergency, he could authorize whatever was necessary. . . .

Sanders was hardly aware that he was moving at all, let alone half running toward the doors, or that, down the middle and far aisles, Minsky with his aide, and Ruskin with his, were pacing him.

"What," he tried again, wetting his Velcro-dry lips, "is 'this thing'?" His tone would have withered the aide on the spot, in any other circumstances. "A Soviet experimental weapon? An AI weapons platform? What?"

"Our experts don't think it's Soviet." The young aide's eyes slid to the Soviet officials just ahead of them, pushing through the doors as if the Soviets and Americans were going somewhere together. "It's nothing we can ID, sir," said the youngster miserably, his hand out to catch the door swinging in Minsky's wake. "But we're sealing everything off. The Security Commissioner's called in Birdie's Marines, and—"

"*On whose authority?* Take me there." They were outside the briefing room and Sandy hadn't realized how goddamn hot it had been in there. He wiped the stinging sweat out of his eyes and blinked at the receding figures of Minsky and his aide, and Ruskin and his, heading toward the Zils already waiting.

"But sir, the area's cordoned off—it's Code Red/Cosmic/

Lethal, out there. Yates just pulled UN rank to get some muscle on-site. . . . Everybody's waiting for your orders. . . .''

"Take me there, I said, sonny!''

The kid actually stepped out in front of Sandy, with his arms spread wide, as if to physically prevent the general from attempting to reach the engagement site.

For a moment, Sanders considered slapping the youngster silly, pushing by him with a flat hand on that pigeon breast, or simply bludgeoning the lieutenant into submission with a combination of aural volume and inherent clout.

But the youngster was right. Command was never at the front. In this man's Air Force, the real battle was one fought hunched over viewscreens and com-grids.

"All right, son. Let's go—back to HQ, and don't spare the horses.'' He followed in the wake of Minsky and Ruskin, glumly hoping that whatever "it" was would blow the two Russians away, if they managed to go to the site instead of their offices, as he must do.

It wasn't until he was in his car and on the way back to HQ that he began worrying that "it" might have more to do with the Kiri alien than with terrorists or deniable Soviet dirty tricks.

The unidentified tanklike thing that he could now view through his limo's data-feed VDT didn't look like anything the Soviets, let alone terrorists, were capable of fielding—at least, he told himself, there was that comfort.

But it wasn't a comfort, not even when he remembered, watching the Armageddon-dispensing tank chew up his damned habitat, how Sultanian had been implying that there were weaponry applications to these A-potential fields that the Soviets hadn't been able to bring to fruition.

The evidence before his eyes was telling him in no uncertain terms that *somebody* had. Montague Sanders knew his weapons classes, and what the alien tank was accomplishing wasn't anything that the Soviets or the U.S. could match anywhere but in a wet dream.

Or in a nightmare. Not in a hundred years.

Chapter 15

VECTORS

"You see where it's heading, don't you?" Sonya muttered as they stepped into the hallway.

"We don't know that for—" Yates said; and stopped speaking when he saw the men coming toward him from the Entry Section lobby.

Two of them. Both big, both young; both in better shape than Sam Yates had ever been in his life.

They were also wearing suits more expensive than Yates bought even now, which gave him a pretty good idea of whose people they were.

"Commissioner Yates," said the one in gray silk. "We've been—"

"Kid, some other time," Yates said. "The shit's really hit the fan." He thrust past them—his body tight with the assurance that they were going to block him physically, going to try. He carried the stunner openly, cocking his arm to point the muzzle skyward.

They moved aside, sucking in their already-flat bellies so that Yates and Yesilkov could pass with no more than a brush of cloth on either side.

"Sir," continued gray-silk, "we've been directed to take you and Supervisor Yesilkov to Mr. McLeod."

Two more of McLeod's men, just as big as the first pair, stepped out of the lobby. Yates had let the first pair box him— had boxed himself, like an *idiot*, thinking just of the first shock while they were thinking a step ahead. Now he couldn't shoot his way through them, even if he'd been willing to try.

Which he probably was.

"Listen, you people!" he shouted, turning toward gray-silk but continuing to back into the lobby. As he'd expected, the men

there fell in alongside but didn't actually grab him, so long as
he faced away from the direction of escape. "Something's shooting the place up, the whole *habitat*! I'll talk to McLeod when
this is over!"

If they were both alive. If *anybody* was still alive up here.

He glanced around quickly. The lobby was crowded with
desks, though there were only three clerks on duty at the moment. They'd had time to grab the emergency breathing apparatus from their desk drawers before the visitors arrived—but
now they waited with their hands in plain sight, their eyes flicking between Yates, those with him . . .

. . . and four more of McLeod's people, standing in pairs
against the walls. Two of them had attaché cases half-open in
front of them. Yates was willing to bet their concealed hands
were gripping something more substantial than needle stunners.

By God, Yates's staff had really taken their commissioner at
his word when he said he wanted his calls held. McLeod must've
been ripshit to send this big a team.

"I'm sorry, sir," said gray-silk, so polite that he actually
sounded apologetic. "Our orders were very specific. But the
sooner we get moving . . ."

Sonya hadn't spoken. She was in—not shock—but a higher
state of agitation even than Yates. Events have different implications for different people, and for a Russian citizen suddenly
arrested by American intelligence personnel—

She couldn't get away, but she could make them kill her; and
if they did that . . .

Yates put his free arm around her. "It's gonna be all right,"
he said. "No sweat. I'm gonna make it all right."

"Balls," she grunted, but she squeezed him fiercely in return.
She didn't want to die; almost as much as Yates wanted her to
live.

A pair of six-place cars stood just outside the door. There
wasn't much other traffic. A few pedestrians were running along
the slidewalks, with frozen expressions and breathing apparatus
clutched in their hands against need. Only a few, those who had
to get somewhere—get to someone they loved—even at the risk
of their lives.

Inside, it was safe. All the units in the habitat could be sealed
off from the corridors. The air circulation system would continue

to work for each individual unit whose own integrity was un-breached.

An orange Utilities Division van passed with its siren and flashers on, moving as fast as batteries could drive its wheel-hub motors; but there were no private vehicles in the corridors. The folks powerful enough to wangle highly restricted vehicles for their personal use didn't know anyone who was important enough for them to risk their own lives.

The pavement transmitted three quick shocks. A moment later the atmosphere merged them into a single blast loud enough—and close enough—to make several pedestrians stumble.

"Get in, please," gray-silk said without expression. His fingers opened Sonya's purse and removed her stunner, flipping it to the man at his side without needing to check whether the fellow was ready for the exchange.

Yesilkov ignored the man gesturing her to the closed vehicle. Instead, she sat down on the middle bench of the open car.

"Quickly." Gray-silk reached forward and gripped Yates's raised weapon between a perfectly manicured thumb and forefinger. He began to exert pressure, while members of his team moved in from the sides.

Yates grinned. "If you really want it, sonny," he said. "But when I let go this dead-man switch, the blast'll clear a square block."

The closest pair of gray-silk's subordinates backed up with a gasp and a curse. Gray-silk didn't move much, but his mouth opened a silent millimeter and his grip on the pistol relaxed.

Yates dropped the stunner—perfectly normal, exactly what it looked like—on Yesilkov's lap. He sat beside her. "Thanks for the loan, Sonya," he said in a loud voice, "but I don't think I'll need it now, after all."

"Well, get moving!" gray-silk snarled to his driver from the car's rear bench. "We're already late!" His partner jumped in beside him as the car accelerated, leaving the closed vehicle behind as the remaining five members of the team scrambled for places.

Yesilkov sighed. Holding the needle stunner by the barrel, she offered it over her shoulder without turning around. After a moment, gray-silk's partner took the weapon.

"This ain't the time to play them games, soldier," she said

banteringly, turning her face slightly away from the man at her side.

Yates's forefinger stroked the rigid tendon in Yesilkov's neck. "There's never a time to let that shit pass, Sonya," he said in as light a voice as he could manage. "It just gets worse in the future."

He looked back at gray-silk and his partner. Their fine young faces were as stiff as Sonya's had been in the lobby when she was preparing to bolt into oblivion. You had to teach them that you might go off like a bomb. Because if they didn't learn that, they kept pushing until you *did* go bang.

You went bang if you were Sam Yates. And that was all he'd ever known how to be.

A Uniformed Patrol vehicle passed in the opposite direction, moving at speed but without flashers and siren. There wasn't enough traffic now to require the warning devices, but from the howls up and down the empty corridors, they were generally being used.

"In the front seat," Yates said. "That was Captain Aramski from Sector Three, wasn't it?"

He was controlling his voice fine, but he couldn't seem to help the way his fingers twined and gripped like a knot of rattlesnakes.

Three hundred meters of corridor lights went out abruptly. The car plunged ahead in darkness for three seconds before glowstrips in the corridor roof activated—a dim alternative, inadequate at the speed they were traveling. The integral rhenium-cadmium power packs would keep the glowstrips illuminated for years.

Maybe the glowstrips would be appreciated by the clean-up crews Earth sent to figure out what happened to everybody in UN Headquarters.

"Yeah," said Yesilkov in the same disinterested tone. "Pretty good officer the day or two he's sober." She paused, then added, "I, ah . . . think I maybe know the other guys, too."

Civilians. Men in civilian clothing, rather. Tall men and so broad for their height that each filled a bench intended for two patrolmen. On their laps were metal boxes with carrying handles, small suitcases rather than attaché cases.

"Yeah, thought you might," Yates said. "Keep your fingers crossed."

"They were guards from the Soviet Mission, Commissioner Yates," gray-silk volunteered unexpectedly.

Yates blinked and looked over his shoulder. The closed car was fighting to catch up with them, handicapped by a slow start and a heavier load. It was rocking along at a distance of five hundred meters. The vehicle's speed, close to fifty kph, was more than he'd thought you could squeeze out of the small-wheeled crawlers used in the colony's interior.

"Thanks," Yates said. "You know where we're going, buddy?"

"To the—" gray-silk began. "Ah, to your office, Commissioner. Mr. McLeod didn't explain why it was he wanted you there."

A shock jounced dust from the floor and ceiling of the corridor. For a moment they were driving through a dry, choking fog. Since the corridors were never darkened, most vehicles didn't have driving lights. It didn't matter in this dust cloud, because lights would just be scattered into a dazzle, but if more of the ceiling lights went off . . .

"Sir, my name's Stuart," gray-silk added.

Sure, why not? "Jeb, I suppose?" Yates said.

"Jim, sir," Stuart replied stiffly. He licked his lips. "Actually, James Ewell Brown . . . But I don't go by my initials."

"One big happy family," Yesilkov snapped.

The closed car jounced over the slideway junctions at H and 3, the intersection the lead vehicle had just crossed. A streak of zigzag fire caromed down the cross street, H, and touched the car in passing. All eight wheel-hub motors exploded in blue sparks. The car ground to a halt, burning.

No one got out.

"Well, we're almost to the office," Yates noted without inflection.

And they weren't the only ones.

"I told ya that's where it was heading," Yesilkov said in gloomy satisfaction.

Chapter 16

INTELLIGENCE COUP

A KGB orientation document that Sonya Yesilkov had been issued during her training for posting on the Moon stated bluntly: *One of the serious problems in planning against American doctrine is that the Americans do not read their manuals nor do they feel any obligation to follow their doctrine.*

The words kept coming back to her, under arrest in the car of the American Imperialist intelligence operatives, despite Sam Yates by her side and the chaos around her. The doctrine of the moment was cooperation between allies. Yet always, when pressured, Americans looked at Soviets and saw the enemy. Even her UN status and her close working relationship with Sam Yates could not protect her from that.

The well-groomed, beautiful young men who had captured her would never have taken her alive if not for Sam. If not for Security Commissioner Yates, she amended silently. She mustn't again be lulled into a false sense of security because Yates fancied her body. In this, American officials were no different than Soviet officials: Intimacy offered no benefits, no protection, to the underling—only to the superior.

How could she ever have forgotten?

Minsky had been right. She was too close to the situation to see the problems. Minsky was always right, or he would not still be the Soviet KGB resident at UN Luna. This was no comfort. Her intimacy with Yates and her special status in the eyes of the alien, Channon, had intoxicated her. Like any drunken Russian, she had then proceeded to fuck up her life irretrievably.

Life is vodka; vodka is life—clear, odorless, colorless life. Why did she succumb to Yates and his little-boy look and let him get his hands under her blouse—every time—when she needed her wits about her, not centered on the receptacle between her thighs?

She was as angry with herself for losing sight of her duty as she was at the Americans for taking advantage of her foolishness. And her body, thwarted, was counseling extraordinary measures; the frustration in her blood had turned to dour fury. If no sex was to be forthcoming in this interval, then violence would suit; it was the wisdom of the flesh.

She must control this desire to escalate tension until it became outright conflict, here in the car amidst the CIA enemy, with their beautiful bodies and beautiful suits and beautiful educations.

She found herself staring out the rear window at the overturned car full of no-longer-beautiful American intelligence operatives, burning with their vehicle, until Stuart shifted so that she could no longer see it.

Then there was nothing to look at back there but Stuart and his partner. Well-trained men, these. They'd taken up thoughtful positions in the back seat, one behind the driver in case he must be shot if he should deviate from his orders, or if Yesilkov tried to comandeer the car by producing a hidden weapon and holding it to the driver's belly, his neck, his ear. The other, Stuart, was positioned behind Yates for the same general purpose: If the hostages became intractable . . .

She shook her head and faced forward, away from the silent stares of the American operatives, preferring the chaos she could see out the windscreen. It suited her mood and reminded her of another old saying, attributed to a German general officer:

The reason that the American army does so well in wartime is that war is chaos, and the American army practices chaos on a daily basis.

The American army was going to meet its match today, on the Moon. As for the Soviet troops up here . . . if throwing bodies upon the thing would kill it, her superiors were willing to spend their entire contingent of soldiers to secure the habitat once more.

Even the infinitely paranoid Minsky, the tow-headed KGB colonel, had not predicted such dire events. Minsky had never spoken of alien enemies, of destroying unknown aggressors at all costs.

Yet, when she had called the alarm in to headquarters, she'd been told that Minsky had left a standing order for just such a contingency: Secure the alien's weapon at all costs, preferably without letting the Americans know that the Soviets have done so.

Minsky had never let on that he was expecting any such thing. Minsky had told her no good would come of her affair with Yates, but that, for now, the Party approved of her giving her body in exchange for the confidence of the Americans. Minsky had told her the Americans would eventually become so proprietary about the alien that she would face disenfranchisement as a result of Channon's favor. Minsky had told her there was a risk, a substantial one, of finding herself in such a car, surrounded by such fine young men, against whom Yates would be unable to protect her.

But Minsky had never told her that the alien would lead his powerful enemy into their midst, so that troops would be mobilized and all their lives at risk.

But then, KGB only told you what they wanted you to hear, in order to elicit the desired result—often untruths, half-truths; sometimes, less than you needed to know.

Now, in the silence broken only by the Americans' strained banter and the wail of dopplered sirens as they sped toward their destination, she remembered all that Minsky had deigned to tell her.

Some of it fit the situation all too well, though she hadn't understood it then. Sultanian, Minsky had said, was close to a solution that would "tap the energy sea" and make the USSR invulnerable to American Imperialist aggression, the undisputed ruler of not only cislunar space, but the universe.

This was brave talk, old talk, talk she had heard often in smoky backrooms when the hour was late. Talk of weather weapons; talk of unjammable communications systems; talk of cold explosions and heat exchangers into other dimensions; talk of ray-gun weapons that could freeze the blood in the enemy's veins and kill his ships, tanks, and planes from great distances—even reach down below earth and water, and destroy guidance systems shielded from all conventional means.

Such talk had been around forever. Such weapons had never materialized. But in Sharyshagan and other secret installations, research had been going on since Yesilkov was a child. Scalar waves were thought to permeate the entire universe, and Sultanian's specialty was treating scalar fields as real fields, rather than as purely mathematical tools, as was done in the West.

But Sultanian and his colleagues had never succeeded in deriving an A-vector potential from the scalar field. That was what Sultanian was doing on the Channon team, Minsky had said with a gleam in his eye. If Channon's communicator could be built, then weapons of unthought power could be derived from the emergent technology—weapons the Soviet Union was more qualified to develop than was the West, which had let the entire area of A-potential research lie fallow.

Thus Yesilkov had been instructed, in that vague and oblique briefing, to watch for anything the alien might say or do that might aid Sultanian—even something that would inarguably prove that such weapons were possible.

That proof was all around them, now. That proof was what was tearing up the habitat as if it were made of papier-mâché. And that proof might destroy them all before any nation had a chance to develop a counterforce.

No wonder the Americans were nervous. But the Americans turned on everyone whenever they were nervous. This, history had taught well: at Yalta, in Chile, in the Philippines, the Levant, Cyprus, Panama—the list was endless.

She had no right to expect Sam Yates to protect her. And she couldn't risk a protracted debriefing at the hands of Taylor McLeod and his friends. Having been twice debriefed by her own people—once by NVD over an internal matter, once by KGB in the aftermath of the Afrikaner affair—she knew better than to think she could successfully hold back anything she knew.

And although she didn't know much, what she knew about Sultanian and Minsky's allegiance to the long-range A-field development program in the USSR was information that she could never allow the U.S. to acquire.

She looked at Yates out of the corner of one eye and touched his hands, knotted in his lap. It might seem unprofessional, but she needed human comfort. She needed to say things her mouth couldn't be allowed to speak, let alone her heart to feel or her mind to think.

And Yates dipped his head, caught her forefinger in his fist, and said again, "Sonya, I told you: It's gonna be all right."

"How is it you can say for sure?" she answered. "When that thing is destroying everything in its path?"

"It hasn't destroyed us, honey," Yates said.

And from the back, Stuart's companion muttered, "Yet."

So she turned, put her arm on the seat back and her chin on her arm, and smiled. Might as well take the offensive, since it was offered: "My country's condolences over the death of your operatives in the follow car," she told the two CIA men, probing.

"Thanks, lady," said the junior, "but it's a little early to start handing out black ribbons; we've got to get through this oursel—"

Stuart elbowed his subordinate. "Supervisor Yesilkov, do your people know anything about this that would be helpful to us in fighting it?"

The carefully worded question brought Yates's head around. The front seat suddenly seemed smaller as he shifted, pushing her against the driver who was steadfastly trying to ignore everything but his route.

"If she knew anything, you think she wouldn't have told us already, kid? You think she don't know it's her ass on the line, too? You think she thinks she's in some other car, goin' to a Company picnic?"

"Sam," she said.

"Shit; damn kids," he said and twisted around again, facing forward, all the tendons in his neck and the muscles in his jaw bulging.

She turned with him, and let her fingers burrow farther into his fist. There were times when human relationships must be allowed to mean as much, not as little, as they could. Facing whatever it was that had six limbs and destroyed anything in its path, you wanted to know that somebody cared.

Right now, husband or no husband, that person—for Yesilkova—was Sam Yates. She was even willing to forgive him for being born an American, since he might be about to become a dead one.

As she might become a dead Russian, momentarily. With calm and rebellious determination, she pulled her hand from Yates's grip, turned his face to hers, and kissed him long and hard in front of the American operatives. Let them put that in their files and ponder it, if any of them still had active files when the shift was done.

Chapter 17

DEAD ON ARRIVAL

The Security Commissioner's office suite had been moved eight years before to a corner location on what was then the northern perimeter of the UN complex. It drove Sam Yates nuts to be so far away from all his line departments, but the Commissioner of the day—a northern Nigerian with the votes of both Africa and the Islamic world backing his appointment—had been more interested in spaciousness.

Spacious it was: Yates sometimes wondered how many other offices on the Moon contained a fully equipped *hammam*. But when he leaped out while the car was still skidding to a halt, he found that the door on the side facing Avenue E was locked and sealed against him.

Hell, it shouldn't have been a surprise. *He* was the one who'd announced the meteor strike, after all.

The wall was polarized acrylic, not regolith, though McLeod had lowered the internal titanium shutters as almost his first act upon commandeering the office (and who else did Sam Yates have to blame for McLeod *being* involved?).

"McLeod!" Yates shouted, raising his fist instinctively as he faced the cameras, which were probably the only view those inside had of the corridor. "Open the hell up! We're here!"

JEB Stuart was erect, looking back the way they'd come—toward the remains of the follow car, sparkling brightly in the distance. The two surviving members of his team eyed him in apprehension.

Yesilkov stood back-to-back with Yates. There wasn't a whole hell of a lot she could do if the intruder appeared—*when* the intruder appeared—but she could watch Yates's back nonetheless. She was keyed up and looking for a way to jump or strike—

but it was a good tension now, rather than the empty blackness of being captured by the intelligence service of a hostile power.

A car was racing toward them from the opposite direction, still three blocks away. For a moment it drew all their eyes, even Yates's.

Then the door-seal sighed and the panel slid open.

"McLeod, you dick-headed jackass!" Yates bellowed as he stormed through the door. "We've got a—"

It was Ella Bradley who'd unsealed the door, and there was nobody with her in the outer office except Yates's own secretary. Sally couldn't help but look beautiful, even though she'd pulled the cup of her emergency air supply over her chin so that she was in instant readiness for depressurization.

"But where's McLeod?" Yates asked, his mild tone a measure of his amazement.

JEB Stuart was a lot sharper when he snapped, "Please, where's Mr. McLeod? At once!"

"Sam, Channon says there's a *Rillian* coming," Ella blurted as Yates headed for the inner office without waiting for an answer to his question. "But you mustn't—"

"Sally, get us pictures of this thing!" Yates said. The inner-office door, keyed to his presence, slid open regardless of whether McLeod had decided to change the programmed unlocking sequence.

"Ms. Bradley, I must know where—" Stuart said.

"Hologram, feed intersection G and 87—project!" Sonya ordered. Sally of course hadn't known what the hell her boss had been ordering her to do, but Yesilkov had sense enough to do the thing herself instead of wasting time in explanations.

"But you mustn't *hurt* the Rillian!" Ella completed in a shout.

The alien—the humanoid alien, the first alien—had Yates's inner office all to himself.

"Sam, he's close!" Yesilkov shouted, which meant closer than they already knew—which meant a lot of things, but mostly that the next couple of minutes probably wouldn't be survivable.

"It comes for me!" Channon said, extending one of his long-fingered hands to Yates's cheek. "You must give me!"

Yates grabbed the Tokarev from the plaque behind his desk and racked back the slide to chamber the first of its eight rounds. There was nothing that said you couldn't keep a collector's item in working order. . . .

"Like hell we give you!" he snarled at Channon. He started to grab the alien's arm to drag him along—thought, jerked open the center drawer of the compudesk instead, and called, "Sonya!"

Yesilkov, at the doorway and trying to watch both Yates and the hologram projection in the outer office, caught the needle stunner he tossed her before he gripped Channon around the waist to carry him forward if necessary. She flipped the charging lever with her thumb, lighting the red LED that indicated the stunner was ready now to fire.

Channon wasn't objecting. His only hesitation was a pause to snatch his helmet from the desk—which showed how badly Yates was thinking. Almost went off and left that.

Directed. Not bad, just focused; and you couldn't focus on every damn thing.

"There's a suit room down on D," Yesilkov said.

"Yeah, and there's *gotta* be some ship ready to lift," Yates agreed, trying to think the necessary distance ahead. Course didn't matter, fuel state didn't matter—just get Channon off the surface and away from this *thing* that was coming after him.

They might not be able to stop the Rillian here on Luna, but if they could lure it out into the killing zone of the hardware orbiting Earth—fusion warheads, X-ray lasers, and plasma weapons that could vaporize a fair-sized city every time they fired—that was a different story.

Toss the Rillian what it wanted and hope it'd go away? Hell, they'd die first.

The commissioner's outer office was set up for meetings. It had the same projection capability as the units which overwhelmed Yesilkov's cubbyhole in Entry Section, but here there was room for a proper display.

The Rillian—the Rillian's ass—filled the image area.

Instead of blowing in each door as it passed, the way it had started to do, the creature was now traversing the blocks in a pair of strides calculated to keep it from brushing the corridor ceiling. At each intersection it stopped and triggered blasts in all four directions—then leaped on.

Unless somebody's changed the camera feeding the display, the Rillian was precisely one block away from the commissioner's office.

"Take the car!" Yates said as he started for the outer door. "I'll hold—"

"I'll go—" Ella said.

"Sir, you can't—" JEB Stuart said, and his two subordinates moved instinctively to block the doorway. Sonya took Stuart and his men out with a burst of her stunner.

The charged needles raked across McLeod's team at solar-plexus height, two or three into each abdomen. The poles of each tiny needle—insulated from one another until they grounded in flesh—set up a fluctuating current that paralyzed the nerves of the victim for some minutes thereafter.

The effect was exquisitely painful to the victim, but he was still alive later, for apologies. The pistol Yates carried didn't have that option—

And he'd been half the weight of the trigger-pull from shooting, anyway. This wasn't a time to screw around; and there was never a time to fail.

Channon leaped the thrashing, writhing bodies of McLeod's men as if he'd practiced the maneuver for a month with Yates and Yesilkov. Yates wasn't pushing, wasn't even guiding him anymore; Channon knew just what he was supposed to do—and did it. Would to God there were more humans like that, but there was Sonya and maybe that'd be enough—the three of 'em.

They jumped from the office. The car skidding along the corridor as its wheels braked against the weight of the four big men aboard almost knocked them down.

The vehicle was from the U.S. mission. The driver and the pair in back with plasma weapons were uniformed Marines, and "civilian" was only a courtesy title for the fellow in front shouting into a radio handset.

A jet of *something* ripped down Corridor 87—not ravening Hell, but a glimpse of blue sky and clouds like cotton balls. It was as though somebody'd ripped away a painted backdrop, to display a ragged line of spring on Earth.

The ceiling lights on 87 went out, and so did those of the block of Avenue E in front of the commissioner's office.

The handset roared with a deafening level of static until the man holding the unit smashed it under his heel as he leaped from his vehicle.

"Sonya, go!" Yates cried. He didn't bother to look around to make sure she was obeying, because he knew she would. She'd

get Channon as far as anybody human could manage while Sam
Yates—

"Here," he said to the Marine with the brilliant red-and-gold
chevrons of a gunnery sergeant clashing with his green uniform.
"I've used these before." He dropped the Tokarev into his
pocket and reached for the plasma weapon.

"Get the fuck outta here!" the gunny snarled, hurling Yates
back with a disinterested ease that suggested he was very fresh
from the higher gravity of Earth. He, his partner, and the civilian from the car ran to the corner proper while the Marine driver
waited.

"The transmission went to hell, but it's gotta be—" said the
civilian.

"Right," agreed the gunny, settling the folding stock of his
weapon against his shoulder. He nodded to the Marine with the
other plasma discharger.

"Go!"

The younger Marine sighted around the corner while the gunny
rolled into the center of the intersection. Yates covered his eyes
with his left arm while his right hand fumbled the pistol out of
his pocket again. Even so, the bolts' blue-white glare was almost
as punishing as the snarling crash of the two miniature fusion
bombs detonated and controlled by lasers within the weapon
tubes.

Yates blinked. The younger Marine ducked back to cover while
the gunny waited the fraction of a second for his weapon to cycle
another round. A sphere of opalescent light formed where the
Marine had been.

And vanished. The floor was cut in a curve perfect enough to
polish concrete and rock into a dull mirror. Air popped to fill a
vacuum harder than what separated the stars.

The gunny's partner triggered his weapon in shocked reflex.
Its muzzle was pointed at the ceiling just over his head.

Rock, concrete, and all the transmission lines running through
the ceiling exploded in a gout of plasma. If either of the men
closest to the blast survived, they were luckier than anyone had
the right to be. The Marine driver was screaming and covering
his eyes too late.

Sam Yates was thrown ten feet back by the concussion. He
landed in a hail of acrylic grit that had been the wall of his office
a moment before. A huge section of the glowstrips which were

just flickering to life had vanished, and the remainder went black again.

Though even the titanium shutters bulged, there was no danger of breaching the ceiling to vacuum. Six meters of regolith top-cover protected the colony from cosmic rays in lieu of a planetary atmosphere.

The Rillian strode into the intersection, carefully avoiding the smooth-sided crater it had blasted there. It stood in a cloud of dust and swirling vapor that blurred its outline against the lights still blazing behind it.

The creature pirouetted like a dancing elephant, to aim its weapon in the direction of Sam Yates.

Yates squeezed his trigger. The red flash and recoil of his pistol told him it had fired even though he was too deaf to hear the muzzle blast. The Tokarev's sights were rudimentary and its grip-angle too steep for a natural point-to-shoot, but this was spitting distance, twenty feet, and the muzzle rocked down to slam out another round and another.

With the fraction of his mind that expected anything but death, Yates expected the Rillian to vanish because that's what the holograms had showed it doing every time it was threatened. Even the light-swift plasma bolts hadn't been quick enough to find a target waiting . . . .

The Rillian didn't vanish, and it didn't sweep the corridor with its own weapon. Instead the vast bulk seemed to . . . to settle, like a whale being crushed by gravity onto the sand where it's beached itself. Sparks of violet light were playing over its surface. Another spark snapped from the suit every time Yates shot, then expanded with the restless hunger of acid devouring zinc.

Within the second-and-a-half before Yates's last round locked back the Tokarev's slide, almost a third of the Rillian had sparkled away. He stared at it, rubbing his eyes against the dust and stinging residues blasted into the atmosphere by the plasma bolt.

When Yates looked over his shoulder to see where Yesilkov and Channon were, he saw Ella Bradley beside him. She was sitting upright, her left hand braced against the floor, and coughing as her right index finger continued its death grip on the trigger of the needle stunner she'd emptied long before.

Chapter 18

STATE OF EMERGENCY

When McLeod slammed his car to a halt in what was left of the intersection before Yates's office, he rubbed his eyes and blinked twice, just to make sure what he was seeing wasn't some weird stress reaction.

Then he sat back in his seat and pried his sweaty fingers from the sticky steering wheel, because Ella was all right. He could see her from here.

He didn't have to admit to anybody that he hadn't had a thought other than her safety in his mind since he'd anticipated where the six-limbed thing was headed. He didn't have to let anyone see his face until there was blood in his lips, until the perspiration dried on his forehead, until he'd straightened his tie and collated what on-site data was available. Then he could get out of this damned car and at least look like he'd been doing his job, rather than breaking every rule in the book so that he could star in his own version of *Prince Valiant Meets Godzilla (And Buys The Farm)*.

The corridor looked like a war zone, which was what it had been, of course. There was a nice shiny crater that McLeod hoped to hell wasn't hot, for the sake of his children to come. There was a Marine vehicle, or what was left of one, with a single live Marine lying in it. Yates's secretary, Sally, held his bandaged head in her lap. There were a few body parts scattered around, enough to account for maybe two more men. The ceiling was . . . shot to hell, right to the regolith in sections, so the light wasn't great.

But his car's lights were on, and the office building's, and that was enough to see the spooky patch of violet-shot scum that looked more than anything like an electrically live shadow.

He toggled his car phone and said in the general direction of the lavaliere mike on the rearview mirror: "Okay, Henhouse. Mother's on-site. Your sighting confirmed. Looks like the thing bought it here. Pull what you can from the Security Commissioner's office system, my authority. I'm seeing Amcits as follows: Commissioner Yates; Yates's secretary, Sally Something-or-other; one Marine, looks like corporal from here; Dr. Bradley—that's it. No Stuart et al; no additional Marines, but a few body parts in uniform. Also, one Sovcit: Entry Supervisor Yesilkova. And our guest, Lucky, seemingly in good health. I'm leaving the car . . . now.''

He didn't wait for Henhouse to respond. If they had anything urgent enough for him and he didn't hear the phone ring, they could beep his car's horn remotely, or feed through into the commissioner's office.

Anyway, he was feeling better. Under control. Less angry about Sandy's behavior. Less rueful over his own performance. Some things couldn't be helped. Extraordinary situations demanded extraordinary actions—from everyone involved.

He cautioned himself to remember that Sam Yates was a part of that "everyone" as he swung his long legs out of the car and the soles of his shoes slipped on the greasy, smoky pavement.

He glanced down at his lapel camera's radiation meter. It was reading low traces; nothing to worry about.

Ella's dull-eyed stare was another matter. She didn't even get up when she realized that McLeod was the man from the car.

She merely watched him come.

Yates, the Security Commissioner, looked like he'd been in a firefight—which he had—but McLeod didn't like the body language projecting, as Yates came toward him, the clear statement that, so far as Yates was concerned, the action wasn't over yet.

The big, lank redneck met him in a dozen loose-jointed strides, palming powder residue or flaked insulation or just plain ceiling dust off his face.

The result wasn't a clean spot, just a patina reminiscent of night camouflage. Yates's teeth were sparkling white against the carbonized smudges as he said, "Little late, there, big fella—party's over." His chin jutted toward the unearthly purple-sparked slick that McLeod had noticed, coming in.

McLeod held out his hand in greeting.

Yates didn't take it. He had a locked-back, obviously empty, antique handgun in his right hand. In his left was a plasma rifle he was using as a swagger stick or a cane, McLeod wasn't sure which.

"The party's not over, Yates, it's only beginning. Report." Damn, McLeod shouldn't let this piece of white trash get on his nerves, but Yates just wouldn't implement even a modicum of courtesy—not even what discipline and relative rank ought to have demanded, if the fool would just use some common sense.

"Report what? It's dead an' gone; so's three of the four Marines who got here when *you* shoulda, with some kind of operational cavalry more than a gunny with a jeep. I suppose you could say this here Rooshin Tokarev was the weapon that killed it, since it was what I had at hand, but I think it was more likely whatever came down when the kid blasted the ceilin' to shit. . . . That's it." Yates sported a wide grin now, and it was the facial rictus of a certain type of man who couldn't cycle down from a combat situation as quickly as most commanders might like.

McLeod exhaled a measured breath and let his eyes stray from Yates to Ella Bradley, still sitting on the steps, her back to the wall. Beyond her he could see Yesilkova and Channon, inside, crouched over something—or someone.

"That's not it, Yates. Where were you? We couldn't find you, or Yesilkova. I sent a team to bring you to Channon. How long have you been here? Where are they?" He fingered his breast-pocket recorder to make sure it was taking this deposition, although he'd enabled it when he'd left the SpaceCom briefing, hard on the heels of Ruskin, Minsky, and Montague Sanders, who ought to rot in hell for letting interservice rivalries enter into something as serious as an alien incursion. . . .

Yates had already started talking when McLeod forced his attention back to the Security Commissioner's words: ". . . can't say I'm that sorry about your live boys, but stunning them was the only option when good ol' JEB Stuart decided to try to physically restrain the movements of the two security officers assigned to the alien's safety. At that time, the hostile alien was bearing down on us and it was the considered opinion of me and Yesilkov that we ought to get Channon the hell out of here. . . ."

Smart enough to lay the right sort of disclaimers into the ongoing record, anyhow. But that didn't excuse much. "Yates, are you telling me you and your Soviet junior turned needle stunners on Agen—on my personnel, who were acting on—?"

"If they was acting on anything but their own *cock*amamie discretion, I wouldn't own to it. Sir. The way it looked right then, and my office transcript'll back me if it survived and took the data, the hostile alien—hell, the Rillian, let's call it what it is—was . . . the Rillian was comin' right into my office to get Channon, like Channon was wearing a homin' device. So we was gonna move Channon, get him outta the habitat to protect all these souls here, and see if we couldn't get the Rillian to chase us into the hardware zone, whereupon we coulda got it dead."

"My men are in there?" That had to be what Yesilkov and Channon were doing in the doorway.

"What's left of 'em. The other car-full got taken out by hostile fire on the way here, unless that burning, overturned car didn't take 'em all with it."

"Terrific. You realize there'll be an inquiry?"

"I can't wait," said Yates, still with that ugly, threatening grin.

"Well, you're going to have to. Right now, take my car and escort Lucky to my offices. There'll be staffers there expecting him. He's got new quarters."

"Great. I get my office back." Yates twirled the Tokarev on his finger like a gunslinger, which, in his fantasies, he probably was.

"Yates, are you angling for a competency hearing or just a unilateral Section Eight? Take . . . Lucky . . . to . . . the . . . U.S. mission. Stay . . . with . . . him. Copy?"

"Roger. Sir." Yates twirled the gun into his pocket.

McLeod took a step forward. Yates took one back.

"And take your Soviet girlfriend with you. I'll meet you there when I'm done here. While you're waiting for me, each of you dictate a full after-action report: everything you remember, no matter how hard it bent the rules. Lucky too. I'll listen to them when I get there. Now get out of my path."

"I'm not sure I can just yet. You're telling me that, when the whole habitat's all shot to shit, I'm supposed to hole up in your Undersecretarial suite and leave the clean-up to . . . who? I got a job to do besides Channon, or don't you care about that?"

"No you don't. You do just what I tell you from now on, Yates. Nothing more. Nothing less. Until I say otherwise. And don't waste time trying to find out whether I can make the orders I'm giving you stick. Now, *move*!''

Dear God, why did he let that cracker crank him up like this?

He knew why: All this was happening in front of Ella's huge, shocked eyes.

He got past Yates, somehow, and forgot him. As he forgot, temporarily, about the slick crater in the floor and the huge purplish stain and the ravaged ceiling and the bluntly delivered news that at least four of his men, and three Marines, had been killed here, as well as the rest of Stuart's team having been stunned.

Channon wanted Yates and Yesilkova; Channon was going to have Yates and Yesilkova. In fact, Channon was going to have exactly and precisely whatever he wanted for the forseeable future. Any representative of a race capable of fielding that kind of firepower, or of having enemies that could, was arguably the premier asset of the United States, and no effort would be spared to satisfy Lucky in future.

That statement, McLeod knew, he could ram home all the way into the Oval Office. He'd have to get rid of Yates, eventually. And Yesilkova, of course, at the first opportunity. But the firefight and the likelihood that he and/or she had pulled a stunner's trigger against McLeod's team would surely provide some sufficient pretext.

McLeod knew what to do, now. He was in high gear, comfortable even with the hostility Yates offered. It was only the difficulty he'd had in thinking like a professional when he'd not known Ella's status that bothered him. And it really bothered him.

As he moved toward her, all he could conjure to say was, ''Are you all right?'' The inanity didn't convey a hint of the concern he felt. It had been as if nothing else mattered until he could find out if she'd been harmed.

The implications of his behavior between when he'd heard the news and when he'd seen her in his headlights were unsettling. He was good enough at what he did to cover the lapse, but there shouldn't have been a lapse.

He couldn't allow another such—especially now, when he and every other cognizant player on the Moon had just been treated to a sample of the sort of technological goodies Channon's culture could offer. McLeod couldn't afford to be distracted, to have a split agenda, to make a single mistake.

He'd never thought of Ella as a liability before. And she wasn't. The depth of his feeling for her was, however, an inarguable debit.

"Are you all right, Ella?" he asked again softly and bent down to lift her gently to her feet.

"Ting . . ." Her voice was quavery, distant. Beside her on the step was a fully discharged stunner. So she'd taken part in the combat. Still, when he'd met her, she'd handled risk better than this.

He had to remind himself that he couldn't assess this from a zero-data base. He hadn't been there; he hadn't yet viewed the tapes. So she was shocky. So what? He had no way of knowing how terrifying it might have been to wait here, watching that thing coming on, destroying everything in its way. . . .

"Ella, I want you to go to Earth. I'll bump somebody from the next lift. I won't hear any arguments. Now, come with—"

"No." She broke free of him.

It wasn't hard; he hadn't tried to hold her against her will. He'd merely wanted to hold her.

"I'm staying with Channon. You don't understand, Taylor McLeod! You don't. I'm the only one who does understand." Her voice was more normally intonated now, although rising toward a hysterical pitch.

"Ssh, shh. We'll talk about it inside. Come on . . ."

But Yesilkova and Channon were blocking the doorway still, helping the stunned collection officers back to consciousness by massaging their solar plexus areas and offering them water.

"No, Ting, listen—before Yates and Yesilkova get away. . . ."

"Get away?"

She was unsteady, backing up the steps. He reached out to her in case she fell, but she scrambled back and up, until she was against the doorframe. Her eyes were absolutely manic.

He wished, suddenly, that he wasn't taking transcript. But it was his job. He didn't turn the transcripter off, just let it run, knowing that the camera in his lapel pin was going to lay this whole little show, including her crazy-looking face, into the record. Forever.

"Ting, Channon wants to talk to the Rillian. He doesn't want us to kill it. He made me promise we wouldn't—"

"It's dead," McLeod said automatically, gesturing behind

him, where the purple-tinged slick was about the size of a downed elephant or a moon truck.

And then, behind her, up popped Channon's head. The Kiri alien came to his feet. He stepped over the reviving body of Jim Stuart and out, taking Ella by the hand.

"Yes, dead. Past. Ella, no fault. No time to explain, then. Now, we agree not kill Rillian, yes, McLeod?"

"Ah—you bet, Channon. Time for some good story, is it?" He hoped to hell the Kiri wasn't implying what McLeod thought he might be implying. But he had to find out. "Are you saying you think there're more of these here?"

"Not this moment," said Channon. "But soon, could come. Humanity not kill."

Yates, whom McLeod at that moment would cheerfully have impaled on the plasma gun the commissioner still carried, butted in: "Channon, we don't know how not to kill it. Fact is, we don't know how we killed it. Take it from me, we don't. So if there's another one out there . . . unless you can help us defend against it, the best we're going to do is kill it next time. The worst . . . it kills us. But capture it? We wouldn't know where to start."

Channon's head had snapped in Yates's direction when he began to speak. Now the alien nodded in that exaggerated fashion of his. "Yes, good. Teach Yates and Yesilkov this, you bet. Defend against Rillian . . . go farside."

Jesus, Lucky really did think there were more where that one came from. "Lucky—Channon, we'll talk good story about Rillians, when I get to my office—to your new quarters. Go with Yates and Yesilkov there—not farside, not now. Agreed?"

"Agree. Not now. Big hurry, not. But need technologists, say thoughts on feasibilities study."

"Right. I'll put some people together. Anything else?"

"Bradley. Need Bradley." He raised Ella's hand, in his. "And you, McLeod: soon."

"Soon as I can, I promise, Channon. Want to tell me what the rush is, when a minute ago there wasn't one?"

"Food, McLeod. Bradley, Channon, not eat until McLeod come: cucumbers and flower tea with honeys."

Yates hooted and, shaking his head, reached out: "Okay, Channon, we'll get you a McVeggie or somethin'. Let's let the folks do their work."

And as he hustled Channon toward the car, Yates shook his head disparagingly at McLeod before he called out in a drill-sergeant's voice: "Yesilkov, get the lead out. We're movin' on."

The Soviet woman left the half-stunned men and brushed by McLeod as if he didn't exist. When she reached McLeod's car, she whispered to Yates before she got in the back, behind Channon.

And Yates called out to his secretary, as he slid behind the wheel, "Sally, sweetheart, you give Mr. McLeod and his boys all the cooperation you can. They've got to call in these casualties and wait for the police and coroner to arrive, which might take a while. And o'course the Soviets'll want to send a tech crew over to smell the Rillian sludge. And then o'course there's the message traffic problem, what with the B-sat out of commission. . . ." He turned to McLeod and waved out the open window. "Thanks for the car, 'Ting.' You know where I'll be when you're finished doin' my job for me."

McLeod didn't bother to respond. Once in a while someone with Yates's group of childish proclivities rose as high as Yates had in the system. But systems were self-correcting. When Yates wasn't needed anymore, Yates would take Yates out. McLeod needn't do a thing. The Lone Ranger and his Ukrainian Tonto were going to find themselves in a box canyon one of these days, and nobody from McLeod's office would be around to pull them out.

That was the way it went in his business. You bided your time; you did your best—and you let accidents waiting to happen, happen.

The only thing was, until the Channon affair was over, McLeod didn't want anything less than the kind of total commitment Sam Yates could bring to the job of baby-sitting the most precious living being ever to come under McLeod's protection.

He only hoped that Yates didn't figure out the way McLeod was reading the data; if he did, he'd be insufferable.

And McLeod had enough problems. One of them was sidling away from him, into the building where Jim Stuart and his boys were doing some lethal bitching about Yates and—as McLeod had suspected—Yesilkova, turning a stunner on them.

They clamped their mouths shut when they saw him.

"As you were, gentlemen."

Everyone started talking at once. McLeod said, "No excuses—there's no need, no reason for them. You all did fine work
here, and I'm sure your verbal reports, to me only, will support
my investigative judgment."

Sometimes he hated walking around wired for sight and sound,
but it helped when things turned into your-word-against-
somebody-else's.

"The only thing I need from you, gentlemen, before you each
get forty-eight hours off and a dinner on me wherever you
choose, is those verbals, and a clear-cut identification of who
pulled the trigger—or triggers—on the stunner—or stunners—
used to take you out of play; whether there were any verbal
orders or hand-signal orders given to initiate the attack, and if
so, by whom, to whom. You know the drill."

They did. Yesilkova's name came out of three mouths as the
shooter; the complaints about Yates were more diffuse. Perfect.

McLeod held up his hand for silence. "Give me five minutes
alone inside and we'll finish up. Meanwhile, call Henhouse,
check in, and handle things for me here as if this were our office.
Stuart, you're acting Security Commissioner."

It was easy to walk right past them, into the inner office where
Channon had been kept, where Ella had just now disappeared.

She was like a waif, a wraith. He didn't understand why she
was behaving this way. He told himself again that it was shock,
but he didn't believe it. It was something more.

She was sitting on the desk and when he came close she said,
"Taylor, if you pull me off this project, things can't go on between us."

"That's a ridiculous thing to say. Or it's blackmail. Either
way—"

"It's neither. You wouldn't pull me out if you didn't care
about me. I can't accept that reasoning. I have as much right to
risk my life here as you do. Or as Yates does or—"

"Don't talk to me about Yates. Or Yesilkov. Or about what I
do. I want you out of harm's way. How can I do my job when
I'm so worried about your safety I can't think straight . . . ?"

He hadn't seen her trap until he'd stepped squarely into it, up
to his neck.

"See?" she said quietly, no triumph in her voice, which
shook. "If you can't do your job because of your feelings for

me, and you won't let me do mine, then . . ." She started to twist the engagement ring off her finger.

"Oh, don't do this to me," he said, not realizing how naked it sounded. "Not now. For chrissake, don't you realize what that alien offers this country—? Don't make me choose between you and my work. . . ." Again, she'd caught him.

He took the ring when she handed it to him. It was small and fragile-looking in his hand, and he stared at it there. The sparkle of the diamond wasn't as bright as the tiny beads of perspiration springing up on the creases in his palm.

The silence was imperfect: His eardrums were thumping out his pulse-rate so that he could hardly hear. "Look," he said, without raising his eyes from the ring in his hand. "I admit you're right. It's a problem we can't solve." He didn't want to do this, but she was forcing him.

"I know," she said. Only that.

He'd always known he'd loved Elinor Bradley. The question had continually been whether there was room in his life and his heart for another lover, when his country took up so much of both. He wasn't sure that he'd ever realized just how much he loved her until this moment, when she was giving him no chance to assure her safety other than forcing her back to Earth and breaking her heart.

But he couldn't do less. He said to the ring he was watching, "I'll get you that Earthbound berth. I can't have you up here like this. I'll instruct my office to notify the guests that the wedding is . . . indefinitely postponed."

He had to give them both that option. Maybe there'd be life after Channon. Maybe there'd be no more Rillians. Maybe, even if there were more Rillians, they'd have worked up a defense by then. Or maybe the Rillians would be happy with just Channon, if it came to that, and whatever collateral damage the Rillians had to inflict on the lunar colony to get Channon.

Get Lucky, he amended in his mind. Which was better than he was going to get.

He didn't expect her to do anything but agree. He never expected a direct order to be disobeyed.

She moved to the far side of the room, to the couch where the alien had sat and slept for so long. And she said, "Taylor McLeod, I'm not going home. You can't make me, especially now. Channon wants me here, you heard him." Her voice was thickening. He didn't want to look up. If she was crying, he couldn't hold his ground.

But he did look up. And she was crying. Brave, silent streams of tears. And she said, "He's waiting for us for dinner. You heard him."

"Damn you, woman," he said, and went over to her. There was too much loneliness, too much misery in the world as it was. "Hold out your hand."

She did. He dropped the ring into it. "I don't have any other use for this. And I . . . don't want to lose you. Just let me pretend that you'll take my orders like somebody on my staff ought to, all right? And I'll pretend I think I can protect you better up here, and do my job just as well with you where I don't need to worry that you'll be struck by lightning on some picnic with another guy. . . ."

Then she was hugging him, and he remembered for the first time in far too long that he was recording all of this for posterity.

Well, he'd deal with the consequences of that. He was too disciplined to try to wipe the tape; too concerned with real problems to create another one by setting a precedent of special treatment between them. What he'd just read into the transcript was close enough to that to last him a lifetime.

She said, "Then you won't bounce me from the team?"

"Not unless something comes to light in the transcripts that shows you acted inappropriately. As you said, Channon wants you here. And so do I."

He wished he didn't. He really wished he didn't.

Twenty minutes later, still in Yates's office, after they'd started behaving like professionals, he got a call from Minsky at the Soviet embassy saying that General Ruskin's Zil had been caught in the Rillian death beam, or whatever it was.

"Our condolences," he told his opposite number from KGB. "What's that do to your team structure, Oleg?"

"It puts me in direct charge, at least temporarily," Minsky said smoothly. Minsky's English was better than Yates's. "This is a tragedy, true, but now the teams have real parity, with you shepherding one, and me the other, yes?"

"Yep." He motioned Ella to pick up an extension. She might as well hear whatever was coming next. He pantomimed the procedure: Punch another line, pick up the handset, punch across into the line he was on.

She did so, just as Minsky said, "We need a meeting, you and I. And we need to put Sultanian in direct contact with the guest, and of course with your technologists as well, as soon as possible, that we may all hear whatever he has to say about this enemy, whom he knows so much more intimately than we."

McLeod squeezed his eyes shut, then opened them. This Jonah Day just wasn't going to quit.

"Well, Minsky, I promised Channon, whom I just left, a private dinner with Ms. Bradley. He's got a wicked crush on her, and I've been asked to chaperone. You know how drunk that alien can get on cucumbers and jasmine tea. But tomorrow morning, first thing, we can have our joint teams present for a situation report and Q & A at my office, about 0800 Zulu time, if it suits you."

It wouldn't, McLeod knew. Those weren't the best confab hours for satelliting to Moscow. But it was, still, McLeod's ball—his alien, his defector, America's star performer.

Minsky sighed in deep Russian angst and said, "You are so cruel, you liberal northern intellectuals. We shall see you then, with bells on."

"Bye-bye, Oleg," McLeod said, letting satisfaction creep into his voice.

Then he motioned Ella to wait, watch, and put down her handset exactly when he put down his.

She said brightly, "Well, I'm glad that's settled. Let's have Sally get us a car. Channon's waiting."

"You know I hate cucumbers," he said. "They give me indigestion."

But it wasn't the cucumbers. It was all the compromises he was making, so early into what was becoming an entirely different sort of mission than he'd first thought.

He called Dick Quint, and then Sandy, before he left with Ella for his office, telling both men of the 0800 meeting, and advising them to bring anybody they thought might have a smidgeon of expertise that could be helpful. Whatever Channon wanted to build, it was time to start building it.

As for security considerations and matters of secrecy, the sort of procedures now required were entirely different.

The whole habitat knew that at least one alien was here. The cat was out of the bag: It was big, and bad, and six-legged—

and it could blow the hell out of anything you sent against it except, seemingly, antique Russian-made pistols.

The first order of business was to declare a pro forma State of Emergency, Luna-wide; the blowback down on Earth was going to be fierce, but only if Step Two didn't fly. Step Two was officially lifting that selfsame State of Emergency within, say, twelve hours. They'd float some story about the six-legged thing being an isolated threat, and a dispatched threat at that.

It might work. But even if it did, history was different, as of the time that thing came bounding into the airlock:

Man was no longer alone in the universe, and the whole damned lunar colony knew it.

That news was going to shake some bedsteads, even if they managed to convince everybody that there weren't any more Rillians where that one came from. Or at least, that none were expected.

Gathering up his fiancée and quickly run copies of the as-yet-unviewed log tapes from Yates's office, McLeod was ruefully wishing he could convince himself that there weren't any more Rillians out there.

Or at least that Channon wasn't expecting any.

Because he didn't know how the hell he was going to tell those guys at tomorrow's 0800 meeting that Channon *was* expecting more company: What did you say?

He tried to envision it: *Friends and colleagues, I'm here today to tell you that whatever we just encountered was, despite luck and appearances, virtually unstoppable. We know only that the enemy is possessed of advanced technology and is demonstrably hostile, and that there'll be more of them in the future, so we'd like you to come up with a quick fix: an elephant gun, a bug spray, a monster-zapper, a big cage with real thick bars—just any old thing you have around in your basements. Because, ladies and gentlemen, not only do we think we need to prepare for another such visit, but our friendly alien, here, doesn't want us to kill his enemy. He wants to talk to him, and he wants us to help make that possible.*

Speeches like that were the kind that got you early retirement.

The only plus that McLeod could see, waiting for a car to come fetch him, was that he hadn't managed to get himself divorced before he got married. He'd have to make sure that Ella was comfortable with matters the way they now stood.

This was suddenly very important. Since he didn't know how much of a future any of them were going to have, really, he needed to make sure that the woman he loved was as happy as possible for as long as possible, even if it did make his job a little tougher.

If he'd wanted easy, he'd have gone into some other line of work.

Chapter 19

AFTER ACTION

"Heard from Bradley you was askin' after us, Channon," Yates said as he drove the conveyance away from the murder scene.

Yates was highly agitated, Channon knew. As was Yesilkov, in the back seat behind him.

"Yeah," said the female warrior. "Wanna tell us what all that was about?"

"All?" Channon said. "I wished warn about Rillian coming. This you find out." He was shaken, still, from the violence. And the two he was with still loudly echoed the rage and fear and combat they'd so recently endured. For the first time in a long time, Channon was frightened of these humans—of their capacity for destruction.

"Warn?" Yates turned his head, away from his vehicle's path, and the side of it scraped the wall, spitting sparks.

Yesilkov spoke a string of words that made no sense except in relation to anatomy and the function of human body parts.

When the vehicle was out of danger, Yates spoke again, this time staring steadily ahead: "Warn, you said. That means you knew that thing was on the way?"

"Knew . . . no. Suspected, yes. Said story before." He struggled with syntax. "Tried to say."

"And we didn't listen. Yeah, he's right, Yates," Yesilkov said in her quick way.

"So Channon asks, bring Yesilkov; bring Yates. McLeod do." He shrugged. "Late."

"You told ol' Ting the same thing? And he underestimated the situation? No wonder he's pissy. What else did you tell him?"

"Go farside, Channon wants. Yates, Yesilkov, Channon: farside."

"So that was what he meant. Well, not now, buddy, unless

you're telling me there's another alien hot on the heels of that last one.''

"Hot heels?"

"Sam, he's not following."

"Maybe we're the ones that aren't. That right, Channon?"

"Some moments, yes. Must thank Yates and Yesilkov for risk, for saving—"

"Hey, bub," Yesilkov said from the back seat and launched herself forward, grabbing Channon by the shoulder so that he flinched. "That's our job; that's all."

"Not worth dying," Channon said, and reached up to take her hand as he'd seen human males do with their females. "Thanks to Yesilkov. Thanks to Yates. Thanks to families of dead warriors—you will transmit?"

"S-s-sure," said Yesilkov in a quivering voice and took her hand away. "Next time I see 'em, sure thing."

"Easy, Sonya," Yates told her severely. "He doesn't understand. Listen, Channon, we don't wanna talk about what happened back there, you read me?"

"Hurtful, yes. Sorrys." He did read the pain trying to scramble over the barriers these two had erected to keep feelings away. This was not healthy, but they surely knew what they were doing.

"Let's get back to threat identification. You want to go farside when the next one comes, right?"

"Right." He nodded vigorously.

"You just say when," Yesilkov told him. "We'll be right there. As a matter of fact, maybe we'd better make sure we can provide the transport. . . ."

"Enough said, in this car, about that," Yates told her in a way that must have transmitted more than a blanket caution.

"Still, Sam, in front of McLeod he said he'd teach us how to defend against Rillians by going farside."

"Yeah, that's so. You did say that, Channon. Want to read us in—tell us what we're up against?"

"Rillians."

"Christ on a crutch, we *know* that—now."

"Said before," Channon was becoming frustrated. "Tell Bradley many times, before too late: need Yates; need Yesilkov."

"You've got us, buddy. Just take it easy and tell us when you think the next attack's going to come, from where, and what kind of preparations you'd like us to make.''

They both were silent, now, waiting for his answer. He didn't know how to ask what he needed to. He couldn't find the words. The vehicle grew uncomfortably full of their tension.

At length, spinning the wheel before him in his fingers so that the vehicle lurched sideways, then shivered, then changed direction, Yates said, ''Well, Mr. Kiri diplomat, we're waiting.''

''When I said give Rillian me, you said not. True?''

''True,'' Yates said, baring his teeth.

''This true next visit, also?''

''You can bet your shiny fangs on that, brother,'' Yates promised.

''Then, go farside. Lead Rillian far from habitat, far from humans.''

''Then what?'' Yesilkov wanted to know.

''Then Channon talk to Rillian before dying. Channon job, done. Yates and Yesilkov go home, safe.''

''No way, asshole,'' Sonya Yesilkov snarled. ''It'd be worth our heads. McLeod's just waitin' for Sam to make some mistake. And as for me, I'm stuck so deep in the middle o' this I gotta win big or I'm not even a pension number.''

''Not understand.''

''She said *no*.''

''Not asshole.''

''Okay, okay, we're sorry, aren't we, Sonya?''

''Channon, you have the apologies of the entire Soviet Union, if it helps. We want to help you capture the Rillian, and get a look at its weapon. You can talk to it; we'll talk to its weapon. Everybody will be happy. Try to think how to do that.''

''And if you can't help with that, then just for my peace of mind,'' Yates added, ''help me figure out how the hell we killed the damned thing, so we can do it again—only, of course, in case of direst need.''

''Never need kill.''

''What is this guy, an alien or a missionary?''

''Both,'' Channon said.

''Sonya, this vehicle's probably feeding everything we say to McLeod. You're going right into McLeod's web, Channon. If you want me, from now on, just dial nine-one-nine on any com system and ask for me by name. Say 'Code Red'; that'll get you through. Got that?''

"Got," Channon said. "Defend against Rillian, Channon will think how. Tell McLeod. Tell all peoples.''

The two warriors exchanged glances in the mirror pointing rearward. Yates shook his head, meaning something negative.

"Code Red. If you even think a Rillian's on the way. How much warning—how much time, did you have on the last one?''

"On?'' He thought. "Since comsat ending; sense probe, earlier time.''

"An hour, a day, what?''

"Sam, never mind. He doesn't think like that. Just as soon as you know next time, Channon. Okay?''

"Okay. But go farside, soon?''

"Are you sensing another one now?'' Yates did something with his foot and the vehicle came to a sudden stop, throwing Channon forward.

"Not now. Later, maybe. Not certain. Nothing certain. But Rillian comes, Channon less danger if farside.''

"He's worried about the civilians, for God's sake.''

"God not need help, Yesilkov. Yates and Yesilkov need help, if Channon to protect.''

"Well, we're all agreed on something,'' Yates said, and made the vehicle move forward once more.

"Listen, Channon, ask for us when and if you want us,'' Yesilkov counseled. "Otherwise, we won't see you again, except for the morning briefing, until you need us the way you needed us today.''

"Too late, then,'' said Channon, and hit the window with the side of his fist. He looked at the fist, shocked at what he'd done, although the window hadn't broken. Then he put his hand carefully in his lap where it could clasp his helmet. The distress of these warriors was co-opting his emotional base. "Need prepare, not confront.''

"You know, for a red-skinned, snaggle-toothed, white-eyed alien, you ain't as dumb as you look,'' Yesilkov said warmly.

"You want to prepare,'' Yates told him, "then ask us for whatever you need. We'll have some transport ready, no matter where we have to get it. Right, Sonya?''

"Right, Sam.''

"This lying. Why lying?" He could feel Yesilkov's heavy heart, her despondency.

"Shit, Channon, don't read people's minds. Ain't polite," she answered. "Because we're just grunts—little guys. We don't make policy. We get paid to put our bodies between trouble and folks like you. Where we gonna get farside transport, except in an emergency—?"

"He wants it, McLeod will give it to him." The snap in Yates's voice was an unmistakable end to that discussion. "Just promise me, Channon, you'll do like you told McLeod, and figure out how we can defend against the Rillians."

"Promise," Channon said, suddenly and deeply sorry for the two warriors who firmly believed that he was leading them to their doom. "Channon wants no harm, only peace. If ship given, Channon leave . . . Rillian follow. . . . No more human death. No death Yates; no death Yesilkov."

"Channon, don't ever let me hear you say somethin' like that again," Yates said very softly. "Don't you even think of turnin' tail, especially not because of us. Our asses are fried if we lose you—it'd be our fault if you disappeared. Promise me you won't disappear."

"Not disappear. Cannot. How could? Must stay unless helped."

"We'll give you help, but not to run away, not to commit suicide by putting yourself in front of the next Rillian you see. Clear?"

"Not."

"He means, do you understand?" Yesilkov said.

"Understand, not agree. Next Rillian, Yates and Yesilkov think more. Now, thinking hurtful. Not want hurt friends, savers of life. Savers hurt enough this day."

Yates waved his hand as if brushing something away. "Man, you won't quit, will you? Look, you just call us, okay? At the first sign of need, or even if you're only nervous. If you have a bad dream. If you miss home cookin'—whatever. That's our job; it's what we do. Take that away from us, and then you're really hurting us. Do you understand that?"

"Understand," said Channon, although he did not. What Yates was broadcasting did not match his noble words. He was angry that there might be another Rillian, that Channon hadn't suggested a simple solution he could accept. He was frustrated and resentful and in need of rest. "Maybe no Rillian other comes."

It wasn't a lie. There was always that possibility. He was no expert on Rillians; no Kiri was. Yates needed comfort, and Yesilkov needed Yates to be calm in order for her to be calm, and, sitting in the car with both of them, Channon wanted only the best for both of them, so that he could restore his own equilibrium. So he added, "Fear unnecessary. Yates and Yesilkov alive; Channon alive. Winning, is this."

"Winning is this," said Yates with a rueful chuckle, and even Yesilkov began to smile.

Chapter 20

INCOMING

The Rillian controller came out of sponge-space with the queasy awareness that the average speed of light in this bubble universe was only 300,000 meters per second, barely 85 per cent of normal.

Normal for the controller. The macro-universe was too great for even the Rillians, its master race, to have plumbed all its reaches.

Yet.

Awareness of the alien environment was unpleasant; the controller's instruments corrected automatically, but the far more subtle and valuable knowledge base within his mind was slower to adjust. While he was still orienting himself, his personal database indicated with a ninety-nine per cent certainty that the Elevener his unit was tracking was here.

There was also data on the soldier whose sector included this bubble universe—the soldier whose failure to report had shunted the controller here unexpectedly (prepared only in the sense that it was his duty to investigate such circumstances and that no Rillian is unprepared for his duty).

That Rillian soldier was dead.

The muscles on the back of the controller's neck twitched. If the controller had had scales—as his ancestors had scales fifty million years before, as the soldiers he controlled still had scales—those scales would have risen into a terrible ruff.

The Rillian controller did not need scales to be terrible, any more than he needed an A-field weapon to kill. But he had been issued with the weapon, and he checked it now while his mind and his instruments prepared to accomplish the duty of a Rillian. . . .

BOOK TWO

TO ERR IS HUMAN

Chapter 21

SITUATION REPORT

Channon's skin was beginning to flake. He needed to get out of his suit and wash. Perhaps it would help the itchiness. Perhaps the flaking was a normal result of stress and the lack of normal grooming; he'd never been so long in his suit before. Perhaps . . .

Perhaps the discomfort was something more ominous: There was no way to determine that the humans were not slowly killing him with their kindness, with their flower water, with their vegetables or with the air they breathed or the primitive magnetic fields and low frequency wave baths in which they lived and worked without apparent harm.

But he knew without doubt that any harm they were doing him was unintentional. Since they had shaken hands as friends in Yates's office, Bradley, especially, harbored only the most beautiful of feelings toward him.

This was in direct contrast to what he'd found the humans capable of feeling toward an enemy. Being present while Yesilkov, Yates, and their friends had battled the Rillian for Channon's life had made that painfully clear. He had known all along that Yates and Yesilkov were of the warrior class, but . . . to be bathed in all his sensory ranges with such murderous intent; to be present when death was all around and be helpless even to guide the departing spirits from their flesh; to be unable to testify to the quality of the lives so profligately spent . . .

. . . to observe the Rillian shock trooper close at hand and to be helpless to do more than crouch, quivering as wave after wave of primal rage washed over him, not only from his enemy but from his protectors, who had made his enemy their enemy . . .

. . . to have every overture he projected at the Rillian ignored, every attempt at injecting a conciliatory atmosphere rebuffed without notice, as if the Rillian warrior were deaf and dumb in all communication bands common to civilized life . . .

None of these thoughts could be completed. He had only memories, which were painfully tactile. It might well be that all that broadcast violence had killed the very cells of his epidermis, and thus he itched. And would itch until he could scrub off the dead layer.

It occurred to him, sitting in McLeod's pastel suite, that it had been so long since his kind had encountered primitive warfare close at hand, that the deadness of his skin could be an indicator of an ancient, forgotten, physiological defense against violence fielded in so many frequency ranges. He wished he'd studied the hostage depositions in the Kiri archives more carefully, but it was too late for that. The depositions were lost with the *KirStar*, part of the background material he'd left when he fled in the capsule. Even had the capsule survived, he'd neglected to migrate such seemingly inconsequential data.

It was far too late for regrets. And if he regretted anything, then he must regret everything: Humans had lost their lives protecting him, some right before his stricken eyes. He'd resolved when he saw the first of humanity's warriors step into the Rillian's path that he would do everything he could for these creatures, even though they were so much more Rillian than Kiri in their ways.

So he'd taken off his helmet when it was clear that the Rillian was approaching, ready to endure the consequences in order to acquire a clearer sense of his enemy. And the inundation of his person had been so painful, so engulfing, so transforming, that he had been, for an instant, one with the Rillian; then one with his human champions.

It had been the most horrible moment of his span; even the destruction of *KirStar* paled in comparison. The death of innocents was difficult to endure; becoming one with the minds of beings intent on killing, even at the risk of being killed, was a torture of the heart.

He had barely withstood the madness all around him.

And then all had become attenuated, more distant, more endurable.

Again he scraped at the skin on the back of his hand. It was darker to the eye than it should be; where his nail passed over it, it turned gray and flaked away, leaving pinker skin beneath.

If there had been another Kiri present, he would have mentioned his hypothesis—that his skin had died upon his body in response to the ELF waves of the combatants, in order to provide him with a type of shielding, a natural armor, a layer of protection. This would explain the lessening of the psychic inundation.

Without it, he might have lost consciousness, unhelmeted, when the Rillian had settled into itself to die.

He was still shaken, even after having shared sustenance with Bradley and McLeod. Now the humans were in rest phase, in other cubicles of the same complex. Bradley had told McLeod that Channon needed rest.

McLeod had said, "He's not the only one. Let's take a couple hours off, get some sleep. We'll have to hustle when we reconvene, though. Channon, how does that suit you?"

He had agreed, thinking of the suit galling him whenever he moved, and so much uncollated experience in his head.

But he'd thought that Bradley would stay with him, as she had in the other place. She did not. She'd brushed her lips against his forehead and said, "We'll be—I'll be in there, right through that door, sleeping. If you need me, Channon, don't hesitate to call. Now let me show you the amenities."

These were an H_2O-sprayer, a waste disposal unit he understood to be just like the one in the other place, and a soft pallet with warm coverings.

He looked around the suite again and got up, slowly, carefully. If he could take off his suit, not only could he scrub the dead skin away, he could examine what felt like open sores upon his hips, his elbows, in his crotch. . . .

The washroom was made of hard tile and he knew there was a surveillance device mounted in here somewhere. He could hear the motor whirring as it followed his movements; he could feel the bounce of the uninterrupted waves off the hard-surfaced tiles.

Still, this might be his only chance. As he ran his nails along his suit's seals to loosen them, he thought of the pair in the next room, who had mated as soon as they left him, and how much violence there was in even that, their most intimate act.

At first it had worried him, when he felt Bradley's excitation; her feelings were so mixed, so discordant in the human female he'd thought he'd come to know.

But male and female humans had difficult relations where situational control was concerned; this he had learned from watching Yates and Yesilkov, and both of them with McLeod.

He pulled his suit carefully from his shoulders and half closed his eyes when he first saw the extent of his discolored skin and the flaming patches under his arms.

Then he opened his eyes wide, surveyed the damage clinically, and pulled the suit down to his ankles. Next he sat upon the tile floor, took off his boots as well, and started carefully licking the worst of his sores.

Where he couldn't reach with his tongue and his own antiseptic saliva, he'd have to use their water. But even though the process was painful, as he worked his way up his trunk, he felt relief: Wherever his tongue had cleansed away the dead skin, the new skin revealed beneath was a healthier color than the ungroomed patches.

He continued until only the H_2O sprayer was left to him, to get those parts of his backside that he couldn't reach. If Terri had been with him, of course, grooming and scrubbing all parts of an afflicted body back to health would have been so much simpler.

He sagged against the cold tile of the shower cubicle then, wishing Terri was here to lick his back, wishing that he could lick hers. His elbows itched terribly; if he could, he would have used his fangs on them, bitten a whole layer of skin off in that moment of frustration.

But there was only the water shower. He knew it was going to sting. He didn't know, however, how hot it would be, coming from that spray head.

He howled with misery and stumbled from the shower, then regained his balance and put both hands on the tile, staring at the spray and the steam.

No human could endure such temperatures, any more than could he. Therefore, there was a regulator somewhere. He found it, felt sheepish, and this time waited until the water was tepid.

It was still filled with foreign minerals and chemicals that stank, and now his skin was scalded in places as well.

Nevertheless, there was no benefit in not following through with the cleansing ritual. What he would have given for a pit of clean sand to bathe in, preferably with graphite sides on which to hone his teeth and nails. . . .

It's simply water, he told himself. Tainted water, but water as might have fallen from the skies of home in ancient times, after a volcanic interval or during an early industrial age. If its chemicals created free radicals when they met his scraped skin, then those tumors were far away and even this blighted race could excise them.

He stepped determinedly into the shower once again. His hosts had died for him with less qualm than he was showing about making use of their culture's bathing facilities. He was overreacting, and he knew it.

There was a fiber mitt in the shower, a wonderful thing he found hanging from the regulator when he'd calmed enough to deal with the strangeness around him.

This scratch mitt was not as good as his tongue, but he could grasp both ends of it, behind his back, and rub himself against it. The sting of the water was bearable, even as the scabs came off under the mitt.

Thus he did not know how long Bradley had been standing there, watching him. He merely turned and there she was, a pale figure swathed in steam.

"Channon?" she said with a flash of discomfort that made him want to cover himself, although he couldn't imagine why she felt that he should. "We heard you yell. I thought . . . If you're okay, I'll be in the other room."

"Bradley, stay is okay. Water too hot, was. Now, better."

She was looking at his reproductive organs, this was certain.

He stopped rubbing his back against the mitt and brought his hand forward. "See?" he said, displaying himself to put her at ease and satisfy her curiosity. "Not great difference: mammal type, compatability not probable, but attempts likely pleasurable. . . . Bradley? Bradley, want examine?" he called after her, but she'd already gone.

He could feel her strange reactions: fear, vulnerability, embarrassment, and something he couldn't name that made no sense. She was a scientist, was she not? a diplomatic person attached to this contact team? a professional female person?

He looked down at himself. His body was spotty looking, but nothing fearful. The licking, the grooming, the water-softened mitt—and her attention—had brought blood to the appropriate places, but he wasn't sure why that had frightened her. At least he had not failed to acknowledge her presence as that of a female within reach of a fertile male. *That* would have been an insufferable slight that forever would have hung between them.

He stepped out of the shower, into the steamy room, and went to the door to say, "Bradley, Channon knows, mated with McLeod. Compliment unwelcome?"

Then he realized that she—or McLeod—had taken his suit while he'd been in the shower. He strode into the next room, which was empty, and into the next.

There was his suit, his helmet, and McLeod, nearly as naked as he, sitting with them on his bed.

"Give suit," Channon said, hands on his hips as McLeod had taught him. "Now. Bradley upset, seeing Channon's organs."

"Yeah, I heard. Well, fella, holster your weapon in the presence of a lady, next time."

"Not understand. Bradley comes to Channon. Wants to see . . ." He stepped forward, hand out now for his suit.

"She didn't mean it . . . like you took it, I'm sure, Channon." McLeod was still holding the suit in his lap. "Cultural differences, okay?"

"Okay. Must amend. Give suit. Channon put on, find Bradley. Kiss head. All better."

"In a little while. This thing's dirty, right? You've got a couple sores there, looks like. Why don't you tell me how, and we'll get it cleaned for you."

"Give suit," Channon said. "Your tongue no good to clean. Channon clean."

"Ah . . . must be some way we can negotiate this."

"Give suit." Channon stood over the human, now. "No secrets in suit. Secrets in Channon head." He pointed to his temple. "Suit just . . . inanimate. Give suit before Bradley comes."

"Ella can handle the sight of you. I'd really like my tech boys to look at these electronics, or whatever they are. It might help us where you're weak—on the theory, as you said yourself, behind the communicator you want us to help you build."

"Channon need suit."

"You know, you're a stubborn son of a bitch."

"Not. Practical. Rillian come, Channon go farside, this time. Rillians chase from habitat, not into. Better. Human dead not even understand reason. Bad deaths, such."

"You know of any good deaths, friend?" McLeod was sitting back now, leaning on both arms, looking up at him.

Channon could have snatched the suit from him, but McLeod, he knew, would react badly to such a move. He said, "Good deaths, of course: in lover's arms, when time comes, when work done, when span past—sleep; go to spirit place content."

"Oh yeah? Maybe where you come from. Here . . . it's not that way. I wish it were." There was a huskiness in McLeod's voice. "Tell you what, let's make a deal. You sit down and clean your suit, right here, and I'll give you a bathrobe—a covering temporarily—and we'll talk awhile. And I'll get a couple guys in here to spec this communicator, the translator or whatever it is, and the helmet. Otherwise, we'll just have to do it later. And I'd like to do it just between you, me, and my boys—no Soviets. So if you let me have this examined now, in your presence, I'll back your negative when you're asked, tomorrow, to give up your gear to have it analyzed out of your sight, where you arguably couldn't get at it in an emergency. Deal?"

Everything with McLeod was a deal. "Deal. Give covering so Bradley come out of closet."

"Not closet," McLeod chuckled. "Bathroom—shower cubicle, like in your room. But I'll get her as soon as you're decent."

"Decent now. No ill effects of witnessing murders; Kiri not suggestible. Evil of thought and deed never contagious to us. Need covering so Bradley come."

"I'll get it. Here's your suit. Sit right down and start licking it, if that's what it takes."

McLeod had white trunks over his reproductive organs. Perhaps protocol demanded this here, for every male. "Give white trunks, too."

"Underwear? You poor sod, you bet." McLeod was in a good humor now. His sense that progress was being made was so palpable that Channon felt buoyed.

Even his sores did not itch or pulse so. He said, "Mating successful, then?"

"Damn, Channon, you don't ask things like that. You're not supposed to *know* things like—ah, that's right. Ella told me you're psychic, or empathic, or some such." McLeod turned from the place he kept his clothes, holding a fuzzy robe and white trunks.

He stared at Channon, who had gathered up his suit and was settling himself on the floor with it.

"Does that mean," said McLeod slowly and with narrowed

eyes, "that you can read minds: ours, the Rillians, or the Soviets, say?"

"Can hear emotions, feel stimuli—rage, pain, fear. Sense lies, truth. Sense Rillians, when come."

"Terrific. Next time, be sure to tell me—not Ella or Yates—as soon as you sense Rillians, okay? Anything else I should know?"

"Many things to know, McLeod. What things?"

"What else can you sense—or hear, or feel—that we can't?"

"Death. Birth. Such events."

"Oh boy. This was no picnic for you, then, what happened at Yates's office."

"No picnic until you came," Channon reminded McLeod, confused by the segue. "Then ate here."

McLeod came over to him, holding out the clothing, demonstrating how to put on the trunks. "One leg at a time like the rest of us, okay? And this, arms through the holes, belt it, simple . . ."

"Thanks, McLeod. Bradley out now?"

"You know women . . . no, I guess you don't. It did scare her a little. I think she thought you were making a pass. . . . I'll explain to her." He started for a door beyond which Bradley was waiting. "Look, Channon, I really need you to understand, diplomat to diplomat, that we—the United States, my country, me as its representative—are your closest allies here. There are rivalries among our governments, like there must be in the Kiri Unity."

"Not."

"Right. Well we're not psychic, so we think there are, here. The Soviets—like Yesilkov—are old enemies of ours; we're just starting to work together. Some of us do, some only pretend. There'll be attempts by other governments to discredit us in your eyes, to prove themselves more capable of protecting you, or more . . . hospitable, I guess. I want you to understand enough of our politics to realize that this may occur, and not to be confused. You've been with us now long enough to know we'll do whatever we must to protect you, that we have your best interests at heart. Once you asked us for asylum—us and no other nation—you became a ward of our state. We'll discharge that duty, whatever it takes."

"Already take lives, some humans," Channon said softly,

pulling the robe about him. "Channon knows cost of life, what protection means." His throat tightened. But it had to be said: "Channon grateful, but sorrowed with your loss. Rillians . . ." He dropped the trunks, trying to gesture his feelings into the conversation. "Rillians very segmented. First one, like Yates. Like humans . . ."

"We're better than that, Channon. You're just seeing us under difficult—under combat—conditions."

McLeod beat him to the fallen trunks and lifted them, then put them into Channon's hands.

"Still Channon wishes beloveds of spent humans most love and finding of each other, when spirits all loose."

"I'll convey that the best I can," said McLeod solemnly. "Now, back to the 0800 meeting: We'll stonewall any attempts to take you out of here. You've got this skin condition—we'll say it might be serious, even contagious; this is what we call a 'white' lie, an untruth for good reason. If you really feel you need to go farside, Yesilkov and Yates will take you secretly."

"Good story," Channon approved, stepping carefully into the trunks under McLeod's watchful eye. "But need Soviet mathematician to build—"

"We'll go into that transmitter later, after my boys have looked at your helmet and your suit. These are very crucial technologies to a backward little society such as ours; you must realize that. If you think another Rillian's coming, let's talk about a containment facility for one, that'll allow you to talk to it."

"Catch, yes. But McLeod say best secret, now: What Channon teaches, not make war with. Good."

"We try not to make war all the time, Channon. Just like your people with the Rillians. But, like the Rillians, sometimes you find that your enemy doesn't want to talk. Then if you don't have equal force, you face many deaths."

"Truth. So give every peoples technology. Keep balance."

"Phew," McLeod said with a shake of his head. "I don't know whether you're my dream date or my worst nightmare, you know that?"

"Get Bradley? All covered up."

"Right, I forgot."

McLeod went to the far door once more and hit it softly with his knuckles. "Everyone's decent in here, madam. You can come out now—ASAP, please. Channon's agreed to let some techs look at his suit while we brief him for the meeting.''

"Now?" came Bradley's muffled voice from behind the door.

"Now, Doctor. Double time." This was a command.

The door swung open so abruptly it struck something within. Bradley, dressed in pale suiting down to her wrists and ankles, came out and smiled at Channon awkwardly.

Then she said to McLeod, "I thought we were going to review Yates's log tapes and see if we could lodge a formal protest about Yesilkov's shoot?"

"Later. Channon's worried you're mad at him."

"Who? Me? Never. I was just . . . surprised, that's all."

"Thought Channon female?"

"Let's *drop* it, okay?" McLeod said sharply. "While we're waiting for the techs, Channon, why don't you tell us what you think might immobilize any subsequent visiting Rillian?"

Channon shrugged, to indicate to Bradley that everything was within tolerable limits, and folded into a squat where he could begin licking the inside of his suit. "Magnet," he said. "Big, two, both sides tunnel: One catch Rillian, second pull weapon other side."

"Christ, you're a damned genius, you know?" McLeod, who was already holding a communicator, palmed it. "I'll get somebody on it, right away. How big, do you think?"

"Big as Rillian," Channon said, looking at Bradley over the rim of his suit's helmet seal. "Bradley want see suit now? Here is . . ." He held it out to her, a conciliatory gesture meant to make things normal again between them.

And that urge made him stop and think. In so short a time, these primitives had begun to matter to him as individuals, not simply as a young species to be protected.

Especially Bradley should be protected, now: Her mating with McLeod had just been successful. If she was not killed by the Rillians, in due time she and McLeod would have a child.

On any world, new life was worth fighting for. On this one, extraordinary measures would be called for to make sure that Bradley, and all the Bradleys he had not met, survived.

Chapter 22

LOCK-DOWN

Ella Bradley was beginning to wonder whether she'd ever truly known the man she was going to marry. Taylor McLeod's ruthlessness, his duplicity, his single-minded devotion to duty weren't necessarily negative traits—unless you ended up on the receiving end.

The 0800 meeting was well under way in the U.S. mission's postmodern conference room and McLeod still hadn't dropped his bomb. Everyone was chatting casually, munching on real New York danish and drinking coffee and juice while they looked at briefing tapes composed by Ting's office.

On the screen, the Rillian blasted his way through the outer airlock, the inner one, and on toward Yates's office with unerring precision—in freeze-frame, stop-action, slow-motion, and with circles, arrows, and highlighted sections added by McLeod's tech boys so that what was suit, what might be alien life form, and what was weapon could be studied and discussed at length.

All of that was standard procedure, nothing to alarm the Soviets or the UN General Secretary's people, or the woman from World Health, or even the Americans present—Marine Colonel Birdwell, Jim Stuart, General Sanders, Dick Quint, and someone who'd come in with Quint whom Ella didn't recognize.

There were fifteen people at the conference table, not counting herself, McLeod, and the empty seat left for Channon, beside McLeod. Of those, only she and Taylor knew that he was merely going through the motions with this brainstorming session. Taylor McLeod was here precisely and specifically to introduce Channon at the proper moment, display the alien's lesions to the group at large, and decree a week-long quarantine, a total lock-down for all "exposed" personnel—for everyone in this room.

Ella wished she hadn't known in advance. Perhaps then she could have summoned some enthusiasm for the meeting. But she did know. And worse, she knew that McLeod neither expected, nor wanted, nor would contribute to, any joint solution of the problem of future Rillian visits.

He'd talked to groundside, and groundside agreed with him (how else?) that whatever the technological advantage here, the U.S. must secure it unilaterally.

"Then why bother with this at all?" she'd asked him, alone in the "clean" (unbugged and maniacally swept) environment of the conference room with its nickle-plated suspended ceiling and its fabric-quilted blue-and-white walls.

"We need putative exposure to Channon's disease," he'd told her as if she were a slow student. "We want as many as possible of the opposition players benched for as long as possible."

"Oh," she'd said. They were facing a new era for mankind, and all Ting could think about was internal threat indices and technological advantage, as if Channon's expectation of a second Rillian attack were totally apocryphal.

She reached out for another cheese danish, not because she was hungry, but because she needed something on which to fix her attention, and bumped McLeod's elbow as she did so.

He misread her, and slipped his hand under the table, where it cupped her knee, then ran up between her thighs. She closed her eyes and told herself that she could kill him later.

This was supposed to be a comforting gesture, here among all the movers and shakers on the Moon, every one of whom he proposed to entangle in one of his intelligence games?

She leaned toward him slightly and said under her breath, "Don't do that here, please."

He broke contact. But then he looked at her, his eyebrow raised, and murmured, "Are we getting the Kiri flu, dear?"

She dropped the danish onto her plate and put her chin on her fist, looking at the screen. She'd helped him lodge his formal protest against Yesilkov, who'd stunned his precious Special Activities Group in the heat of battle.

Now she wished she hadn't. Ella didn't blame Yesilkov. She probably would have done the same thing herself, had she been trained as a fighter, in the face of imminent danger, when Stuart and his boys tried to obstruct Yates, acting in the line of duty. . . .

Sometimes she absolutely detested all governments, though she prided herself on being a good bureaucrat. And she knew, even now, that McLeod was a better one. As good as men in this sort of work got.

Minsky, the Soviet team leader, whom Ting said was KGB but who was a Soviet Undersecretary of Commerce or something, was calling for the tape to be stopped.

A hidden projectionist obliged only when Ting raised a hand to shoulder level. The lights came up when he swiveled that hand parallel to the desk and made short lifting motions.

"You have the floor, Comrade Minsky."

"This weapon, which here is encircled in red, what do we know about it?" Minsky asked generally.

Quint from Space Sciences said, "It destroys matter. Real well. Real quick. Without any apparent power pack or reload mechanism. The beam's invisible, at least to my eye—if it is a beam. Sometimes when it's shot, you see little puffs of blue sky and fleecy clouds . . . so there's a secondary effect."

Sultanian raised a chubby hand from across the table. "Too, when it is fired, the Rillian is suddenly invisible—not before, I think, but when—at the moment of energizing. This, I submit, is why nothing we shot at it did damage. All this is consonant with the projected effects of A-field weap—"

From down the table, Silov, the egg-bald Soviet astrophysicist, interrupted: "I beg to differ, Comrade. When the Rillian ceases to be viewable is when something is fired at it, not when it fires at something. It is not hit by our projectiles, or burned by our plasma, because it is not present in our spacetime when the weapons reach the strike zone it so recently inhabited. This is the meaning of the stuttering of the Rillian in the visual spectrum."

"Nah, that's not right," said the unfamiliar somebody who had come in with Quint. "I'm Jones, and I'm sure I'll get introduced around later. Looks to me like the thing has some kind of shielding which just makes it seem invisible; it has to shoot through it, so it takes it down only long enough to fire out, then puts up the shield again. . . . Bingo, when we shoot, it's not there. When we don't, it's shooting, so then it looks like it's there. But it's there all the time."

"What is your expertise, Mr. Jones?" Minsky wanted to know.

"Weapons, Mr. Minsky. U.S. Space Command weapons," Jones responded, crisp and prickly.

"And Soviet ones, of course." Minsky craned his neck to take a closer look at the American serviceman, then cast a glower down the table at General Sanders, and finally turned in his chair to fix McLeod with a carefully arranged smile reminiscent of a patient tutor dealing with an obstreperous child. "I was hoping this meeting would be confined to our respective teams, Mr. McLeod. These newcomers cannot add anything—"

"You wanted the UN and World Health people, Comrade Minsky, not me. Once the party started getting bigger, I couldn't refuse Sandy's requests for a couple more seats, especially since the U.S. Air Force considers UN staffers less than neutral."

Ella Bradley wanted to cover her eyes or sink down under the table. Maybe she could take her danish with her. . . .

"So, we are not off to the best of starts. We must remedy this. Where is our guest?"

"He wasn't feeling well," said McLeod with a sad headshake and deep furrowing of his brow. "Yates and Yesilkova will bring him along as soon as he's able. This should suit your overwhelming thirst for parity, Comrade Minsky. Until then, I suggest we return to the briefing tape. Agreed?"

"Agreed," said Minsky with a gusty sigh.

"Unless anyone else has another comment? Dr. Sultanian, Dr. Quint? Jones? Anyone?"

Ella shook her head along with the rest of the herd, and at McLeod's signal the lights dimmed once more and the tape started rolling again.

The tanklike Rillian stutter-stepped gracefully down a half-destroyed corridor, death blooming from the wishbone-shaped weapon he carried.

Every so often the tape would shift abruptly, or blare to white, as a camera position was destroyed and another edited into place to continue the sequence.

The tape could have been better, if there'd been more time. There wasn't any time. Ella knew there wasn't. But woman's intuition didn't count in government work, which this had unequivocally become since the Rillian had blown the outer lock at Entry One.

Yates and Yesilkov didn't arrive with Channon until the tape was nearly over—but not quite over; McLeod wasn't missing a trick.

And when the two security officers escorted Channon to his place at the head of the long table, the alien was still wearing Ting's white terry bathrobe. A nice touch.

Before anyone could ask a single question about where Channon's suit and helmet were, McLeod stood up as if surprised, rushed over to Channon and whispered in his ear.

Another man entered the room by himself, wearing a white coat with a medic's patch on it. He too conferred with Ting and, apparently, with Channon.

This charade continued while people started talking to one another up and down the long table. The murmurs were so thick that Ting had to raise his hand to be heard.

"Friends and colleagues, most of you have met Mr. Channon, who is a protected person of the United States government, meeting all requirements for political asylum under the United States Code, Title 11, Section 10, subsections as pertinent. Under those regulations, we have the right to declare a health emergency of limited scope, which we are now doing. Mr. Channon, as you can see, is suffering from an increasingly painful skin condition. Anyone not willing to risk contracting this condition should leave the room now."

Only the World Health woman got up, and she strode over to talk to the U.S. mission medic in whispered tones.

"The rest of you, be advised that, with or without the concurrence of the UN, we are declaring said health emergency: a quarantine of all exposed persons for one week, enforceable on our citizens, at least, by house arrest. We can't have whatever this is, spreading unchecked among the Luna population, if it's contagious to humans. Again, anybody want to leave now?"

Ella looked down the table, and up the other side. The whispers were increasing; chairs scraped. But nobody left.

Was this what Taylor wanted? For a moment, she wasn't sure. Then she realized it was. This way, no one could say he or she hadn't been warned. Once they returned to their own facilities, they couldn't get back in here. And he had his lock-down—he wouldn't need to open the U.S. mission to anyone, for any reason, for at least a week. In that week, if the Rillians didn't descend upon the colony in force and kill every living soul, Ting would get what he wanted from Lucky: complete, secure debrief.

No one could convince McLeod that Sultanian really knew any more than the U. S. experts about A-field potentials. But if Sultanian did, McLeod was going to acquire whatever data Sultanian had, personally, during this meeting; or later, by videophone.

Minsky was staring at Taylor McLeod as if looks could kill. But there was nothing the KGB man could say.

There was always the chance that Channon's sores and pink-mottled skin were a sign of some contagion. She could see Minsky rubbing his wrist.

Up and down the table, people were scratching their necks and looking covertly at their hands. But everybody would sit this meeting through: Each knew that, if contagion was a real risk, all had already chanced it.

And Channon said, "Good to meet you, all peoples. We have threat to learn, Rillian to stop, all together in friendship."

Ella had coached Channon on his opening statement. He eyed her and she smiled. He nodded vigorously and took his seat, gingerly settling into it as if he really were as uncomfortable as Ting was making out.

God, she hoped he wasn't really sick. She further hoped, if he were, that it wasn't contagious to humans. Suddenly her own left arm began to itch fiercely.

She refused to scratch it. Even knowing that there was minimal risk didn't help the itch, though.

Sometimes she wished she'd gone into gardening, or watercolor painting. She used to be a fair artist, in high school. She could be sitting on some beach somewhere with a couple of kids, pruning her beach plums so that they'd look just their absolute best when she painted them. . . .

But no, she'd had to have adventure; her life had to mean something.

Watching Channon study the convened humans through his pale, opalescent eyes, she knew she wouldn't have traded this moment for any other possible life—not really. Channon might have brought mankind to the brink of disaster a little quicker, but they were almost there, anyhow.

And from Channon, Ella had learned to value hope.

There was hope for everything, Channon was certain—for the

Kiri Unity, for peace with the Rillian empire, even for Ting McLeod. Channon was sure that Ella was pregnant.

When she'd gotten over the shock, she'd been pleased. Channon spoke of her egg hardening its surface against additional sperm as if he were a gynecologist.

She didn't understand how he knew such things, but she was beginning to understand that he was from a race much older, so it didn't hurt too terribly to have to think of them as "superior."

That was the rough part, she knew, for many of the men at this table: the fear that they were facing a superior force, not just militarily, but in all ways.

Only she and McLeod, and perhaps Yates and Yesilkov, had spent enough time with Channon to realize that, from the Kiri Unity at least, humanity had only the Kiri's enemies to fear.

The Kiri themselves, if man could save their representative and thereby gain entree into their interstellar society, were in receipt of enough wisdom to save even mankind from itself.

If, of course, a bunch of paranoid, primitive humans could help Channon save his Kiri Unity from the Rillian menace, the way Channon was hoping to do.

Chapter 23

BUSINESS AS USUAL

Sam Yates liked to brace himself against the furniture. This chair in McLeod's office was too damn compliant; no matter which way Yates twisted or angled himself, the chair was right there to support him, with no pressure but that of gravity. As if lunar gravity weren't more coddling than anybody'd want to begin with.

"Phone," Yates said. "UN Security Commission. Personnel Section, Superintendent Trefusis." He got up and tried some isometrics against the ceiling. At least *that* hadn't been raised out of useful range.

Ella Bradley wasn't the reason Yates didn't like McLeod. Wasn't much of the reason, if he had to be perfectly honest; there was always a sense of—honest again—ownership about a woman you'd had. It was there, but you couldn't let it get in the way. Anyhow, nobody was really going to own Ella Bradley for long.

He wasn't sure Taylor McLeod understood that. The thought bent Yates's features into a boyish grin.

The phone was clucking to itself. Par for the course. Half the time, Yates's own system would futz around for this long, too— and without the excuse of all the spreads, cutouts and interlocks built into a call made from the fucking CIA Station Chief's office.

McLeod was a type. *No expense is too great, no amount of money spent on my comfort is sufficient, since I'm willing to run the lives of all you grubby little worms.* McLeod was probably good at it. Smart, decisive—willing to put himself on the line.

Thing was, Sam Yates had known a lot of guys who were willing to put it on the line. For about thirty thousand of 'em, that meant they rode back from Central America in a steel box around a plastic bag. And even those who'd come back in a more normal fashion, with nothing much in the way of scars on their bodies—Sam Yates, for example—didn't much like the way the Taylor McLeods had taken care of them and the other "little worms."

Well, life wasn't perfect.

"Desk Seven!" snarled the phone. "Who the hell is it?"

"Last time I looked, Alan," Yates said mildly, "it was your boss. I got a moment and I want to catch up on the, ah, damage."

"Omigod," Trefusis murmured on the other end of the line. "Chief? My God, I'm glad to hear from you! We thought you bought the farm yourself."

"Naw, I'm just working out of the office," Yates said, grimacing as he set his back on the wall and tried to straighten his legs against the immobile curves of the desk. "Bit a damage there, too, y'know."

He'd been half hoping the desk, a spidery bit of boron-resin composite, would rip from the flooring. It seemed to be proof against anything short of a nuke. Which figured.

"Right, ah . . ." Trefusis said, temporizing while his mind raced. "Look, I don't know for sure who's got a damage cumulative—maybe al-Aziz on the Patrol desk. Do you want—"

"Alan," Yates said, his eyes closed as his legs strained to move something that wasn't going to move, "if I wanted hardware, I'd have called Patrol. I want to know what happened to *my* people; and I want to know about civilians. Maybe when I've gotten that down I'll worry about things that don't bleed—but not any time soon. Okay?"

"Sorry, Commissioner," Trefusis said. "We're all . . . you know. I'm loading Personnel Movements for the past three days, that's the simplest way. What d'you want for an address?"

Christ, speak of dropping stitches. "Sorry, Alan. The usual, but slug it with the one-seven-six prefix. That's supposed to work. If it don't, I'll start rattling cages till it does."

"Right," Trefusis agreed. The speaker of Yates's phone murmured dully as the man on the other end of the line set up the data transfer. "You're in the American mission?" he added brightly.

"Alan . . ." Yates said, but he was smiling.

"Sorry, chief," Trefusis agreed, cheerful also. "It'll take a minute or two, is all.'' Either he was glad that Sam Yates was alive—or, considered from the viewpoint of the Superintendent of Personnel—things were bad enough that *any* one fewer casualty was a blessing.

The holotank that was Yates's for the moment pulsed iridescently, waiting for a signal it could convert into images. Air-formed holograms were great for meetings, but even the best weren't going to approach the sharpness of images in the controlled medium of a holotank.

''Say, chief?'' Trefusis asked diffidently.

''Yeah?'' Yates had relaxed, finding the chair comfortable now that he'd managed to stress his muscles . . . stress them good and let the fatigue poisons take the edge off the adrenalin.

''What was it really? The, ah . . . ?''

''For the record, Alan,'' said Yates, opening his eyes because he didn't like what he saw, what he felt, when he closed them, ''it was a meteor. A mother-huge meteor.''

Numbers were forming crisply in the holotank. They had a firm connection.

Score one for McLeod—especially since events had screwed up his organization at least as badly as they had UN Headquarters Security.

''Yeah, but off the record?''

''On this line, Trefusis? Dream on!''

''Sorry, chief.''

''No sweat,'' Yates said. ''Thanks for the feed. I'm out.''

Sam Yates looked at numbers and played with the Tokarev he took from the right-hand pocket of his suit. Maybe when all this was over, the Russians'd provide him with a holster for the damn thing. An extra magazine, at least. At the moment he was carrying his remaining seven rounds loose in the left pocket as a slight counterweight to the pistol.

He'd given one round to McLeod's tech people to slice apart, microphotograph—quantify literally to individual atoms through neutron-activation analysis. They'd wanted more, but Sam Yates had started with a box of twenty-five. One round was all he was parting with until somebody shipped him up another case.

The chamber of the Tokarev was loaded now. Nobody had to tell him how dangerous that was with a pistol that didn't have a safety, only a half-cock notch.

Well, people had been saying similar things about the gun's owner. For a long time.

When all this was over. And he'd called Trefusis a dreamer!

Twenty-three dead. Only seven injured; four of those when a pair of loaded Patrol vehicles collided at an intersection more than a kilometer from the Rillian. Lunar gravity was low, but inertia was the same everywhere. Hitting a wall at forty kph was a pretty good way to take yourself out of play.

Twenty-three of Sam Yates's people dead.

Not so bad, considering. Not bad at all—if you could treat 'em as numbers, so many chips that you'd lost before your luck turned.

His hand was mottled with the force he was using to grip the Tokarev. He had to put the pistol down on the immaculate desk, because of the way his index finger kept curling toward the trigger.

His dead. Other people's dead. Jungles, corridors stinking with the residue of plasma discharges and burned human flesh . . .

Sam Yates knew people to whom these numbers were just like any other numbers. If one of those guys had stepped through the door just now, he wouldn't have left the office under his own power.

You have to relax. You have to never ask why it was the guy you played cards with and not you.

Never ask that. Because there probably isn't an answer.

He'd scrolled to the end of the list. Each entry had a slug number that'd let him call up data from the corridor cameras and watch the individual "events" in as much detail as he needed. Maybe later.

One more name. Reason for Absence from Duty: Termination Proceedings.

"Oh, my," Sam Yates said in a bubble-soft voice. "Oh, my."

He got up, dropping the Tokarev back into his pocket. "Holo, off," he ordered, remembering that others might stick their heads into the office while he was gone and see what was up on the tank.

Sam started for the door. As an afterthought he turned and said, "Phone—U.S. mission. Taylor McLeod."

The unit clucked to itself. With no more delay than a series of glass-hard lock-tumblers turning, a pleasant female voice said, "Seven-five-six-one?"

"This is Sam Yates," he said, his voice a little more musical than usual because of the trill of hormones underlying it. "Will you tell Mr. McLeod, please, that I'm coming to see him?"

"Sir, I'll check with the Undersecretary, but—"

"*Stop!* Honey, read my lips: I'm *coming* to see McLeod. Now! Phone out."

He stepped into the outer office. Sonya looked up from where she and Channon sat in front of another holotank, chatting about God knew what. God and the surveillance system knew what.

"Have a nice nap, Sam?" she asked.

Yates blew her a kiss as he walked past. McLeod had moved three doors up the corridor, that was all. "Hell, babe, I been sweatin' over paperwork. That's what they pay us high executives to do, y'know."

"Sam?"

"Just gotta see some people," Yates threw over his shoulder as he reached for the door. "I be back."

Maybe he'd fooled Yesilkov. But from the way Channon was drawing into himself, arms and legs folding for protection, the gentle alien knew *exactly* what kind of mood Sam Yates was in.

Chapter 24

RISK ASSESSMENT

First: If the Eleveners could have defended themselves against Rillian attack, their ship would not have been destroyed with an ease which justified the naval commander's scorn.

Second: Therefore the single Elevener survivor—without resources beyond what he could drag from his crashed escape vessel; very possibly injured himself—could not have killed a Rillian soldier.

Third: Therefore the soldier had been killed by the indigenes . . . who had, to be precise—as a Rillian controller was always precise—sprung from the oxygen planet rotating around a common center with the cold-cored satellite on which the Elevener had landed.

All that was clear, but . . .

But the indigenes seemed even less capable of achieving such a result than was the refugee Elevener. The more the controller—hanging in vacuum, close above the surface of this nearly airless ball—probed, correlated, studied, the greater his puzzlement and unease grew.

He had come, certain he would find a dangerous opponent. He was aware—

The controller's neck muscles twitched, and nictitating membranes covered his eyeballs, though they were only shimmers rather than the scales of translucent horn that would have turned the claws of an opponent from the controller's fifty-million-years-removed ancestor.

He was aware that somewhere in the vastness of the macro-universe, there *might* be a race which could deny the Rillians as their overlords.

But not here. Surely not here . . .

Nothing on the satellite where the Rillian soldier had died was a *threat* to a Rillian soldier—unless the controller was missing something in the clutter of chemical rockets, solar accumulators for energy, and a habitat armored against energy loss and radiation by being dug through rock.

All the indigenes' techniques worked badly, partially, inefficiently. Yet—unless this habitat was a confinement facility, and a quick probe of the main planet invalidated that almost-hopeful hypothesis—it represented the indigenes' cutting-edge technology.

Such folk *could* not have destroyed a Rillian soldier armed and equipped with all the power of the energy sea.

The controller's nictitating membranes flickered back and across; back and across. Their horny equivalents were surgically removed from soldier-recruits at birth, lest reflex half-blind him when he needed to see his instruments. His body was already protected by armor that was infinitely more effective.

But not effective enough.

Had the soldier's A-field weapon been mistuned, wrapping him in a jet that raised the combination-potential of chlorine instead of oxygen? Had the soldier's suit failed by coincidence?

Would the controller's own suit fail?

Rillian soldiers did not think of their own deaths; that was not their job. It was the controller's job to consider anything that might prevent him and the troops he controlled from doing their duty. So . . .

Hanging above the rock, icily indifferent to—impervious to, at any rate—the *wrongness* of stellar motion and the light with which the stars bathed him, the Rillian controller gathered data. When his instruments failed to display any dangers, any pitfalls, he probed with his mind—despite the pain, the risk of insanity, involved in thrusting his psyche unprotected into an ambience where things were not as they should be.

Nothing; still nothing. Unless the controller was already mad and hallucinating a technical substructure little advanced beyond the Stone Age.

Mad or sane, he had his duty.

There were ample evidences of the Rillian soldier's passage through the habitat, shrugging aside all opposition in the security of his weapon and his armor—

Until the armor had failed, and his life with it.

The navy could vaporize the habitat with its weaponry, could drop the satellite itself as a molten missile onto the surface of the primary with which it now rotated. But the vast ships of the Rillian fleet were not here, and what the controller could do with the weapons at his disposal was more limited.

But surely sufficient.

First he would take the habitat's power plant. When he destroyed *that*, the atmosphere recirculation and general life-support would shut down as well. Then he would deal with the Elevener.

And if the indigenes expected the controller to be bound by the network of corridors as the Rillian soldier had been, then they would be still more disconcerted when the controller closed on his prey in a vector that ignored the rock and metal intervening in *this* spacetime.

Chapter 25

HARDBALL

Jim Stuart was coming down the hallway, with long strides and a worried expression. When he saw Sam Yates, he started to run—but Sam was already between him and his boss's door.

"Hold it right there!" Stuart shouted.

Yates looked back without slowing. "Jim," he said, "I'm sorry about yesterday, but this—"

Stuart grabbed Yates's right shoulder. Yates turned with the motion and slapped the back of his fingertips across the younger man's diaphragm.

It wasn't much of a blow. In the likely event somebody was recording the incident, Sam hoped it'd look more as if Stuart had jerked Yates toward him rather than Yates's own calculated attack.

But McLeod's manicured puppy had taken three stun needles across his belly a day before—right along the line Sam Yates traced with his fingernails. Stuart doubled up with a shriek as his tortured muscles cramped again.

"Kid, I'm sorry," Sam muttered as he opened the door to McLeod's office.

And he *was* sorry.

Sorry Stuart had gotten in the way. Sorry he'd gotten hurt—again. Sorry Stuart was pissed at him, because he seemed like a decent kid—no doubt a credit to his nation and family. On the other hand, if Our JEB survived the next few days, he'd be a lot less likely to get his ass blown away the next time he ran into a Sam Yates.

That was a pretty big "if," of course.

Sam half expected McLeod to have set up shop in a briefing room or the like, but the station chief still had an honest-to-god office. Only one room—with no sign of the secretary who'd taken

Yates's call—but a desk and all the data/communications electronics you could ask for.

As well as three extra chairs and enough space to use them comfortably. Compared to the broom closet Sam'd shunted himself into when Channon took *his* office, this was a palace.

Come to think, five desks had opened up in this corridor of the U.S. mission when McLeod's follow-car got in the way of whatever the hell the Rillian was shooting. Well, there was more room than usual in the Patrol substations, too.

"Sit down, Yates," McLeod said. His hands were spread on the desk in deliberate ostentation, but his body was poised to react if it had to.

"Naw," Yates said, wiping his forehead and eyes with the palm of his right hand. He was afraid of what was coming—maybe more afraid than McLeod was. "Look. Personnel actions. Says Sonya's out. That's canceled."

His speech was coming in little spurts, each a self-contained datum. He couldn't organize his sentences any better way because his mind wouldn't concentrate on words.

"Why don't you sit down, Yates," McLeod repeated. His tone was calm, but his eyes were flicking between the door he hadn't had time to lock—if he'd wanted to—and his visitor.

Then back to the door.

"I thought this might come up," McLeod said. "I've asked Undersecretary Minsky to be present, if you don't mind. As a UN representative."

"Fine," Yates said, "Great. Call a meeting of the Security Council. But it's no go."

His eyes met McLeod's and he added, almost as an afterthought, "Jim's outta this one, right? Not his problem. But he'll be OK."

McLeod's expression grew very quiet. His eyes refocused, and his fingers arched slightly.

Sam Yates smiled. "McLeod, I don't *need* a gun for you. But sure, I've got it. I think you ordered me t'carry it, didn't you?"

He took the Tokarev from his pocket and set it on the desk, butt toward the station chief, muzzle toward a wall. "Careful. There's one up the spout," he said.

"I don't believe—" McLeod began. Yates braced his hands against the ceiling and strained as though he were in a gym—or at least in *private*, not bursting in on . . .

The door burst open. Jim Stuart pivoted in with a broken-backed gracelessness, holding a Smith and Wesson that should have been checked into the arms locker as soon as he entered this corridor. He pointed the gun at Sam Yates and shouted, *"Freeze, you sonuvabitch!"*

A small part of Taylor McLeod's forebrain was praying that the pistol was loaded with the frangible bullets normally issued for carry in vacuum habitats. They wouldn't ricochet.

Oleg Minsky, wearing a professionally bland expression, stood in the doorway behind Stuart. McLeod couldn't even begin to imagine explaining how the KGB resident came to be killed by a ricochet in the American mission.

Sam Yates started to laugh.

Stuart, who by now had had time to notice that his target was pressing the low ceiling with both hands, glanced sideways at his chief and saw the Tokarev. He began to tremble.

"Jim," McLeod said, "would you give me that, please." He nodded toward the S&W.

Stuart, white-faced, rotated the weapon so that the butt was forward, then handed it over.

The sweat on the contoured grips chilled McLeod's fingers as he ejected the magazine. "Jim," he went on calmly as he jacked back the slide, "you're to consider yourself on suspension for two hours or until further notice, whichever is sooner. Go to your quarters, please, and don't leave them."

The cartridge that lunar gravity spun from the chamber in a slow arc had the gray-white tip of a ceramic-cored frangible, thank *God* for small favors—not that it mattered now.

Stuart nodded, turned, and strode out of the room. He looked perfectly normal, down to the half-smile that decorated his lips; but Minsky had to jump aside or the young American would have walked right into him.

"You Americans," Minsky said as he stepped into the office. He cocked an eyebrow at McLeod; McLeod nodded.

Minsky closed the door. "You Americans," he repeated.

"I think I'll take that seat you offered, Taylor-buddy," Yates said.

His angled face changed as he sat and added, "Look, I'm sorry I laughed like that. Don't be too hard on the kid. He lost a lotta friends yesterday. So far as I'm concerned, he's got a free throw for anything that happens the next couple weeks."

McLeod couldn't tell how much was real concern, how much was playacting . . . and he had a feeling that all the electronic analysis he'd run on the recordings of this scene weren't going to help decide that, either. The stress needles were probably flatlined at the top of their range, anyway.

He looked at the Tokarev, lying innocently in front of him. God save him from this murderous idiot—who maybe wasn't *quite* as stupid as he seemed!

Undersecretary Minsky sat down also, mopping his face with a patterned blue handkerchief. McLeod hadn't been the only one aware of the possibility of ricochets.

"Undersecretary," Yates said as he crossed a knee over an ankle and leaned back insouciantly, "I was telling my friend Taylor, here, that there'd been a personnel screw-up, terminating Supervisor Yesilkov. And that I'd canceled it."

He smiled at one man, then the other, his expression false but as hard as a diamond.

"Yates—" McLeod began.

"Even though Taylor's not in my chain of command," Yates added to Minsky.

Did the stupid son of a bitch still doubt that McLeod—that CIA—had horse-traded this one with Minsky before executing it?

"Yates," McLeod said, speaking with the same calm certainty he'd kept in his voice while demanding the gun from young Stuart, "the Security supervisor in question attacked three of my men, shot them down with a stunner and left them incapacitated during the . . . events yesterday. I've demanded that she be removed. Undersecretary Minsky—who is, as you choose to put it, in your chain of command—fully concurs in the matter."

Minsky nodded with a smile of amusement rather than mere politeness. He'd stuffed the handkerchief into a side pocket; a corner still peeked out.

"I appreciate that," Yates said, gripping his crossed leg with both hands. His voice sounded fairly normal, but the mottling of his knuckles hinted at the strain. "Going to get somebody you trust a little farther to watch Channon, eh? Channon and me. But *I* don't concur, and I'm the Commissioner of Security."

McLeod started to rise, despite himself. "*Yates,*" he snapped, "if you're going to pretend you can cowboy—"

"No, I'm not," Yates said tightly.

"—around without taking orders from—"

"*McLeod.*"

Yates closed his eyes for a moment. That was good, because McLeod hadn't liked what he saw in them, the unfocused stare that made McLeod's own glance flick toward the Tokarev.

Yates turned. "Undersecretary Minsky," he said, his voice trembling, "the Secretariat can give me an order. One order. My job. In my department, my job. You want the job?" He pulled his suit coat open with one hand, and, with two fingers of his other hand, dipped into the inside pocket for his UN identification.

Minsky looked at McLeod from the corner of his eye.

McLeod shook his head almost imperceptibly. He'd been holding himself rigid. For an instant he was afraid that the necessity of responding would set him off in a paroxysm of rage.

If he hadn't *needed* Sam Yates, he'd have throttled him with his bare hands.

"I don't think you fully understand, Commissioner Yates," Minsky was saying in a detached tone. "Your resignation would create a great deal of publicity that would gravely embarrass Citizen Yesilkova's country. Shooting down several American functionaries, after all . . . While I can speak only as a member of the United Nations Secretariat, I fear my compatriots would regard the scandal as a very serious piece of anti-State activity."

He smiled. There was a gap between his front teeth. "For which the death penalty still applies, of course."

Yates closed his eyes again and shrugged. "I can't help that," he said. "I won't fire her."

Minsky's face lost even the semblance of good humor. "You think I am joking, Commissioner Yates," he said.

"No, Undersecretary," Yates answered tiredly, meeting Minsky's eyes. "I know you mean it; I know you can do it." He licked his lips, locking his hands on his ankle again and staring down. "I can't control what happens. But I can control what I do. I won't do that. Sonya did what I told her, and that's *my* heat, not hers."

"Yates, we've got the whole scene on recording chip," McLeod said, interlacing his own fingers very tightly. "You gave *no* orders—"

"I gave her the fucking stunner!" Yates shouted, rising with the same grace McLeod had seen on the recording as the Tokarev rose through the haze of dust and gases to begin slamming shots into the Rillian. "That's an *order* to use it to save Channon, and that's *just* what Sonya did."

"She didn't—"

"McLeod," Yates went on in the tired voice again, "if it'd been a shotgun, I woulda given it to her. And that woulda been OK, too. Because there wasn't much time, and your boys didn't know their ass from a hole in the ground."

"Listen, you . . ." McLeod said, very softly—still seated behind his desk.

"Minsky," Yates said, "who's the complainant on this one? The kid who just ran in here with a gun?"

Minsky looked at McLeod and raised an eyebrow.

McLeod said nothing.

Yates shrugged. "Everybody's pretty revved," he said. "It's no sweat—I been on the wrong end of a gun before. But let's let this'un lie, shall we? Unless—"

He looked at McLeod—looked down at McLeod—and continued, "Unless Taylor-baby wants to prove that he understands what I mean by not letting my people take the heat for what I ordered. Just tell us for the record that you ordered Stuart t'stop me however. So his running in here with a gun was your own fault. Go on, show us what kinda man you are."

"Undersecretary Minsky . . ." McLeod began, certain of nothing except that he didn't want to speak to the cretin who was grinning at him.

"Guess we knew the kind already," Yates said with a death's-head grin.

"We have responsibilities!" McLeod glowered, rising to his feet at last. "Can't you get that through your skull?"

"Nothing as important as not selling out my people, McLeod," Yates said. All the banter, the crowing, was gone.

"Your whore, you mean."

For a moment—

"Ella Bradley's a fine woman, McLeod," Yates said softly. "You oughta watch your language."

They do it, Sam Yates thought, because they don't think you'll respond. Will respond, can respond. Dare respond. Because you're all little worms for them to prod.

Minsky was as still as he'd been when he'd seen Stuart's

pointed gun, but he could have been back on Earth for all the other men in the room cared just now.

"Right," Yates said at last. "I'll go back and see how Sonya and Channon are doing."

"Get out of here," McLeod whispered.

"I'll take this too," Yates said, pointing at the Tokarev with the same two fingers that had offered his ID card. "For the next Rillian."

"Get *out*."

Yates slipped the pistol into his pocket and left with only a cursory nod toward the Undersecretary. He'd pushed McLeod as much as he was gonna get away with today.

You use what you got. Maybe you didn't like yourself later.

But you use what you got.

Chapter 26

TARGETING

The Rillian controller was having a problem. In fact, he was having several. His directive—to consider and anticipate anything which might prevent him or any troops he controlled from doing their duty—included reporting the result of his reconnaissance before he began his moonwalk and the dance of death to follow. So far, he had been unable to transmit his initial scans.

Equipment failure was unheard of, as an excuse for nonperformance. For a Rillian controller, there was no excuse for nonperformance. There was only *mission incomplete; operator missing in action.*

There were, of course, reasons for nonperformance, such as the controller's current dilemma. But there was no such thing, in the Rillian armed forces, as survivable failure. There was no precedent, even, under which to report failure.

You did the mission, or you were lost, doing the mission. No middle ground existed; no fail-safes were engineered into the system; you triumphed or you died trying.

Died as had the first Rillian to come across the enigmatic, horrid infestation of bipeds in this solar system, whose gravity-wells, in a thin and confuted spacetime, created a series of physical special cases which were negatively affecting the controller's equipment.

Equipment failure was one thing; temporal maladjustment was quite another. The controller might be able to jury-rig his transmitter to send his interim report once he'd solved the temporal phasing problem, but he must first solve that problem.

All of his equipment was calibrated to Ril standard time, capable of bridging n-space on any of the appropriate T-2 vectors, and self-correcting on the other end, back to Ril standard. Thus were messages sent, regardless of the varying speed of light and processional time throughout the cosmos, to be received and logged during an interval congruent to what the controller (or any controller) would consider the immediate future of the moment when the message was sent.

Up the X-Y (or North-South) axis of the forward-moving arrow of time, which split his com-grid longitudinally; somewhere in the right-hand quadrant north of the A-B horizontal line; across that same grid, which determined where events could take place in real time, he should be able to situate his message blip and send it.

The blip would then turn from red to green, signifying an event in current real-time had occurred. Hanging in space over the airless satellite's dark side, an arm's length above a crater wall to prevent being accidentally discovered by primitive radars, he doggedly kept trying to accomplish this simple feat. Every time he performed the requisite, rote operations, the blip would slide to the west on the A-B axis, as if he were creating an advance wave—a message that could be received only in the past of the moment it would be sent.

No matter what he did, he couldn't steady the event blip long enough to send a message anywhere but to the past.

It was a result, he was nearly certain, of the confuted spacetime here, which promised so many positive effects when considered in terms of combat.

This place was slow to his biology, slow to his equipment's calibration, slow and thus physically malleable. The speed of light here was far below the cosmological average in the spacetime native to Rillian exploration. This meant that many tactical advantages were his. But the solar system was complicated by many elliptical orbits, by a far-distant dark dwarf star, by a rigidity of processional real-time that separated the Time-2 space, which was the controller's native one, from the Time(-1) space of the sort that had spawned the first Rillian trooper and all soldiers of his ilk.

Rillian culture still raised its troopers in asymptotic spacetimes. It helped make them the killing machines they were, beings of hardened physique and expanding presents, mind-blind to anything more than biological time, unable to adjust their presences to more or less than the speed at which their cells determinedly replicated.

A Rillian trooper carried his single available spacetime matrix with him, mated to his mass, and it automatically adjusted to the spacetime he was in, without enough physical discomfort to impair his effectiveness.

The Rillian controller was more evolved. He had a broader mandate. He had an organic sensor sensitivity range that went from extra-low frequency to far beyond the one hundred GHz that was all these indigenes could acknowledge, even with mechanical aids. But he was only a controller, not an engineer. The problems associated with these air-breathing races and the way their infestation of spacetime deformed manifolds were engineering problems, not controller problems.

So far, the engineers had not solved the deformation problem associated with air breathers. Until they did, the containment and subsequent eradication of air breathers was the problem of Rillians like the controller.

Still, there must be an interim solution for the on-site deformation problem that the controller now faced. Rillian Control would not have put him in a no-win situation. Nor had his briefers given any hint that this spacetime would, as a result of its deformation and the rigidity of its boundaries, lock out T-2 transmission lines.

He had been given a T-2 matrix transmitter, if not a receiver. Logically, somehow, he *could* transmit.

Therefore, he continued to attempt a transmission that would light his transmitter's targeting grid green, on the requisite event line, in the proper quadrant. Once that had happened, and he got a *transmission sent/transmission received* indication—the green blip turning blue, a second event coming up green, "forward" of the then-blue event of his transmission—he could do the accursed job he'd been punched in here to do.

Rillian Command didn't waste controllers. His training and equipment were too costly, not to mention his entire incubation and the special hatching and tutelage systems necessary to create a combat-ready controller.

Therefore, there was a solution to this dilemma, one that was eluding him because his very brain was being forced into attenuated function by the rigidity of the spacetime around him.

He chewed on his helmet's fang-file absently, catching the dust with his tongue. He could probably get away with punching out of this spacetime, now. He could rebase and deliver a verbal report—it was within his orders, given a stretch of interpretation.

But such a thing had never been done before. He would be branded a dullard or a coward, because this sort of thing never could be kept quiet. His wife would smash their eggs, eat their hatchlings, and burn their nest to the ground. No one would want to drink with him. . . .

No, there must be a way, and he would find it. He began thinking about light cones, forty-five-degree angles based along the event line.

He recentered his targeting grid for transmission, using a "now" positioned as closely as possible to the crossing of the event- and time-lines, just slightly to the east of the center.

The blip didn't slide.

He tipped his head and slid his first fang back and forth across the file with deep satisfaction: progress! He could feel the tremor along his arm as he considered immediately enabling the push.

But he didn't. Not yet. He rechecked everything: carrier-to-noise; loss, free-space and other, including pointing; transmitter power; energy-per-bit to noise density ratio; antenna noise temperature.

He recalibrated that to eleven other factors, including receiver noise temperature at HQ, and then once more he paused.

He looked at his radiated power rate; he considered his non-coherent previous result. He computed his probability of error with a flick of his dewclaw.

Then he swore like a trooper, accidentally biting down on his tongue with his newly sharpened fang. The taste of blood cooled his temper. And it did something else: It excited a part of him not previously engaged in solving his problem—his kill instinct.

He got out his A-field automat; he calibrated it for a point a mere bodylength away from his suit's extended antenna. He reconfigured his inboard micronic servo to lock the elapsed-time meters of the communicator and the A-field automat together, and sequenced a *shoot/send* into both systems.

There was more than one way to skin an opponent. This, of course, was why no one had bothered to train and equip him specially for the discrete problems of this spacetime: He'd had what he needed, all along, slung across his front shoulder.

It was truly simple. If you didn't like the spacetime, change spacetimes. But no one had counted on the dislocating mental effect of being shunted into a venue where both T-2 and the part of his brain accustomed to quantizing T-2 information would be muted.

This no doubt explained why the Rillian trooper had been defeated by so inconsequential a bunch of indigenes: Even a primoRillian had need to *think*.

The controller hissed in pleasure as he added an addendum to his message, warning that future combatants in this and similar locales be alert to T-2 related reasoning dysfunctions. That would get him a Purple Claw, if he performed the rest of his mission without error.

He shut down his configurator ruefully, thinking what a shame it would have been if he'd failed to see the obvious, been lost out here, and a high-echelon commander was then dispatched, as protocol would then require.

These primitives did not deserve such an honor. The problems here were not born of their cleverness, or of their warmaking prowess, or of anything but this freak of a convoluted manifold that they no doubt considered a normal environment.

No wonder the Kiri scum was here. The Kiri slime would be right at home, like a snail in its shell.

Now that he was ready to transmit his Go code, the controller windowed his system—just in case—to perform one final check, a discretionary caution.

He now knew he was not as sharp as he'd previously assumed he was. So he must confirm that the Kiri really *was* still here. A new targeting grid came up before him, this one simple and decisive in its micronic clarity, giving him multiband wave confirmation:

Yes, there was the Kiri, in a place it perceived as safe, hiding under rock and metal with the indigenes. His signature-detector confirmed the distinctive Kiri ELF.

Content, sure that he was error-free, the Rillian controller toggled back to his communicator, now slaved to his A-field automat.

He raised the weapon, sighting down it visually with one eye, while his splatter-vision kept tabs on the communicator grid.

He would squeeze his trigger when the barrel lined up with the counter and the X's merged. The hole in spacetime he subsequently punched would clear a path for his push all the way to T-2, when the communicator's instructions would kick in.

The transmitter would then take over, calibrating with T-2 in passing and splashing on, into the energy sea itself, where Ril substations would do the rest.

The *X*'s meshed. A red circle popped up around them: Fire.

His finger squeezed, ever so gently. All the subsequent enabling was micronically initiated. He must only not sneeze at the wrong moment.

He didn't. His suit/automat system kicked him out of the accursed indigene spacetime; his communicator initiated while he was indisposed; his transceiver spat the push across nonlinear eons, into the energy sea.

And the controller snapped back, into the exact position he'd formerly occupied, above the crater's rim, with the communicator's targeting display before his eyes happily blinking: *Message received.*

An amusing moonwalk, and the conflict beyond, were now his for the taking.

Chapter 27

GOOD STORY

Channon could not fathom why the humans were so outwardly complacent during the interminable conferences McLeod insisted on scheduling, even though each person was inwardly seething.

Channon was feeling much healthier. He had his suit back. Inside it, his skin was responding well enough to its recent cleansing, especially with the addition of the balm that Bradley had given him, telling him it was "baby oil." Although at first he was hesitant to make use of the oil of human infants, it had soothed the dryness. Wearing his helmet whenever he could seemed to be helping, also: When his suit was sealed, the wave baths in which he now dwelled were greatly reduced, both the organically generated ones and the inorganically generated ones.

This he should have realized previously. But despite his concern that further exposure to this alien environment, coupled with even the lesser violence of humanity's ELF, might again make him itch and peel, he could not bring himself to wear his helmet during McLeod's briefings. When he did, those around him were discomfited, their suspicions aroused, their tensions raised.

So again he sat bareheaded among them, listening to their words and trying not to heed their contrasting broadcasts.

McLeod was unhappy, even though his lips announced that the participants were "making substantial progress." He was brooding and uneasy, sitting sprawled in an upholstered chair, with all but his bottom layer of clothing removed and an iced drink in one hand.

Part of McLeod's distress was, Channon knew, explained by the presence of Sultanian, who had chosen to be quarantined with Channon, rather than wherever he normally stayed.

This, Ella had told Channon, McLeod thought to be a "Soviet trick." But since the opportunity for this "trick"—defined by *Webster's* as a device or action designed to achieve an end by deception or fraudulent means—had been the "white lie" of Channon's illness that McLeod had fabricated, McLeod's anger was, rightly, turned inward.

Yet McLeod was broadcasting a blanket hostility—not only toward Sultanian, but directed at everyone in this third serial briefing, held in an evening room of beauty and soft pallets and low, pleasant light. He seemed unwilling to confront the necessity to prepare for a second Rillian visit while Sultanian was present. Thus very little was being accomplished, and this made everyone else—Ella Bradley, the warriors Jones and Sanders, Quint the scientist, and even the redoubtable JEB Stuart—ill-tempered. Yates and Yesilkov had not even bothered to attend these meetings.

Sultanian was asking once again, "But Channon, my good friend, there must be much more which you can tell us. Yours is a great nation, a homeland and part of a confederation, facing a furious and implacable enemy, yes? Then you must know more about this enemy, all of which we must know, to help you fight him. So tell us, have no fear. The hour grows late."

Channon fingered his helmet, upside down in his lap, fighting the urge to put it on his head and go to sleep. The humans would not know until he failed to respond to one of their questions—most of which, in any case, he was not qualified to answer.

His throat was sore from talking. If he did not truly believe that he was as healthy as a spacefarer in his circumstances could be, he would be beginning to credit McLeod's white lie. But he was healthy; his tongue had proved that to him; the oil of babies had done the rest.

He said, "Friend Sultanian, again Channon says good story. This time listen better. Ears there for hearing, use. Rillians use weapons, A-potential. Kiri do not. Weapons biggest, worst sort. Unnecessary evil. Arguments, many, among Kiri Unity about building for Kiri use. Some say, never. Some say, yes, against Rillians. But even if yes, must learn to build, ourselves. Not now know this. Channon not know; Kiri technologists not know better than theory. Practice different. Control A-field, difficult. Opening spacetime surface to access inside energy: How stop up hole, after? Punch it hole, easy. Close up, harder. Out energy comes, how direct? How regulate? Spacetimes many; energy sea, supporting all. Rillians not care if spacetimes hurt. From different ones, across Rift.''

"I don't get this," said Jones, leaning his head on the five spread fingers of one hand so that his whole face was distorted. "They're blowing up your ships, maybe your habitats or planets for all I can figure, and you're letting them? You're not fighting fire with fire?''

"Fight fires after Rillians start. A-field imported fire . . . ignites Kiri atmosphere. Clinging many-bombs of other matter, make . . . inert . . . matters combust: explodes oxygen in air, other atoms.''

"Jones means, Channon"—McLeod entered the conversation for the first time in a long interval—"that he doesn't understand why your people haven't developed a countering technology, since you know the theory.''

"Said that: Kiri debate going. Not want A-field weapons, best of us. Only good story for warmaking. No other use, where not something else as good. Stability of peoples—and places—more value.'' Channon hoped he was making his point. The thought of the infinitely destructive A-field technologies in any hands—Rillian hands, or the hands of this eager young warrior race—was disquieting to the Kiri mind.

"So you let them turn your atmosphere volatile whenever they want?'' said Sanders. "Let's say I buy that—which I'm not sure I do. What's the good of that to them?''

"Rillians not breath same. Your . . .'' He closed his eyes and searched for a correlate. ". . . chlorine, partly, they breathe. Rillian not want Kiri Unity planets. Want no Kiri Unity on any planets. Then use other planets in systems, maybe.'' He knew he was oversimplifying, perhaps not making himself understood at all. He clicked his tongue; they still didn't know what an impolite sound that was. "Or not. Kiri not know. Finding out, Channon's mission. Go Rift, see Rillians, talk peace. Make peace.''

"Same thing in a forty-four mag,'' Sanders muttered.

"Say again?'' Channon asked, using a phrase he'd picked up from Jones, who was the least compartmentalized of all the participants.

"He is saying,'' Sultanian spoke up before Sanders could, "if again I'm not mistaken, these Rillians want only to cut Kiri noses: genocide; utter eradication. Like my nation. Like the holocaust.'' His large, bulgy eyes were sparkling as if their water would fall out onto his cheeks, as Bradley's eyes had once lost theirs. ''And he's saying, if again I hear the truth, that these weapons are too terrible—that this debate is ongoing among his people. What we know of A-field supports this. And because it does, dear friends, I, for one, am going to my room you have so generously provided, to get some sleep. If the Kiri are afraid to use such power themselves, even if Channon knows the key to its management, he is not going to give such a thing to us. Why should he? Would you, if the circumstances were turned around?''

Sultanian lumbered to his feet, shuffled papers into his box, closed the box and hefted it under his arm. ''Happy sleep, everyone. In the morning, you will tell me of your progress, I am sure.'' With a twist of his lips, the bulky man waved a hand at them and headed for the door.

No one spoke until he had gone and the door had closed behind him. Then Jones said, ''Well, law of averages: Eventually, you get a break, no matter how bad your luck's running. Want to get down to business now, Ting?''

''I thought we were,'' said McLeod. Bradley arose from her seat and went to his, where she leaned down and said softly, ''I'm going too, Ting. I'm no help to you here.''

Channon said, ''Me, also. Go with Bradley.''

McLeod reached up to Ella Bradley's face. ''Looks like you're staying. Sorry. We're still running a log here, folks. Sultanian can access it in the morning. But go ahead, Jones. Try your luck.''

Jones said, ''Quint and I have been looking at the suit data, and we think we can make a stab at some sort of transmitter, Channon, if you have any idea where you want to transmit *to*. It's a big universe out there.''

''Rift. Kiri substations in Riftspace. Can help, with astronomical dictionary.''

''Charts, yeah. We'll get 'em.''

''Truth?'' Channon's heart leaped; his ears pricked in Jones's direction. Was it possible? Could it be that all was not, truly, a matter of choosing ways to die? A second Rillian probe had tickled his senses earlier in the meeting. Since then, he'd been turned in upon himself, savoring life and the sound of blood in his veins, the feel of his healing skin in his suit—all things. He would have preferred to leave with Bradley, to go and sleep, to prepare himself for what was coming.

And now this glimmer of hope. Providence, in this lost corner of the universe, was capricious or, at best, inscrutable to tease him so. Yet hope was a wellspring no Kiri could resist.

Jones was telling him fervently: "We can copy what you've got there. We're good little monkeys. Give it more power. We just don't want to hurt anything. We'll have to take the communications system you've got in that suit and helmet apart . . . but you can be there when we do. We'll be very careful."

Apart? "Deconstruct? Then what will Channon do for helmet? For—" He stopped himself. Sacrifices always must be made. But he must have his helmet—have the choice of whether or not to wear it for his confrontation with the approaching Rillian. "Later," he suggested.

"Later after when?" Quint said, raising his eyes from his lap, where he had a device of some kind balanced on crossed legs.

"Later after next Rillian. Channon need helmet for next—"

"Jesus, McLeod, can't we confirm or deny this 'next Rillian' business?" General Sanders got to his feet, up from the long soft couch, and began walking back and forth.

"Figure of speech, Sandy. I promise," McLeod said.

"Not," Channon warned.

McLeod rose, too. He put his hands on his hips and came over to Channon, where he stood spreadlegged and said very softly, "Channon, quit jerking us around, okay? Everyone's tired. We spent all that time talking about Kiri history and ideology and the price of monster-eggs, while Sultanian was here. You think there's another Rillian on the way—as in imminent ETA—then I want to know *(a)* how you know; *(b)* when you expect it, to the closest picosecond; and *(c)* what the fuck you want us to do about it without any commensurate technological base? Which I still think you could give us if you wanted to."

"Said before, McLeod, what to do. Agreed, right? Electromagnets, two. Tunnel: corridor—Channon in one end. Lure Rillian. Put electric current through first one: grab Rillian. Then second: pull weapon, other side. When ready, McLeod?"

"Yeah, we're working on it." McLeod shook his head and held up his hand.

Channon knew, as clearly as these others must, that McLeod

didn't want to discuss that option further. Again the secrecy problem was apparent in his broadcast: He didn't want Sultanian to know of that private discussion between Channon and Mc-Leod. But then, how could the nations be working together to deal with the Rillian threat?

Channon looked to Ella, confusion carefully displayed on his face. She shook her head, also. Then Channon realized that the nations of humanity were not working together to help Channon talk to the Rillian. Only McLeod was doing that, and he without haste, hoping for some magic defense to be forthcoming from Channon.

He must convince McLeod that there was none such. "Must hurry McLeod. Time short. Second Rillian incumbent."

"Incumbent?" Sanders said in an aroused fashion.

The two men, both of whom were moving about the room, met each other in its center and whispered together.

"Channon"—Bradley got up with a grunt and came to him, taking his hand in her ugly, deformed one—"are you saying you're sensing another Rillian at this moment?"

"Not this moment. But recent moment. Trace. Enough to know coming. Not know closeness yet: different Rillian."

"You bet, unless the other one had nine lives," said Jones, who had short dark hair of almost Kiri density. He rubbed his hand over its brush. "You're not saying that, though, are you?"

"Saying different Rillian segment."

Quint said, "Oh-oh. Different in what way?"

Channon felt the sudden upstep in tension. The pressure of all their eyes and all their attention on him made his skin crawl. He hoped he wasn't going to begin to itch again. How could he explain what he sensed? What his race was only postulating?

"Channon talk hypothesis, now. Okay?"

"Okay," McLeod assured him. "Talk."

"Types of Rillians: at least three. Same . . . *evolution* is word. Young, old, older—no, not correct words: *primitive, civilized, socialized*—warrior class, technocrat class, diplomat class. Like humans."

Someone laughed explosively, and the noise chilled Channon. It was Sanders, and the sound was one like the sound of pain.

Bradley said, "Good Lord."

Quint said, "I guess we asked for that."

Jones said, "Puts me in my place."

McLeod said, "No shit, Sherlock."

And JEB Stuart asked McLeod, "Sir, should I secure a status report on the electromagnets?"

"Yeah, do that, Stuart. And check the security preparations, as well." Then he turned to Channon. "You knew this all along. Why didn't you tell us before?"

"How would help you? Help me? Not certain, said: *hypothetical*. Rillian probe sounds different, so now pertinent. Could have been second Rillian just like first warrior. . . ." He didn't know why he felt suddenly apologetic. Perhaps because McLeod's broadcast was accusing him of holding back information that might keep Humans from dying. "Not change troubles," Channon added softly. "McLeod knows Channon wants no death, Humans."

"All right. Easy, everybody. Let's sit down and take it from the top. You too, Channon. I'm not blaming you."

"Are." But Channon sat back.

"Well, not consciously, whatever you think your psychic skills sense. I'm just worried, that's all."

"Not need worry. Never useful. Bring Yates. Bring Yesilkov. Channon go—"

"Farside," McLeod nearly shouted the word simultaneously with Channon's vocalization, then continued by himself in a voice that finally matched the emotions seething inside him: "Look, you thick-headed alien, you're not going farside. Clear? No way. I'm having trouble with Yates and Yesilkova—Yesilkova especially. You saw them shoot my people the last time. Do you want to trust them with your safety after that? I'd like you to agree to another pair of bodyguards. Stuart can—"

"Yates. Yesilkov. Brave warriors. Not think too much."

Sanders made a noise that might indicate choking, then said, "Hey, Ting, let him have 'em. What difference does it make? If the electromagnets don't work, they're dead meat, anyhow."

"Pulse magnets as Channon directs, work. What is A-field, responds to—"

"Christ, McLeod, he's *giving* us a leg up on the potential tech. Why didn't I realize . . ." Jones was baring his teeth to McLeod and nodding vigorously.

Channon nodded vigorously, too.

". . . let me go huddle with the guys doing the electromagnetic setup, okay?" Jones asked McLeod.

"Okay, go. Everybody, go. Meeting's adjourned. Go make your wills and call your wives or get a steak or whatever," said McLeod.

Most of the humans left quickly. Bradley did not. "Ting, I want to stay with you."

"That's up to you."

Channon said, "Mates should be together."

Bradley said, "I'll handle this, Channon."

She did not want Channon to spoil her surprise, she'd said. This meant that McLeod was unaware that he'd made a child with her.

Channon felt sorry for the deaf and blind humans, and a deeper sadness that McLeod might not have a chance to share Bradley's joy. But this was a different world, with different customs. He was diplomat enough to respect her wishes.

"Okay, but want Yates now. Need Yates and Yesilkov."

"I'd back the fuck off, Channon, if I were you. Now that we're all by our lonesomes, you're going to tell me whatever you know about the differences between this type Rillian and the last one we encountered. Then, when I'm satisfied that you've done that, you can have Yates and Yesilkov. For as long as you all shall live."

"Okay," said Channon, and nodded vigorously to ease the waves of worry and anger coming out of McLeod. "Time enough to say one more good story before Rillian comes."

And he pulled back his lips at first one of the stricken humans, then the other.

When McLeod put his arm around Bradley, he added, "Channon proud of McLeod, proud of Bradley: Humans very brave."

Because they weren't brave at all, in that moment, faced with a threat they were unable to assess, let alone meet on their own.

Chapter 28

KITCHEN BALLISTICS

"Dr. Jones, my name's Yates," Sam said to the little man who frowned and muttered—perhaps in concentration, perhaps into a voice recorder—as he stepped from the conference room. "Got a minute?"

"Probably not," Jones said with a bright smile that dared Yates to doubt that he meant exactly what he said. "Certainly not, if there's any truth in some of the suggestions I've just heard."

He nodded crisply and strode off down the hall.

"Sam?" said Ella Bradley, slipping from the conference room before the door had closed behind Jones. "Can we talk?"

Jones paused in midstride—he'd been on the Moon long enough not to pogo-stick even then—and turned. "Sam Yates?" he said. "Commissioner Yates?"

Sam gestured to Bradley with two fingers, indicating he wasn't deliberately ignoring her, though his attention was on the weapons researcher. "Sumpin' like that, yeah," he said. "Look, I need to figure out what happened to the Rillian."

Jones flashed his metallic smile again. "The first Rillian?" he said.

Yates shrugged. "That's why *I* care, you bet."

"Well, come along then," Jones said. "Even crises pause for Nature's call."

Yates grimaced mentally as he fell into step. In a *real* crisis, you learn quick that you can wash out your trousers afterwards—if you're still alive to do it. Aloud he said, "I need an expert to look at some data. There—"

He paused, turned. "Ella," he said. "Wanna come along?" His tongue touched his lips. "After all, you were there."

"No thank you, Sam," she said primly, touching one perfectly manicured hand to the peaked swirl into which fashion had twisted her hair. "Perhaps another time."

She was back in the conference room before Yates had rejoined Dr. Jones's impatient frown.

Sam had met enough of Jones's type in the past not to mistake the prickliness for hostility. Personal hostility, at any rate.

The luck of the draw had left Jones shorter than Yates by ten inches, and lighter by eighty pounds in Earth gravity. That wasn't anything Jones was willing to forget, even if Sam tried to; and any attempt by the bigger man to push or patronize would lead to a real explosion.

Jones obviously felt the difference in size was at least balanced by their relative IQ's. That was fine with Sam Yates. It made Jones safer to be around than lots of little guys who had to depend on hardware as an equalizer.

The loo two doors down from the conference room was the size of a vehicle facility. Jones ducked into it when he saw Yates was following again. There was no room for two people inside at one time—the dry-chemical lavatory filled all the space that the toilet left open—but the scientist blocked the door open with the back of one heel while he stood to urinate.

"All right," he said when Yates's shadow darkened the door opening. "What do you need? I really am busy, you know."

"Yessir," agreed Yates, trying not to smile. "I shot the Rillian. Other people shot *at* the Rillian, and their bullets passed through where he oughta be. I need to know why I hit—so, you know—I hit the next time. All the next times."

"We don't know you did hit,"Jones said, sealing his fly as he turned. He'd weighed the situation now and dismissed it. "Best conjecture at this point is coincidence. The, ah, event collapsed in on itself as a result of the forces it was unleashing. If another *event* occurs before we've got the information we need from Lucky, wear a Saint Christopher's medal and keep your fingers crossed."

He stepped past Yates, on his way back to the conference room.

"*Sir,*" said Sam Yates.

Jones turned, wide-eyed.

Yates was squeezing his fingertips together before him and staring at the operation. The muscles of his jaw were bunched, and his cheeks were flat planes.

"Sir," he said to his fingers in what was almost a whisper. "This ain't sexy. There's no scalars and supercomputers, none a that. But we got a dead Rillian, and I'm telling you: I shot, and the thing sparked, and the thing started t'die."

"It seemed to you at the time," Jones said cautiously.

"Bullshit," said Sam Yates. "At the time, it seemed like noise and muzzle flash. And the—and the smell."

He shuddered and put his hands down. "Sir. But on the recordings, it's there. And the earlier ones—other guys, you know—the bullets zip right through where it *ain't*, we got that too."

"I'd conjecture that instead of . . ." Jones murmured with a faraway look in his own eyes. His features sharpened. "All right, what is it that you want *me* for, Commissioner?"

"Sir, I know which end of a gun the bang comes outta," Yates said. "I can gather the crap, the data, and there's nothing wrong with the Commission's *processing* capacity. But I need somebody who knows what questions t'ask."

"How long do you foresee this taking?" Jones asked crisply.

"I dunno, Doctor," Yates replied with his thumbs on the points of his pelvis. "How smart are you?"

"Touché, Commissioner," Jones said with a cold—but rather friendly—smile.

He tried the door beside which he was standing. It opened. Inside was a steward with a doughnut halfway to his mouth and his feet propped up on the counter of the kitchenette adjoining the conference room.

The steward hopped to attention. The doughnut escaped in a slow arc that ended in a splatter of jelly on the ceiling.

"Gentlemen?" said the steward. He was white, but he spoke in what sounded like a Jamaican accent. "If you need someting, you are to buzz, dat is de way, and I bring it ASAP." He pointed to the door connecting the kitchenette with the conference room.

"We just need your phone," Jones said dismissively as he peered at the unit on the wall beside him. He looked up at Yates. "Unless you've got your data with you on chip?"

"Ah, no sir," said Yates. "Ah, I can call it up, sure, but we'll need a holotank. I thought—"

"This'll do," said the scientist as he unhooked from his belt a flat device about the size of a hand with the fingers extended.

He set the unit over the phone's keypad and fitted its right-angled extension into the card-slot.

"There," he announced with a pleased expression. "Call up your data and we'll project it right here. I'm used to this."

I'm not, thought Sam Yates, but he didn't speak while concentrating on hitting the right sequence of tiny buttons to transfer his project files to this electronic address. It would have been a lot simpler if Jones's gadget hadn't disabled both the full-sized keypad and the card-slot—which, with Sam's ID inserted—would have given him vocal control of switching.

Of course, there wouldn't be anywhere to switch to then.

Anyhow, it didn't matter whether Sam Yates was comfortable with this toy. And he was sure Jones would tell him so if given the opportunity.

A thirty-centimeter ball of diffuse light formed above the phone, which had just been converted into a data terminal. The steward watched it as he wiped his hands repeatedly with the towel he'd used to clean away the doughnut. Then, unsummoned, he disappeared through the connecting door, with a large carafe of coffee.

Instead of clucking to itself, Jones's miniature holounit made the air quiver with tiny electronic chimes.

"Lovely little thing, isn't it?" Jones said, beaming at his hardware as though it were a sheaf of baby pictures. "Indonesian, you know. I tell you, one of these days—"

The implication of a future recalled him to the present, and his normal demeanor. Jones looked sharply at Yates and said, "How can you be sure other bullets passed through the event? Rather than bounced off or missed when the event vanished from the operator's targeting array?"

Which was a funny way to talk about a pistol's sight picture, but Sam wasn't looking for somebody who thought the way *he* did.

There were hard amber images in the air above the phone, now: *BF #1/ARAM**. Rather than trying to explain verbally, Yates keyed the buttons carefully to bring up the incident at E and 17.

Computer enhancement brought the Rillian's purple image to sharply defined but jerky life at the intersection. One of Yates's patrol officers stood on Corridor E, raising her needle stunner, while a man in civilian clothes knelt in a doorway off Corridor 17.

"That's the main entrance to the Cuban mission," Yates explained. He cued a pulsing orange arrow to draw attention to the weapon cradled in the man's arms, then focused down on it. Gas and muzzle flashes spurted as the gun began to fire.

"Probably a standard Defense Forces' issue Balaguer," Yates continued calmly as the image of the wall—with door and gunman—dissolved in choppy waves like those of a windswept pond. "We didn't recover it, but we got the brass, while over here—"

The image expanded, jumped back in time, and then shifted to the wall of Corridor E, kitty-corner from the hunched gunman. That façade also began to flash and crumble, but under discrete impacts and on a much slighter scale.

"Using explosive bullets, y'see," Yates commented. "Now, watch *this*."

After two false tries with the tiny controls, he got the combination he wanted. The scale steadied to show the entire intersection again. In freeze-frame, narrow orange lines traced the tracks the bullets must have taken through the Rillian—which vanished each time as though it were an image on a prismatic reflector.

"And from this angle—"

The Rillian reappeared in the gunsight image that was wholly computer-generated, blinking out of existence each time a bullet track crossed the portion of spacetime it appeared to occupy.

"Now," Yates said, "*exactly* the same thing happened when the needles hit—didn't hit, you know—from the, from ah . . . Patrol Officer Xavier. We've recovered the needles from the far wall."

"Here, let me see it," said Jones, reaching for the keypad. He looked at Yates again. "You're using ConForm software? That's HQ-standard, isn't it?"

"Huh? Yeah, I guess."

Jones's face made a sourly disappointed moue, but his fingers were already playing with the keypad—orange lines down Corridor E at a much flatter angle, through the target—the target area, flickering in and out of the image.

"You can—" Yates started to say, but the weapons scientist already *had*, merging the two sets of data, submachine gun and needle stunner, into an X-pattern of orange lines at different rates of pulse while the Rillian danced a spacetime ballet within their intersection.

"There!" Jones muttered. "There, he's swinging toward the shooter, but he only moves when he's in sight." He looked at Yates sharply. "Is that a software artifact? Is that something you've created here?"

"No *sir*," said Yates, glad to be asked a question he could answer. He was standing in a formal at-ease pose, feet spread and his hands crossed behind his hips. He felt comfortable for the first time in—quite a while. "That's true on the unprocessed files. And at the, you know, real-time when it was . . ."

"Well, why the hell didn't somebody tell *me*?" Jones grumbled as his fingers danced on the keypad. One of the sidebars expanded into a mass of figures, displacing the image of the doorway as it and the man sheltered there lapped into a different universe.

Because you folks working on Channon are the very cream of what's available, Yates thought, *but there's some real low-order questions that oughta be asked, too.*

And more or less by chance, there were a couple real low-order cops "on the team" to ask them.

Aloud he said, "It kept moving after I hit it. And then it, you know, started to go down. Like a balloon. But it was *there*—"

Yates's eyes went unfocused and his voice changed. He didn't realize the difference, because his mind watched his pistol lift into the afterimage of the muzzle flash, felt the recoil against the web of his thumb. . . .

Hell. "None of my slugs—or Ella's needles—were recovered," Yates finished, feeling his skin crawl with embarrassment at the way he'd dropped out, dropped into memory. "The rest— we think we got all the rest when we looked where the cameras said look."

Jones was watching him with a quizzical expression, but whatever he saw or thought he saw in Yates's eyes hadn't been enough to untrack the scientist. The sidebar he'd expanded to fill the holofield was the file that held the projectile data: types, weights, numbers, and available subsorts for composition, burst-frequency and gridded location of use.

The meeting in the conference room had reached some sort

of formal break. The gabble of voices within the room rose in volume. A pair of men, speaking a Slavic language and either furious with one another or faking it beautifully, headed past on their way to the john.

Jones ignored them. Without bothering to ask for help—or needing to—he keyed a subdirectory, translated Yates's simple headings, and displayed the file that gave quick-and-dirty estimates of the composition of the projectiles fired at the Rillian.

Damn! but it was good to work with an officer who knew what he was doing.

"All right," Jones demanded. "Was anybody using a weapon just like yours?"

"No sir," Yates said, reaching into the side pocket of his coat, "but the jacket material's a pretty close match with a couple others including them Cuban rounds you watched. Bullet jackets, I mean. Do you want to see—"

He already had the Tokarev out of his pocket—muzzle high, butt forward so that Jones could take the weapon safely.

"Good God, *no!*" the scientist blurted with a tone and an expression that might've been justified by an offered chance to go down on a menstruating leopard. "Do you have to carry—" He caught himself. "Yes, of course you do. But please, I don't need to see it."

The steward poked his head into the kitchenette; just long enough to get his own glimpse of the pistol disappearing.

"Christ!" Yates muttered. "I never shot anybody I didn't mean to," he added, before he had time to realize what a bad idea it was to say that.

Jones grimaced again, but his fingers were working the keypad and his attention was on the holofield. "All right," he said, "if the difference isn't in the composition of the projectiles, let's look at—"

The data set voided, to be replaced by a schematic of the Rillian mapped with calculated impact points of all the shots that had been fired at the creature. Hundreds of orange pips, smears, and blotches were scattered all over the Rillian's body.

Christ, there'd been a shitload of people trying their damndest to stop the thing. Some of them folks were doing their job, patrol officers and guards of one sort or the other; but some were just people, like the guy who'd hurled a vase he'd just bought through the center of where the Rillian would have been if it hadn't winked out at the right instant. . . .

And they were dead now, most of them; but so were a lot of people who'd taken the sensible course of ducking under a desk that went coruscant when the Rillian happened to spray death in that direction. Maybe when you were dead it didn't matter, but Sam Yates had always figured he'd sooner go with his teeth in a throat.

Sanders, the Air Force general—looking like an angry bowling ball in a tailored sky-blue uniform—thrust in through the door from the conference room. "Jones!" he snapped. "What are you fucking around here for?"

Yates smiled at him, wide-eyed. Sanders blinked.

"Hi, Sandy," Jones said, glancing up and then back at his hologram display. "I ordered the commissioner here to assemble some data on kinetic-kill probabilities. I'll be with you soon as I can, but"—he met Sanders' eyes again—"I think this takes precedence."

"Oh," said Sanders. He scowled, but his heart wasn't in it. "Well, I want you back ASAP anyway to vet the log. I'm sure that little kike Sultanian understood something from what Lucky just said."

"As soon as I check this out, Sandy," Jones agreed offhandedly as his fingers danced on the keypad. "Anyway, he's Armenian."

The general disappeared back the way he'd come, shaking his head.

"Thanks," Yates said.

"Tsk," Jones said, rotating the image so that he had the Rillian from all angles. "Couldn't take a chance on you shooting my boss when I'd just got him trained. With your gat, do you call it?"

"I call it a Tula Tokarev TT-30," Yates said stiffly. "And I wasn't going to shoot General Sanders."

"Sure, you're a pacifist," Jones agreed as he peered face-on at the image. "That's why McLeod says he needs a leash and muzzle for you."

The eight Tokarev rounds were in blue—not a bad group, under the circumstances. Green marked the twenty-seven of Ella's needles which were calculated to have hit in the target area, and *that* wasn't bad either. Around and about the effective hits were the pips of other shots that should have hit but hadn't, and the broad orange smears of the plasma bolts fired vainly at the Rillian, instants before Yates started shooting.

"Beats the hell outta me, Commissioner," Jones said matter-of-factly as he toggled back to a video display of the actual event. He squinted. "Why's it fuzzy? Is it the image?"

"Negative, sir," Yates said. "It's dust. One of the Marines just blew a chunk outta the ceiling with a plasma gun."

Jones frowned in amazement.

Yates shrugged. "It happens," he said without emotion. "Wait till you're there. Anyway, there was a lotta rock in the air. Concrete too, I guess."

Still frowning, Jones manipulated the image to focus on the cratered ceiling rather than the Rillian, using the software to create the scene from fragmentary data. "It wasn't just rock and concrete, you know," he said carefully. "There were conduits in that ceiling, plus the lights and the glow-strips."

He glared at Yates. "Do you know what the composition of all *that* was, Commissioner?"

"I will," said Yates, clicking through a mental file of who he'd grab in Utilities Division—which was also on a crash schedule, repairing damage, but Teilemann or maybe Butkus would appreciate that it might be more important to worry about the *next* time. "You think that's it?"

Jones shrugged. "I think something masked the event's—that does sound silly, doesn't it? I think something masked the creature's sensors so it didn't react when your bullets hit it. If that was just lime dust, fine . . . but if it turns out to be vaporized copper or what-have-you, I too would like to have some of that handy the next time."

Yates reached out with a hand scabbed from the violence of the day past and scarred by years of other violence. As he shook with Jones, he grinned; it was a measure of mutual respect that Jones didn't flinch at the big man's expression.

"You bet, Doc," Yates said. "You go talk to Channon and the spook brigade about death rays; but I'll put some stuff to-

gether, so you'n me can figure out what *really* kills the bas-
tards.''

Yates walked out of the kitchenette with his hands in his pockets, playing with the pistol and the loose rounds. The refrain of
the song he whistled was, ''And now you're lyin' dead on my
barroom floor!''

Chapter 29

RED/COSMIC/LETHAL

The phone in McLeod's office rang—again. He was already on one call, with two more waiting, his console lit up like a Christmas tree . . . or a Halloween jack-o'-lantern. He let it ring; his secretary could handle this and all subsequent incoming calls. The voice yelling in his ear wasn't one you put on hold.

It wasn't McLeod's day—but then, none of the days since the Kiri had walked into Entry One were among his fondest memories.

Nobody, but nobody, was handling the events surrounding the alien in a professional, cooperative, nonemotional or even vaguely efficient manner, himself included. Which, he knew, was the way it always went: When you needed people the most, they failed you, every time. You could count on it.

Usually, though, Taylor McLeod could count on himself not to lose control, and command. The way he'd lost it with Yates—in front of Minsky, yet—still bothered him, not so much because he'd shown anger, but because he hadn't followed through and forced Minsky to accept Yates's resignation there and then.

But he knew why he hadn't: McLeod was way out on a limb, anticipating the bough to break and the baby to fall, the way this morning's message traffic was telling him was imminent. And since he was the baby—the guy who'd come in out of left field and usurped whatever authority was necessary to get the job done—he'd gotten cautious at just the wrong moment, when he'd had a chance to take Yates out of play permanently.

But he couldn't risk it in front of Minsky—not right before the lock-down Minsky hadn't known was coming. If Yates was officially out as Security Commissioner, then Stuart's temporary appointment wouldn't hold. The next Security Commissioner,

under those circumstances, would almost certainly have been a
Soviet national. Minsky, for one, wasn't stupid.

And now Minsky and every other privy national and UN official on Earth and the Moon were pissed as hell at Taylor
McLeod. Well, there were lots of ways to lose your job, to waste
your career, to shove yourself into the shredder, dick first. It
didn't matter that the possibility was there, because the possibility was always there, in his business. It mattered that the
reason was worth the price.

He kept telling himself that Channon was worth any price.
And that if Channon wasn't, then saving what he could of the
Luna installation had to be. *Had to be.*

Between the Stars and Stripes and the UN/Luna flag, McLeod
slumped over his desk of polished moonrock, one hand shielding his eyes, the other sweating on the secure handset he held
to his ear.

"Yes, sir, I realize that, sir," he said to his director during a
pause in the tirade coming up from Langley. "But you must
realize that I don't see any other option worth initiating. I can't
lift the State of Emergency and I won't back off the alert level."

McLeod had been chewed out, this morning, first by the UN
Secretary General's office, who threatened a Security Council
meeting unless he had Stuart, the acting Security Commissioner,
rescind the State of Emergency and lower the alert status; then
everybody nearside whom the Secretary General thought could
pull his chain, including Sandy, who'd apologized and read him
a rote statement meant for McLeod's jacket.

Then, when none of that worked, the calls from groundside
had started coming. He was short four staffers and Stuart was
seconded to Security, which meant McLeod was right here, at
his desk, because he needed everybody else more elsewhere.
Thus he was catching flak like some idiot bureaucrat, instead of
being out of communication the way a good intelligence officer
ought to be when he was trampling every known rule of procedure underfoot and didn't intend to stop until either the job was
done or somebody stopped him, physically, before he could get
it done.

He'd been taken to task by everybody he might be expected
to heed from groundside, in ascending order. The opening salvo
had been one from the State Department's intelligence liaison,
who ought to have been intelligent enough to have more sense.

When McLeod had said so, the first groundside call had been
followed by one from the Luna ambassador, whose Cabinet-level
post had had him in DC since before Lucky delivered Armageddon to Luna base in his red, six-fingered hand.

Next, when that didn't work, he'd gotten a lecture on Rules
of Engagement in internationalized zones by a four-star from
the Tank.

And now this: an official remonstrance and inquiry from the
top of his own chain of command, with whom, except in the
direst of emergencies, he was to have no contact, since his Luna
post was (still?) a nonintelligence cover. It wasn't fair, but it
was hardball, and McLeod had brought his catcher's mitt.

McLeod's director was saying: "You don't see another option? Then find one, Mr. McLeod. This comes straight from the
President. The newsies are picking up on this State of Emergency even as we speak, despite the downed satellite. We can
only keep them off your back for so long with smoke about
jammed transmission lines. They know damned well we could
shuttle them feeds to their own sats if we wanted to cooperate.
The definition of covert, in case you've forgotten, is 'activities
planned and executed in such a manner that the identity of the
sponsor is concealed, or at least so that the sponsor has plausible
denial of involvement.' Are you maintaining that this alien gam-
bit, complete with an official State of Emergency, falls into this
category?"

"No sir," McLeod said so quietly that his director demanded,
"What?" and he had to repeat his comment: "No sir, I'm not.
But Security Commissioner Yates's office floated some nonsense
about a meteor strike without checking with us. You can't blame
the newsies for digging into as tantalizing a piece of obvious
deception as that—it's like dangling a prime roast before a starv-
ing guard dog. Since Yates is uncooperative in the extreme, we've
replaced him temporarily with one of ours, and shifted Yates to
close support for Lucky, but we had to enlist the USSR's aid to
do even that much. You've got to remember, sir, that this isn't
happening in a vacuum—yet, thank God—or in a friendly national venue, but in a highly polarized international community
with disparate goals and a communal interest only in survival.
You bet, under the circumstances, we're going to step on some
toes."

He'd only spoken to his DCI personally twice before in his

career. He hoped this wasn't going to be the last—of both. But he couldn't lift the SOE in good conscience. That was what he'd told State, and the Lunar ambassador, then one of the Joint Chiefs, and now his own director, who claimed to be speaking for the Chief Executive.

"Then perhaps, Mr. McLeod, you'd clarify for me just which category of your oversight assignment this mess does fall into. Clandestine operations are planned and executed in such a manner as to hide the fact that an operation took place at all. You're surely not expecting to write Lucky up as clandestine, after this public posturing."

"No, sir, I'm not, sir. But you're not taking into account the subtext of—"

"Maybe," said the voice from Earth, which must not have paused for his response at all to have cut into his answer, despite the transmission lag, "you're thinking of this as a 'special' activity, which we're still defining as per Executive Order 12333-4/12/81: 'intelligence activities conducted in support of national foreign policy objectives abroad which are planned and executed so that the role of the United States Government is not apparent or acknowledged publicly. . . .' "

"No, sir, I know we're not appearing to meet any such guidelines," Taylor McLeod said, making a conscious effort to keep his voice audible and level. He knew where this was going— He was going to be waved off. He'd almost have welcomed being cut from Operation Lucky Break, if he thought that would get him and his out of harm's way. But it wouldn't. And right now his job, including pension and health benefits, didn't seem like awfully much to risk, considering what else was at stake here.

"Then you're telling me you're purposely engaging in overt activity up there?" thundered the director as if he were right here, spitting into McLeod's ear, instead of sitting in his Langley corner office on the seventh floor, watching cherry blossoms fall off the trees beyond his office window.

"Sir, if you mean"—McLeod could cite page and line with the best of them—"overt as in 'operations planned and executed in such a manner that no attempt is made to conceal either the operation itself or who is sponsoring it'—no sir, I'm not doing that, although I know it looks like I am. I'm trying to use whatever can't be concealed as cover for what can. I know it's irregular, but this whole thing is irregular. I really wish you'd wait for my interim report to reach your desk.'' To himself, he added: *If I'm not dead by then, I can make a pretty good case for what I'm doing, and why, you fat political appointee.*

"And when will that be? General Sanders is suggesting that a state of martial law might be appropriate, and the military brass down here concurs. They want to raise the DefCon to Three—that's milspeak for Defensive Condition, in case you're amnesiac, and it means you've failed, in any terms the military considers pertinent. It's difficult to argue the other side when, despite your best efforts at security, it's painfully clear to everyone on the Moon and half the goddamn population of Washington and Moscow, if not the entire Earth, that the planet's been attacked by monsters from outer space, against whom you and yours have been entirely ineffectual.''

"Not the planet, sir. The Moon. And only as a byproduct of a squabble we're not central to, sir. My report's cued up and spooled to transmit, but there's a lot of message traffic right now. . . .''

"Moon, schmoon. I want a reason to go to bat for you, McLeod. If I don't have it by the end of this conversation, I'll have to bow to Executive pressure and turn control of this alien over to the military, let them have their declaration of martial law . . . the whole nine yards.''

McLeod took his hand from his eyes and stared blankly at the far wall. One of the stress regulation tricks he'd learned was that of focusing on a wall-ceiling juncture and taking deep breaths. He did that.

Then he said, "Sir, I'd like to point out that Sandy and every Joint Chief in the Tank together haven't clout enough to declare a military emergency up here; that's a UN prerogative. If the UN Peacekeeping Force up here takes control, then we lose access to Lucky. Perhaps permanently. I'd also like to state for the record that it's my considered opinion that Lucky represents the most crucial intel batch-file in operational history. If we lose Lucky to the U.S. military, they'll lose him to the UN forces, and then he's as good as Soviet property. I'm still not satisfied that my—that our—interrogation brief, in this situation, can be preempted by our military, let alone anybody else's. And I'm maintaining that stance. I'm not finished with Lucky. Security leaks on something of this magnitude can't be helped. As our director, you're surely familiar with the maxim that all operations of this sort blow, eventually. We're facing a second possible alien incursion of unpredictable magnitude, from an enemy of inestimable force. That opposition is overt in nature. Therefore at least one compartment of our response must be equally overt. Removing Lucky from my care and providing more general access to any information he might be holding can only be construed by the Agency as contrary to the security interest of the United States, not to mention curtailing the effectiveness of any response by my team—the only on-site authority. In my capacity as that authority, I'm officially recommending against declaring martial law, and equally against lifting the current health advisory—i.e., the Moon base ought to remain under general quarantine. Nobody we haven't got up here already can help us now, and we don't need any more persons at risk.''

McLeod paused for breath and to await his director's tirade—this time, well deserved, since he'd lost his temper in midstatement and let a snide remark slip out.

The pause from the other end was so lengthy that McLeod had begun wondering if the line hadn't gone dead before the director's next words reached him:

''Ting—that's what your friends call you, I'm told—you'd better be right about this. Not just the UN bigwigs, but the Mars Observer Group is complaining that you're negatively impacting their effectiveness with your tactics. And there'd better be something in that report of yours I can use to back you up. Right now, it's just your word against that of a number of others who have the President's ear.''

''Among other things, I'm sending down the X-ray photos we took of Lucky's equipment, plus computer work we've already done toward reverse-engineering from that data.'' *All gotten*, McLeod thought in a silent addendum to the conversation, *when I swiped his suit while the poor bastard was parboiling himself in my shower at exorbitant cost to the U.S. taxpayer, but you're not going to care about any of that.*

''Let's hope it's good enough.''

''It will be, sir. Now, if that's all, I've got to go tend to Lucky, who's expecting a second visitor any time now.''

''A . . . second . . .''

''That's what I've been trying to tell you, sir.'' *Did tell you, you overfed dolt.* ''That's what all the wrangling's about, sir. So perhaps now you understand why I'm not overly concerned with what, on the overt side, leaks, and when. Barring a decision by Lucky's enemies that he's not worth any further trouble, you're going to be getting sound bites for the evening news, unless your friends in the Press Office can slap a security gag on the press corps, or unless everybody up here who can and would send such feeds is already dead by then, or all our transmission equipment fried to hell. So if you'll let me get on with my chess game, sir?''

There was a whole lot of heavy breathing on the line. Then the director said, "Mr. McLeod, you have our best wishes and strongest support. Break a leg.''

"Yes, sir. Thank you, sir.'' McLeod uncurled his cramped fingers from the handset with some effort. He used to wish this Administration would quit handing sensitive government appointments to movie actors who'd stumped for the President when he'd been a candidate. Now he didn't mind so much. Maybe the director was an all-right guy after all. Maybe he could deliver his lines with enough verisimilitude to keep groundside off McLeod's back for a just a little while longer.

A little while was all he needed. A little while was all it was going to take to find out if Lucky's plan would work—if the incoming Rillian could be immobilized.

If it couldn't, and the small group of defenders couldn't then duplicate the conditions that had killed the first one (even though, according to Lucky, this one was different), then it wasn't going to matter what groundside thought. Not to McLeod. Not to Elinor Bradley or her pet alien.

Not to anybody on the Moon. And maybe not to anybody on Earth, if Lucky's fears that the Rillians would sterilize any planet inhabited by technologically competent airbreathers weren't unfounded.

If Taylor McLeod had ever been in a situation where an alert status of Red/Cosmic/Lethal was totally justified, this was it. And if it was making them nervous groundside, then that was nothing compared to what they'd be feeling if the whole lunar installation ceased to exist. Or if the Rillians decided to clean up the Earth while they were in the neighborhood.

McLeod kept thinking about letting the Kiri alien go farside, if worse came to worst. It was a long shot, sure. But it was a shot at saving Earth, if not the lunar colony. And shots were seeming to come at a real premium, lately.

He looked at his com console, still blinking with cued calls waiting for his attention. Then, instead of punching a lit button, he paged through to his secretary: "Get me Ella Bradley; she'll be with Lucky still, I think. Tell her it won't take long, but I have to brief her personally on the meeting I had with Yates and Minsky—at her soonest pleasure, please."

He let up on the toggle. You took your shots at a time like this—all of them. The last thing he needed in the middle of this crisis was Ella hearing somebody else's version of Yesilkova's termination hearing. There was never time for an error of omission, no matter how short time was beginning to get.

Chapter 30

LAB WORK

"Glad you called us, Channon," Yates said when Bradley and the Kiri alien arrived at Science Module 20, under the protection of JEB Stuart's Special Activities Group—or the four who were left of it.

The module was white and silver and dove-gray and gleaming, where it wasn't blinking and beeping and chattering as banks of rack-mounted electronics burbled away at their appointed tasks.

White coats with affiliation patches bustled to and fro, none turning a hair at the appearance of a fully suited fellow with no recognizable insignia and six fingers to his gloves.

But then, these were America's most highly cleared lunar technologists. Yates had had to go through the clearance officer to get Yesilkova the plasticized badge that hung from a beaded chain around her neck. It read: *TTS/SCI/COSMIC*, the last clearance level being the only one that had anything to do with UN procedures, and that one a NATO designator.

Minsky would have been proud of her if he'd seen her sporting her deep-penetration U.S. badge. With it, she could have gone anywhere—if there was anywhere worth going when compared with where she was.

But there wasn't. Channon, whom the Americans called Lucky among themselves, was the only game in town. Of this, she'd become certain when Minsky had phoned her to say that, "for the duration, Yesilkova, the entire resources of the USSR are at your unilateral disposal. Orders have been given. Whatever you need, take. We will perform the paperwork after this crisis is past."

It had been nice to think that Minsky expected the crisis to pass, and that paperwork would then once more be important.

If his spoken words had not hidden an unspoken reiteration of his desire to acquire the Rillian weapon, she would truly have been comforted by them. As it was, Minsky's was just one more demand to do the impossible, a demand that could not be obeyed—or, if obeyed, could not be fulfilled by a dead Yesilkova.

She'd told Yates, who'd been looking at her questioningly after she'd hung up, "Well, Commissar, you'll be piss-pleased to know that the USSR gives us whatever we wish that your country won't, no paperwork required. Ain't that the damndest thing?" It always took her a moment to recapture colloquial American syntax after speaking Minsky's brand of bureaucratic Russian.

Yates had hugged her tight, raised a glassless toast to the Party, and hurried her off to his "secret-secret test facility. Have yer miniaturized videocamera ready." And winked.

There was something wrong in Yates's demeanor. He was keeping something from her, this she knew. What it was, judging by his bright smiles and overt affection, was serious, and had to do with her. She knew this because she knew the man, his volatility range, his defenses, his responses. Sleeping with Yates had recently seemed like an error in judgment; then, because of Minsky's support, a triumph. Now she was regretting it again. If they had not been so close, perhaps he would not be acting so strangely. If he was trying to protect her from something—from everything—this might explain his close-mouthed behavior, his exaggerated lightheartedness.

But it did not explain his deepened voice, the distance behind the closeness. She worried that he was beginning to think of her as the enemy, as a Soviet agent, which of course she was . . . but never an enemy. Never.

She told herself that he knew, without her having to tell him, what sort of pressure she was under. She assumed he was enduring the same—and had her assumption confirmed by the lengthy clearance process he'd expedited but still had to go through to allow Yesilkova into the lab.

Now, in the presence of Channon, Bradley, and the beautifully dressed commandos from CIA here in America's most secret lunar laboratory, she felt proud of her country. Excluded from Yates's confidence, Mother Russia's was what counted.

All this American competency, and his superiors would not give Yates so much as a moon truck to take Channon farside.

They did not trust him with the alien. While her country had laid its every resource at their disposal. If this ever ended, the contrast between her freedom and Yates's continued subjugation to paperwork and protocol would be a fine feather in the USSR's cap. Assuming, of course, that anyone had a head to put such a cap upon.

It remained only to get the alien alone and tell him that his wish for a trip farside had been granted—over the objections of the USA, by his friends in the USSR. She hoped Yates would forgive the way such a statement must be put, but she too had officials to whom she must answer.

Bradley was on Channon like a leech, holding his arm, walking him through the aisles while she and Yates, surrounded by the SAG personnel, followed.

Stuart was talking very carefully to Yates about the electromagnets: "We'll position them in Corridor Nine B, given that we think Lucky's already been targeted as being in the U.S. mission. Now, that may change, and we could have a problem moving these big pieces of equipment in the maintenance tunnels quickly, but that'll be part of your job, Yates—tracking the Rillian's progress."

"Don't tell me what my job is, sonny. You're Security Commissioner until the grownups get back—fine. Go tend to the While-You-Were-Outs on my desk. Leave the Kiri and the Rillian to me. That's the way we worked it out, your boss and me, remember? Or are you looking for another two-hour suspension?"

Stuart flushed visibly and turned to the alien. "Mr. Channon, if you'll come with me, Dr. Quint wants to discuss some of the preparations with you," he said stiffly, still staring defiantly at Yates over Channon's shoulder.

Bradley looked between the two American men and caught Yesilkova's gaze. She rolled her eyes upward and indicated a quiet corner with an inclination of her head.

Yesilkova did not respond. Her job was to watch the Kiri alien. Channon was shaking hands with Quint, who was in a lab smock, while Yates stalked over to run his hands along the electromagnetic assembly that was nearly as tall as he.

The Kiri alien also began examining the huge wire-wound electromagnets on wheels, while Quint was explaining, "We'll be running shunts to the mission emergency generators, so we won't lose power whatever happens. The timing of the two start-ups—for Magnets A and then B—we've computerized, so even if everybody's unconscious, it'll still work . . . it's just . . ."

"Just? Meaning consistent with moral right; fair, equitable?" Channon said. "Device not so. Only usage tells if—"

"—it's just that you don't happen to know how much to pulse these with, do you?—how much'll immobilize the critter without collapsing his suit and killing him, and how much is too much?"

"Not kill Rillian," said Channon warningly. "Killing force, too much. Show Channon controlling device?"

"Computer?" Quint said. "Sure, right this way. We've put a teraflops machine on this, fastest we've got, to go with the su-perconducting ceramics of this cable we're using. You think we need fast, Jones said. So you've got fast as we can give you. Even the switches are Josephsen; the arsenide circuits cut the resistance some more. The whole electron flow's optimized. The question we see is, how big an area do you need to cover, really? How far's this thing's arm from its ass, sort of. . . ."

The two wandered away, white-coated scientist arm in arm with space-suited alien. Yates followed close behind, asking a sharp question the tone of which was combative, delivering words Yesilkova couldn't catch, beyond the single phrase, "sometime before Hell freezes over."

Stuart then scratched his head and said in a mild voice aimed vaguely at Bradley, "Guess I'll go back to the office. If you need anything, our boys'll be at the door, Ms. Bradley. Yesil-kov." He saluted her smartly, with something like mockery in his manner, and let himself out the double doors, using his ac-cess card.

That left Yesilkova face to face with Elinor Bradley, and Brad-ley's glance still suggested that something must be discussed between them.

Bradley said, "Come on, Sonya, let's get coffee while we can."

American coffee was terrible, weak and thin, but Yesilkova went along to the dispenser and received a cup from Bradley.

She made a face when she sipped it.

Bradley said, "You can say that again. Can't we do something about this, before it scuttles everything we're trying to do here?"

"The coffee?" Yesilkova stared at her cup, then at Bradley,

with exaggerated puzzlement. Whatever 'this' was, Bradley must be forced to explain.

"You're not wired, are you?—for sight and sound, I mean. Because this has to be off the record."

"Here?" Yesilkova looked around as if searching for eavesdroppers, while neatly avoiding a direct negative answer to Bradley's question. "There is no security, Ms. Bradley, but what one's own self can provide."

"Great. Well, can we do something or not? Tell them to cut the crap, if nothing more. That you're not angry, that you understand why Ting did what he—"

Yesilkova still had no idea what Bradley meant, but now she knew she needed desperately to learn. "Tell me what Mr. McLeod told you," she bargained.

"He told me . . . everything, I think." And she smiled weakly, as even she realized what a ridiculous statement that was. "About what happened between Ting and Sam, about Minsky being there, about . . . the deal they made."

"Please?" Yesilkova was becoming distinctly uncomfortable. Anger quickened her pulse. Her mouth dried up. Her face felt flushed. Yates had told her nothing. Minsky had told her nothing. They were professionals. This Bradley would tell her everything. "Deal? Which deal?"

"Surely you know . . ." Bradley tipped up her styrofoam cup and stared at Yesilkova over it. Then she lowered it and sighed. "Well, if you don't, you're going to be very unhappy; if you do, I don't see the point, but here goes: Sam and Ting and Minsky got together to argue your termination—"

"*Pizviets!*" swore Yesilkova. "And you, how do you know this?" she demanded.

"They didn't even tell you that much?" Bradley shook her head pityingly. "Now I don't feel that it's all my fault—that I'm the cause of everything."

"*What, Amerikanski, is everything?* From the beginning, please." Yesilkova crossed her arms, her cup in one hand, carefully held just short of overflow. She would make sure Minsky learned that she'd heard this from an enemy—from Sam's former lover. Minsky could have saved her at least the shock.

"The beginning . . . Taylor and I filed charges for an inquiry over you stunning the SAG officers. Termination orders were issued. Yates protested. Minsky, as Yates requested, appeared at a closed hearing as UN representative, since Sam works for the UN. The discussion got very personal. Everyone said things that were regrettable. Sam offered his resignation, saying you were only following orders and if anyone was terminated, it should be he. Taylor and Oleg Minsky didn't accept it. Things got more unpleasant. . . . My name came into it, Taylor said—he didn't want me to hear it from anyone else.''

"*Da,*" said Yesilkova. It was the most she could manage.

"Now they're acting like two bullies on a playground, who've both been punished for fighting during recess."

"No, they ain't. They're actin' like two guys been screwin' the same bimbo and aren't sure whether the one that was or the one that is, is winnin'." She couldn't help it. She was furious. "You wish to solve this, Ms. Bradley, you do something. Sam has no problems you and your overreaching fiancé ain't creatin'." Why did Bradley simply stand there, staring at her woodenly?

Bradley said, "I see. Very well, I'll do my best, given your input, to take care of things." She carefully put down her coffee and moved away from Yesilkova.

When she reached Yates and Channon, Ella Bradley touched Sam's arm and he bent his head to talk to her.

Suddenly, Yesilkova was even more angry than before. Didn't these people realize how much was at stake? How dare they have personal problems, when the survival of the colony—perhaps the entire species—depended upon their performance?

As she watched, so angry she was shaking, Channon detached himself from the knot of folk around the giant electromagnets and came purposefully toward her.

When he reached her, he said quietly, "Yesilkov, Channon feels pain. Where hurt, Yesilkov? Channon help Yesilkov? Want Yates? Want medic? Want—"

"I don't want nothin', Channon. I'm fine, hear? Just fine. People just . . . don't always get along, that's all."

"Not get along because of Channon, Channon help," said the alien. "Need friends, Yesilkov."

"Channon," she said quickly, "it's not you. I just . . ." She took a deep breath and plunged forward, seeing an opportunity, a one-in-a-million chance that she was angry enough to take. "My country wants to see the Rillian's weapon, wants to understand the Rillian technology, and the Americans—Yates's country—aren't going to let us. They're not going to share with us, Channon, and that will be my fault—unless you can help.''

"Channon help. Give Yesilkov help, whatever kind. Please to smile and be happy. Faith, Yesilkov. Faith.''

"If you say so, Channon," she said, and smiled, though it wasn't a pretty smile and it wasn't a happy one. Satisfaction would do, in a pinch. It always had, before she'd met Sam Yates. It must again. "And in good faith, on my part, I'm offerin' to take you farside, just like you want, wherever you want—in one of our trucks. I dunno if you wanna tell Sam, it's up to you. But any time, Channon. Any time you say, you got your ride farside—long as McLeod don't find out first.''

Maybe it was wrong, but maybe it was right. Maybe it was the only way to win on points, and maybe it was the only way to save everything—and everybody—Sonya Yesilkov had spent her life protecting.

She hated like hell not to have told Sam first. But it wasn't like he was telling her everything she needed to know, either.

Then Channon reached out and touched her arm, saying, "Now, Yesilkov? Go farside, now? Rillian coming, now.''

"We know, Channon—soon, right? So soon we'll go farside, as soon as I can sneak—''

"Now,'' said the alien. "Rillian here now.''

"Shit," she said. "You mean *right now*, don't you?'' She turned and yelled to Yates, "Sam, Channon says it's here now— the Rillian. As in any minute. Let's get that stuff into position. *Move it, Yates! Quint, let's go!*''

Farside was just going to have to wait.

Chapter 31

WALK-UP

Throughout the collection/communication phase of the operation, the Rillian controller had remained in the shadow of a crater, hanging in near-vacuum. Now he shifted to the vicinity of what he had decided would be his first target. The instant of sponge-space, where the constants *were* constant, was as refreshing as feeling the blood of prey gush across his lips at a formal banquet.

The controller returned to local standard within fifty meters of his target—directly above it, drifting down as planetary rotation shifted his impact point slightly, insignificantly.

Quite acceptable. For this *damnable* spacetime, genuinely praiseworthy.

He landed above the reactor vessel, which was buried a further thirty meters beneath living rock. For this purpose, the indigenes had gouged a cave instead of excavating a hole and backfilling to cover it. He balanced on all four legs, making a game of the fact that he was able to alight squarely instead of bouncing, because the flexure of his muscles had overpowered this satellite's minuscule gravity.

The controller checked his surroundings again. Optical devices were staring at him, and he could hear the trill of emergency signals. The material substrate had not changed, nor had what passed for energy constants in this spacetime. So . . .

The Rillian controller stepped into the reactor compartment.

The indigenes had cut a ramp down into the regolith, to their switch room. The dozen technicians on duty there were armed, and doubled as guards. The rear wall of the switch room was a massive airlock, opening onto the reactor room itself. There was no other access to the reactor except through the rock.

The Rillian controller dropped through the regolith, under the gentle tug of lunar gravity, skewing his atomic structure so that he slipped through the rock with the same ease and rate at which he had fallen through near-vacuum a moment before.

Inside the containment structure there were more optical devices and an amusing array of emergency signals both above and below the Rillian's normal auditory range. There were no indigenes within the facility: Were the warnings meant for *him*?

Surgical precision was unnecessary, but the controller chose to exercise it nonetheless. He aimed his A-field weapon at the vat containing the water moderator, set it for a tight beam, and fired.

Instead of a neat line ripping across the surface, a three-meter sphere of matter exploded into fireballs scattering more energy than their corner of spacetime had ever before contained.

The controller had either misadjusted his weapon, or he had miscalculated the type or degree of anomaly in this subuniverse. Either way, a personal failure—

But not an operational one. The fission pile was devouring itself with a roar that blanketed the radiation spectrum, all the way from X-rays to sound at the level the indigenes could hear.

Still, it was in an access of rage that the controller swung his weapon onto the sodium heat-exchanger. He triggered what was intended to be an engulfing blast that would match the fury drawing his lips back over his fangs.

A brilliant line, less than atomic radius in breadth or height, razored across the controller's target. The vessel bulged and the severed top lifted in a gout of light metal vaporizing. Apart from that, the unit could have been reconstructed without any material loss at a level the indigenes could detect.

It was the kind of effect the controller had wished to achieve with his first shot.

Was it the weapon, or were these *temporal* anomalies that were causing his problems? Had the Rillian soldier who died in this morass managed to kill himself by intersecting his own weapon at a *time* in which his suit did not protect him?

Damn all soldiers. Damn all Eleveners.

And damn this spacetime, which would be gutted to flatline nonexistence if the controller could convince his superiors when he returned from his mission. For now, he would be sure to attempt a surgical effect with the burst *preceding* the one with which he eliminated the Elevener, because the controller very much wanted a trophy to carry back to his own spacetime. . . .

He paused, balancing his atomic structure again while the ravening destruction he had loosed bombarded his suit and forced him out of the local spacetime. When he had the equation correct, he stepped through the wall into the switch room.

Some of the indigenes wore protective garments or had started to don them. All carried weapons. They turned to the controller, shouting words that were far beneath his auditory frequencies—and his interest.

Rather than be bothered by them—better to slay twice than never, as the old saying went—the controller ignited the room's atmosphere with a burst from his weapon. None of the indigenes wore coverings that were sufficient to survive the blast. It drove the Rillian himself back into sponge-space for some moments, while the effect dissipated.

As the controller waited, he reviewed the remaining stages of the operation. He would use the indigenes' transmission lines, the switching capacity of his suit, and his weapon as a power source to pulse portions of the habitat which the Elevener had frequented. After that additional disruption, the controller would walk into the habitat to destroy the Elevener.

And he would kill everything he met on the way.

Chapter 32

LOSING ON POINTS

"Yates," said Dr. Hugh David Jones to whoever stepped through the door behind him. His eyes were shuttling between a holo-tank, a thirty-centimeter flat-screen display, and the length of hard copy—curling even in lunar gravity—in his left hand. "How do I get him?"

"He's down in Module 20," General Sanders said in a tone just to the positive side of a snarl. "Why aren't *you* in Module 20? And what the hell business do you have with that whacko, anyway?"

"Take a look at this, Sandy," Jones offered mildly.

Here on the Moon, almost no one was cleared to enter Jones's office, so he ought to learn to check who'd come in before he made offhand demands on them. . . .

But at least he'd learned not to argue directly with his two-star boss. That was almost as bad an idea as giving Sandy honest, direct answers to the questions he barked out.

Sanders bent over the holotank, scowled, and let the scowl deepen as he peered next at the flat-screen. "Jones . . ." he said in a dangerous voice as he realized he didn't know the data's frame of reference.

Besides, he was fairly certain the symbols wouldn't have meant a damned thing useful to him, even if he'd known whether they involved particle physics or a sure-fire way to handicap the ponies.

"Our event seems to be a chlorine breather," Jones explained, pointing to the spike in the filter-bed results Yates had gathered from the habitat's air plant. "The probability's above the third standard deviation, even with the slop in the data. You just don't *have* that volume of chlorine available for release up here."

"So what?" said Sanders, watching his subordinate's fingers play with the pad of his phone bank. Jones didn't like to use oral controls for his hardware; whereas any human in the civilian's neighborhood seemed to be fair game for his demands, no matter how many stars the subject wore on his shoulders. . . .

"Used to breathe," Jones said, correcting himself. His phone threw *YATES, S. W./UN COM SEC* onto its display in green letters.

"You see . . ." he continued as his fingers loaded with three key-strokes the conclusion from the file displayed on his holo-tank, then sent the data over the phone line with a tap of his left pinkie. The sheaf of hard copy floated gently to the littered floor. "You see, I think this gives us a line on how bullets stopped the event last time, and—"

"Does it tell us how the thing's weapon works, Jones?" Sanders demanded. "Does it give us a leg up on the Russians, do you mean?"

"Well, not exactly, Sandy," Jones said, squeezing the bridge of his nose with his left thumb and forefinger in a transferred attempt to bring his boss's concern into mental focus. "I'd say it gives us a hell of a lot better chance of being alive after the next event, though. You see, rhenium is the six-shell reciprocal of chlorine in the periodic table—the elements that occur outside a lab. Now, we can be pretty sure from calibrated results—as well as U.S.-normal design parameters—that the event's weapon was calibrated *not* to affect chlorine in normal use. That—"

General Sanders had taken a light-pen from his pocket. It was the form of control with which *he* was most comfortable; and, though Jones never used a light-pen himself, his equipment was configured to accept that form of direction also.

Sanders pulsed the data-field of the holotank. The figures quivered, then blanked to a charged point in the center of the display. Moments later, the blip expanded into a frozen image of the Rillian a matter of seconds before it—stopped, died, vanished. . . .

The scientist frowned, sucking his lips between his teeth.

"Jones," the general said, "I don't *want* to live if the Russkies take over. And they will, you bet your ass, if they get that weapon and we don't."

The pen—its diode emitting white light as a pointer instead

of the yellow-green charged with control codes—steadied on the stocked wishbone in the Rillian's arms.

"Sandy," Jones said carefully, "the Russians aren't going to get a jump on anything that happens down in Module 20, believe me."

He raised his hands. "These weren't made to solder wires, and that's all I could do down there to help at this point. Sandy, we may never have another event, but if we do—"

The screen of the telephone began flashing blue as the unit's speaker warbled its Emergency Message indicator. That stopped abruptly as the room's overhead lighting went out and the hologram image blurred to nothingness, much the way the Rillian had vanished in reality.

For a moment, the only sound was the soft sigh from the air ducts as the ventilating fans spun down. The general's pen was a bright needle into the heart of the blank holotank.

"What in the name of—" Sanders started to say.

"Christ, it's the whole—" Jones started to say, tangling his feet with his chair legs in the sudden darkness that quivered with the start-up of the glowstrips in the corridor.

The holotank exploded with a pulse of energy never meant for its circuits. A blue-white arc shot up the track of the light-pen. All General Sanders' personal hardware and the metallized braid on his uniform blazed in multicolored coruscation for a fraction of a second.

Jones leaped out the door. Behind him, Sanders was still toppling in the low gravity. Smoldering hair gave a disconcertingly angelic touch to the corpse.

Chapter 33

CONTACT

Down in Science Module 20, Channon could *feel* the Rillian— its savagery, its determination, its hunter's eagerness. It was totally focused on its mission, its quarry—on killing Channon, now that it had found him.

The first overwash of Rillian presence made these humans' pathetic problems pale to insignificance. No matter that the humans were struggling with each other, and with forces of nature they understood no better, in hopes of saving Channon, and thereby themselves.

Once the Rillian touched his mind, it was as if all the humans disappeared. Yesilkov was reduced to a two-dimensional image whose mouth was offering special assistance while her body radiated treachery, uncertainty, and fury born of pain.

Quint and his technicians were no more than walking interrogatories buttoned into white coats covering their pale, mangy, vulnerable physiques. Their loud voices were squeaks which Channon had no time to decipher as they tried to convey a false courage, one to the other, in the face of imminent death they could not confront because they did not understand. Under other circumstances their jerky movements and desperate bravado would have concerned him, as all indicators of distress and dissembling among the humans who'd elected themselves his protectors had come to concern him.

Now, not even the sadness radiating from Bradley and the impatience of her once-mate, Yates, reached his heart. Channon still felt most protective toward Bradley, carrier of new life, but not even that blanket emotion was enough to cut through the immediacy of the Rillian contact.

All the humans before him receded in status to what they'd been when first he'd encountered them: barely rational, minimally conscious creatures scampering about, performing hard-wired acts of socialized herd behavior, none of them much different from the next.

He still recognized his duty to protect them. They were living beings, possessed of at least the possibility of true consciousness, given evolutionary leisure and the favor of Providence. Terri and he had always shared a love for the wild and uncontrolled behavior of lower life forms, gloried in what studying it could teach a sensitive observer about the similarities of goal and structure among all conscious life.

But these specimens of the human race had lost their individuality for him. They were like any spooked herd on a plain or a hillside. Even the pregnant one was no more than a gravid female among a milling crowd, the behavior of which was no longer that of discrete beings but of a social order of animals. . . .

Terri would have been angry to learn he'd reduced humankind to a mere genus, retreating into genetically programmed survival behavior himself.

But Channon *was* determined to survive, now that a discourse with the Rillian was providentially close at hand. He must. Every fiber of his being was already reaching out to that Rillian presence, steeling itself for the submergence of empathic contact which must precede discourse.

For Channon's skill depended on understanding his opposite number. No Kiri negotiator had ever done less. He could not do less now. Despite the murderous intent of the Rillian, he must come to a sympathetic understanding of Rillian needs, else he would fare no better than his mates on the *KirStar*, or all the dead Kiri before him who'd encountered Rillians and learned nothing but how to die as prey or as captives.

His breeding, his training, his genius and his heart all demanded a special kind of sacrifice only a Kiri conflict-negotiator could make.

And he made it, in the midst of the deaf, dumb, and blind representatives of humankind. He simply stood still, his back against a wall to support him if his knees would not. Then he expanded himself toward his skin, even as he shook himself loose from mundane contact with his own nerves and flesh. He slowed his heartbeat and his respiration; he both gathered and dispersed the knowingness that was the Channon entity, until his entire cognizant being rested well above his brainstem—and equally was concentrated along the ELF receptors of his sinuses and his epidermis.

Then he separated that body of energy which was Channon from the biological body housing that Channon, and sent his intelligence questing toward the Rillian.

It wasn't hard to find the midsegment being once again. It was harder to embrace it, silently; to become it, ephemerally; to look through its eyes and have his own thoughts overwhelmed by its thoughts.

It was wading through the physics of humanity's universe in a sea of its own fear. It was cold and uncomfortable in its hunting. Its eyes saw everything as semipermeable; its soul saw everything as hostile and yet mindless, an unfriendly environment in need of sterilization. It was sinking into a pit in which it would meet the enemy, and from which only it or its enemy could emerge.

There was no calm in it, only the lure of battle. There was no thought in it, beyond thoughts of targeting and technical means. There was no mercy in it—but then, mercy was none of its job.

It was a Rillian controller. It came on the heels of a lesser killer, fully alerted that whatever had vanquished its predecessor was lethal. It had a right to live that could be assured only by triumphing over those who had triumphed over its predecessor.

Channon's mind tiptoed into the Rillian's mind unnoticed; settled there; nested there. He saw a targeting array, a squish of lunar regolith that was, to the Rillian, the texture of mud. He saw a ready-light on an implement of destruction that used the energy sea between the worlds as its power source and the suit of the controller as its power pack. He saw in a different spectrum. He understood what it meant to experience the speed of light itself as unnaturally slowed.

And he shared the Rillian's repulsion for the human infestation it was about to raze. He was suddenly privy to the emotions as well as the technical expertise of the Rillian controller. Channon understood its job and its weapons intimately. He understood the consequences if the Rillian controller should fail.

As the targeting mechanism, suddenly so familiar, blinked, Channon shook himself free of the controller's mind. His own body shivered with the effort. His twelve fingertips dripped with the sweat of his close call.

He'd gotten out of there just before he'd had to witness—to be a party to—murder on a scale vast enough to horrify any Kiri. He could still feel the fierce pride the controller took in his work.

He'd gotten out of there just in time—before the actual carnage had begun. Otherwise, he'd have been a party to it. Otherwise, he'd have had to try to reach the consciousness of the Rillian controller—to stop it, to reason with it, to plead if necessary.

And he'd learned from that brief but more than sufficient contact that reaching the mind of the controller was useless. The controller would not show mercy. The controller would only do his job. As would the Rillian that must follow, if this one failed.

If this Rillian could be kept alive, there would be no third Rillian. But only Channon, in all the universe not privy to the intricacies of Rillian command structure, had the faintest notion what that meant.

The third Rillian would not be a mere controller. The third Rillian would be a different matter.

Yet Channon could not morally hope that this Rillian would end its span, not for any reason, especially not for those of Channon's safety or Channon's needs.

He now knew enough to use this Rillian controller as a negotiating tool—if only the opportunity presented itself. If he lived, and the Rillian lived, and enough humans lived to facilitate a dialogue. If, when the A-field weapon in the Rillian's hands ceased firing, there was anyplace to stand on humanity's moon, and anyone to stand there.

If.

Chapter 34

THE WAITING GAME

"Look," Sam Yates said with his head bent toward Ella Bradley and his fingertips pressed tightly together. "If McLeod's gonna make putting me in my place his first priority, then it's gonna be my priority too."

He met her eyes. Her scintillant contact lenses woke memories which, in turn, crooked a tiny smile at the corner of Yates's mouth. It was so damned hard to remember how things had been—how they got the way they were now. . . .

When they *were* the way they were now.

"Ella," he said, "I showed my ass. Some people I owe apologies. You. I'll tell you why sometime, but I owe—"

"I know what you said, Sam, and it doesn't—"

Yates flicked a hand dismissively. He glanced around the module, partly to see if there was anybody in listening distance. There wasn't.

Partly because he wanted to get out of this conversation, and it just came naturally to look for an escape route.

"Then you know," he said. "Sorry." But he wasn't so sorry he'd have given up that chance to twist a knife in McLeod, not the way he'd been feeling when he said it.

Hell, weren't things bad enough from the outside?

"Sam," Ella said, putting her hand on his upper arm. It made his whole body prickle with embarrassment. "I apologize for my part in the problem, too. But now with the future of the—"

Sam laid two fingers across the back of Ella's hand to silence her. He'd wanted to touch them to her lips—or walk away—but since she'd starting talking, he had to go on.

God *damn*, why did people think they had to talk about these things? And talk about the wrong parts of things.

"Look," Yates said, "he knows my buttons. If he's gotta

push 'em, I'm gonna react. I'll try, but there's a lotta history there that's Taylor Fucking McLeod under twenty other names, all right? I *really* want Channon safe, and no, I don't wanna die—I'm no fucking kamikaze. But he's *gotta* not push.''

"Sam," Ella replied earnestly, though those fire-opal contacts made Sam feel like he was having a deep, meaningful conversation with a pimp's hood ornament, "I'll talk to Taylor. I understand your concerns—"

Bullshit. But maybe she could cool McLeod out . . . and let Sam cycle down before he did something he'd really regret later.

"—and I want you to know"—she swallowed, twisting her hand so that she held his fingers in hers—"that we've been more than friends, you and I. If there's anything I can do to—to make this easier for you, Sam . . ."

Jesus God.

"Ella, Ella, doll . . ." Yates said, laughing because that was the best emotion to let out just now. "Look, free's one thing but charity's another, and I won't need charity while there's ten bucks in my pocket." He patted her hand and disengaged it. "Well, maybe a hundred, prices up here bein' what they are, but—"

"—the Rillian! As in any minute." A new, urgent voice jerked his attention away from Ella.

What the hell?

"—into position. *Move it, Yates!*"

Sonya was shouting. Channon was staring at a patch of wall that looked as blank as anything else in the lead-sealed science module. The Kiri's ears were pricked forward and seemed twice the size Sam remembered them being.

Sam Yates held the Tokarev, which he knew—better than anybody else in the room—wasn't going to be a damned bit of help this time around. He turned, sweeping the exit and the other people in the room with his eyes while he speed-cocked the weapon by sliding the burred hammer down his thigh, hard enough that he'd have a bruise tomorrow.

If there was a tomorrow.

"*Quint, Let's go!*" and Sam Yates was already moving, toward Channon, toward the pair of meter-square electromagnets with a core length of twenty centimeters, when the lights stuttered and a redundantly secure phone console in the corner spewed a dozen whips of violet electricity as though it were a tesla coil.

One of the crackling arms touched a technician. Sam expected her to scream, but instead she went rigid and toppled in the direction inertia carried her. An explosion in the guts of the phone bank ended *that* light-show, but a spike of blue-white fury ripped momentarily from an equipment bay and gouged across the ceiling tiles with a stench of ozone.

Yates backed toward Channon, uneasily aware that there were a lot of phones in the module, and God *knew* what other hardware tied into the mission's communications net.

And the comnet seemed to be having lethal problems just now.

"Sir!" called a technician at a computer terminal. "I got dumped! The power went out!"

Either the fellow had a lot of guts to stay in his chair, or he was too focused on what he was doing to figure out what Sam Yates just had.

"The power's not—" This, from somebody hidden behind a bank of equipment.

"Our reactor's powering the whole mission!" called a big, soft-looking redhead at a control board. His hair was long enough to spill over his lab coat except when he turned quickly; as he did now, his eyes searching for Quint, Colonel Quint, who was probably in charge of this ratfuck. "I think the—"

"Rillian comes to me," Channon said, his eyes as brilliant as Ella's and his tone just as earnest. He'd laid one of his six-fingered hands on Sonya's arms, while the other one waggled the helmet it held toward Dick Quint as the Space Command scientist's mouth opened to snap orders to his subordinates.

"Yeah, we know," Sonya snapped. "We're gonna get this crap up in place t'meet it, too."

She'd drawn her own piece, not a needle stunner this time but a military-issue Richter: 5mm, high-velocity, dual-magazine— and as useless as tits on a boar right now, except as a security blanket.

Which maybe wasn't so useless after all.

Pairs of technicians had started to push the electromagnets toward the door. The casters on which the magnets were mounted were too small for either speed or good control. Yates grabbed a projection that would do for a handle on top of one unit. The iron-cored windings were heavy, even in one-sixth g, but a couple grown men ought to be able to lug them—

"No, Yesilkov," Channon was saying. "The Rillian comes to *me*. When he stops—"

The Kiri paused, setting his helmet on a cold holotank, but Yates had heard enough. He took his hand from the magnet, feeling it slue away as one of the technicians cursed. Yesilkov had understood also, and so had Dick Quint—only the three of them—while men and women in white lab coats rushed to move the electromagnets and the necessary support array.

To where it wouldn't be a damn bit of good, unless they moved Channon with it all, as bait.

The Kiri stood beside the holotank, with one finger touching his helmet. A pseudopod flopped itself out of the helmet's face-plate and dangled like the root of an air plant among the connector cables.

Yates, Yesilkov, and Quint stood with their mouths open, Quint's tongue twisting to countermand the orders he'd just given his staff. The holotank flashed with an image as crisp as if it were graven from stone rather than phosphor dots.

"Christ, it's the power plant," Yates whispered before the others recognized the scene. Security of the main reactor was part of his job, a vulnerable part of the habitat that made him real nervous at normal times when there wasn't an alien with a death ray out to destroy the place.

He should have realized the problems weren't mutually exclusive.

The Rillian stood in a sparkling shambles that had been the reactor control room.

Everything flammable was gone. Including the crew, save for sticks of charred bone poking up out of a floor covered with gummy ash that had once been human also.

It had a reversed crossbow like that which the first Rillian used, but it was holding the weapon in contact with the—

A blue spark leaped from the hologram weapon to the hologram power-grid controls. Simultaneously in Science Module 20, a computer terminal threw out a trident of lightning to skewer the operator who'd first shouted that his unit had been dumped off-line.

The hologram shivered into darkness as the technician screamed and burned. The line dangling from Channon's helmet was now attached to the holotank's input jack, but the connec-

tion obviously depended as much on the Kiri personally as on
his hardware. . . .

''Hold it,'' said Quint, laying a hand on the shoulder of the
nearest of the men shifting the magnets. ''We'll set up the trap—''

''Right,'' Yesilkov said, turning to the red-haired man at the
module's power-control board. ''Dump everything. Break all
connections with the—''

''What the hell do you—'' Quint said.

Right, thought Sam Yates, *or more than a—*

Another phone burst into shrieking, buzz-saw circles of
sparks. This was how you drove rats nuts: random application
of terror.

*—few pieces of commo equipment were going to go. The Ril-
lian would notice the emergency generator and pulse* that *through
the main power grid.*

''Can you do that?'' Yates demanded of the frightened technician.

''Yeah, but if we do that—''

''Like *hell* we're going to—'' shouted Quint.

Yates turned as the Space Command colonel sprang toward
him.

Channon had already moved, putting his hand on Yates's right
hand. He said, ''Please. Humans not to kill humans. Not now.
Please.''

''Cut it off,'' said Ella Bradley. She turned the wide-eyed
technician back to his console. ''We have to. Or it'll all be for
nothing, all the deaths.''

Her face was very white. She and Channon were staring at
one another. Both of them were stiffly erect and shivering with
the emotions that bathed the room.

The same emotions that brought a flush to Sam Yates's skin
and brightened his eyes.

With a convulsive gesture, the red-haired technician crashed
down the knife-switch on the right side of his console. ''Well,''
he muttered, ''it's what it was designed for. Uninterruptable
power for Science Module 20 . . .''

Simultaneous fiery explosions wracked three phones and two
terminals—the pair that were tied into the mission mainframe
instead of the module's own shielded data bank. Arms of hissing
violet linked the units. In the seconds that they wavered in their

deadly handshake, they burned through partitions, equipment racks, and at least one more man in a lab smock. The survivors flattened.

All but Ella and the opal-eyed alien. Those two stood, waiting for the electrical discharges to dissipate, waiting for the screams to die down. Ella wiped her eyes with the back of her hand.

Channon put his helmet on. The dangling wire remained connected to the holotank.

"Right," said Yates to Quint as they both hunched to their feet again. The room seemed silent for lack of the sizzling roar that had dominated it. "It's changed tactics. Maybe that means—"

Channon's holotank was live again, though the power switch was clearly toggled off. The Rillian was walking out of the ruined power plant, his weapon in his hands. The creature's legs scissored so swiftly and smoothly that there seemed to be more than four of them.

Something looked wrong.

"Get the magnets set up at the door to the emergency staircase," Quint ordered flatly. "The elevators are dead now, so that's the way he'll be coming."

"Unless the shaft . . . ?" ventured a technician.

"Shit," Quint whispered. "Okay, set it up right here. In the module."

The holographic Rillian was scuttling across a holographic lunar landscape like a spider hunting by daylight. That was as it should be. *But something had been wrong before. . . .*

"Lucky," Quint said. "In the power room, it looked like this one's smaller than the first. Is that correct?"

About the size of a horse, not an elephant or worse. But that wasn't . . .

Channon was nodding, making his helmet's pseudopod wobble. "Second Rillian segment," he said. "Not so big as first segment. Worse than first segment, very worse."

The thing that was wrong . . . was that Sam Yates was pretty sure the Rillian hadn't bothered to open the power plant's doors on his way toward the habitat proper.

Chapter 35

TRIAGE

The lock-down had been Taylor McLeod's own idea, but the reality of it was already making his skin crawl. Being confined—confining himself—to the U.S. mission compound was very like wearing the same suit at all hours, every day. Uncomfortable, even with a good suit.

And this time the suit had Russian lice in its seams.

Well, that was operational expedience. Operational expedience meant that you were never quite comfortable with the circumstances; that you dealt on terms of brotherhood with people you'd sooner not have seen on the street; that you said what was necessary, knowing that it was only coincidentally the truth and *never* the whole truth.

Because you couldn't trust the efficacy of truth, anymore; just operational expedience.

"Yes, Madam Ambassador," McLeod said calmly, trying to allow for the lag to groundside so that he didn't clip the words of a woman who was already angry enough. "We fully realize the necessity of avoiding links between the U.S. mission and the damage to the United Nations habitat. We're—"

She'd paused for breath before ripping on as though McLeod hadn't tried to fill the gap with something useful—or at least mollifying.

The spreads and compression built into both ends of this communications system made the ambassador's voice sound even more like a bandsaw than usual. There were three Priority One calls stacked precariously, LEDs pulsing on the base unit of McLeod's phone—two of them from Earth, with the A com satellite nearing the horizon and no B-sat to take over. . . .

You might think she was a jumped-up anchorwoman with the intellect of a turnip. Everyone you *knew* might think that. But you didn't offend someone with a Cabinet post and access to the President's bed—unless you were as bent on career suicide as Sam Yates.

"Yes, ma'am," McLeod attempted. "We appreciate that the linked Russian involvement may be even more of a negative in the eyes of Third—"

She'd just been taking a breath again.

McLeod wondered how Sam Yates *would* handle the American ambassador to the United Nations. He sighed. Fuck her brains out in a broom closet and wind up advising the President on intelligence policy, the way Yates's luck had been going. And Taylor McLeod's luck.

The lights went out—all of them, even the phone indicators. For an instant, the only sound was McLeod's intake of breath and the faint click as shutters in the ventilating system clicked closed since there was no power for the circulating fans either.

Vivid light blazed from a distant office, blue-white but yellowed where it reflected from the hall paneling. Somebody screamed. The self-powered glowstrips in the hall flickered on.

When the arms cabinet lost power, did the locks freeze closed or open?

"Stuart!" McLeod called as he moved cautiously to his door and opened it fully.

He wasn't sure whether it was Stuart or one of the SAG's other two survivors on duty this shift. Everybody'd had to double up with the extra workload, but Taylor McLeod had been *on* ever since that ape Yates broke the news at Ella's party. Sure, he dropped a few stitches, but nobody could be at a hundred per cent all the time under these—

The lights came back on as Jim Stuart appeared at the head of the corridor. Stuart looked calm, but he was moving fast enough that his coattail lifted back to expose the holstered weapon he wouldn't need to get from the arms cabinet after all.

"Sir," he was saying, "a secure data terminal in—"

Something that sounded like a cross between a bomb and a cat fight went off in McLeod's regular office, empty now that Lucky and his babysitters were down in Science Module 20. If all the office's electronics had simultaneously shorted out, it might have sounded like that.

"—Section Alpha has burned out and injured the operator," Stuart completed, with only a half-step pause and a tick in his jaw to indicate he was aware of the snarl and actinics from the empty office.

McLeod glanced behind him. The green blip on the phone meant it was ready to go, but the ambassador and the waiting calls had been dumped before the relay kicked the mission onto emergency power.

"Jim," McLeod said, "stay right here. Don't let anyone in." He swung his door almost closed before Stuart could nod the unquestioning obedience that both knew was the only acceptable response in a crisis.

The door—like every door on this corridor of the U.S. mission—was solid titanium with a multibolt locking system. McLeod didn't dare close and lock it. Jim Stuart provided adequate security, and McLeod couldn't be sure of *these* locks any more than he could about those on the arms cabinet if the power failed again.

There was always something the SOP didn't cover. *In event of attack by aliens from another universe, doors in secure areas are to be opened lest total power failure segregate operatives in discrete locations without the ability to coordinate responses. . . .*

The ventilators remained closed and dead, proof even without the blue warning dot on each of the light fixtures that the mission was on emergency power. McLeod knew he wouldn't be able to call anywhere that required going through the habitat's normal communications net, but that was the least of his worries.

The SOP did cover reporting when it looked like this might be the last chance you or anybody in your circuit would have to report.

McLeod left the handset on the base unit, pressed his left thumb on the SEND button, and tapped out his authorization with his right forefinger. It took three seconds for the phone to chuckle, then beep readiness. Only then did he lift his thumb and stab 1* into the keypad—with unintended violence.

"Three-one-seven," Taylor McLeod said crisply. When his tongue touched his upper lip, he tasted the sweat there, but there was no nervousness in his voice. "The UN Lunar Habitat has lost all power for approximately"—how the *hell* long had it been?—"two minutes. The US mission is operating on its emergency reactor. At least one data terminal has failed—"

The quivering ambience of electricity arcing wildly—and the

sound of screams—filled the corridor. A single spark bounced through the crack between McLeod's door and the frame. It melted a sepia stain into the flooring as it cooled.

"—catastrophically, suggesting that an outside source is pulsing the communications net or power grid. I suggest that—"

There was a ground shock. The lights and phone went out—stayed out—but the dim orange of the corridor glowstrips still crept into McLeod's office.

Taylor McLeod rose and groped his way to the door.

He couldn't be sure the A-sat was above the horizon. The Secretariat staff was still arguing about whether to shift the orbit of the C comsat as a stopgap or wait until the B-sat could be replaced.

Taylor McLeod had just stuffed a note in a bottle; and he assumed he'd be dead before he learned whether the tide washed it back to lie beside his corpse.

Most of the color in Jim Stuart's face came from the glowstrips as he turned to his superior in evident relief. There were three clerks in the hallway—out of an on-duty staff of seven. One moaned while the others tried to salve a figure-eight pattern of burns across his face and chest.

Sultanian was shrieking, index finger raised, at Stuart. The Russian mathematician had been reviewing the logged recordings of Lucky; they couldn't refuse him access, and it'd seemed better to give him the data in *this* corridor than to send it to a less secure part of the mission complex.

"Sir, hardware's been blowing up," Stuart said. "Turned off, dead, it still—"

Christ, the other four members of the Commo/Encryption team . . . ?

"Mr. McLeod!" Sultanian was shouting. "I am the guy who must return at once! No buts, no maybe—"

Equipment in several offices, including both the phone and holotank behind McLeod, shorted in simultaneous ravening fury. A beam of violet light flashed through an open doorway and scored a palm-sized patch of the corridor wall.

The burned code-clerk whimpered.

"Right," said McLeod. "Has there been a report from Module 20?"

Sultanian was watching the two Americans now instead of speaking.

"Negative, sir," Stuart said, licking his lips. "Dr. Jones was going past when you called me from the checkpoint. He said he was going there."

"Right," McLeod agreed. "And we'll go there too."

"And I will come," the Russian said.

"Dr. Sultanian," Stuart said in a polite voice, "shut up or I'll shoot you in both knees."

McLeod didn't comment.

The three of them strode down the corridor. The door to the checkpoint at the hub of the mission's top security area was closed.

"Is it locked?" McLeod demanded. Of course Stuart would have shut it behind him as he rushed to his superior. . . . "Can we get out?"

"Yessir," Stuart said, "this door." He was fumbling in his pants pocket. Another shock bounced grit from the ceiling and loosened one of the wall panels. "And yessir, we can."

He slid the panel covering the electronic locking mechanism sideways and reached in with the object he'd taken from his pocket. He fumbled again for a moment in the dim light before extending a pair of three-inch metal arms.

"It's not really a key," Stuart explained apologetically as he began to turn. "It's a crank to retract the bolts. When the power is off."

"That's all right," said McLeod, pressing his fingertips together. "Just get on with it."

Sultanian opened his mouth as though he were about to speak again. Then he looked at Stuart and said nothing.

The crank stopped turning. Stuart swore as the narrow handles slipped and jabbed his palms.

McLeod reached past his subordinate and put his weight against the door. It opened against inertia and the drag inevitable from even frictionless hinges.

"Thank God," whispered Taylor McLeod as he stepped into the circular hub, scarcely aware of his two companions. The door to the Module 20 stairwell was open.

They were halfway across the hub when the paneling covering solid rock between military turf and the General Access corridor blurred, shadowed—humped into something violet.

The Rillian strode into the hub with them, his weapon raised. Taylor McLeod suddenly realized that all the training in the world couldn't give the Jim Stuarts of this world the instinct to shoot without having to think about it. For that, you needed somebody Sam Yates's farther distance back down the evolutionary scale. . . .

A dazzle of white light crackled from between the yokes of the Rillian's weapon, filling the room with a pattern as ragged as the web of a black widow spider.

All McLeod's body hair stood on end. His eyes blinked with multiple afterimages as the Rillian began to sink through the concrete-and-stone floor.

Sultanian was falling also. The mathematician bled from the mouth, but the fist-sized hole through his chest had been perfectly cauterized.

Jim Stuart's right arm ended at the wrist. His hand and the pistol he'd finally drawn were sailing toward the wall in a slow arc.

There was nothing wrong with Taylor McLeod, except that he wanted to vomit because of the stench of burned flesh that filled his nostrils.

Chapter 36

THE WON-LOST COLUMN

Thirty meters of corridor ceiling shattered in Channon's holo-tank. Simultaneous with that image, the groundshock jolted Science Module 20. Loose bits of glass and metal jingled.

"What the Rillian sends—" said the speaker on Channon's chest.

The Rillian, looking sharper than a hologram had any right to do, strode into the bouncing rubble and paused.

"—I show."

Everything around the creature vanished completely, as if it were in hard vacuum instead of the center of a subsurface habitat. When it walked forward, normal surroundings closed in around it again.

"If it's got a data link," muttered Dick Quint to himself, careless of who else could hear, "then there's more of 'em coming."

The Rillian was in an office; not in the corridor anymore. Half a dozen clerks screamed silently and ducked behind furniture. Sheets of hard-copy and objects from the desks flew up in the long, slow arcs characteristic of lunar gravity.

Quint tugged his nose with a thumb and forefinger. "If there's anything left here to come to."

A jagged white line ripped from the Rillian's weapon, awakening visual echoes from every metal surface in the office. A young woman arched up like a gaffed trout, propelled by the frozen lightning blazing from her hair combs and silver-lamé jumpsuit.

"He's not . . ." said the red-haired technician. "I mean, it isn't like the reactor control room where he really cut loose. . . ."

The Rillian ignored both the bodies and the survivors in its wake. It brushed away several desks, breaking the metal-strong adhesive that tacked the furniture to the floor. At the back wall of the office, it paused.

"Maybe he's worried about his own weapon," Quint said. His face hardened. "Lucky," he demanded, "is the intruder afraid of the backblast of his own weapon with the volume of the whole habitat to feed it?"

The Rillian's image stood alone in the holotank. The creature took a step, two steps—and a plush private suite formed around it as if the surroundings were just coming into focus.

"Rillian afraid," Channon's suit said. His helmet nodded the way the Kiri had learned to do almost as soon as he came in contact with humans. "Rillian much afraid to fail."

"I know the feeling," said Sam Yates in what was more a prayer than simple agreement.

A line of spluttering beads danced from between the arms of the A-field weapon. They bounced around the suite, igniting flammables while the Rillian quickstepped onward. The image flashed and quivered whenever one of the little fireballs should have intersected the creature which loosed it, but this time it was the background rather than the Rillian itself which seemed to vanish.

" 'Bout time t'get the noncombatants outta here, Quint," said Sonya Yesilkov, looking from the holotank to the module's door. Her hand kept dipping the Richter toward its holster beneath her dress jacket, but she never quite completed the motion.

"Noncombatants," the Space Command scientist repeated bitterly. "That's a joke."

The Rillian strode into another corridor. Its weapon swept both directions with a dull red glare that settled slowly, like a heavy gas. Humans running along the stalled slideways began to dissolve.

"Open the door here," said Sam Yates, gesturing with his Tokarev toward the module's airlock.

"What?" said Quint. "Don't be—"

"It walks through fuckin' walls!" Yates blazed. "We need it there, right?" His pistol bobbed angrily between the magnets. "The only way we got to channel it's t'leave the door open. Make it easy."

Quint gave a quick nod. One of his underlings tapped a switch to cycle open the massive portal, big enough to accommodate any equipment that fit the cargo elevator serving the module.

"Anybody who wants to leave, go ahead," Quint said in apparent calm.

A few of the technicians looked at one another. No one moved toward the door.

In the holotank was a large room with dormitory-style bunks for scores of people. It filled with dust and blood under invisible hammer blows from the Rillian's weapon.

"I mean it, dammit!" Quint shouted. "It's coming here! Get out while you can!"

The red-haired man on the control board licked his lips and said, "Sir, here we got power. Maybe a few places besides, maybe the Sov mission—" He looked at Sonya and licked his lips again. "But what the hell."

"Yeah, there's that," Quint agreed tiredly. "Ms. Bradley? I'd really rather you were not . . ."

Ella shook her head, a tiny chip of motion. She'd turned so that she didn't have to see the holotank, even from the corner of her eye. Her left hand rested on the shoulder of Channon's suit, her fingers kneading him gently.

"Then we might at least get our heads down," Yesilkov said. "So he don't take us all out when he waves hello."

"We got a while yet, Sonya," said Sam Yates. The hologram of an office interior glowed white, then began to cool while plastics and flesh burned. "Coupla minutes, maybe. Hasn't reached the U.S. mission yet."

"Yes, it has," Ella corrected emotionlessly. "That was the Academic Extension Office on Corridor BB, between 90 and 91. I deal with them frequently. They all—"

"Quint, is this hardware gonna work even if we're . . . ?" Yates waggled his Tokarev.

"—recognize my voice on the phone."

Quint nodded curtly.

"Used to recognize."

A waist-high equipment bank doubled as a counter. It ran most of the module's width, facing the door to the anteroom. It wouldn't stop the Rillian, but the creature's weapon seemed to operate line-of-sight . . . about half the time, anyhow. You use what you got, so—

"Channon," Yates said, "we better get you down in a back corner where—"

Another ground shock bounced soot and shattered ceramics from the floor.

The door to the emergency staircase beside the elevator flew open. A technician screamed.

The door should have been locked, even though the main security checks were at upper level, not down here in the module itself . . . but the locking mechanism was electronic, and it wasn't on the same circuit—

A target in the Tokarev's narrow sights.

—as the module.

"Christ, Jones!" shouted Dick Quint. "Are you trying to get yourself *killed*!"

Yates backed off the pressure on the Tokarev's trigger. He closed his mouth. It felt dry. Sonya was cursing in Russian, phrase after phrase without repetition.

"The event's headed this way!" Jones gasped. "I'm sure it is! All power and commo's been cut off up there and I couldn't warn you!"

"Right, it'll be coming the same damned way you—" Quint began. Jones entered the module, stepping between the magnets and skipping forward abruptly when his eyes understood what they saw.

"Sam," said Sonya Yesilkov.

Yates turned. Sonya was looking at Channon; Channon was looking at the module's high ceiling.

The Rillian in the holotank stood amid the guttering wreckage of the U.S. Mission's high-security area. The heads of the elevator and the emergency stairs—the latter's door swinging open as Jones had left it—were in the image, but the Rillian was facing away from them.

The ambience froze to blankness as though the creature were about to step through another wall.

There weren't any walls nearby.

"Rillian comes," repeated Channon in doleful satisfaction.

But there was a floor.

"Sonya, get'm the fuck out!" Yates shouted as the shadow coalesced against the ceiling—

Only as big as a horse . . . but a horse is huge when it's dropping out of what should be solid roof.

—and the Tokarev blasted brittle echoes around the module.

Fire, fire again. Red muzzle flashes, and only flickers from the slowly dropping Rillian, ten feet away, maybe nine. The bullets punched neat holes in the drop ceiling, ricocheted off the module's lead sheath, and key-holed back out through the ceiling in angry tears.

Fire. Fire again, fire again.

The Rillian hit the floor. One of its forefeet landed on the holotank Channon had been using, crushing it in a sputter and a mass of phosphorescent vapor, but the Kiri was gone—leaping toward the door, half-driven by Sonya's left arm around his waist.

Dick Quint and his technicians scattered in every direction. Ella jumped onto the counter, toppling backward because she was trying to face the Rillian, spread her arms, and fumble in her tiny purse for the needle stunner that she hadn't drawn before because it was so foreign to her instincts.

Trying to shield Channon with her body as he bolted toward momentary safety.

The Tokarev's muzzle was a finger's breadth from the Rillian's domed helmet. The creature should have had an odor, but only the stench of dead electronics and dead humans wrinkled Sam Yates's nostrils.

Sam fired. A computer across the module exploded as the bullet punched through circuits still energized by the emergency power plant.

The Rillian pointed his weapon away from Channon and fired, as if clearing its throat. A meter-long cone of orange light, its base on the yoke of the weapon, flashed in momentary brilliance. A microsecond later the orange cone was replaced by its reciprocal, apex to apex, white and ravening. The glare blasted a spreading tunnel through the module and thirty meters of the regolith beyond.

Sam's senses were too stunned by the blaze and roar to be certain that the Tokarev was firing, but after his third squeeze the slide locked back and the lack of recoil proved he'd felt the recoil before.

The Rillian swung its own weapon like a broadsword. A needle-narrow line, black as the heart of a dead star, slit everything it touched in an arcing plane toward Channon.

It would reach him before he reached the stairwell. It would section him like a microtome.

Ella must have fallen, because she wasn't in the way when Jones vaulted the counter to grab one pole of the A-field weapon in either hand.

For a moment, Sam Yates thought he saw the tableau reversed: the Rillian on the door-side of the counter facing Jones, and both figures hanging upside down in the air. Then there was a flash and implosion where Jones had been.

Channon was up the staircase, far enough to be out of sight; Sonya was turning with the pistol she hadn't had time to fire yet; and the Rillian's stumpy legs pistoned him with the authority of a bulldozer in the direction of his quarry.

The counter was a meter thick and packed with equipment hardened to survive nearby nuclear blasts. It flew apart as the alien struck it, headed for the big doorway and the—

When the paired electromagnets tripped, the buzz they made was almost an explosion in its own right.

The A-field weapon clanged against the magnet to the right of the door. The Rillian itself struck the other unit. The creature twisted and flattened visibly along the axis of the core—

But it stuck there, by God!

Sonya fired a three-shot burst from her Richter. The Rillian quivered as the bullets slapped sharply at hardware further within the module. She triggered another programmed burst, bracing herself against the stairwell door as one of Channon's orange-suited arms reached from behind in an apparent attempt to stop her.

Yates had a worse problem with what was happening. "Sonya!" he cried as he lurched to his feet. "Don't hit the mag—"

The Rillian's suit flattened to two dimensions, then slipped down as it lost polarity and there was no longer anything for the magnets to grip. The weapon dropped a moment later, when the computer cut power to the magnets.

The air seemed dead without the crashing sound of current reversing at high frequency.

Sonya lowered her pistol and walked forward. Channon slipped past her, intent on the Rillian. There was no Rillian, only an empty violet suit. Even that was blurring away, without the electric sparkles which had dissolved the first of the creatures.

The head of the power-board technician lay sightless in a spill of its fine red hair. The Rillian's first blast within the module had driven a cone thirty meters into the rock beyond and snuffed through anything else which chanced to be in the way.

Near the meager remains of the technician was a headless body. That casualty had been Dick Quint when he was alive.

Sam Yates stepped through the gap the Rillian had torn in the counter. Ella was rising on shaky legs. Her expression was that of someone who'd cheated death but wasn't quite sure of it yet. It was a mirror of Sam's own face.

He put his left arm around the woman and hugged her, hard enough that it would have hurt if either of them had been less numb.

Yates's eyes were watering. Partly with dust, partly with ozone from arcing electronics; partly . . .

He was looking for Dr. Jones.

But there was nothing left of the little scientist who'd figured things out just in time to save all their asses at the cost of his own.

Nothing left except memory.

Chapter 37

BODY COUNT

Once the Rillian intent on murdering Channon was killed by the Kiri's defenders, all strength of purpose in the humans bled away and divisiveness took over. There was fear. There was recrimination. There was self-doubt and paranoia. And there was mourning so intense that it made Channon stagger.

Unlike the Rillian's soul, native to a different spacetime, the souls of the murdered humans in Science Module 20 had brushed Channon's heart as they went their way. All were gone now—the male and female technicians; the redhead; Quint. Even Jones, who'd taken a different path—left this universe complete and whole, flesh and soul and all.

Channon tried to block the outpouring of grief from his human allies. His own shock helped, when he realized emotionally, not simply intellectually, they could not see or hear the clear and certain evidence of a soul's survival after death. This was the root of the fury in the warrior classes: the way Yesilkov and Yates subsumed their fear in rage and thus made something paralyzing into something energizing. But it did not make the cascade of raw emotion in the room easier to bear.

So much wild emotion threatened to drown him, to carry him with it, to make him forget all he knew of life and all he held dear: the valor of duty, the significance of willful action, the honor of right action. None of these children of the universe understood the gift they spent or the value of striving, of death as well as life, of making way for what was to come.

What came to Channon, in those confused moments after the Rillian's suit crushed it and the suit itself dissolved, was a despair as deep as the abyss and as wide as the gulf between the Kiri and human races.

These creatures had clumsily killed their best hope when their

237

crude computer-guided magnets had crushed the Rillian. They killed out of reflex. They could not be stopped by reason. Like the Rillian, they were preprogrammed entities at their core. The genetic information that had made them the ruling species on their planet overrode their volitional minds in crises. So no matter what they promised Channon, or what they believed in their tiny hearts, in the end, confronted with a threat, they could only either eradicate that threat or die trying.

The fate of the human named Jones proved that beyond doubt. Jones had demonstrated a quirk of genetic programming defined as species altruism: He had risked sacrificing himself for the survival of the group. But since there was obviously no way to convince the humans that a living Rillian was tantamount to the survival of that group, this trait—even if it could be triggered by Channon—would do him no good in the future.

In future. When the next Rillian arrived. Which it must. On the staircase, Channon sat despondent, his helmet off now and his fist supporting his chin, watching the survivors and thinking things through as best he could.

When the torrent of human fear and horror and loss abated, he told himself, thinking would be easier. Now, they shocked his nerves with their wildly broadcast energies. They were looking for culprits among the living, affixing blame and barking at each other, analyzing performance, shouting over their fear.

The smell of burned humans—dead humans—was especially noxious. It even affected Bradley, who was leaning against a wall. She had emptied her stomach into a container, and the smell of that was one more irritant, along with the roasted flesh and burned hair, the exposed intestines and excreted feces, the boiled blood and braised bone from the dead. Channon, aware that all smells were composed of tiny particles, narrowed his nostrils to slits and prayed that he would not become ill, or be forced to put on his helmet to screen the stimuli. He was much less threatening without his helmet.

No one here needed to confront an additional threat. The survivors were volatile in the extreme, goaded by the crying of the wounded, trying not to mourn where others could see.

The physically undamaged few scrambled over the wreckage of Science Module 20. Yates, Yesilkov, two of McLeod's functionaries that Channon recognized, three more men in uniform whom he did not—these tended their wounded with a black determination that was manic.

All the while Yates demanded answers to questions that only the dead scientists, Quint and Jones, or their technicians, might have understood.

And Yesilkov repeatedly swiveled her head to glance conspiratorially at Channon. She had the Rillian weapon over her shoulder on a makeshift sling that had been her belt.

But it was Bradley's emotional storm that finally forced Channon up from his seat on the step, and back into analytical mode sufficiently that he could decipher the words of human conversations, not simply recognize the tones as interrogatory or declarative.

He made his way toward Bradley, hoping to comfort her enough to stop her broadcast so that he could think. As he stepped over smoking wreckage and carefully around Quint's headless corpse, a few of the survivors' words penetrated:

"—get word outta here, Sam. I gotta call the Sov mission; there's nothin' left here—nothin' worth security shutdown. We need help from some—"

"Sonya, once we've taken care of our wounded, okay? Once we've got a body count. Once we see whether we've got a Security Directorate to represent, or it's just you and me. You wanta talk to one of your own, try and raise Sultanian. But *after* we figure out just what the hell that Kiri alien was doin' with that holotank and whether he can do it again. I gotta review that log tape. That Rillian was comin' right through the damned floor, and we got it on the record. I want to know how Channon managed to interlock that fractal geometry program with—"

Channon reached Bradley's side. "Ella Bradley," he said softly to the human female, "grief not; baby needs Bradley. Think life, not death. Death a door, Bradley. Like Rillian when go through door, can't see other side. But side there. Have heart, beating, Bradley. Alive is now. After alive, later. Be here, Bradley. Not send Channon so much pain. Work for doing, save Bradley and baby. Bradley, time let father know."

"Christ, Channon," Ella Bradley said, swiping eyes that threatened to leak fluid again, "if you tell Ting about this supposed pregnancy, now, in the middle of this, I'll never forgive you."

"Not forgive what?" He focused on her face, seeking an explanation. He found only anger and pain and fear. Perhaps it was the language barrier once again. . . . "Bradley explain why father not know. Needs to know."

"He doesn't. He's got too much to worry about. It'll distract him, screw him up. We're all screwed up enough already. Anyway, it's my choice, right? My body, you stupid alien twit. Maybe I won't have it. Maybe I won't want it. Maybe none of us will live long enough to—" Her voice seemed to be dying. It was quieter and quieter and it trailed off in a rasp.

"Bradley will live that long. Baby is; Bradley is mother. Now, Bradley. Be now." Even while trying to cheer her, Channon knew she needed more help than he could give.

"Channon, go bother somebody else. What did I ever do to you to deserve this?" Now her eyes were leaking profusely and through the liquid she glared at him as if he were her enemy. Her whole person broadcast that assessment.

He realized that in her terms, he was, finally, defined as a threat: None of this would have happened without Channon's presence here. He had forgotten, seeing how poorly they dealt with tragedy, how little they comprehended or marshaled their own reactions. Or how he, an alien, had underestimated the degree to which they were driven by competition and technological greed. Whichever, the rest would, like Bradley, eventually understand him to be at the root of their difficulties: The Rillians were here looking for Channon, and for no other reason.

Suddenly he was afraid of Bradley, of all the humans around him. In their midst, he was no safer than the midsegment Rillian had been. He said, "Bradley, listen . . . to . . . Channon with all ears. The Rillians send another, yet. For Channon. Channon say this, repeatingly. Humans not listen, not understand. Now understand. Humans cannot fight Rillians—not enough evolved. Channon go farside. Humans need not be killed by Rillians. Next Rillian must not be killed by hu—"

"The hell we can't fight them," Bradley blazed. "That's two dead Rillians, by my count. We gave them a run for their money." She palmed her mottled cheeks.

"An' about a hundred an' thirty dead humans, by a quick head count," Yesilkov said from behind Channon. "An' that's only what we've figured so far by callin' around: five techs in here, Quint, Jones, everybody at the power station, couple o' code clerks, four Commo/Encryption officers and their clerks, everybody on the next four floors who happened to be in harm's way . . .'' Yesilkov's eyes, too, were very bright. She slid one buttock onto a ruined desk's upended side. "I called up the mission floors. Found Stuart in sickbay. He says Sultanian bought it, too. So that's all the science types, gone in one hosing.'' She slapped the Rillian weapon at her side.

"Ting?'' said Bradley, loading the single word with an emotional tonnage that made Channon's chest contract.

"On his way, Channon,'' Yesilkov said. "Which is why—since I overheard and agree—I'm here. Let's go. You and me'll move the targeting zone outta here—''

"Thank God he's all right,'' said Bradley, and Channon could breathe once more.

"Yesilkov and Channon, go,'' he said softly. He reached out to touch Bradley's shoulder as the humans did to comfort one another. She shied from contact.

"Bradley,'' Channon began.

"Yesilkov, bring that thing over here,'' Yates bellowed from the far side of the ruined module.

"Which thing's that, Sam?'' Yesilkov quipped. "An' is it animate or inanimate?'' Her eyes swept from Channon, over Bradley, to the weapon she held but did not understand how to use.

Channon turned to look at Yates and saw that the big man was reloading his projectile gun, pellet by pellet. As Channon watched, Yates dropped a pellet, swore, and bent to retrieve it. From his crouch, he said, "All of 'em. I wouldn't want to lose track of anybody—or anything—in this mess.'' His expression was challenging.

Yesilkov took Channon's arm. "C'mon, you're humanity's last, worst hope, Lucky. Let's tell Sam what he wants to know about that computer trick you did so's we can get the hell out of here.'' The last statement was said softly, with a furtive glance at Bradley. "Remember what I tol' you before, Channon.''

He remembered. She didn't want Yates to know about the offer of her people to take him farside. He was learning, finally, about the human race.

Bradley said, "I'll be along when I'm ready,'' stony and tense.

Yesilkov was pulling on his arm. "Suits me.'' And, when they'd crossed the obstacle course in the middle of the room: "Don't mind her. She'll snap out of it.''

"She waits for McLeod."

"Don't we all," said Yates, meeting them halfway. "Channon, can you get that holotank working again, the way you did before?"

The phones in the room were beginning to ring.

"Show Rillian movement? Rillian not here."

"We know, Channon. But the data must have saved . . . okay, the data didn't save. How come is that?"

"Not . . . familiar . . . with terminology, procedure," Channon said. Then: "Reconstruct, okay?"

"Okay, hell yeah," said Yates, whose face finally moved from its set expression. "Come right this way, sir . . ." Yates was behaving as if something truly mitigating had just happened.

Channon reconstructed the interface and let his helmet feed the holosystem. "You save this time, Yates." He was concentrating when he said it. The data was in his suit's system—all the Rillian's log sends, plus the fractal matching he'd done to give the humans something they could view, even though it was a simulation . . .

. . . and to keep from them what they should not, as well as could not, understand. He had no interest in teaching this fierce, amoral young race about A-field weaponry, even enough to allow them to operate the weapon Yesilkov had commandeered.

When he had dumped enough data into the crude terminal to allow the reconstruction and Yates was immersed in studying the data, he toggled the cable back into his helmet and caught Yesilkov's eye. "Now?" he said.

She motioned with her hand.

They were heading toward the open door with as much consonance of intent as he'd ever managed with a human being when McLeod appeared in the open doorway.

"Hey, folks," said the disheveled man whose face was rosy with reaction to radiation he'd been exposed to earlier. "No time to be leaving the party."

Yesilkov muttered incomprehensibles.

Channon said, "Channon not needed here, go now."

"Sorry, Channon, we've got after-action piecing to do," said McLeod, his pale eyes darting around the room until they found Bradley. Channon could feel the man relax—slightly. "Yesilkov, let's see that."

He held out his hand for the Rillian weapon.

Yesilkov didn't offer it.

The two stared at each other and Channon felt the urge to move away from both. He did not. "Rillian weapon not teach humans; not work for humans. Need Rillian suit components, not have."

"My tech boys'll still make something out of it." McLeod's open hand didn't waver.

Yesilkov shifted on her feet. From the single operable holotank console, Yates came toward them determinedly, head down, shoulders hunched.

When Yates noisily kicked over a piece of wreckage, Yesilkov looked in that direction, despite the ringing phones and the muted cries of the wounded still in the air.

"Okay, McLeod, here y'are." Yesilkov unslung the Rillian weapon and handed it by one wishbone-end to McLeod. "Now, I promised Channon he didn't have to sit here smellin' the stink of the dead and the frightened, okay? Gonna be a while 'fore y'know what questions y'wanna ask, right?"

"You two go ahead, then," said McLeod. "My quarters, no stops. Copy?"

"You bet—sir." Yesilkov prompted Channon with a pat on the back. "Let's go, Lucky. You're gonna get yer wish."

Channon knew that Yesilkov was warning him not to discuss their private arrangement in front of McLeod.

But there was something else: "McLeod, talk to mate. Ask right question. New life, Channon congratulates."

McLeod's brow furrowed, but Yates was upon them, saying, "Well, glad to see there's something left of the Special Activities contingent. Lord knows we need all the Special Activities we can get, the way this last round went."

"Back off, Yates. You and I are due for a long sit-down."

"Maybe when this is all over, if we're both around to sit down," Yates said to McLeod.

Channon could feel the waves of antagonism issuing from the two faced-off men as Yesilkov guided him out the door.

At least it would be quiet, farside. Freedom from the incomprehensible internal affairs of humans was beckoning. As for the weapon, Channon would never have used it, even if he could.

BOOK THREE

THE KIRI WAY

Chapter 38

DAMAGE CONTROL

"How the fuck could we *not* have killed it, you sanctimonious son of a bitch, and stayed alive ourselves? Do I look like God to you?" Yates flared.

"I simply said," Taylor McLeod reiterated, hands safe in his pants pockets, "that you failed in your mission—which was to utilize the magnet program to immobilize the alien. Can you spell that, Yates? I-m-m-o-b-i-l-i-z-e. Maybe now you can look it up in *Webster's*, the way Lucky doubtless did. The definition neither implies nor imputes anything about taking potshots with an outdated Soviet popgun at an armored alien the size of a horse. In terms of mission definition, you shouldn't have been doing anything but standing over that program, ready to interrupt and stabilize it *as soon as the alien was in the field.*"

McLeod turned away from the single working holotank in the ruined science module. "You're shown clearly, by this logged data, as flagrantly disregarding agreed-upon mission parameters—"

Yates's white finger stabbed three buttons in quick succession. The holotank went blank. "What log? This whole program just flatlined."

"Come on, Yates, wiping data's a prosecutable offense in a situation like this."

"That isn't real data, it's Channon's reconstruction," Yates said in a choked voice from deep in his throat. "And you weren't here, so don't tell me what's prosecutable. On-site commanding officer's got some leeway, McLeod, and you weren't anywhere near on-site." Yates's pupils were pinned; his face was in full rictus.

"Yates, you're going to be a civilian when this is over," McLeod promised aloud in spite of himself. He wasn't about to argue rules of engagement with this fuse before him. Yet everyone was listening; they couldn't help it: Yates was nearly shouting.

And Ella was slowly threading her way toward them; he saw her step over somebody's headless corpse.

So he had to say something to reassure the onlookers that discipline wasn't breaking down. Once people started interpreting their orders instead of following them, you got the sort of results that lay all around him, complete with high body count, failed mission, fumbled objective.

Yates must know as well as McLeod that if they had a live Rillian captive, nobody would be scrutinizing the reasons that they *didn't* have one.

The next time McLeod gave an order he needed to know that it would be followed to the letter, not simply approximated in somebody's adrenalin-drenched opinion.

"Yates, table the aggression and demonstrate some ability to function in a crisis with more than a handgun, or I'll sideline you right now, right here." Two of his SAGs had arrived—there were six security men here now as well; follow-through wasn't the problem. "And that's not a threat, it's a warning."

"Don't push, McLeod." Yates was physically trembling now. "I'm beggin' you, man, don't push."

McLeod was running a situation log, as usual. He had to be careful. He had to be precise and appropriate and well within the bounds of legality. Which he was, he knew. He was beginning to think that Yates was fucking up for perverse, personal reasons. People did it all the time. And if that wasn't the case, then the sucker was just out of his depth. Crazy wasn't an excuse for anything, but it demanded certain countermeasures.

"Commissioner Yates, if 'pushing you' is what it takes to put a situation report together, then I'm going to push until I've got that report. Until every question is explained to my satisfaction, and hopefully to my superiors'."

McLeod didn't have enough time, personnel, or technical resources left to risk working with a spoiler, subconsciously motivated or not. And there was the problem of Yesilkova's loyalties. All in all, if Yates jumped him and thereby provided McLeod with an actionable offense, incontrovertibly logged, it might be a blessing. Yates under house arrest would allow McLeod to decouple Yesilkova.

With two less wild cards in this deck, things certainly wouldn't be any worse.

Yates started four sentences without finishing one of them: "You can't—" "I don't—" "Nobody ought to—" "If we hadn't been shootin', Ella and—"

"Ella what?" said McLeod's fiancée, joining them with an insouciance belied by her red-rimmed eyes.

Did she know that she'd reached them at a critical instant? Did she realize what she was interrupting? Even after all that had happened, was she still trying to protect Sam Yates from the consequences of his own crazy actions?

McLeod took a deep breath and let one hand emerge to steady the Rillian weapon slung over his shoulder on its makeshift sling. He hadn't gone rushing over to Ella immediately. He could see she was unhurt; he had to handle this like the executive officer he was.

Right then, he wasn't even sure if she understood that much. Or that it mattered if she did. She ran her hand up Yates's arm and squeezed, then let go. "Sam?" she said softly. "What's going on here?"

All that time her eyes were locked with McLeod's defiantly, making him wish she was still wearing her contacts.

"I'm tryin' to tell yer boyfriend it wasn't our fault that the Rillian got crushed, is all. Funny, I keep gettin' the feelin' he doesn't want to believe me."

"Taylor, I was here the whole time. If you want to discuss this . . ."

"When I'm finished comparing notes with the Security Commissioner," he said stiffly, "I'll take your deposition. Now, if you don't mind, we're conferencing."

He thought she'd flinch at the rebuff; step back; walk away; give him the space he needed. He was on the record and she, of all people, knew that—knew enough not to bring up personal considerations.

But she did none of those eminently rational and professional things. Her chin came up, her hand returned to Yates's arm, and she said, "Ting, now. I need to talk to you *now*."

"Fine. If it's a security emergency, then talk. Commissioner Yates is sufficiently backgrounded where you're concerned." McLeod moved back, the alien weapon still in hand, until he could lean against the holoconsole. It occurred to him that he

ought to take the weapon and run it upstairs to sickbay, where
he might yet find somebody with the expertise to analyze it who
wasn't at death's door. It made more sense than airing dirty
laundry in public.

Yates was looking at Ella too, with an expression in his eyes
that McLeod couldn't name, but which was healthier than the
flat, opaque stare he'd been wearing moments before.

"Channon wants me to tell you," she said to McLeod, "that
he thinks we're going to have a baby."

He waited for the rest, but nothing followed. Dear God, how
did she expect him to respond to that, here, now?

Yates was staring at her, and she was staring at McLeod, and
everybody's breathing was too labored. So he said, "Well, living
that long's hypothetical at this point, thanks to Yates and—"

"Thanks to Channon, you mean." Yates rounded on him,
shaking off Ella's grip with a shiver. "You are a bloodless bastard, you know that? Keeping that Kiri under wraps in here,
where all your best people were bound to go down tryin' to do
the impossible. That's what you keep insisting on—people doin'
the impossible. It don't work that way, cowboy. People's just
people."

"Sam—" said Ella.

"Naw, he oughta hear it. Channon ought to be farside somewhere for the next round of this, if there is a—"

"He says another one's coming, and soon," Ella interrupted.
"I think he and Yesilkov were discussing something like that,
but I'm not sure. . . ."

"What about you, Yates? Are you *sure* whether Yesilkov and
Channon have a backup plan?"

"First I heard of it, but it's a damned good idea. If you
weren't so book-and-page when you ought to be usin' your forebrain, you'd realize that."

Neatly done; no complicity admitted. "They'd better be in
my quarters when I get there." No matter that he'd been thinking
the same thing himself: Yesilkova was a Soviet national; farside
was a big place.

"Shit . . ." said Yates, and started to walk away, shaking his
head.

"Ting . . ." said Ella pleadingly.

McLeod decided to let Yates go. "What?" he answered, his
hand over his lapel mike, which wouldn't do much good, but

would do something: give him a sense of privacy he needed to talk to her they way she obviously needed to be talked to.

"Don't do this. Sam can't handle what you're throwing at him."

"Obviously."

"Then is that the point?"

"Ella," he found himself gripping the little bead mike between his thumb and forefinger so that it was buried in his flesh, "the point is to get through this alive, to use the best people most effectively in a scenario designed to save lives and meet objectives. We're running on emergency power. We've got a couple weeks' worth, even with the whole colony tied together, unless we get parts resupplied—if there's anybody here alive to resupply. If you're pregnant, I want to try to send you home, now. I'll risk whatever disciplinary measures come later, to do it. Just say you'll go if I can steal a seat for you on something that'll get you there. Every live dip Lunaside is scrambling to push the same buttons I'll need to . . ."

"Nobody's going home, Ting, and you know it. Not until this thing's settled—if it is. Maybe not after, until everyone's stories are squared. I haven't been with you this long without learning something. If you sent me, you'd have to let others go. . . . No. Anyway, Lucky trusts me."

"Lucky trusts Yesilkova." He shrugged dismissively, still holding the mike.

"Promise me you'll let Sam alone."

"I'd love to do that. He won't let me. He's still playing parallel command chain, and the result of that's all around you. He almost got you killed today, from what I saw there. You stay away from him." The last came out of him sounding like a growl.

She retreated a pace, but steadied. "If I do, you'll stop riding him?"

"With pleasure." He'd have said anything to terminate this conversation. Since he couldn't figure out what might do that, he changed the subject: "You think Yesilkova and Channon are talking about farside?"

"I think yes, from what I saw and heard."

"And you think Yates is competent?"

"You know I do."

"Yates," he called over the general low-intensity chaos, "get up to my quarters. Tell Lucky you'll take him farside as soon as he's been debriefed. Then debrief him into my study's system. Use whatever equipment and personnel you need, but make sure that if he wants to go farside, he goes under our protection—not the Soviets'—and with our best support. Take Yesilkova with you if you like, but keep her away from Minsky. Now, on the double!''

Yates came sauntering—slowly—their way, not close enough to count the pulse-beats in his throat, but almost. As he passed by, the tail of his jacket swept aside to receive the Tokarev he was holstering on his hip, he said, "Nice work, Ella."

McLeod didn't acknowledge Yates in any way; it was a point of honor, a demonstration of control, not to. He kept watching Ella's face, the way her eyes followed the rangy security man.

When she turned back to him, she said, "And us?"

Something in him relaxed. "We'll be fine. I'm going to sickbay. See Stuart and the rest of the wounded. See if anybody can make heads or tails of this." He slapped the wishbone-shaped weapon that dangled nearly to his knee. "Like to come?"

"As far as your quarters, yes. I need to be there in case Channon needs me."

"I see," he said, though he wasn't at all sure he wanted to see what he thought he saw.

If she was making a personal choice, that was—of course— her option. But whatever the emotional fallout of this mess, she was arguably safer in his quarters than anywhere else on the Moon—especially once Lucky was out of there, and on his way farside where the next Rillian was sure to follow.

They'd just started toward the door when one of Stuart's SAG boys came up with an itemized list of casualties for McLeod to sign.

Sandy's name was on it. He hadn't known that Sanders had been killed. He hadn't dreamed any particular casualty would jump out at him, make him momentarily dizzy with implications, make him sweat.

He'd considered the farside option himself, and discounted his instinct, earlier, as too difficult to justify or get others to support. If he hadn't, Sandy and everybody on the list he was holding might still be alive. He ran the back of his hand across his upper lip and said, "Go ahead, Ella, go on up. Mister, send somebody from Security with her—my quarters. I'll be along when I'm done here.''

She didn't argue or even look back.

Which was a good thing. He needed to sit down, to think for a minute, to catch his breath. With Sanders gone, where did that leave him?

In the hot seat, was where: as the highest ranking American official Lunaside. So what was so damned paralyzing about that? How many times had somebody handed him a nasty bag full of insolubles and said, *Here, kid, fix this for us*? He couldn't count that high.

But always, the missions had been survivable—if not personally, for the players, then at least nationally.

He tried to read the rest of the names on the list in his hand, which shook. There were too many he knew, and for a moment he couldn't think of anybody whose name wasn't on that piece of printout.

Then he reminded himself that Ella was safe and sound, and Stuart was up in sickbay, making wisecracks about low-bidder prosthetics, and that the competent young GS-13 who'd handed him the list was waiting for a response.

He had to sign it. He had to hand it back with a wry grin and a word of encouragement. He had to get hold of himself, shape the hell up. So what if he was the tasking officer for Armageddon?

He'd been that in practice, if not in theory, since Yates came into the UN mixer and tossed him a live grenade named Lucky.

He had too much to do to fall apart now, and no time for a crash-and-burn of any sort, let alone stress reactions. The colony power grid had to be dealt with: UN and Soviet functionaries had to be contacted; spare parts jury-rigged into a system; America's soft, high-intensity solar arrays unveiled, deployed and integrated with less efficient civilian solars. What wasn't in storage must be ordered; what hardware was on hand had to instantly become multinational property. A power-grid team, once appointed, must feel free to cobble together an entire new power plant from everybody's back pockets.

That job alone, in any less life-threatening circumstance, would have taken six months of wrangling. The call for spares currently off-Moon but accessible to be dropped—not landed— was going to go down hard among all the security-conscious nations who had personnel here, especially when the highest-ranking among them were screaming on backchannels for lift-offs.

So what was it about losing Sandy that made his guts churn? Circumstances of death, was what: Guys like Sandy died in the arms of escort-service superstars, in expensive hotels, and on golf courses. Worst case, they commandeered experimental aircraft they were too old to handle and flew them into the Arizona desert nose-first because nobody had the clout to tell them no.

When you start losing four-stars in combat, the whole universe takes one step to the left. When you're next up to bat, that same universe shrinks down around you like a stiff, new shroud.

If Ella'd been thinking, she'd have realized that this was no time to be talking about having babies.

He scrawled his name at the bottom of the printout and handed it to the youngster, saying, "So much for top-loading the heavies. Get me a roster of the newly promoted. Until Stuart's up and around, you've got his desk." McLeod let his mouth quirk and his level gaze meet the younger man's.

"Yes, sir. Thanks for the vote of confidence, sir," said the SAG officer, all grace under pressure, gung-ho and ready to please.

The kid didn't make him feel any less alone, or any more capable of defending, with the meager weapon between his ears, the whole of Luna base—and arguably the human race—from the Rillian incursion.

But then, feelings of inadequacy had never stopped him before. Only this time, there wasn't anybody else ahead of him on the high wire who had *Made in USA* on his skivvies.

McLeod still didn't think he was in shape to talk to anybody, let alone see Stuart or join Lucky and Ella and Yates in his quarters, when Minksy's call came in.

"Want me to stall him, sir?" asked the youngster he'd just field-promoted.

"Nope. Patch him here." He patted the holoconsole's top.

McLeod had no idea how he was going to handle the KGB resident. But he wasn't feeling quite so terribly alone. When you're faced with an alien enemy, even an old foe is company. If you wanted to stretch a point, you could say that McLeod's interests and Minsky's were finally mutually compatible.

Chapter 39

SHAKE OUT

"But will the weapon work for you, if we can get it back from McLeod?" Yesilkova asked Channon, who was sitting calmly on the couch in McLeod's study now that Yates had finished debriefing him into the desktop secure recorder.

Sonya Yesilkov was pacing. She couldn't help it, even with Yates watching from behind McLeod's desk and Bradley slumped against the wall nearby. She wanted Bradley to go see to her own kind, to her fiancé, to her baby's needs. She wanted Sam to leave so that she could slip away with Lucky. But Sam showed no signs of leaving and the Bradley woman was as proprietary as ever where the Kiri alien was concerned.

Yesilkova desperately wanted Channon to say yes. She wanted the weapon with them. She had orders to secure that hardware as a prime objective.

She could have the whole of Directorate 8 personnel at her disposal, whatever KGB-run Spetznaz boys Minsky had on Luna, if only she could say she had that weapon in hand.

Minsky would detail a command vehicle for Lucky's farside trip, a personal commando to massage her toes if that was what she wanted, or Lucky wanted. But without the weapon, she must wait . . . at least until she could explain why she was forming a sortie party when she had no chance of securing the weapon as a result of that trip.

KGB was not a charitable organization. Neither was it a public relations bureau. The Rillian weapon was more central to Minsky's interests than was Lucky's good will. Of course, if she could speak privately with Minsky, perhaps she'd find that view changed because of the immediacy of the Rillian threat and so many dead to prove it.

But she could not speak with Minsky, not with Bradley and

255

Yates here, and not at all from McLeod's redundantly bugged office.

She could only speak with Lucky. "Please, Channon," she prompted when the Kiri alien did not respond. "Can y'operate the weapon? Could we protect ourselves with it on the farside sortie if McLeod'll give it t'us? Fer yer use, and yours alone? We won't touch it. Ask Sam. But we need a plan. We can't just run blind, hopin' the fox'll chase us. . . ."

She was standing in front of the Kiri alien now, pleading openly. She'd have snuck away with him well before now, if only McLeod hadn't intervened, demanding the weapon where she had to hand it over. "C'mon, Channon, say somethin'."

The alien was turning his helmet in his lap. His red-bronze hands were chalky-looking, as if he had a bad dry-skin problem.

He looked up at her with those abalone eyes and his lips stretched back enough to bare fangs that still chilled her spine.

"Yesilkov want weapon; weapon useless against top-segment Rillian."

"That's why he took so long to answer you, Sonya—didn't want t'tell us that," said Yates sharply. The Security Commissioner got up and came around the desk. He put both hands on her waist and pulled her back against him as he settled onto the desktop.

She pulled away and glared at him. "Not in front of your old girlf—"

"Hush. Channon, that right? This is a clean suicide call— you, me, and Supervisor Yesilkov out there to draw fire? Then you think the Rillian'll go home happy? Leave mankind alone?"

"No, not happy. Not alone, mankind. Not suicide. All wrong, Yates. Trust Channon."

Ella Bradley burst out laughing. The sound had an hysterical edge. She choked it off and said, "Let me talk to him."

Yates put his hands, thwarted from making physical contact with Yesilkova, on the desk and let them try to choke the inanimate desktop to death. "Go ahead, sweetheart. Meanwhile, I'm ordering an executive moon truck, the one they outfitted for the Mars Observers. It'll carry the magnets an' us—just me, Sonya, and Lucky. So talk your heart out now. You got forty minutes or so, while I figure out how I'm to deploy and power those magnets once I get us there."

"I'm going with you, Sam. Ting'll support me on that," Ella Bradley announced.

"With you carryin' his brat? No chance. Even if he will, I don't want that on my mind."

Yesilkova looked between them, only slowly realizing what had just been said.

"Channon," said Sonya Yesilkov, "I'll take you by my lonesome—this don't have t'be no tourista excursion. My people'll supply some low-profile transport. I'll just call an' verify—"

"Sonya, don't pull this shit," Yates said, but didn't move to stop her as she went around behind McLeod's desk.

Her mouth was gluey: "Sam, you got troubles that's impingin' on yer abilities here. I ain't takin' no pregnant professor into a free-fire zone, not when the daddy's a high-powered spook who's real hostile t'me because o' national origin, and t'you because o' . . . whateverall. Now, I'm gonna make this call, on his damn transcripter phone, and it's all aboveboard. Minsky'll give me whatever I ask for. . . ."

As she picked up the phone, Yates leaned back on the desk and put his thumb on the base unit's disconnect.

"Sam!" Yesilkova protested.

"Smart, Sam," Bradley said, and came over to sit by Channon, taking his chalky six-fingered hands in hers.

"Yates, Yesilkov: not argue," said Channon. "All come, okay. Humans dead, too many. Too bad. Channon find solution. Not need weapon. Not need magnet; magnets kill Rillian. Channon, Rillian, talk good—"

"—story, we know, Channon," said Yates, his thumb still on the base unit of the phone. "Okay, everybody goes. Far be it from me t'argue with alien wisdom. My career's shot anyhow; McLeod so much as promised me. Takin' Ella ain't gonna make nothin' any worse."

Yesilkova could have bitten his throat out. "Obstructin' my attempt to report ain't makin' nothin' no better, Sam Yates." She started to slam the phone's handset down, hopeful of smashing his thumb in the process.

He removed the digit just in time. "Now, now, Sonya. You shouldn't be reportin' to anybody but me, I figure. Executive privilege, an' all, while I still got it. I'll find some UN higher-up to vet this, if there's a live one anywhere around before we debark. Right now, we need suits, provisioning, a logistics checklist. What do we take for how long? Conventional weapons, for my nerves' sake. You want to do somethin', get us up and runnin'."

"Yes sir, Commissar," said Yesilkova acidly, flopping into McLeod's soft, expensive chair. "Channon, how long you want to be farside? What sort of equipment will you want with you? How much food, air, that sort of thing? Extra suits? Armor? Spare generator? We're gonna set up the magnets anyhow, once we get a setup zone. . . ."

Her mouth went through the required list of questions while her mind fumed: How could Sam do this to her? There was just no hope for any of them—they deserved this.

To die with Lucky farside was so apt, so fit a punishment for all the treachery and duplicity, for all the personal disappointments so evenly distributed among the three of them, her dark Russian soul was beginning to look forward to it.

Then Minsky would mourn her. Her whole country, so long as there continued to be one, would know she was a hero of the Cause. At least, those with security clearance would know. And she would not be standing by, helpless, when the Rillian fleet arrived in a multitude to raze every living being on the Earth.

She liked the idea of heroically dying farside, striving bravely to help Lucky negotiate the impossible with the implacable, much better than the alternative of running and hiding and losing and then, at the end, dying with the rest of the cattle.

If she hadn't wanted to be more than another cow, she'd never have gone into this line of work in the first place.

Sometime during that meeting, Sam came around behind McLeod's chair and let his fingers trail in her hair. She reached up and caught his hand defiantly, right in front of Bradley, and then pressed his palm against her cheek.

She knew what he was thinking, because her body was prompting her to think the same sort of thoughts. There'd be time for a quick clutch, somewhere in what was to come. They'd make time. Both of them needed to feel a heart beating next to theirs, skin on skin—all the life-affirming actions that meant, yeah, you were human. You had feelings. You were proud and free and acting on your own, not just as an extension of some ideology, a piece of hardware that wasn't halfway hard enough.

There'd be time. She'd see to it.

Meanwhile, there remained Lucky's crazy denials that anything but air and food were needed for their next confrontation with a Rillian Channon knew to be approaching.

They'd learned not to doubt Channon, that was something.

But when the Kiri alien said, "Need Yates, need Yesilkov; meet Rillian on respecting terms," Bradley nearly burst into tears and demanded, "But you don't need me, right?"

"Represent self, Bradley. Choose course. Like Kiri. Rillian not need, but maybe Channon need. For inspiring. But risk new life? Bradley choose."

"I told you before, Channon: I'm coming."

"She ain't got no reason to be here, you six-fingered goon," said Yesilkova, trying to force Bradley out with brutality. "Her boyfriend's less than pleased with all o' us—her too."

"Shut up, Sonya, Jesus," Yates said softly, not understanding.

But Channon understood. She knew it by the way he raised his chin, the way his lip bowed back over those fangs, and the way he shook his head at her. "Wrong thinking, Yesilkov. No trick; pure truth, from now forward. Otherwise, all lose."

"Channon, can we get it straight about the Rillian weapon?" she retorted, swiveling McLeod's chair so she could put her booted feet up on his desk—and shoving Yates away as she did so. "You say we can't use it, you can't use it. But you understand it, right? Then why can't you use it? Only if we need it, of course. . . ."

"Power pack . . . transformer—energy conditioning—in crushed suit. No time, fabricate other. Not win by force, this visit."

"Yeah? Keep talkin', maybe we can figure somethin'," said Yates, interested at last in something more than suicide preparations.

"There aren't any science types left, Sam," said Ella with a quaver in her voice. "Not at the level Channon needs. And we're on a tight time-line."

"There are Soviet scientists," said Yesilkova stiffly.

"Yep, she's right, Ella. Sorry I doubted you, Sonya. Wasn't thinkin', one more time. Go ahead, call Minsky. I'll call McLeod. Tell him we got twelve hours, tops, to get outta here. If they can put somethin' together, we'll haul it out to the fire zone. Why not?"

Channon didn't realize the question was rhetorical. The Kiri alien got to his feet, came over to the desk, put his hands on his hips and thrust his head forward in a good imitation of human anger, saying: "Not need weapon of Rillian. But take, to show top-segment Rillian that have. Confrontation, this time, different level. Must let Channon lead."

"Lead's yours. Lead the meeting, if you want; lead the sortie, no sweat; lead us to the promised land, if you can." Yates's voice had a ragged edge. "Hell, you can lead my ass on a sight-seeing tour of the Kiri Unity, for all the use it's going to do me here after this is over—if I still got an ass."

From the couch where Channon had been sitting, Bradley said quietly, "You people turn my stomach, you know that? With so little time left, we should be asking intelligent questions, at least."

"Morning sickness, honey, that's all," Yesilkova snapped, and turned back to the alien.

Yates said, "Since you're comin' along, Ella, we're gonna have all the intelligence we can stand, right there beside us, farside, whether we need it or not."

Yesilkova met Yates's glance. He winked. She knew him well enough to recognize, finally, where he'd been guiding matters.

He had no intention of letting Bradley come along. Yesilkova could feel her own eyes widen as she realized it.

Yates prompted softly, "Sonya, you were going to call Minsky?" Then he turned to Bradley and said in a challenging voice: "Maybe you'd like to make the arrangements for the Mars Observer coach, Ella, since you know all those folks by name and they'll listen to you. Or do I need McLeod's clout behind me? I'm not sure he'll okay anything I—"

"I'll do it. I'll be back in half an hour," she said, not seeing the trap because Yates was that good.

Until Bradley huffed out to "Ting's bedroom to use a private phone," Yesilkova suffered under the weight of an awful intuition that Channon understood exactly what they were pulling and would say something to stop them.

But the alien said only, as the door closed behind Bradley, "Good story. Bradley bears new life."

Chapter 40

A LITTLE KNOWLEDGE

When Ella Bradley came out of McLeod's sleep chamber, Channon noticed that her cheeks were mottled and her lips were blue. She was radiating frustration and she smelled even more pungent than usual. These signs must have been obvious to the other two humans, for they fell immediately silent.

No one moved. The tableau made Channon feel as if he'd walked into some painstakingly crafted natural history display back home, until Bradley said: "I've been on hold for nearly half an hour." She sighed and raked at her short hair. "Ting finally deigned to take my call, long enough to tell me *he* was on hold with Minksy, and that if I want to talk to him about the weapon, to come up to sickbay and bring Channon."

The other two exchanged a conspiratorial glance and continued their silence. Channon sensed a subtext here, but was unsure of its significance.

So he said, "Bradley, want Channon go sickplay?"

She motioned him to get up. "That's right, Mr. Wizard. You're going to tell Ting what you think will render that Rillian hardware operational."

His helmet tucked under his arm, he followed her to the door, feeling Yesilkov's consternation and Yates's caution like physical curtains parting as he passed through them.

"Have a nice day, Channon," said Yesilkov.

"Yeah, don't forget to write," Yates added.

Bradley halted in midstride, nearly colliding with Channon as she turned to tell her compatriots, "You two . . . Never mind. Play your little games. Sonya, I forgot to give you Ting's message: Minksy'll be up in sickbay as well. If you need to know that, he said."

"Whoa, this is gettin' deep," Yates remarked lightly.

Channon didn't understand any of the exchange, which was so colloquialized as to bear little or no relationship to a word-by-word decipherment using *Webster's* as a key. But he had no doubt that Bradley's message was perceived by both the warriors as duplicity, if not an openly hostile attempt to thwart the warriors' plans.

The tightening of the bond between the two combatants was as clear to him as the rush of blood into Bradley's cheeks when Yesilkov said, "Great. Just have Channon back here when we're ready to leave."

Channon. Not Channon and Bradley.

He put himself in Bradley's line of sight, as if he could break a circuit by that means. It seemed to work. Bradley said, "Come on, Channon, some of us have to do the real work. With any luck, we'll get everything resolved sensibly up there and we won't need the Lone Ranger and Tonto."

This was totally incomprehensible.

Yates responded, "Take the security men outside with you when you go. Sonya and I can take care of ourselves. The last thing we need is you two trippin' over a live wire and McLeod tellin' me it was my fault somethin' happened 'cause I neglected to issue any coverage."

The Security Commissioner fingered a toggle on McLeod's console, speaking into it in a low voice.

Outside McLeod's quarters, two uniformed humans fell in behind them at a discreet distance. Channon could feel Bradley's reluctance to discuss anything of import with others listening.

Still, he must speak to her: "Bradley, so little time. Tell Channon what hurts."

The security guardians behind were discussing routing. One called out, "Ma'am, the second lift on your right's the best bet for sickbay."

Bradley took Channon by the arm and headed for it. "Channon, you've got to let people feel what they can't help feeling, without demanding explanations. When we want to talk about our feelings, we verbalize them."

"Not. Always not, but sometimes. Not talk emotions to mate, Bradley. Rightful parts, not said. But felt. Always felt. Makes confusions, humans."

"If you mean those two back there, that's not confusion, that's subterfuge. As for Ting, he and I'll do fine, thanks. We just haven't had time.''

"Have time now, Bradley. Maybe not have time, later."

"God, you're like my mother sometimes, you know?"

"Mother? Channon not female—"

"Oh no, no. Don't show me. I remember. I believe you." She grabbed his wrists. "We've been through all that."

The guardians came up behind them. One reached around Bradley and pushed a plaque until a button lit and the doors drew back. They all piled into the transfer lift and the same man pushed another button.

The two guardians then pressed themselves back against the opposite wall, as far from Channon as they could get, and stared at their feet.

Bradley, too, looked at hers. This was a customary place for silence and contemplation. Channon looked at his suit's toes. He, too, could use a moment of peace.

In that interval, a course of action became clear to him. To implement it, he must keep the humans from killing the third Rillian who would come here in the wake of the second one's demise. Never had a Kiri negotiator had such an opportunity. He was no longer even concerned with the message beacon that once had obsessed him. The Rillians were providing more than a simple message beacon; their own message traffic was a rescue beacon for all concerned. He need only find a way to save the third Rillian, and he could save himself as well, the Kiri Unity in all its splendid diversity, and even humanity—if he was up to the task.

And he was. His contact with the midsegment Rillian's mind had taught him what he needed to know, and more. He understood the weaponry of the Rillian enemy as had no Kiri before him. He understood the psychology and the hierarchy of the Rillian enemy as none of his kind ever had. Terri's spirit would be overjoyed, when they next met, to learn what he had learned. But because he *had* learned it, it was now incumbent upon him to use that information where it would do the most good, no matter what tactics he must employ. This new wisdom could not be allowed to die with him, where only Terri's afterliving soul would ever hear of it.

He must bring his new understanding of Rillians to the Kiri Unity. To do that, he must bring it before the top-echelon Rillian

who would come seeking him. These were no longer personal
goals; their fulfillment was worth any price. He could not let
these confuted, savage human beings destroy all hope for peace
in the civilized universe with their personal antagonisms. He
could not.

He looked to his right, where Bradley stared at the ceiling of
the lift. She was nearly leaking her misery once again.

He looked away, at the two motionless guardians Yates had
sent. In them was only the feral alertness of their kind.

Once again, he felt that he'd fallen in among wild beasts. Yet
the sacrifice of young life was not the Kiri way. Providence had
sent him Bradley, and the new life she carried, to make sure he
did not forget, did not succumb to temptation and consider these
creatures as expendable as they themselves did. Though it might
be expedient to discount humanity in the equation now forming
in Channon's mind, he could not, and retain his honor.

Therefore, he must develop a scenario in which all participants survived. Or none would. And none of these had Terri's
spirit arms awaiting them, no comfort waiting beyond the flesh.

They would kill the Rillian on sight, without compunction,
for its kind had killed their own. They were first cousins to the
Rillians in thought, if not yet in deed. He must remove the
A-field weapon from their hands, as he must remove all weapons
from the negotiating field. Their nature must be tempered by
reason or by subterfuge, before it destroyed their own hopes for
survival as well as his.

Even for a Kiri conflict-negotiator, this was not a simple task.
He needed a plan, constructed from all that he had learned,
taking into account the predilections of his hosts. When the lift
drew to a halt, he still did not have one.

Once the door opened, the guardians exited first, looked both
ways, and then allowed them to exit as well.

"No threat present," Channon said generally, puzzled. "No
need for worries."

"There's always a need for security, sir," said one of the
guardians, who stepped smartly aside at another doorway. "In
here, please."

Bradley went first.

Channon, following, hesitated.

The complex was full of punctured humans, burned humans,
humans on wheeled pallets, and humans in white rushing around,

radiating as much unhappiness as did the injured ones they
tended.

"You can wait here," Bradley told the guardians, who stepped
obediently aside and stationed themselves on either side of the
doorway, without comment.

"This way, Channon," she said and he followed her gaze as
well as her footsteps, and saw McLeod sitting by a bed at the
far end of the crowded chamber.

"Bradley," Channon said softly, "want talk? Sadness too
much, Bradley. Survival possible. Hope necessary."

She'd been one step ahead of him. Now she slowed and said
quietly to her feet, "You don't get it, Channon. My feelings are
. . . I'm disappointed. In my friends, or supposed friends. And
in you."

"In Channon?" He tapped her shoulder, signifying the need
to halt and make eye contact.

She did that, in an aisle between suffering people whose discomfort, angst, and disorientation rolled over him like a storm
tide.

"You want *them* with you, not me, farside—Yates and Yesilkov, and their killing power. If all you said were true, you
wouldn't be opting for firepower over brainpower." Her lip
curled. "So you lied to me, Channon—all the way along. This
Kiri Unity of yours is no better than the damned UN. Or I was
hearing what I wanted to hear, not what you were saying."

"Need Yates and Yesilkov, show Rillian, only. No lies you,
Bradley. By honor of Channon's family, no lies yet."

She peered up at him. "I probably believe you because I want
to believe you. But I'm always believing in the wrong ones: I
believed in Ting, and Yates, and even Yesilkov—that they'd do
the best they could under pressure . . . the right thing, if you
will."

"Channon will."

She made a sound and took his arm. "That's not what I meant.
I know *you* will, but they won't. Come on, Ting's seen us. And
that's Minksy, the pale-haired man with him. Be on your best
behavior in front of Minsky."

"Bradley warns," he ventured, "because not best behavior,
Yates and Yesilkov?"

"I thought they were my friends. We'd been through so much
together. . . . Nobody likes to be betrayed—to find out conven-

ience, not loyalty, is at the heart of a relationship." Her voice
shook. "It's ethical differences, Channon. You ought to be able
to understand the principle, if not the specifics. I . . . wanted
so much to go through this with you, to help, to learn, and
nobody cares anything about any of that, just point-averages and
personal play-offs."

"McLeod tries save everything . . . whole settlement: not blame
mate. Yates, Yesilkov: warrior class, reflex-driven. Bradley
want . . ." He sorted through *Webster's* in his mind for a suitable example. " . . . pig to fly. Pig not fly. But pig not bad.
Pig, pig."

"Phew. Channon, please stop making me ashamed of myself.
We've got a bear and an eagle waiting up ahead. Maybe I'm just
resentful that nobody thinks I'm making any significant contri-
bution, not even you."

"Bradley only sign of hope, whole race, Channon sees," he
said truthfully.

'Oh great, that's terrific. Don't tell Ting that." But her shoulders straightened as they came through one aisle of the wounded's beds and turned down another, at the end of which waited
McLeod and the paler Minsky, beside a damaged man sleeping
in an electronic nest.

"Tell Ting, Bradley, all truth, should."

"God, Channon, not with the Soviet resident right beside
him." Again Bradley slowed. She turned and said with clear
desperation: "We're bad little humans, factionalized in your
terms, suspicious and surrounded by enemies you can't distin-
guish—I understand that. You take my word that Minsky is one
of those enemies, friendly only to Yesilkov, and that's stretching
a point. Don't offer any information unless Taylor asks for it.
Follow my lead."

"How else?" he wondered, and let her guide him down the
corridor marked off by beds. He knew precisely what she was
saying. More, he was in accord: He'd decided in the lift to with-
hold as much data as possible while still securing cooperation.

Yet among all these broken humans, it was well that Bradley
had reminded him. Serendipity at work. If all these perished,
and their homeworld was saved by their sacrifice, history would
consider it a victory. Channon must try to attain such a per-
spective.

"Friend Bradley," he said in the last moment before McLeod

and Minsky would be able to hear, "Channon has respect, honor, heart-love for Ella Bradley, Pee Aitch Dee. If humans saved, you did, not Yates did, not Yesilkov did. Bradley teach Channon what works, humanwise."

He bent down and kissed her on the forehead as he'd seen McLeod do.

She broke stride and McLeod rose immediately, coming around the bed, hand out.

For a moment Channon thought that the human was angry because Channon had laid lips on his mate. But then the expression on McLeod's face made itself clear: a pleasure smile, not a fury smile.

"Well, aren't we cozy? Channon, Ella, you've both met Comrade Minsky before. Stuart's pretty doped up, I'm afraid. . . ." He motioned to the mutilated human who had only a bandaged stump where a hand should be, and who was sleeping soundly amid machines monitoring his bodily functions.

"*Privyet*, comrades," said Minsky, coming to the foot of the bed, his own hand extended for Channon to clasp.

He did what was expected of him, and flesh-to-flesh contact jolted Channon with the depth of Minsky's distress—and caution, and acquisitiveness.

"What's this about, Ella?" McLeod said.

Channon knew that McLeod knew the answer, but wanted a different thing said aloud.

Yet time was short. Before Bradley could respond, Channon said, "McLeod, need farside transport. Need Yates, need Yesilkov. Yesilkov needs Rillian weapon. Yates needs magnets and power source. Go farside now, McLeod. No time for games playing with comrade."

McLeod chuckled and Minsky stroked his chin. "How long did it take you to rehearse this, Undersecretary McLeod?" said the pale human called Minsky.

"Not my doing, Oleg—honest. Ella, is this the whole agenda? We're trying to put a power-station working group together, in case there's somebody left alive up here next week to bitch if we haven't got one."

"Uh . . . I believe Mr. Minsky has spoken with Yesilkov on this, from your office as a matter of fact." Bradley looked unwaveringly at McLeod.

It was as close an attempt to utilize ELF information-gathering techniques as Channon had ever seen between humans. The mates watched each other as if no one else was present, hearing and seeing with all their might.

After a lengthy pause in which the wounded Stuart groaned and shifted, McLeod said, "Oleg neglected to mention that. We're short on time. You said something about the Mars Observer coach—it's yours, Ella. I've cleared it. The weapon you require, Channon, will be in the coach when you get there. We're still examining it for our records."

"And then, of course," said Minsky, "*we* must examine it for our records. It was acquired by the joint efforts of our . . ."

". . . two nations, Oleg. We know. Nobody's arguing. Especially when you've got more live techs up here and we're data-sharing the intelligence."

"Channon need weapon for Yesilkov," said Channon.

Minsky lowered his head. McLeod made a soft noise in his throat. Ella touched Channon's arm. "Yesilkov needed to make sure Minsky saw it, Channon. He's going to see it. We'll just tell Yesilkov that and she'll be happy."

"Not," Channon predicted. "Minsky not happy now. Yesilov, Yates not happy. Channon take Rillian weapon farside: show Yesilkov, show Yates, show Rillian. Friend Comrade, A-field not good for human warriors. Winner is all, or none, of race."

"And if, my friend from outer space, *alienski*, the Rillians you led here attack the Earth—then with what will we defend ourselves? You owe us a fighting chance—the key to this technology. Comprehension of a technology guarantees an eventual counterforce."

"Don't get doctrinaire with him, Oleg. It's useless. I've tried. Channon doesn't understand A-field himself. He says the Kiri don't use it. Isn't that so, Channon?"

"Kiri not use," said Channon, avoiding a response to McLeod's earlier misrepresentation. "But Channon show Rillian—give Rillian weapon back, Rillian." Once, he had not understood the A-field technologies. Since he'd entered the mind of the Rillian controller, he understood enough to know that those of the Unity who had resisted developing it were right. Without A-field mechanics, species so disparate as Rillians and Kiri would never have encountered one another. The universe had divided itself into dimensions and kept those dimensions separate for good reason.

Yet now that the greatest sea between cultures had been crossed—the energy sea itself, where time was manifold and the speed of light was no longer a determiner of what species could coexist in a spacetime—negotiators like Channon had before them the greatest challenge life had ever faced.

Could beings with so little in common coexist? More to the point, on what grounds could they try to form a framework for negotiations? Without A-field mechanics, the Rillians would have been locked into their bubble-universes, and the Kiri-type in theirs.

Looking at Minsky, so anxious to have a weapon he understood only as uncounterable in his hands, Channon knew he must explain. This would be his last chance. He said, "Minsky, friend, listen: Channon say good story. A-field opens air to fish for living in; opens eyes of moles for seeing. But not make natural. Humanity very young, very angry, very intolerant—like Rillians. Need learn not to kill different life. Too late for alone learning; learn now where all life sees. Explorers, you. Explore selves. Make readiness. Kiri Unity protect young life. A-field opens . . . places, spacetimes, options . . . unfit for human life."

"That's a waste of time, Channon," said Bradley very softly. "Even Ting wants it more than anything else."

"Very interesting, Mr. Channon," said Minsky. "But we must protect ourselves from these aggressors. You see what helplessness before such an enemy leads to. . . ."

"Channon make peace with Rillians. Why here. Why Rillian come."

"Right," said McLeod with a quirk of his lips. "We've noticed how peaceful this negotiation's been up until now. Channon, we've got work to do. If you don't have anything constructive to add, we can do without the lecture."

"Not lecture. Knowledge."

"A little knowledge is, as the Americans say, a dangerous thing, yes?" Minsky said, and sat on the edge of the white bed where a maimed man slept under electronic guard.

The smell of blood and trauma was beginning to make Channon dizzy. "Rillians dangerous, yes. Humans dangerous, yes. Kiri not dangerous. Kiri welcome humans, someday."

"If we don't build these weapons, right?" McLeod was struggling to understand, but disappointment and bitterness radiated from him. "Someday, when we're older and wiser."

"Not get old and wise with A-field shooting one another."

"That's it," said Ella. "Enough. He won't—or can't—help you with your tech problems. He needs the weapon. He's got to face another Rillian. If either of you two were in his position, it'd be name, rank, and serial number only. He's done more for us than we have for him."

"Yeah, I was hoping somebody'd come along and get a couple hundred of the lunar residents killed. Leaves more for the rest of us," McLeod said, crossing his arms and watching Channon steadily.

"Channon admit responsibility in deaths. Channon want going farside, from earlier. Channon fix Channon trouble. Humans fix human trouble as good."

"Ting . . ." Ella's hand was on Channon's arm now. "He thinks we've got a time pressure. If you and Mr. Minsky are concerned about additional casualties, you ought to let us get started."

"No one, Comrade Bradley, is holding you here." Minsky got up from the bed. "We will have the weapon in your coach within the hour, Channon. Or should I say Ambassador Channon? Know that the greetings of the Union of Soviet Socialist Republics are extended to you, personally, and to your people, and to the Rillian people if, as you hope, you are able to open a dialogue with our mutual enemy." His eyes glittered. "And if you should, we will expect reparations for the Soviet citizens' families and the Soviet property destroyed here during this conflict, of which we were never a part. Information on A-field weaponry, merely enough to protect us against future such incidents, will be considered by my government payment in full."

"Mine too, Channon," said McLeod, "if you're alive to start handing out favors. Meanwhile, Ella—you're got whatever you want. Tell Yates I'm working on the magnet situation. We'll have them loaded on the coach. I'll figure something for a power source—feed you from the A-sat, maybe. Now, if that's all . . . ?"

Ella pulled Channon away, making polite noises at the other two, once McLeod had dismissed them.

When they were out of human earshot, Bradley said, "See? I told you. It's hopeless. All they care about is killing power. All of them. And I'm just as bad: I didn't even bother to see how poor Stuart was doing . . ."

"Not hopeless, Bradley," Channon reached down and pressed his palm against her still-flat belly.

"Channon!"

"Life cares about life, Bradley. Afraid, is all. Big fear of death; big fear of suffer. Big fear of Rillian. Channon fix. Rillian never come here more. Channon promise Bradley's unborn."

That much he was sure he could deliver to this benighted huddle of hairless apes staring fearfully into the black and starry night.

Chapter 41

SIGHT PICTURE

There wasn't any lack of ways to feel trapped. . . .

You could watch an elephantine Rillian pivot toward you with a weapon that had already devastated much of the habitat you were supposed to be guarding. You could live with a woman who snapped at you every time you failed—and was twice as vicious when you told her about your successes. You could lie at the edge of a jungle trail, lit only by muzzle flashes as guerrillas left their ambush positions to police up weapons and to finish the moaning American wounded.

Or you could stand in your quarters, looking forward to a future in which Taylor McLeod made it his business to ruin you personally and professionally.

As he could do.

As he would surely do.

"Sam . . ." said Sonya Yesilkov.

"Don't mean nothin'," murmured Sam Yates as he turned to the holotank in the alcove that converted his kitchenette into a home office.

"Sam . . . ?" Sonya repeated, stepping closer to him as worry dimmed her determinedly bright expression.

"Holotank," he ordered, "ARAM star, messages," but he stretched out his left arm for the woman's embrace. He knew what she wanted, needed, now that they were finally alone. He'd take care of it the best way he could, because she'd earned it; because she was as close to a friend as Sam Yates had in this universe; and because it was nice to think that in all of this, *somebody's* needs were being serviced.

What Sam Yates needed was a hole he could pull in over him. This time there wasn't one. Nowhere at all . . .

"Look, big fella," Sonya was saying, "if you don't wanna—"

but the gentle force with which he drew her softness closer silenced the rest of her protest. She deserved better; but hell, they all did. Even Taylor McLeod deserved better, if you wanted to look at it the right way.

Yates nuzzled the woman, keeping his eyes on the data scrolling up the holographic display. His dick had shrunk to the size of his little finger, but that was something he'd take care of when he put his mind to it. The people who thought fucking was something bodies did all by themselves weren't very good at fucking. . . .

Messages from frightened people—chiefs of mission, Secretariat honchos . . . Security staffers who didn't know Sam Yates wasn't their boss any more or didn't care, just wanted somebody to hold their hand while they were feeling trapped.

"Oh, Jesus," said Sam Yates softly, as one of the message slugs penetrated the brown dome over his mind, as neither the others nor Sonya's insistent hands had been able to do. He kissed the woman firmly on the lips, then leaned his torso back and said, "Sweetheart, I've got to check this one. Now."

To the holotank, he continued, "Holo, run contents of File Jones HD."

"Right, Sam," said the woman as she disengaged herself. "I'll just—"

"You'll wait right here," Yates said, gripping Sonya's wrist so that she had to face him again, despite the expression she couldn't blank and the glint of tears in her eyes. "Because you're all I got in the world, Sonya . . . and because if Jones did what he figured he could, there might just be a world for us'n everybody for more'n the next twelve hours."

As he spoke, he guided Sonya's hand to his groin. Her eyes widened, though it shouldn't have been a surprise. There was nothing so exciting—in all ways—as a win when you didn't think there was a prayer of winning.

A chance to win, anyway. A chance for the world, though not for Sam Yates.

The orange-amber letters in the holofield read:

Commissioner:
70% probability the rhenium in the glowstrip power pack
was the key. Full breakdown appended. Suggest plating pro-

jectiles by vacuum deposition—thickness of coating insig-
nificant. Good work and good hunting.
Jones

The message was followed by the schematic of a glowstrip
and a mass of figures that would have meant nothing to Yates if
he'd had a lifetime to study them. That was part of Jones's job,
and the little scientist had done it perfectly.

Sam Yates's job was to kill Rillians, and Jones had just given
him a way to do that without trusting to luck or prayer.

"I don't get it, Sam," Yesilkov said. She didn't have the context, the question that Yates had to put to Jones—and which
Jones was answering three hours after his death. . . .

"Shoot," Yates muttered, blinking because his eyes suddenly
stung and blurred. "He was a sharp little bastard, you know?
I'd have backed him any day."

He reached into a drawer and—very carefully—handed a very
sharp knife to his doubting companion. It was substantially
sharper than any knife Sam Yates was likely to need for the
preprocessed foods that passed through his personal kitchenette.
"Sonya," he said, "could you pry loose one a the glowstrips in
the hall for me? Their batteries're plated onto the backs."

"You bet, Commissar," Sonya said without inflection. She
strode to the door, picking up a chair in her free hand as she
went; she wasn't tall enough to reach the corridor ceiling unaided. Her face gave the benefit of the doubt—not to her boss's
sanity, but at least to the question of whether he was imminently
dangerous.

Yates had the laser drill—which he'd borrowed without explanation from Utilities Division two days before—set up on the
kitchenette table by the time Yesilkov returned. She held a
glowstrip; flecks of ceiling paint dusted her grim expression.

The strip was two meters long and twenty centimeters wide,
with edges which were almost knife-sharp themselves. She'd been
lucky not to carve herself good when it flopped loose unexpectedly, especially since she'd been squinting against the flurry of
paint chips.

"What the hell's that?" she growled to Yates as he started to
thumb long copper-washed cartridges out of the Tokarev's magazine.

Sam set the first round in the drill's integral vise and tightened it down. A protective shield covered the workpiece, but the hologram that sprang to life above the unit showed the tip of the bullet magnified thirty times. Sighting cross hairs were centered on the polished nose.

"Remember when that Marine blew the glowstrips outta the roof?" Yates muttered as he stroked the control knob forward. "Jones figures it was the rhenium in their batteries—dust, vapor, whatever—that coated the Rillian's suit and—you know, held the Rillian long enough to let bullets get through."

The unit whined at two levels: with the sound of high-frequency relays operating, and the softer purr of the fan beneath the shield sucking away vaporized metal. The sighting hologram didn't show the miniature laser beam that spurted from the drill-head, but a precisely controlled cavity grew in the workpiece.

"So if we put rhenium on the bullet," he continued as he slipped the hollowed round out of the vise and replaced it with an unmodified one, "maybe we don't have to wait around for somebody with a plasma gun to do the wrong thing at the right time. . . ."

The drilled tip was warm but not hot. Sam spat on it anyway to be sure it wouldn't cook off. He had only seven rounds; and anyway, even though the bits of flying metal were unlikely to really harm him or Sonya, they didn't need loud surprises.

Sonya took the cartridge from him. "Okay," she said as Yates bent over the drill again, "how we gonna get the whatium on the bullets, Commissar? Vacuum-plating, your late buddy says?"

"We're gonna scratch the hollow points over the back of the strip and hope the edges of the steel jackets gouge out enough rhenium to do the job, doll," Yates replied. He handed her the second round and set the third in the vise with his left hand. "Here, spit on this, will you?"

Yesilkov leaned over the sink and ran a trickle of water from the faucet, enough to quench the warm metal. Quick and dirty; but it just might work—there couldn't have been much of the crap in the air when the first Rillian bit the big one.

The woman's short, powerful fingers scraped the round across the glowstrip, chiseling a sheen of silvery metal over the bullet's jacket of copper-coated steel.

"So we kill Bugger Number Three," she said, her eyes on Yates's face. "And then what, big fella?"

He drilled the third round and reached for the fourth. "Then

I go look for a job downside," he said without emotion. "Maybe private, maybe . . . a lotta police forces still like t'hire veterans, you know. I'm not real fussy."

"Not gonna fight'n stay here, then?" Sonya demanded challengingly while her fingers fed the round with—maybe—a rhenium coating into the Tokarev's magazine.

"You don't fight the ones you can't win!" Yates snarled, a sudden flash that proved how thin were the sidewalls separating anger from the box holding his present calm. "He—"

His face calmed as abruptly as it had broken into rigid planes.

"Sorry," muttered Sam Yates. He looked back down at his drill, his hands splayed on the table, and then completed the operation on the third round. "Sonya," he continued quietly, "if it was in-house, if it was me'n some bozo in the Secretariat who wanted my ass—maybe."

His fingers swapped rounds in the vise. Yesilkov raked the drilled pair across the glowstrip, one and then the other, her motions mechanical and as emotionless as her face.

"But I'm not just Commissioner of Security for UN Headquarters, I'm an American citizen," Yates said. "If my own government asks for my head on a platter, that's what the UN'll give 'em." The anger returned for just an instant, the quiver of lightning across a summer horizon. "Who's gonna go t'bat for me, sweetheart? Minsky?"

"McLeod ain't the whole USG, is he?" the woman asked her hands as she plowed the nose of the fourth bullet down the glowstrip. The thin metal trembled on the table with the sound of distant thunder.

Sam Yates turned and put a hand on Sonya's cheek to raise her face to his. "Taylor McLeod's the only part of the U.S. Government that cares about Sam Yates one way or the other," he said softly. "He'll get what he wants because there's nobody who'll take the *time* to get in the way of somebody as high as McLeod and as mad as McLeod is on this one. And anyhow . . ."

Yates's lips brushed Sonya's forehead. She lifted herself to return the kiss. "And anyhow . . ." Yates murmured a moment later into her short blond hair, ". . . McLeod's right. When the Rillian came, I did what I knew how to do—instead a'what he told me my job was. Disobeying orders in the face of the enemy. Hell . . . your people'd"—he nuzzled the base of her neck—"let me hold one in the back a'the neck."

"You need a truck outta here fast?" the woman whispered, her whole body tingling from the touch of his lips and the doubled images he'd just triggered, love and death. "If—if that's the choice, I can maybe arrange it. . . ."

"Oh, McLeod won't shoot me," Yates said, vaguely amused. She was wearing a dress rather than a skirt and blouse; he massaged her breast through the soft fabric. "That'd be uncultured. He'll just let me—"

"Sam," Sonya said, tilting up her face and pinning his hand firmly against her beneath one of her own.

"—twist."

"You know Ella pretty good," Yesilkov said in the tone she'd use to discuss something important, like the title of a report due to go before a standing committee. "Look, if that's what it takes—"

Yates was shaking his head, smiling with his mouth and his eyes . . . and then with his mouth alone as bleakness swept back over the surface of his mind. "Naw, that's all right," he said with only a slight catch to the words. "Naw, I thoughta that, but she's not gonna change his mind—not this time, not ever. And I thought—"

He paused and hugged Sonya again, but with the gentle pressure of kinship rather than lust. He just wanted her to be looking at his shoulder instead of his face as he continued, "And I thought I'd do it—I'd fuck her, because that I could manage, you bet, poor pitiful Sam. And he'd know but he'd never do anything, say anything, just know it for the rest of his life. And I didn't do that—"

Yates leaned back again so that the woman could see his bright smile, neither wholly forced nor wholly sincere. "—because Ella's a nice kid, and because that's not what fucking's for, and because—"

He reached down for her groin. She spread her thighs greedily.

"—you're a lot better in the sack anyway, doll."

"You're a goddam crazy bastard," Yesilkov grumbled as she reached for the closure strip beneath her left sleeve, "but I guess you're my kinda—"

"And I'm not going to blow McLeod away, either," Sam murmured in her ear as his fingers fluffed her skirt higher to get beneath it.

Yesilkov froze. "I didn't ask . . ." she said, eyes closed and no muscles but those of her mouth moving.

"Yeah, but I didn't want you to get the wrong idea," Yates

explained calmly. "Maybe help the wrong time, you know? It's okay. I'm not going to try'n arrange a tragic accident, him catchin' a round meant for Rillian Three, whatever."

"Sam, I didn't *ask*!" Sonya repeated, meeting his steady gaze fiercely.

"I'm telling you anyway, doll," Yates said. "And I'm tellin' whoever's listening to the bugs CIA, KGB, and probably the UN Janitorial Service have plastered all over my rooms by now. So you know I mean it. The only thing is—"

He swept the room with his smile.

Sonya felt his body stiffen. She glanced around, thinking the threat was external, but there was nothing except what was in Sam Yates's mind.

"—I'm not going to have a lot then t'lose. So Taylor baby'll believe me"—Yates's voice was as cold as the sword in the hand of a corpse—"when I say that if he tries to come down on you too, I'll find him and I'll kill him."

"Shit, Sam," the woman whispered against his shoulder.

"It's no sweat," he said, soft now and trembling. "It won't happen. I just needed to get real clear, 'cause that sort, they don't always hear what people like me say, y'know?"

Sonya was blinking at tears. Her mouth pursed, but there were either no words or far too many of them for her to speak.

"Hey, don't mean nothin', doll," Yates said, bending to kiss her gently. "Chances are the next Rillian's gonna solve everybody's problem—McLeod's and mine and all of us."

Yesilkov slid the dress closure down, letting the silk chiffon gape open. "If I'm such a great lay," she said without meeting Yates's eyes, "then how come we're not fucking?"

"Well, I got the brass band laid on fer a little later," said Sam Yates as his hands rolled down her transparent bandeau without bothering to completely remove the dress beforehand. "But sure, I'll see what"—he bent—"I can do."

"Say, doll . . ." he murmured a few moments later, "you want your bullets drilled too?"

He smothered his laughter in the welcome flesh of her breast. After a time, Yesilkov began to laugh also, though her chuckles were interspersed with Slavic curses.

Chapter 42

FINAL APPROACH

The Rillian commander received news of his controller's destruction with regret—not for the controller who was, of course, expendable, but because the commander must now deal with whatever was good at killing Rillian shock troopers and reaction controllers.

And he had to leave his game. He put down the dice he'd been shaking just in time: The automated sequence kicked in and his body kicked out of its staging spacetime.

His ready-room disappeared in a blink. The data feed in his helmet was full. His orders were systemic. He knew exactly what to do, though he'd never known anyone who'd had to do it before.

His name was Komida and he was a master. His solution needed no higher authority; his was the authority to speak for all Rillians, on-site, as he willed.

Life or death of a race hung in the balance. The Rillian hegemony was at risk. He would do what he needed to do.

As his senses reeled and his suit micronics spat him into the same jump coordinates that had received both soldiers under his command, he was aware that he trod in the footsteps of the dead.

The moon below him was dead here. The surface was lifeless. The indigenes lived below ground, some distance away.

He drifted slowly onto the surface, tapping his belt-computer to calibrate his suit to this spacetime so that the regolith here would be solid to his suited feet. No use sinking into muck.

He was not a trooper; he was not a controller. He was a master, a commander. He would do as he saw fit here.

No Rillian of his rank could admit to fear, but Komida could admit to consternation. There were few guidelines for a situation such as this.

One made history for the first time, and one must be ready.

He went about establishing a base camp, snapping components off his belt and aligning them in this spacetime with adroit taps of his dewclaw. He paced off his perimeter with all four feet hitting the ground in rhythmic, calming strides. Then he sat in the clear bubble of atmosphere he inflated, thinking.

One did not wish to make an error. One must not bring shame—or destruction—upon the Rillian armada. This might be some Kiri trap. The Eleveners might have purposely drawn the Rillians to this spacetime, where they had a secret ally, a monster race of horrible strength and aspect, waiting.

Or it could be simply luck. The Rillian commander must analyze his situation, his enemy, and then draw the Kiri negotiator to him. That was still a priority.

The Kiri quarry, at least, was a known quantity. Its allies were totally unknown.

The Rillian commander set up his single-station listening post and settled in to think. He had the entire controller's log to review. Then, if he had not already been discovered, he would let the murderers know that he was here.

He wanted, suddenly, to groom himself all over—to bite his fur, to chew at the tough, scaly skin between his clawed fingers, to gnaw the leather of his hind feet. He wanted to defecate, too, and to urinate along the perimeter of his station: to mark his turf.

This was the first Rillian station in this repulsive excuse for a spacetime. If the Kiri negotiator lived to step inside this perimeter, then the horrid-looking Kiri enemy would be on Rillian territory.

The very thought of smelling a Kiri next to him was enough to make him want to howl. But he did not. He had work to do. He had a plan to construct. He had a decision to make that would change the course of Rillian history, however he chose.

What was this formidable race which had destroyed a trooper and a controller bred for centuries to be unstoppable? What was this new and diabolical union between the Kiri Unity and a slow-moving race of whom no one knew anything?

The commander, who was named Komida like his father before him, knew that death was here. The whole place reeked of it. But there were options, beyond a planet killer rigged to explode with the cessation of his heartbeat.

There were options.

He must only find them.

Perhaps there was some key to this dilemma in the controller's log. He began to view it, settling into a comfortable position on the rock. Having slowed his biology to match the situation, he must now do the same with his mind.

The accursed Kiri conflict specialist was out there somewhere, alive, laughing at him.

He must develop a response, or the response triggered by his death would obliterate this entire gravity-well and everything in it.

Chapter 43

BLOWING SMOKE

When Ella Bradley and the Kiri alien got back from sickbay, Yates didn't waste any time. He'd made up his mind; gotten things straight with Sonya the best he could; he had his rhenium slugs. The last thing he needed was to sit around wondering if there was a better way to do what he had in mind.

If the cliff between you and your objective was there yesterday, it'll still be there tomorrow, so you might as well jump now and avoid the stress points.

"Ella," he said, "McLeod sent somebody by just a minute or two ago to say he needs you back up in sickbay—alone. Somethin' about not being able to talk when Minsky was there and the phones being dicey." The baldfaced lie sounded plausible enough. He just had to hope Sonya would go along with him, even though he hadn't exactly warned her—and that Channon wouldn't flat-out call him a liar, if the Kiri do-gooder was as smart as Yates thought.

Channon looked Yates straight in the eye and blinked like an overgrown owl.

"Damned bureaucrat," Ella Bradley said, "I knew that wasn't the whole of it. Look, before I go: Ting promised he'd let us know as soon as the Observer coach is ready. He's working on a power source for the magnets; he'll have the Rillian weapon on board."

"Great," said Supervisor Yesilkov. "When'd he say that'd be?"

Yates held his breath. *Did* Sonya realize what he was doing? More to the point, did she agree that leaving the possibly inoperable Rillian weapon and the probably unpowerable electromagnets was a good choice, so long as that meant they could leave Ella Bradley here, too? The math went: Subtract Bradley and you'd be subtracting worry about a pregnant female non-combatant, as well as McLeod and any number of hidden agendas, plus bureaucratic oversight. The sum of that equalled fifty per cent added to the survivability of their mission, by Yates's estimate. If the Rillian really only wanted Channon, maybe there was hope yet. If not, there were the rhenium slugs in the Tokarev. . . .

"Ting *said* as soon as he could," Bradley replied to Yesilkov in a sharp, defensive tone and crossed her arms.

Channon was staring a hole in Yates's chest. Sonya was picking at lint on her breast pocket.

Nobody spoke to Bradley's comment. Nobody moved. Yates could see the whole scenario flushing right down the toilet. God preserve him from women: You couldn't live with 'em; you couldn't shoot 'em.

The truism didn't cheer him. He knew without doubt now that Sonya had tripped to what he was doing; he could only hope she'd play along.

Finally he threw a prompt into the silence to see what would happen. "Well go on, then—go see Our Leader and find out what the hell he wants, Ella. If it's some damn excuse why he can't deliver any or all of what we need, let me know right away. If we're not here because you took too long, we'll be down lookin' over the Observer coach."

Now, for sure, Yesilkov was clear as to what the agenda was. Her head came up. She looked squarely at Yates and opened her mouth.

Before she could verbalize whatever it was, Channon spoke up: "Hurry, yes, Bradley. Rillian make self home, farside. No wasting time. Channon go Rillian, or Rillian come Channon. . . ."

"Here? Now?" gasped McLeod's fiancée. "Why didn't you tell me that before? Never mind. I'm going, Channon. As fast as I can." Ella Bradley's cheeks were flushed as she spun on her heel and stamped out the door, leaving Channon staring after her until it had closed.

"What the—?" Yesilkov began.

"This ain't the place, Supervisor," Yates warned. If Sonya'd had a change of heart, or hadn't really understood what he was saying before, then he'd deal with it—but not in McLeod's quarters. "Channon, let's go see if we can hurry them up down there. You too, Sonya."

Yates herded them out the door, doing everything but putting a finger to Sonya's lips to keep her from asking the wrong question. For sure, he wanted to avail himself of Soviet hospitality, like she'd been tacitly urging. For sure, he was counting on her to deliver the Soviet transport she'd been bragging about. And for sure, he couldn't risk saying it in so many words. Not here. Not anywhere they'd been earlier or would be later—until they were in that vehicle.

But she kept eyeing him, all the way to the lift station, until he realized he was going to have to say something, or risk her saying the wrong thing in front of Channon. Here in the hall he could see smoke damage and dangling wires where some ceiling panels were melted. Half the equipment in the U.S. mission was dead, anyway. He'd have to chance it.

The lift opened. As they piled in on either side of the big alien with his helmet under his arm, Yates said, "First stop's the suit room. We need spares and extra oxygen—in case of an emergency or some screw-up with what got loaded onto the Mars Observer coach—more than we need electromagnets or the Rillian weapon."

He couldn't make it much clearer than that. The only way they were getting out of here without Bradley, any time soon, was by blowing a little smoke and sneakin' out the back door while everybody was lookin' the other way.

He knew Sonya needed the weapon to satisfy Minsky. He knew almost as certainly that McLeod was no more planning to put the weapon on the Observer coach than he was planning to turn himself into a frog and hop home to Earth.

Sonya ought to know Yates well enough that he shouldn't have to declare treasonous intent and explicate extenuating circumstances; he'd said what he could when they'd had the time to talk. Minksy's agenda couldn't matter now, any more than McLeod's did.

"You saying 'fuck the weapon,' Yates?" she had to ask.

"Sonya, don't act like a girl," Yates replied, and Channon looked between them with puzzlement—or what Yates thought passed for puzzlement—on that harelipped, fanged, white-eyed face, his ears pricked forward.

Damn, it was one thing to flush your career down the toilet, throw your weight behind a Soviet agenda, and generally muck up your life for human reasons. It was another to do it for something that looked like Channon.

But then, he wasn't doing it for Channon. He was doing it because he'd started it—the whole mess. It had been Yates's bright idea to grant the Kiri alien asylum.

You pay as you go in life, but Yates's pockets were nearly empty.

He regretted everything, for an instant. Then he got hold of himself and regretted only that there was no way around hauling Yesilkov's fine plump Soviet rump into the dumper along with his and Lucky's.

But she'd asked for it. Shit, she'd damned near demanded it. She would have left him here playing pocket pool and run off with the Kiri by her lonesome, if she could have—that was the difference between them.

Yates could envision a scenario wherein Yesilkov might have enough shards of a career left when this was over to make a new start—assuming there was life in her, and a Soviet resident to report to, and a green planet in the night sky so you cared about reporting-chains.

As for his own chances: Hell, he'd be better off hitching a ride with Lucky than facing the consequences of even a complete and utter success, once he'd snuck them out of the lunar garage's back door in a Soviet moon truck, without leaving so much as a suicide note behind.

In McLeod's eyes, any human survivors of this mission were going to be traitors, Soviet agents—including one Samuel Yates.

Well, that was what the extra couple of mundane rounds loose in his pants pocket were for. Whatever happened out there, he and Yesilkov weren't going to die a slow, painful death at the hands of Rillians, Americans, UN forces, or even the Union of Soviet Socialist Republics.

Sam Yates might be getting old and stupid, but he still had a healthy respect for the concept 'death with dignity.'

Except that, even when the lift breathed them out onto the garage level, he still hadn't come to terms with his own worst-case estimate.

And in all that time, Lucky hadn't said a goddamned word.

Neither had Sonya Yesilkov. Yates said, ''This way, folks. One extra suit apiece; as many extra tanks as we can carry.''

He was almost hoping somebody would stop him. There wasn't much damage down here, almost no sign of the catastrophe above—except that the power to the corridor lights was flickery, and only half the normal complement was lit. And there was nobody in the halls.

It was as spooky a walk as he'd ever taken, down that corridor, with the Kiri alien next to him and Yesilkov stretching her legs to keep up. He wasn't so sure now that he was doing the right thing, but that figured.

There was no way to avoid pre-action jitters. It proved to him that he wasn't altogether crazy. If you're crazy, you don't worry about whether what you're doing's crazy. Or survivable.

Except he knew, deep in his heart, this wasn't survivable. He could almost feel Yesilkov's warm body against his—tactile memory, because his body wanted to prove to him he ought to do whatever was necessary to keep it safe.

He wished they'd say something.

But they didn't. The two of them just paced him, into the suit room, where he and Yesilkov suited up in UN-standard equipment, and they each shrugged on an extra air pack.

Suddenly the spares didn't matter—if he lost the truck, where was he going to hike to? He told Yesilkov, "Fuck the rest; just the extra air pack'll augment what's on board well enough."

She grunted like an infantryman; she wouldn't meet his eyes.

He was holding his helmet under his arm when Channon said, "Fill Channon's atmosphere tank?"

"Jesus Christ, how we gonna do that?" Yesilkov exploded in a short, nervous burst.

He felt even more foolish than she must have. He should have remembered; Lucky'd asked for replenishment enough times.

"Here, Channon, let's figure out how to mate these nozzles. . . ." Yates said.

The time it took to realize the systems weren't going to mate; to slash a chunk of hose from another suit; to find some composite tape and construct an airtight sleeve, was enough time for Yates to begin to sweat.

He kept expecting somebody to waltz in with backup, saying, "Hands up; against the wall, traitors!"

But nobody came.

When Channon, looking at something inside his helmet, announced, "Fullness," Yates's knees went weak.

"Okay, folks: next stop, farside."

Yesilkov ducked through the doorway into the hall ahead of them, her hand on the service pistol at her hip.

Then Lucky, and Yates himself exited. The suit room closed up behind them. He wished he'd dared bring heavier weapons, not because he needed them to handle the opposition, but because he was pumped up to the point where he felt naked without at least a rifle cradled against his chest.

But that would be telling.

So would entering Russian garage-space with the bareheaded alien. "Put on your helmet, Channon; I'm putting on mine. Check your air flow now, and try to match frequencies with me so we can talk privately. I'll send you an A440 test tone until you've locked with me. . . ."

He didn't need Sonya having to explain his presence, either, if anybody from SovSec recognized the UN Security Commissioner's face.

He settled his helmet over his head, checked his seals, his own atmosphere delivery system, and started broadcasting the test tone while Yesilkov's mouth, beyond her faceplate, guided Channon's search for the UN-Security-dedicated frequency.

Finally Yesilkov gave Yates a thumb's up; he stopped sending his test tone. Channon's voice thundered in his ears, reciting what might have been numbers, or the alphabet, in a language that was probably Kiri, judging from the interstitial clicks and growls that were like no sounds on Earth.

"Okay, Channon! I copy, but turn your damned volume down before I go deaf." He dialed his own comset back.

Then he motioned Yesilkov, who was bareheaded yet and would remain so until they'd secured the Soviet moon truck, to lead on.

They still had to saunter into the Soviet garaging area, listen through ambient receivers to Yesilkov sputter Russian that Yates couldn't follow, and walk calmly down the aisles of vehicles until they found the right one.

When they did, Yates was prayerfully glad for a moment that he'd let Sonya call Minsky from McLeod's office: The moon truck was big, capable, Soviet-milspec—Luna cammo, armor, and conventional cannon under stubby, transatmospheric wings.

"Thank Minsky for me," he said succinctly on the all-com which linked their three suits.

Yesilkov punched the belly-plate combination lock and the little TAV's hatch/ramp descended with a sigh he could hear through his helmet's exterior mike.

"Thank the war-game planners, yours and mine," said Yesilkov's tinny voice in his ears. "Please, Channon, be my guest: Once up that ramp, you are in Soviet territory. We must make it clear to those who'll view the garage log that no force was applied to bring you aboard." Yesilkov bowed low, with an exaggerated sweep of her arm.

Channon's voice rode a carrier wave with a hint of feedback to it: "Thanks, Yesilkov. Thanks, Yates. Go now, hurry fastest."

The alien trod quickly up the hatch/ramp and ducked inside, then turned back and peered out the door to make sure they were following. The Kiri had one arm propped against the hatchway, looking for all the world like any suited pilot taking care of his passengers—if you didn't notice the extra fingers or know your gear well enough to realize you weren't looking at anything human. . . .

The way the guards at the garage checkpoint and the Soviet officer who'd passed them through and given Yesilkov the keycodes had pretended they didn't.

Yates's pulse was pounding in his ears as he ascended the ramp. It didn't calm until the hatch had closed up behind them, the pressure lamps had lit, the REMOVE LIFE SUPPORT indicator was green, and he and Yesilkov were strapped in the two front cockpit couches, going through preflight checks.

By then his helmet was on the hook beside his acceleration couch and Sonya was talking a mile a minute in Russian to the garage-level's flight controller.

It really seemed, for one hyperacute instant of Yates's life, that he had it all together: the mission, the motive, the means, the consequences—the whole drill.

And then Lucky stuck a bare head over his shoulder and said, "Hurry, Yates. Rillian wait so long, only. Then come looking. . . ."

"How the fuck can you know that, Channon?" he demanded, finally, where only the Sovcraft's black box could be recording for an increasingly unlikely posterity. "Strap yourself into that there navigator's g-couch and hold on for dear life. Neither of

us is what you'd call a fighter-ace.'' Still, no matter how hot this
"truck" was, they'd fly it.

"Rillian call Channon, mind-line. Summons Channon's ELF.
Must respond, beacon—with person. Rillian not hear answer;
Channon tries and tries.''

"Oh, good,'' Yesilkov said, palming the bead mike on her
headset. "Just what we need, Channon—more pressure. Why
don't you try the radio in front of you? If you can reach your
Rillian buddy, tell him we're on our way, ETA less than two
hours, depending upon his exact coordinates. Which, by the
way, I could use right now. Farside's a big place. . . .''

"Channon say again: not reach with ELF. Not reach with
radio waves. Rillian in secure bubble, awaiting fix of Channon's
locus. Rillian's locus, can give Yesilkov.''

"Then let's *have*, it, Channon,'' Yesilkov said with a toss of
her head and a grim smile. "History's waiting.''

The next thing Yates knew, the TAV was moving along and
up the sparsely lit subterranean runway, toward the pressure
doors that opened onto the surface of the Moon.

Chapter 44

TURNABOUT

McLeod had just gotten Minsky off his back when Ella came waltzing down the aisle of casualties that marked humanity's first contact with alien life forms.

He looked at her and then down at Stuart, beside him on the bed. He was going to sit here until Stuart woke up so that he could say what he wanted to somebody who deserved to hear it. Then the context surrounding her solo approach, here, now, penetrated.

Damn, why wouldn't anything go right? You see your intended, unharmed amidst so much harm, you're happy she's safe: a normal reaction. You're preoccupied with Soviet-American game-playing because the Soviet resident's just left and he's been too cooperative, too forthcoming, too much a team player, even for this emergency, so you don't cycle the data as fast as you should.

Minsky hadn't been giving him half as hard a time about getting Soviet hands on that weapon as Ting had expected. It was almost as if the first A-field weapon to materialize in this part of the universe didn't matter; it was almost as if Minsky actually believed this crisis was laying the groundwork for Soviet-American cooperation on a grand scale. All of which had read, to McLeod's disaster-shocked brain, as if Minsky didn't think there was any long-term future to worry about.

So McLeod had been sitting where he was, letting the implications of Minsky's behavior cycle and trying to get a handle on what to do next. He'd given orders to prepare the Observer coach, but not to deliver the weapon there—or the magnets. There wasn't any use. He couldn't find a way to justify dedicating a single solar array to the electromagnetic defense of a coach that size, not when he had power problems colony-wide.

He waved to Ella and she waved back. Maybe Yates had gone down to the garage, checked out the coach, and sent her up here to hassle him. That was fine with him; he had no intention of letting Ella go with Yates and Channon. His last-ditch ploy was trading Yates the weapon for Ella.

It was that tense between them. A little serious social hardball wasn't going to make things any worse.

And if Channon was what the Rillian wanted, then the place for Elinor Bradley was nowhere near either of them. Even if such fielded duplicity bought her only a few extra hours of life, then that mattered more than how angry she was going to be with one Taylor McLeod. He was doing his best for all concerned, on his own recognizance, standing squarely in the face of enough blame already.

If he was wrong, and the Rillian didn't go away happy once it had Channon, he'd just cost the human race its collective life. So hours, minutes, and seconds were precious. He admitted, as he watched Ella's lithe form take long strides in the lunar gravity, that he'd kept the electromagnet battery just in case he could steal enough parts and power to retrofit it back together. He had this vision of going one-on-one with the next Rillian, standing in the ruins of his mission, with Ella behind him.

Things never went the way you expected, but if they went that particular way, he'd hate to be the fool who played by the rules and sent the only known working defensive weapon off to the farside on what might be a wild-alien chase.

His tech boys were working feverishly to see if, somehow, they could make the Rillian hardware perform. If they could, or if they could reverse-engineer a counterpart, and if there was enough time, the current SDI stations could be converted to Rillian-kill-capable. All they needed was twenty years or so. . . .

"Hi, Ella." He got up from Stuart's bedside, came around to meet her. Rebelliously, because it occurred to him, he took her in his arms, right there in public. Pulling her against him, he felt a savage satisfaction in this undecorous, emotional, human act of comfort and possession.

She was stiff for a moment. His lips found hers, seeking them gently with tentative kisses down her cheek, until she relaxed.

Then she gripped him hard in return and he could feel her heart scrambling in her chest like a trapped animal.

"Hey," he said, leaning back far enough to see her expression "it's going to be all right."

"Yates said you wanted to see me. . . ." Her voice was still soft from the emotions that a public embrace in this war zone had loosed.

"Uh-uh," he said candidly. "Must be crossed wires. I wanted to make sure you knew where I was, but that was—"

She pulled away. She hugged herself. She stepped back until her thighs bumped Stuart's couch. "No. Not crossed wires." She bit off the words. "Sam said you said it was stuff you couldn't talk to me about with Minsky here. You say you sent no such message?" Her eyes widened, and then narrowed. "He's going to sneak off without me."

"Don't worry, the coach isn't ready yet: no magnets, no Rillian weapon." Christ, if Yates would do that—slip away without Ella—McLeod would almost be ready to call them square.

But he wasn't supposed to want that; he couldn't show his feelings. "Let's go down to the garage and see how the prep's going." He needed to get out of here, he realized at last. Just because they were his casualties didn't mean that sitting a vigil was going to help them, or him, or those who were still up and around.

He knew he should be reacting faster. Ella was furious, her face flushed. "Ting, if you had anything to do with this. . . ."

"Ella, hold on."

She was moving away, hurrying down the aisle of beds. "What?"

"Come back here."

She stood still, and it was as if the entire circumference of the moon stretched between them.

Then she started slowly toward him, and he went to meet her halfway.

When they were an arm's length apart, he said very quietly, "I love you. I wouldn't game you."

"I thought I knew you," she whispered dismissively, disbelief in her rigid form.

"I don't want you to go, that's true." He took another step toward her. "Not with Yates; he's a suicidal cowboy. But I wouldn't use subterfuge to stop you. Believe me."

"I'm trying."

"You're convicting me without evidence—we don't know they

aren't still in my quarters, or on their way to the Observer coach right now.''

"Ting, I'm going down there. I'm getting in that coach, if it's still there, and I'm going with Channon to meet the Rillian. You're right: Yates can't handle this on his own. Somebody with some common sense must be there to temper his reactions—''

"Ella, I promise you, if that coach is still there, you'll be on it—if that's what you want. Even if I have to chaperon you.''

"You promise? Then call the garage and tell them not to let it leave without me.''

"I just said that's a promise. Now hold on while I call down.'' He left her waiting, used the nursing station phone, and confirmed that the coach was where it ought to be.

Then he rejoined her, lightly touching her elbow. "Now, m'lady, your coach awaits. . . .''

It never truly occurred to him that the coach wouldn't be down there, waiting, or that Yates and Yesilkova and Channon would be nowhere to be found. "They must be on their way,'' he consoled her when he couldn't raise them as she insisted he try to do.

By then he was beginning to harbor a dim, flickering hope he dared not confront straight on—yet. All the way to the garage he tried to ignore the feeling; all the way to the garage Ella fed it with her certainty that Yates wouldn't have lied to her without good reason.

And there was only one logical reason that Yates would want Ella Bradley separated from the traveling party. McLeod wanted to believe Ella's instinct. That was why he'd given no orders to obstruct any attempt by Yates's party to leave when ready.

When they entered the garage and he saw the Observer coach sitting there, he pretended he was relieved. It was there; he had to face the problem head on: He couldn't let Ella go off with Yates and Yesilkova, Channon or no Channon. He just couldn't.

The Mars Observer coach was more a liner than a truck—she had the same specs as a passenger transatmospheric: cushy seats, lots of food in her galley, suit room for EVA's, and a multifunction power plant that could switch from rocket to airbreather without a single passenger spilling his drink.

Looking at it, McLeod was tempted to fill it with his nationals, his wounded, and his fiancée and burn out of here, back to Earth, where at the least a few more days of life were likely.

It was simple enough, logistically. The coach had an AI Associate program that could navigate, fly, reenter atmosphere, and land on a sixty-foot square in zero-visibility, even if her standard complement of human pilot and copilot had both suffered massive heart attacks and were stone dead at her controls.

All he had to do was give the order and get those he chose on board before the rest of the lunar population realized what he was doing and stormed the garage complex to tear him, and his, limb from limb.

But he'd given the order that nobody went home until this was over. He had to stick to it.

He kept watching Ella, leaning against a security kiosk as he phoned around, looking for Yates again because she insisted he try. Beyond, men were sitting on their pumpers and their electronic test carts, swinging their legs and drinking coffee.

Once he'd satisfied himself that Yates was unreachable, he could have gone to her and told her something comforting. But he was beginning to credit the nagging hunch at the back of his mind, composed partly of his assessment of Yates's personality, and partly of Minsky's strangely civilized and nonconfrontational behavior, and partly of the instinct that made him what he was.

A good intelligence officer makes connections between seemingly unconnected data that others might miss.

So he thumbed the security phone's disconnect and rang Minsky's office. When he got a voice-only connection, he was nearly sure he'd guessed right. Adrenalin and noradrenalin flooded his system in a rush that made his hands shake.

"Gee, Oleg, I wish we had video for this."

"I am so sorry, Undersecretary McLeod. Something is amiss with my mission's electronics, due to the event, no doubt."

"No doubt. You know, Oleg, I'm down at the mission garage and I thought I'd see you and yours down here."

"We have been very busy, Taylor."

"Yep, so I'm beginning to realize. You know, Yates and Yesilkova and Channon aren't down here, either."

"Is this so? I assume that the Rillian weapon and the electromagnetic weapon that you promised them have been loaded by now?"

"That was why I was wondering where your boys were, since they were so anxious to see the alien hardware."

"I have someone viewing what is purported to be that self-same hardware right now, in one of the UN science modules that your people commandeered. Perhaps this is a time mix-up?"

"Ah, something like that, I'm beginning to think. Any idea where Yates, Yesilkova, and Channon might be?'

There was a long silence. In it, McLeod weighed the benefits of being out of phone range—and blame range—if what he was now postulating as the actual situation turned out to be correct. He also weighed the consequences and the responses if it turned out that a U.S.-protected person named Channon had been shanghaied—on Taylor McLeod's watch—by the USSR.

"Minsky? Are you still there?"

"Yes, ah . . . I'm here. I believe Yesilkova put in a request for transport—an emergency request—and my office approved it. Without my knowledge, of course—my direct knowledge. I'd left a blanket authorization that Yesilkova might have whatever logistical support she requested."

"You son of a bitch. What did you have to gain—?" Stupid question. "Never mind. You're saying there's no use looking for the Kiri alien or Yates either, I suppose."

"I believe not. Of course, we have no reason not to help you determine the location of Yesilkova's vehicle. . . ."

"I'm so pleased to hear that. I'll get back to you, Oleg, and when I do, you'd better have those coordinates. . . . I'm making one assumption I'd like you to confirm or deny."

"Yes, what is that?"

"That you haven't taken Channon by force; that Yesilkova's vehicle isn't headed for Earth, but is providing transport to the farside meeting that was part of our joint agenda."

"Da, da. You see, Undersecretary McLeod, we do understand one another."

"Oleg, that makes me feel a whole lot better. Like I said, I'll get back to you."

He slammed the handset into the secure cradle and came around the kiosk, to where Ella was waiting.

"You were right, Ella. They did leave without you—in a Soviet vehicle."

"Without the Rillian weapon? Without the magnets? Without—" She broke off and turned away, staring at the Mars Observer coach.

"Look, I'll take you out there. To keep the record straight for posterity, to cover my ass in case we've still got a government when this is over, and because I just can't give Minsky the satisfaction of having to ask him what the hell happened out there, once it's over."

She turned back and her eyes were shining. "Really? Can you?"

"Just let me get the coordinates and ETA of the Sovcraft from Minsky. And the Rillian weapon, in case it proves useful some way. Won't take but a minute."

"Thank you, Ting. Thank you."

"If we live through this—you and I and whoever that is Channon thinks you've got there—then thank me."

Right now, if he could have thought of a way to do it, *he* would have left her behind. But there was no way out now, not for any of them.

Somewhere farside, if Channon could be believed, the future of mankind was about to be decided by two alien races.

He had to be there, if only to bear witness. It wasn't the sort of thing he could leave to the Soviets, or to someone like Sam Yates. And Ella had earned the right to be there. He couldn't deny that.

Chapter 45

COMING TO MEET

As the human craft drew closer to its rendezvous with the Rillian commander, Channon began reaching for the mind he was coming to meet, flesh to flesh, on the dark side of an alien moon.

But it was difficult, because of the agitation of the minds closer to hand. The humans stank exceedingly in the close confines of their little warship. The normally rank odor of the carnivores was augmented by the sexual pheromones of each, plus their fear, plus the glandular muskiness of aggressive excitation.

All Yates could talk about was the power of the ship he piloted—its underwing cannon, its vertical landing capability, and the futility of his compatriots' pursuit:

"I dunno what McLeod thinks he's doin', comin' after us. Or Minksy, lettin' him. They think there's going to be enough of us left when this over for arrest an' trial, they're dreamin'."

"Sam, relax," replied Yesilkov, from the seat beside him, poking at her instrumentation. "Just in case there *is* somethin' left o' us, I gotta give 'em the coordinates they're askin' for—unless Channon's got a salient objection."

The female warrior was as battle-ready as her mate; she was sweating profusely as she turned in her seat to demand, "Well, Channon—what say, can I give 'em the data? They're gonna get it, anyhow, once we land. We ain't invisible. And McLeod just ain't that far behind. They can vector him in on our signatures, if he hasn't got chase-and-lock in that tub o' his."

"Do this, okay; whatever required, okay. Except kill Rillian—this not okay," Channon said and, in desperation, put on his helmet, within which waited some respite from the dizzying broadcast of the human warriors.

With his helmet on he could attempt an official contact with

297

the Rillian, using the universal hailing frequency or a scan for a working Rillian com channel.

As he searched for the contact, the boundary between the moon's bright and dark sides whizzed under them, and was soon far behind the human ship. With it went the light.

Through his external audio sensors, he heard Yates call his name, saying, "Are you sure about McLeod and Bradley? We went out of our way to ditch 'em."

He could even hear the sharp intake of human breath as they waited for his answer. He thought he could hear their hearts pounding. They were so biologically prepared for fight or flight that unless he could intervene they would manufacture an enemy to confront, even if they had to misconstrue the actions of some of their own.

He didn't want to take off his helmet. They didn't realize how uncomfortable they were making him; they couldn't help their wild emotions even if they did understand. He felt so sorry for them, in that instant, he transiently forgot all the English he had learned. In his own language he told them, "Be calm, children. Be patient. Bravery is prevailing over the animal in us all. Triumph is understanding how not to become enemies. Strength is declining to resort to might. The universe demands only change, not destruction."

Then he realized that the Kiri litany, even in English, would not hearten such creatures as these. So he pushed his translator button and his suit speaker said, "Tell McLeod come, see, witness. Tell Minsky, no problem. Tell both, not interfere Kiri way. Yates, Yesilkov, too: not interfere. Channon do this, Rillian do this. Humans win life, Channon way. Humans try human way, all die."

"Don't try to scare us, Channon." Yates's words were nearly indistinguishable, a feral growl. "We brought you out here; yer our responsibility. Maybe we don't have rhenium slugs in those cannon, but it's better than bein' unarmed."

"Come on, Sam, lighten up. I gotta call this in." Yesilkov turned to her instrumentation, a hand cupped over the microphone depending from her headset.

Channon waited until she had finished. It was becoming clear to him that he must not count on Yates and Yesilkov obeying him out of respect, or because they'd given their word. Their own survival was at stake. They were experts at survival. In their terms, with the survival of the human race riding on their shoulders, any action that might work was right action.

In that interval he reached again for the Rillian mind, and for the Rillian's hailing frequency, to make sure he was correct in his assumptions, to reinterpret the fleeting contacts he'd made with the Rillian—to finally decide how much to tell the frightened predators who flew him toward a final confrontation with the archetypal enemy of their primeval nightmares. For it had become clear to Channon that he and the Rillian represented all that humanity had feared for its entire climb up from the slime: some race smarter, some race stronger, some race more vicious and xenophobic than even itself.

Humanity had survived and prospered by being the most unflinching exterminator among all Earthly competitors; it had wiped out half the other species on its birth-world. It could not look into the star-strewn blackness of the universe and envision anything less than a more powerful version of itself. Even its gods, he'd long surmised from *Webster's* and the times at which men called upon them, were violent and partisan and vindictive.

Therefore, Channon was a conundrum to representatives of the warrior class, such as Yates and Yesilkov. He still hoped he was less so to the diplomat class like McLeod. But the presence of Yates and Yesilkov was necessary in meeting the Rillian, who respected warmaking prowess—who counted deadliness as a precursor to negotiation.

It was thanks to Providence that Channon had been marooned here, among all the races of the far-flung worlds, to ally himself with such a race before meeting a Rillian face to face. Terri, who was on his mind increasingly as the human craft sped toward the waiting Rillian, would have understood eternity's joke.

It seemed to him, somehow, that she did, as if the world of flesh and the world of spirit had bled together in the meeting place of his mind. As he reached out to the Rillian, he felt her close to him. He could nearly see her face. It was as if she were only a short distance away; as if he could look out the window and wave to her, and she would see him and wave back.

But out the window was only darkness, and the pitted face of the much-battered human moon.

The Rillian, when he reached its mind, was hardly clearer: It was blocking all but tertiary contact. At first it wouldn't respond to his com beacon. It wanted him to come to it; it was making its location and its determination clear.

Then, abruptly, it appeared in his mind's eye, with its tongue lolling over its fangs. It wiped its big black lips in exaggerated fashion.

And its words burst from his helmet's receiver, while the inboard translator labored to keep up: "Come to me, Kiri abortion. Show me how it is you have prevailed against my brothers. Prove to me that you are worthy of discourse. And be warned: One false move, one bit of treachery, one blink of cowardice, and this moon, the planet it satellites, and even their gravity-wells will cease to exist. There will be a rain of destruction, a hail of sterilized planetoids—and then the peace you Kiri try to impose upon the universe will reign here. These are my terms: Show cause why we should treat with you, bring the allies who are worthy, or die as you Eleveners always do, whining and scrabbling and calling out for the peace of death."

When the Rillian ceased its challenging, it sent an additional mental image of itself, ears pricked forward, eyes glowing. It waited for his response.

Channon cast a furtive look at the humans before him, then closed his eyes to concentrate on his answer. He'd forgotten that the humans were deaf to all but sound waves. What went on inside his helmet was hidden from them.

As he must hide them, and their buffeting emotions, from the Rillian during this sensitive initial exchange. He did not want the Rillian to get a taste of the humans—not yet.

He sent the Rillian an image of himself that was as true as he could make it, not idealized, not optimized. Doing this focused him enough that he was reasonably certain nothing unintentioned would reach the Rillian.

And he broadcast from his transmitter: "Rillian commander, you have come here to negotiate—not as a favor, but because events have proved you wise to do so. The Kiri and their local allies send me, Channon, with condolences for your dead and in the company of warriors. An honor guard follows, more respect for your station. But let us not forget the obvious: Two attempts to destroy me have failed; your best attempts have come to naught. With respect, we submit that had the Eleveners of the Kiri Unity known previously that we needed only to destroy Rillians to bring Rillians to the bargaining table, we would have commenced long since. Now, be ready to meet us without subterfuge—your death and mine will serve no purpose. Neither my government nor yours sends such as us to die, but to treat, to live, to create solutions.''

He broke the contact. Though he desperately wanted to see and hear what effect his words might have had on the Rillian commander, he wasn't sure he could sustain the ruse much longer.

He took off his helmet. He'd verified what he'd suspected: The Rillian commander was a negotiator of quality, if of feral heritage. The opening of dialogue was at hand. And the results of failure would be utter and complete, not only for himself, but for the Rillian and the race called mankind.

Having confirmed his suspicion as well as his hopes, he spoke once more to the stench-drenched humans accompanying him. ''Rillian brings planet-killer, Yates, Yesilkov. Needs success, or all die this day: Moon, Earth, humanity—Yates, Yesilkov, Rillian, Channon . . . all gone. Negotiations succeed only with help, Yates, Yesilkov. Trust Channon?''

''Spit it out, Channon. Whaddaya want us t'do?'' Yesilkov said before Yates could respond.

''Now you're telling us this?'' Yates's eyes were mere slits that raked Channon before he turned back to his controls.

''Need fibs. Comply, Yates, Yesilkov?''

''Fibs?'' Yesilkov said with her explosive laugh that still made Channon shrink away, back into the padding of his seat, behind and midway between theirs.

''What d'ya know, Kiris lie just like everybody else. Sure, what do you want us to say—and to who? We gonna meet the Rillian?'' Yates wanted to know, and touched his hip where his projectile weapon was strapped.

''Channon say humans new Kiri allies—not lie, fib only. Will be truth, if Yates, Yesilkov comply.''

''Jesus yeah, no sweat,'' Yates replied. ''That is—Sonya?''

''Whatever works, Sam. Channon, are we really going out there with you?''

''Rillian come see Channon's warriors. Say killed Rillians, proudly, if asked. Say Kiri allies, if asked. Say Channon best friend, universe, if asked.''

Sonya Yesilkov pushed the headset down until it collared her throat. "Channon, are you serious? All that's true, as far as I'm concerned."

"Me too," said Yates in a scratchy voice. "What's the catch?"

"Rillian want proof. Rillian weapon, not have. Must prove otherwise, you killed former Rillians. Rillians ritualize, much. Killing . . . confers . . . respect; precondition for negotiating. Kiri not know this, before now. Sorry not have weapon. Think of way . . ."

"Wanna bet we won't have?" said Yates with a baring of teeth only slightly related to a human smile. "Sonya, get McLeod on the horn."

"Aw, Sam, you don't wanna . . ."

"Yeah, we do."

Channon watched the two humans, wondering if they understood what he was implying, as Sonya Yesilkov spoke into her microphone.

While she was busy, Yates tilted his couch back until his head was very near Channon's and said, "Big fella, if there's any chance of pulling this out, no matter what it takes, we do it. Whatever it is. Even if it kills us. You got that? First's doing the job; second's personal survival; third, if there is a third, is pickin' up the pieces. . . ."

"Channon pick up all pieces," he promised with as much sincerity as he could deliver in the unwieldy foreign tongue. "Pick up Yates, pick up Yesilkov, if live. Make Kiri heros, both you. Celebrate you, light-years from star to star. Be brave only, follow Channon lead, not fear. Okay, Yates?"

"Okay, Channon."

Yates stuck out his deformed death-pale hand and Channon, expert now at nonverbal human assurances, took it firmly in his six-fingered one.

Then Yesilkov was saying, with a look on her face as if she'd tasted something foul, "I got McLeod here, Yates. And he's not happy with us. But he says if we don't fuck with him no more, he'll hand Channon the weapon after we make landfall— personally. You want a piece o' this, seein' as yer as much a 'traitorous Commie' as me, in his opinion?"

"No thanks, Sonya. Tell him we'll see him there," Yates said, and winked broadly at Channon before he restored his couch to the upright position where he could put a hand on her leg to transmit tactile support.

Channon, alone among savage friends and soon to be facing a savage enemy, wished desperately that Terri was here to comfort him and receive his comfort in return. In that instant it seemed almost as if she were with him.

He could hear her in the back of his mind; he could see her delicate lips drawing back over her beautiful teeth; he could make out the words she wanted him to hear: "I'm here, best beloved. We'll be together soon. Providence will preserve you until then."

He slumped in his seat, shaken from the sharpness of the image, the reality of the contact. The mourning mind could do amazing things, even part the curtain of death.

For a long while the humans before him and the Rillian he was destined to meet didn't matter. Only Terri mattered, and the hole in his heart where his love used to be—

—and would be again, when he shed his fleshly form. But until then, there was only the work before him, and the fates of all the living, including his own, to fill the void.

Chapter 46

ONE ON ONE, PLUS TWO

The Kiri slime arrived in a primitive-looking vehicle that none-theless settled down onto the ruined regolith on gouts of flame, its nose pointed straight at him—and its weapons as well.

A show of force from a Kiri negotiator? It confused Komida; then it enraged him. His data-gatherers had been in error. He should have brought a display of might, himself.

But he had not. He got up, arched his back, and exited his bubble once he'd put on his helmet. There, with his spacetime bubble behind him (only a four-step back to safety, even if he had to snap the planet-killer from his belt), he waited for the Kiri to emerge.

He knew of the second craft, and coming forth before it too had landed was a show of courage.

The Kiri weren't supposed to behave like this. They were craven; they made deals for hostages; they groveled for mercy; they were soft and foolish and unworthy.

Or so he had been told.

Komida four-stepped to the right, slightly, so that he could keep his bubble in sight and still be able to watch the Kiri emerge from the conveyance.

The hatch opened, made a ramp. The Kiri came out first, without even opening communications. Inside his own helmet Komida let out a howl of frustration. Then he read the time and date into his log com, the base unit of which was safe in the Rillian-universe bubble and would not be destroyed no matter what happened on the surface of this arid moon.

And added: "The Kiri comes, out from the craft. Two similar-sized indigenes follow at a respectful distance. A second indigene ship is now visible, ETA imminent. The first craft is armed, no doubt with whatever destroys Rillians.

"Komida now meets the Kiri. To my nest, all my goods, if I should not leave here. To you is my vengeance."

The formula complete, he put the log on automatic and trotted forth.

The Kiri was large and Komida felt an urge to stand on his hind legs to meet it. He smothered the instinct: He would not offer his underbelly.

Instead, he chose a spot halfway and sat on his haunches. With his four feet on the ground and his arms crossed over his chest, he waited, his right hand closed over the planet-killer on his belt. No death could come quick enough to avoid a response: Either he would snap it free and all would die, or the cessation of his heartbeat would trigger it. Either way, the Kiri's reinforcements would not change the outcome.

They would find common ground, or this slow and warped spacetime would be minus one threat to Rillian suzerainty.

The Kiri's first words were: "Greetings, Rillian commander, honored Komida, the valiant. I am Channon, Kiri conflict-negotiator, here to create a basis for understanding between the mighty Rillian Pact and the Kiri Unity."

"Then what," Komida nearly barked into his helmet com, "are all these weapons, this second ship now landing, and those behind you? A Rillian comes alone."

"A Kiri comes with proof, as the Rillians have asked."

"I see no proof, only aggression."

"These with me will go to the vehicle now landing, and then present the weapon of a slain Rillian—a weapon they took as a prize in battle. We will return this weapon to you, as proof of our good intentions."

"Our? Who is this 'we'? With whom do we treat?"

"With the Kiri Unity."

"And these warriors are a part of that Unity?"

"They are our newest allies. They protected and nurtured Channon at great cost. You know that cost. You sent two war-making segments, and many casualties were sustained. Reparations will be due in good course."

"Two Rillians were killed. Reparations must be set," said Komida uneasily. The Kiri was walking forward as he spoke, so close now that if he did not sit, Komida would have to rise. Behind the Kiri, two similar-looking four-limbs were headed to the rear of the first craft, where a second one was landing.

This was not fair. This should have been one on one, not one on one plus two, plus . . .

Komida stopped the rage building in him, with a snarl and a shake of his head. He was here because force was inappropriate—that is, ineffective. Rillian troopers and Rillian controllers could not be profligately wasted, thrown into confrontations they could not win. The dispatchers had made an error. This entire solar system could have been obliterated, if only the Kiri negotiator hadn't been so slippery.

Someone had wanted to justify his error of letting the Kiri escape in the first place. That was the first mistake. If Komida lived to find the fool, his nest would destroy the nest of that fool. But decorum and law now demanded a settlement.

The Rillian way could not be ignored. You treated with those you could not destroy. This was the value of having become civilized. Without limits, without laws, without ritual and restraint, Rillians would not be the masters of so much spacetime, respected overlords to so many client species deemed valuable enough to preserve.

Somehow, the Kiri Unity had managed to become worthy of respect. Reality could not be argued. Komida wanted to howl for hours, but that was immaterial. When an enemy is fierce and strong, there is no shame in concluding a treaty.

But it was difficult to think of the Kiri Unity thus. They had been designated as prey. They had been designated as vermin. That label had been unchallenged since Komida's indoctrination.

He had been dutifully hating and despising the Kiri enemy for cycles. He must forget all that, and do what only a Rillian master could do: construct a body of law and rule to protect both species, or the destruction of both was inevitable.

The Rillian way was the way of survival.

Yet Komida wanted the taste of blood between his teeth, and imagined it—racial memory. His back spines stood up, snagging on his suit, a trait left over from when his kind were much larger, scaled, and incapable of negotiation. Turf that could not be won at acceptable cost must be marked; everywhere in the universe there were borders. It was Komida's task to determine the borders in this case.

No one had realized what tricksters, what sinister gamesters, the Kiri were. He could not keep his eyes in one place: He must watch the ones at the second ship; he must watch the first ship for signs of aggression; he must watch the approaching Kiri who now was closer than the Rillian liked.

"Sit down, Kiri Channon. Sit upon your haunches and treat with a Rillian commander. Otherwise, I must assume aggression on your part."

"I sit," said the Kiri identified as Channon.

"How were my brothers killed?"

"By their own aggression," said the Kiri.

Far to the rear, Komida could see the two ambulatory four-limbs returning. One held a Rillian weapon in his hands.

This proof made Komida wish once more that he could howl in rage. This time, though, his hand clutched the planet-killer tight. He could simply pull it free, and all this embarrassment would be over with, for him at least.

But then his nest would be filled with shame, and killing this warrior world was not killing the whole Kiri Unity. No, it was too disgusting an alternative. It fed only his backbrain and the glands in his mouth.

"By whom were they killed? Where are the warriors?" he demanded of the Kiri negotiator. "I must sniff the truth of this."

"They come, with their trophy," said the big, ugly representative of the Eleveners. "They are native to our part of the universe—they live at the Kiri rate; they belong to our nature; they are our children. We will negotiate with you a boundary all can respect—a boundary based on the speed of light, and the conditions natural to our respective spacetimes. There will be no shame. But there can be congress; there can be enlightenment; there can be peace. Or there can be mere avoidance."

"How can there be avoidance? You exist; we exist. One cannot pretend the irrational."

"Are you saying," the Kiri wanted to know, "that you will begin negotiations on these terms?"

"I am saying," said Komida, watching the Kiri troopers approach, "that you have brought warriors to this negotiation. I have not brought warriors."

"You brought warriors who died. You asked to see the victors. I am showing you those victors. We are returning the trophy we took—we are here in good faith."

Two more four-limbs had come out of the far craft, and these were approaching very slowly, following in the footsteps of the first pair.

"Bring the warriors forth, then," said Komida.

They were coming, anyway—with one of the Rillian's own weapons in hand. Komida wasn't sure whether their suits were up to firing the rifle, but he didn't want to find out.

"They come." There was a click and Komida could hear the Kiri talking to the troopers, who answered unintelligibly in a low-frequency range.

"Just the two," Komida warned. "I told you the consequences of treachery—I hold my final option in my hand."

"Just the two. The others will stay by the craft."

And the Kiri called Channon spoke again on an open channel, albeit incomprehensibly, to the troopers.

The first two quickened their pace. The second two waved to show they understood and would comply.

These were intelligent, well-disciplined troopers, even if they were small by Rillian trooper standards. Komida was rather relieved that they were not huge and armored; it was enough to be outnumbered by somewhat larger creatures.

How could the intelligence-gathering on this race have been so wrong? It must have to do with the difference in the space-times, he told himself. It might be that the Kiri was right. The Rillians were masters of their own native topologies, unable to comfortably adapt to the physics of this asymptotic part of the universe. It therefore followed that, on their home turf, native races would have an advantage.

When the two approaching four-limbs reached Channon, they sat down beside him and handed Channon the weapon. If not for the helmets all were wearing, Komida could have judged something by the look in their eyes. Warriors' eyes always told their hearts.

The other pair, behind, had reached the foremost craft and they stood there. Komida heard some more indecipherable babble, and then Channon spoke once more to him:

"Here we present you with the trophy, the weapon of your lost and valiant warriors. Our warriors do not speak your language; we neglected to bring translators for them. They wish to extend their respect and admiration, and their hopes of a peace of strength and honor, with no unnecessary humiliation on either side."

"This is a good basis for a beginning," Komida said, picking the simple words precisely because they were simple, and could not be wrongly construed or loaded with too many implications. "I will take the weapon now."

As he stood up on all four legs to reach forward far enough to take the weapon in his hand, something in the sky caught his eye.

"Traitor!" he snarled, and threw the weapon up against his shoulder. It came in contact with his suit and, without prior calibration, he fired at the Kiri ship that had suddenly materialized high above the landed indigene craft.

The weapon spat forth . . . nothing.

It was damaged. It was broken. It had been subjected to rigors of combat too great for its structure. His throat closed up. "Kiri trickster!"

Komida stutter-stepped around, holding the weapon in one hand, now. His other hand was firm on the planet-killer. "Why did you do this? How can you break a sacred trust of word, and bring your—"

The Kiri had one hand on each of his warriors. Channon's answer made his ears close up, so loud was it: "I tell you, I didn't know she was really alive! I didn't know. . . . She rode your beam in, that's all. There are no weapons there, aboard that ship. Sit down, Komida, I beg you, and you will see I speak the truth. The final option is still yours in any case."

There was nothing better to do. And it was clear that the warriors themselves had not expected the Kiri spongeship. The pair close at hand and the pair by the landed craft were both staring upward.

On the open com channel Komida could hear much babbling he couldn't understand. So he said, "Kiri called Channon, I accept this token of good intentions. I propose we end this meeting, since too many others are present, and reconvene it at a time and place you and I will decide."

"Yes. A good idea. A brilliant idea." Channon named a time and a neutral beacon in the Rift. Then: "Farewell, Komida. You have the weapon. You have seen our warriors. May you never cross paths in aggression with us or ours again."

Komida was already retreating, backstepping carefully, toward the bubble of Rillian spacetime behind his back. "When next we meet, I want a translation program so that I can speak personally with your warriors, and accept their condolences in my own ears. Then the reparations on all sides shall be determined.''

He didn't care that much if he ever again saw the four-limbs, but he wanted to assert himself, lest it look like he was beating a hasty retreat into his bubble, and safety.

His backside preceded his front into the bubble, and he didn't even wait long enough to put down the weapon before he enabled his return to the Rillian staging area.

As the moon blinked away, its dimension left behind, he was thankful for the mangled, inoperable weapon he held. Without it, even though he'd run a log, Komida might have trouble getting the ones who counted to believe his story.

And he needed, more than anything right now, to drink with his fellows at the staging area, to be congratulated, to accept the rounds bought him by his admirers.

After all, he, Komida, son of Komida before him, had just changed history.

Chapter 47

MUTUALITY

"What the fuck, Channon?" Yates was staring up at the huge ship descending without any visible rocket burn.

Yesilkov was saying, at the same time, "Where'd the Rillian go?"

"Rillian back to own spacetime. We meet again, arranged," Channon explained what, because of language, the humans hadn't realized. "Yates, Yesilkov, see Kiri ship. Mate of Channon, come take us for negotiations. Bring Yates, Yesilkov back soonest, okay?" Best to make the entreaty sound as if the humans had already agreed to it.

McLeod and Bradley were hurrying toward them. McLeod's voice in Channon's phones was saying, "Channon, what the hell are you pulling? Yates, Yesilkov—you're not going anywhere."

And Bradley's voice joined in: "Channon, you *gave* that weapon to the Rillian, and now this ship—I don't know what to think."

"Think?" Terri's ship was settling, only a short distance away. "Think saved, Bradley. Channon promise, Channon deliver: Earth, Moon, Bradley, McLeod, baby—all safe. Channon need Yesilkov, need Yates, for keeping safe, this place. All places. McLeod, Bradley not stop. Please."

"Goddamn," said Yates's voice, and Channon looked away from McLeod and Bradley, who were no longer running, but had their helmets together where they stood.

Yates put an arm around Yesilkov and said, "Well, whaddya think, Sonya? Gotta be better than what we got waitin' for us back home."

Yesilkov's helmeted head turned Channon's way. "You really need us, Channon?"

"Need Yates, need Yesilkov," said Channon, and held out both hands.

Beyond them, McLeod and Bradley had finished conferring. They walked slowly forward. McLeod's voice said, "Channon, if I let this go down, you owe me one. Those two are real close to being firing-squad ready. What am I supposed to say happened here?"

"One owed McLeod," Channon agreed. "Any one, whenever time. Say Channon need Yates, Yesilkov—for safety of homeworld. This all humans understand."

"For how long, Channon?" Bradley's voice was thick. Channon knew with certainty that her eyes were leaking. "Bradley, friends come back. Channon bring, one day. See baby of Bradley and McLeod. Not sad, Bradley. Good story: humans winning, Kiri winning. Bradley say, Bradley make humans part of Kiri Unity. Promise, someday. This day, Channon take Yates, Yesilkov—now."

"Okay. You got a deal, Channon. Take them," said McLeod and came the rest of the way toward them, offering his hand.

Channon almost forgot to shake it.

Terri was standing in the open hatch of a Kiri ship, ready to take him home, her welcome radiating so strongly that even his suit couldn't dim her joy.

Or his.